The Land of Footprints

by Stewart Edward White

Copyright © 7/1/2015
Jefferson Publication

ISBN-13: 978-1514797938

Printed in the United States of America

# Contents

I. ON BOOKS OF ADVENTURE ....................................................................4

II. AFRICA ................................................................................................6

III. THE CENTRAL PLATEAU .......................................................................13

IV. THE FIRST CAMP ................................................................................14

V. MEMBA SASA .....................................................................................16

VI. THE FIRST GAME CAMP.......................................................................23

VII. ON THE MARCH..................................................................................27

VIII. THE RIVER JUNGLE ...........................................................................31

IX. THE FIRST LION ..................................................................................35

X. LIONS..................................................................................................42

XI. LIONS AGAIN .....................................................................................46

XII. MORE LIONS......................................................................................48

XIII. ON THE MANAGING OF A SAFARI .....................................................54

XIV. A DAY ON THE ISIOLA.......................................................................59

XV. THE LION DANCE ...............................................................................63

XVI. FUNDI...............................................................................................65

XVII. NATIVES ..........................................................................................70

XVIII. IN THE JUNGLE ..............................................................................74

XIX. THE TANA RIVER...............................................................................89

XX. DIVERS ADVENTURES ALONG THE TANA ...........................................93

XXI. THE RHINOCEROS.............................................................................97

XXII. THE RHINOCEROS-(continued)........................................................102

XXIII. THE HIPPO POOL ..........................................................................104

XXIV. BUFFALO ......................................................................................108

XXV. THE BUFFALO-continued ...............................................................112

XXVI. JUJA..............................................................................................119

XXVII. A VISIT AT JUJA............................................................................121

XXVIII. A RESIDENCE AT JUJA..................................................................125

XXIX. CHAPTER THE LAST.......................................................................131

APPENDIX I ...........................................................................................131

APPENDIX II ..........................................................................................132

    GAME ANIMALS COLLECTED .............................................................132

APPENDIX III .........................................................................................133

APPENDIX IV. THE AMERICAN IN AFRICA ...............................................135

    IN WHICH HE APPEARS AS DIFFERENT FROM THE ENGLISHMAN ..........135

APPENDIX V. THE AMERICAN IN AFRICA .................................................139

WHAT HE SHOULD TAKE........................................................................139

# I. ON BOOKS OF ADVENTURE

Books of sporting, travel, and adventure in countries little known to the average reader naturally fall in two classes-neither, with a very few exceptions, of great value. One class is perhaps the logical result of the other.

Of the first type is the book that is written to make the most of far travels, to extract from adventure the last thrill, to impress the awestricken reader with a full sense of the danger and hardship the writer has undergone. Thus, if the latter takes out quite an ordinary routine permit to go into certain districts, he makes the most of travelling in "closed territory," implying that he has obtained an especial privilege, and has penetrated where few have gone before him. As a matter of fact, the permit is issued merely that the authorities may keep track of who is where. Anybody can get one. This class of writer tells of shooting beasts at customary ranges of four and five hundred yards. I remember one in especial who airily and as a matter of fact killed all his antelope at such ranges. Most men have shot occasional beasts at a quarter mile or so, but not airily nor as a matter of fact: rather with thanksgiving and a certain amount of surprise. The gentleman of whom I speak mentioned getting an eland at seven hundred and fifty yards. By chance I happened to mention this to a native Africander.

"Yes," said he, "I remember that; I was there."

This interested me-and I said so.

"He made a long shot," said I.

"A GOOD long shot," replied the Africander.

"Did you pace the distance?"

He laughed. "No," said he, "the old chap was immensely delighted. 'Eight hundred yards if it was an inch!' he cried."

"How far was it?"

"About three hundred and fifty. But it was a long shot, all right."

And it was! Three hundred and fifty yards is a very long shot. It is over four city blocks-New York size. But if you talk often enough and glibly enough of "four and five hundred yards," it does not sound like much, does it?

The same class of writer always gets all the thrills. He speaks of "blanched cheeks," of the "thrilling suspense," and so on down the gamut of the shilling shocker. His stuff makes good reading; there is no doubt of that. The spellbound public likes it, and to that extent it has fulfilled its mission. Also, the reader believes it to the letter-why should he not? Only there is this curious result: he carries away in his mind the impression of unreality, of a country impossible to be understood and gauged and savoured by the ordinary human mental equipment. It is interesting, just as are historical novels, or the copper-riveted heroes of modern fiction, but it has no real relation with human life. In the last analysis the inherent untruth of the thing forces itself on him. He believes, but he does not apprehend; he acknowledges the fact, but he cannot grasp its human quality. The affair is interesting, but it is more or less concocted of pasteboard for his amusement. Thus essential truth asserts its right.

All this, you must understand, is probably not a deliberate attempt to deceive. It is merely the recrudescence under the stimulus of a brand-new environment of the boyish desire to be a hero. When a man jumps back into the Pleistocene he digs up some of his ancestors' cave-qualities. Among these is the desire for personal adornment. His modern development of taste precludes skewers in the ears and polished wire around the neck; so he adorns himself in qualities instead. It is quite an engaging and diverting trait of character. The attitude of mind it both presupposes and helps to bring about is too complicated for my brief analysis. In itself it is no more blameworthy than the small boy's pretence at Indians in the back yard; and no more praiseworthy than infantile decoration with feathers.

In its results, however, we are more concerned. Probably each of us has his mental picture that passes as a symbol rather than an idea of the different continents. This is usually a single picture-a deep river, with forest, hanging snaky vines, anacondas and monkeys for the east coast of South America, for example. It is built up in youth by chance reading and chance pictures, and does as well as a pink place on the map to stand for a part of the world concerning which we know nothing at all. As time goes on we extend, expand, and modify this picture in the light of what knowledge we may acquire. So the reading of many books modifies and expands our first crude notions of Equatorial Africa. And the result is, if we read enough of the sort I describe above, we build the idea of an exciting, dangerous, extra-human continent, visited by half-real people of the texture of the historical-fiction hero, who have strange and interesting adventures which we could not possibly imagine happening to ourselves.

This type of book is directly responsible for the second sort. The author of this is deadly afraid of being thought to brag of his adventures. He feels constantly on him the amusedly critical eye of the old-timer. When he comes to describe the first time a rhino dashed in his direction, he remembers that old hunters, who have been so charged hundreds of times, may read the book. Suddenly, in that light, the adventure becomes pitifully unimportant. He sets down the fact that "we met a rhino that turned a bit nasty, but after a shot in the shoulder decided to leave us alone." Throughout he keeps before his mind's eye the imaginary audience of those who have done. He writes for them, to please them, to convince them that he is not "swelled head," nor "cocky," nor "fancies himself," nor thinks he has done, been, or seen anything wonderful. It is a good, healthy frame of mind to be in; but it, no more than the other type, can produce books that leave on the minds of the general public any impression of a country in relation to a real human being.

As a matter of fact, the same trouble is at the bottom of both failures. The adventure writer, half unconsciously perhaps, has been too much occupied play-acting himself into half-forgotten boyhood heroics. The more modest man, with even more self-consciousness, has been thinking of how he is going to appear in the eyes of the expert. Both have thought of themselves before their work. This aspect of the matter would probably vastly astonish the modest writer.

If, then, one is to formulate an ideal toward which to write, he might express it exactly in terms of man and environment. Those readers desiring sheer exploration can get it in any library: those in search of sheer romantic adventure can purchase plenty of it at any book-stall. But the majority want something different from either of these. They want, first of all, to know what the country is like-not in vague and grandiose "word paintings," nor in strange and foreign sounding words and phrases, but in comparison with something they know. What is it nearest like-Arizona? Surrey? Upper New York? Canada? Mexico? Or is it totally different from anything, as is the Grand Canyon? When you look out from your camp-any one camp-how far do you see, and what do you see?- mountains in the distance, or a screen of vines or bamboo near hand, or what? When you get up in the morning, what is the first thing to do? What does a rhino look like, where he lives, and what did you do the first time one came at you? I don't want you to tell me as though I were either an old hunter or an admiring audience, or as though you were afraid somebody might think you were making too much of the matter. I want to know how you REALLY felt. Were you scared or nervous? or did you become cool? Tell me frankly just how it was, so I can see the thing as happening to a common everyday human being. Then, even at second-hand and at ten thousand miles distance, I can enjoy it actually, humanly, even though vicariously, speculating a bit over my pipe as to how I would have liked it myself.

Obviously, to write such a book the author must at the same time sink his ego and exhibit frankly his personality. The paradox in this is only apparent. He must forget either to strut or to blush with diffidence. Neither audience should be forgotten, and neither should be exclusively addressed. Never should he lose sight of the wholesome fact that old hunters are to read and to weigh; never should he for a moment slip into the belief that he is justified in addressing the expert alone. His attitude should be that many men know more and have done more than he, but that for one reason or another these men are not ready to transmit their knowledge and experience.

To set down the formulation of an ideal is one thing: to fulfil it is another. In the following pages I cannot claim a fulfilment, but only an attempt. The foregoing dissertation must be considered not as a promise, but as an explanation. No one knows better than I how limited my African experience is, both in time and extent, bounded as it is by East Equatorial Africa and a year. Hundreds of men are better qualified than myself to write just this book; but unfortunately they will not do it.

# II. AFRICA

In looking back on the multitudinous pictures that the word Africa bids rise in my memory, four stand out more distinctly than the others. Strangely enough, these are by no means all pictures of average country-the sort of thing one would describe as typical. Perhaps, in a way, they symbolize more the spirit of the country to me, for certainly they represent but a small minority of its infinitely varied aspects. But since we must make a start somewhere, and since for some reason these four crowd most insistently in the recollection it might be well to begin with them.

Our camp was pitched under a single large mimosa tree near the edge of a deep and narrow ravine down which a stream flowed. A semicircle of low mountains hemmed us in at the distance of several miles. The other side of the semicircle was occupied by the upthrow of a low rise blocking off an horizon at its nearest point but a few hundred yards away. Trees marked the course of the stream; low scattered bushes alternated with open plain. The grass grew high. We had to cut it out to make camp.

Nothing indicated that we were otherwise situated than in a very pleasant, rather wide grass valley in the embrace of the mountains. Only a walk of a few hundred yards atop the upthrow of the low rise revealed the fact that it was in reality the lip of a bench, and that beyond it the country fell away in sheer cliffs whose ultimate drop was some fifteen hundred feet. One could sit atop and dangle his feet over unguessed abysses.

For a week we had been hunting for greater kudu. Each day Memba Sasa and I went in one direction, while Mavrouki and Kongoni took another line. We looked carefully for signs, but found none fresher than the month before. Plenty of other game made the country interesting; but we were after a shy and valuable prize, so dared not shoot lesser things. At last, at the end of the week, Mavrouki came in with a tale of eight lions seen in the low scrub across the stream. The kudu business was about finished, as far as this place went, so we decided to take a look for the lions.

We ate by lantern and at the first light were ready to start. But at that moment, across the slope of the rim a few hundred yards away, appeared a small group of sing-sing. These are a beautiful big beast, with widespread horns, proud and wonderful, like Landseer's stags, and I wanted one of them very much. So I took the Springfield, and dropped behind the line of some bushes. The stalk was of the ordinary sort. One has to remain behind cover, to keep down wind, to make no quick movements. Sometimes this takes considerable manoeuvring; especially, as now, in the case of a small band fairly well scattered out for feeding. Often after one has succeeded in placing them all safely behind the scattered cover, a straggler will step out into view. Then the hunter must stop short, must slowly, oh very, very slowly, sink down out of sight; so slowly, in fact, that he must not seem to move, but rather to melt imperceptibly away. Then he must take up his progress at a lower plane of elevation. Perhaps he needs merely to stoop; or he may crawl on hands and knees; or he may lie flat and hitch himself forward by his toes, pushing his gun ahead. If one of the beasts suddenly looks very intently in his direction, he must freeze into no matter what uncomfortable position, and so remain an indefinite time. Even a hotel-bred child to whom you have rashly made advances stares no longer nor more intently than a buck that cannot make you out.

I had no great difficulty with this lot, but slipped up quite successfully to within one hundred and fifty yards. There I raised my head behind a little bush to look. Three does grazed nearest me, their coats rough against the chill of early morning. Up the slope were two more does and two funny, fuzzy babies. An immature buck occupied the extreme left with three young ladies. But the big buck, the leader, the boss of the lot, I could not see anywhere. Of course he must be about, and I craned my neck cautiously here and there trying to make him out.

Suddenly, with one accord, all turned and began to trot rapidly away to the right, their heads high. In the strange manner of animals, they had received telepathic alarm, and had instantly obeyed. Then beyond and far to the right I at last saw the beast I had been looking for. The old villain had been watching me all the time!

The little herd in single file made their way rapidly along the face of the rise. They were headed in the direction of the stream. Now, I happened to know that at this point the stream-canyon was bordered by sheer cliffs. Therefore, the sing-sing must round the hill, and not cross the stream. By running to the top of the hill I might catch a glimpse of them somewhere below. So I started on a jog trot, trying to hit the golden mean of speed that would still leave me breath to shoot. This was an affair of some nicety in the tall grass. Just before I reached the actual slope, however, I revised my schedule. The reason was supplied by a rhino that came grunting to his feet about seventy yards away. He had not seen me, and he had not smelled me, but the general disturbance of all these events had broken into his early morning nap. He looked to me like a person who is cross before breakfast, so I ducked low and ran around him. The last I saw of him he was still standing there, quite disgruntled, and evidently intending to write to the directors about it.

Arriving at the top, I looked eagerly down. The cliff fell away at an impossible angle, but sheer below ran out a narrow bench fifty yards wide. Around the point of the hill to my right-where the herd had gone-a game trail dropped steeply to this bench. I arrived just in time to see the sing-sing, still trotting, file across the bench and over its edge, on some other invisible game trail, to continue their descent of the cliff. The big buck brought up the rear. At the very edge he came to a halt, and looked back, throwing his head up and his nose out so that the heavy fur on his neck stood forward like a ruff. It was a last glimpse of him, so I held my little best, and pulled trigger.

This happened to be one of those shots I spoke of-which the perpetrator accepts with a thankful and humble spirit. The sing-sing leaped high in the air and plunged over the edge of the bench. I signalled the camp-in plain sight-to come and get the head and meat, and sat down to wait. And while waiting, I looked out on a scene that has since been to me one of my four symbolizations of Africa.

The morning was dull, with gray clouds through which at wide intervals streamed broad bands of misty light. Below me the cliff fell away clear to a gorge in the depths of which flowed a river. Then the land began to rise, broken, sharp, tumbled, terrible, tier after tier, gorge after gorge, one twisted range after the other, across a breathlessly immeasurable distance. The prospect was full of shadows thrown by the tumult of lava. In those shadows one imagined stranger abysses. Far down to the right a long narrow lake inaugurated a flatter, alkali-whitened country of low cliffs in long straight lines. Across the distances proper to a dozen horizons the tumbled chaos heaved and fell. The eye sought rest at the bounds usual to its accustomed world-and went on. There was no roundness to the earth, no grateful curve to drop this great fierce country beyond a healing horizon out of sight. The immensity of primal space was in it, and the simplicity of primal things-rough, unfinished, full of mystery. There was no colour. The scene was done in slate gray, darkening to the opaque where a tiny distant rain squall started; lightening in the nearer shadows to reveal half-guessed peaks; brightening unexpectedly into broad short bands of misty gray light slanting from the gray heavens above to the sombre tortured immensity beneath. It was such a thing as Gustave Dore might have imaged to serve as an abiding place for the fierce chaotic spirit of the African wilderness.

I sat there for some time hugging my knees, waiting for the men to come. The tremendous landscape seemed to have been willed to immobility. The rain squalls forty miles or more away did not appear to shift their shadows; the rare slanting bands of light from the clouds were as constant as though they were falling through cathedral windows. But nearer at hand other things were forward. The birds, thousands of them, were doing their best to cheer things up. The roucoulements of doves rose from the bushes down the face of the cliffs; the bell bird uttered his clear ringing note; the chime bird gave his celebrated imitation of a really gentlemanly sixty-horse power touring car hinting you out of the way with the mellowness of a chimed horn; the bottle bird poured gallons of guggling essence of happiness from his silver jug. From the direction of camp, evidently jumped by the boys, a steinbuck loped gracefully, pausing every few minutes to look back, his dainty legs tense, his sensitive ears pointed toward the direction of disturbance.

And now, along the face of the cliff, I make out the flashing of much movement, half glimpsed through the bushes. Soon a fine old-man baboon, his tail arched after the dandified fashion of the baboon aristocracy stepped out, looked around, and bounded forward. Other old men followed him, and then the young men, and a miscellaneous lot of half-grown youngsters. The ladies brought up the rear, with the babies. These rode their mothers' backs, clinging desperately while they leaped along, for all the world like the pathetic monkey "jockeys" one sees strapped to the backs of big dogs in circuses. When they had approached to within fifty yards, remarked "hullo!" to them. Instantly they all stopped. Those in front stood up on their hind legs; those behind clambered to points of vantage on rocks and the tops of small bushes: They all took a good long look at me. Then they told me what they thought about me personally, the fact of my being there, and the rude way I had startled them. Their remarks were neither complimentary nor refined. The old men, in especial, got quite profane, and screamed excited billingsgate.

Finally they all stopped at once, dropped on all fours, and loped away, their ridiculous long tails curved in a half arc. Then for the first time I noticed that, under cover of the insults, the women and children had silently retired. Once more I was left to the familiar gentle bird calls, and the vast silence of the wilderness beyond.

The second picture, also, was a view from a height, but of a totally different character. It was also, perhaps, more typical of a greater part of East Equatorial Africa. Four of us were hunting lions with natives-both wild and tame-and a scratch pack of dogs. More of that later. We had rummaged around all the morning without any results; and now at noon had climbed to the top of a butte to eat lunch and look abroad.

Our butte ran up a gentle but accelerating slope to a peak of big rounded rocks and slabs sticking out boldly from the soil of the hill. We made ourselves comfortable each after his fashion. The gunbearers leaned against rocks and rolled cigarettes. The savages squatted on their heels, planting their spears ceremonially in front of them. One of my friends lay on his back, resting a huge telescope over his crossed feet. With this he purposed seeing any lion that moved within ten miles. None of the rest of us could ever make out anything through the fearsome weapon. Therefore, relieved from responsibility by the presence of this Dreadnaught of a 'scope, we loafed and looked about us. This is what we saw:

Mountains at our backs, of course-at some distance; then plains in long low swells like the easy rise and fall of a tropical sea, wave after wave, and over the edge of the world beyond a distant horizon. Here and there on this plain, single hills lay becalmed, like ships at sea; some peaked, some cliffed like buttes, some long and low like the hulls of battleships. The brown plain flowed up to wash their bases, liquid as the sea itself, its tides rising in the coves of the hills, and ebbing in the valleys between. Near at hand, in the middle distance, far away, these fleets of the plain sailed, until at last hull-down over the horizon their topmasts disappeared. Above them sailed too the phantom fleet of the clouds, shot with light, shining like silver, airy as racing yachts, yet casting here and there exaggerated shadows below.

The sky in Africa is always very wide, greater than any other skies. Between horizon and horizon is more space than any other world contains. It is as though the cup of heaven had been pressed a little flatter; so that while the boundaries have widened, the zenith, with its flaming sun, has come nearer. And yet that is not a constant quantity either. I have seen one edge of the sky raised straight up a few million miles, as though some one had stuck poles under its corners, so that the western heaven did not curve cup-wise over to the horizon at all as it did everywhere else, but rather formed the proscenium of a gigantic stage. On this stage they had piled great heaps of saffron yellow clouds, and struck shafts of yellow light, and filled the spaces with the lurid portent of a storm-while the twenty thousand foot mountains below, crouched whipped and insignificant to the earth.

We sat atop our butte for an hour while H. looked through his 'scope. After the soft silent immensity of the earth, running away to infinity, with its low waves, and its scattered fleet of hills, it was with difficulty that we brought our gaze back to details and to things near at hand. Directly below us we could make out many different-hued specks. Looking closely, we could see that those specks were game animals. They fed here and there in bands of from ten to two hundred, with valleys and hills between. Within the radius of the eye they moved, nowhere crowded in big herds, but everywhere present. A band of zebras grazed the side of one of the earth waves, a group of gazelles walked on the skyline, a herd of kongoni rested in the hollow between. On the next rise was a similar grouping; across the valley a new variation. As far as the eye could strain its powers it could make out more and ever more beasts. I took up my field glasses, and brought them all to within a sixth of the distance. After amusing myself for some time in

9

watching them, I swept the glasses farther on. Still the same animals grazing on the hills and in the hollows. I continued to look, and to look again, until even the powerful prismatic glasses failed to show things big enough to distinguish. At the limit of extreme vision I could still make out game, and yet more game. And as I took my glasses from my eyes, and realized how small a portion of this great land-sea I had been able to examine; as I looked away to the ship-hills hull-down over the horizon, and realized that over all that extent fed the Game; the ever-new wonder of Africa for the hundredth time filled my mind-the teeming fecundity of her bosom.

"Look here," said H. without removing his eye from the 'scope, "just beyond the edge of that shadow to the left of the bushes in the donga-I've been watching them ten minutes, and I can't make 'em out yet. They're either hyenas acting mighty queer, or else two lionesses."

We snatched our glasses and concentrated on that important detail.

To catch the third experience you must have journeyed with us across the "Thirst," as the natives picturesquely name the waterless tract of two days and a half. Our very start had been delayed by a breakage of some Dutch-sounding essential to our ox wagon, caused by the confusion of a night attack by lions: almost every night we had lain awake as long as we could to enjoy the deep-breathed grumbling or the vibrating roars of these beasts. Now at last, having pushed through the dry country to the river in the great plain, we were able to take breath from our mad hurry, and to give our attention to affairs beyond the limits of mere expediency. One of these was getting Billy a shot at a lion.

Billy had never before wanted to shoot anything except a python. Why a python we could not quite fathom. Personally, I think she had some vague idea of getting even for that Garden of Eden affair. But lately, pythons proving scarcer than in that favoured locality, she had switched to a lion. She wanted, she said, to give the skin to her sister. In vain we pointed out that a zebra hide was very decorative, that lions go to absurd lengths in retaining possession of their own skins, and other equally convincing facts. It must be a lion or nothing; so naturally we had to make a try.

There are several ways of getting lions, only one of which is at all likely to afford a steady pot shot to a very small person trying to manipulate an over-size gun. That is to lay out a kill. The idea is to catch the lion at it in the early morning before he has departed for home. The best kill is a zebra: first, because lions like zebra; second, because zebra are fairly large; third, because zebra are very numerous.

Accordingly, after we had pitched camp just within a fringe of mimosa trees and of red-flowering aloes near the river; had eaten lunch, smoked a pipe and issued necessary orders to the men, C. and I set about the serious work of getting an appropriate bait in an appropriate place.

The plains stretched straight away from the river bank to some indefinite and unknown distance to the south. A low range of mountains lay blue to the left; and a mantle of scrub thornbush closed the view to the right. This did not imply that we could see far straight ahead, for the surface of the plain rose slowly to the top of a swell about two miles away. Beyond it reared a single butte peak at four or five times that distance.

We stepped from the fringe of red aloes and squinted through the dancing heat shimmer. Near the limit of vision showed a very faint glimmering whitish streak. A newcomer to Africa would not have looked at it twice: nevertheless, it could be nothing but zebra. These gaudily marked beasts take queer aspects even on an open plain. Most often they show pure white; sometimes a jet black; only when within a few hundred yards does one distinguish the stripes. Almost always they are very easily made out. Only when very distant and in heat shimmer, or in certain half lights of evening, does their so-called "protective colouration" seem to be in working order, and even then they are always quite visible to the least expert hunter's scrutiny.

It is not difficult to kill a zebra, though sometimes it has to be done at a fairly long range. If all you want is meat for the porters, the matter is simple enough. But when you require bait for a lion, that; is another affair entirely. In the first place, you must be able to stalk within a hundred yards of your kill without being seen; in the second place, you must provide two or three good lying-down places for your prospective trophy within fifteen yards of the carcass-and no more than two or three; in the third place, you must judge the direction of the probable morning wind, and must be able to approach from leeward. It is evidently pretty good luck to find an accommodating zebra in just such a spot. It is a matter of still greater nicety to drop him absolutely in his tracks. In a case of porters' meat it does not make any particular difference if he runs a hundred yards before he dies. With lion bait even fifty yards makes all the difference in the world.

C. and I talked it over and resolved to press Scallywattamus into service. Scallywattamus is a small white mule who is firmly convinced that each and every bush in Africa conceals a mule-eating rhinoceros, and who does not intend to be one of the number so eaten. But we had noticed that at times zebra would be so struck with the strange sight of Scallywattamus carrying a man, that they would let us get quite close. C. was to ride Scallywattamus while I trudged along under his lee ready to shoot.

We set out through the heat shimmer, gradually rising as the plain slanted. Imperceptibly the camp and the trees marking the river's course fell below us and into the heat haze. In the distance, close to the stream, we made out a blurred, brown-red solid mass which we knew for Masai cattle. Various little Thompson's gazelles skipped away to the left waggling their tails vigorously and continuously as Nature long since commanded "Tommies" to do. The heat haze steadied around the dim white line, so we could make out the individual animals. There were plenty of them, dozing in the sun. A single tiny treelet broke the plain just at the skyline of the rise. C. and I talked low-voiced as we went along. We agreed that the tree was an excellent landmark to come to, that the little rise afforded proper cover, and that in the morning the wind would in all likelihood blow toward the river. There were perhaps twenty zebra near enough to the chosen spot. Any of them would do.

But the zebra did not give a hoot for Scallywattamus. At five hundred yards three or four of them awoke with a start, stared at us a minute, and moved slowly away. They told all the zebra they happened upon that the three idiots approaching were at once uninteresting and dangerous. At four hundred and fifty yards a half dozen more made off at a trot. At three hundred and fifty yards the rest plunged away at a canter-all but one. He remained to stare, but his tail was up, and we knew he only stayed because he knew he could easily catch up in the next twenty seconds.

The chance was very slim of delivering a knockout at that distance, but we badly needed meat, anyway, after our march through the Thirst, so I tried him. We heard the well-known plunk of the bullet, but down went his head, up went his heels, and away went he. We watched him in vast disgust. He cavorted out into a bare open space without cover of any sort, and then flopped over. I thought I caught a fleeting grin of delight on Mavrouki's face; but he knew enough instantly to conceal his satisfaction over sure meat.

There were now no zebra anywhere near; but since nobody ever thinks of omitting any chances in Africa, I sneaked up to the tree and took a perfunctory look. There stood another, providentially absent-minded, zebra!

We got that one. Everybody was now happy. The boys raced over to the first kill, which soon took its dismembered way toward camp. C. and I carefully organized our plan of campaign. We fixed in our memories the exact location of each and every bush;

we determined compass direction from camp, and any other bearings likely to prove useful in finding so small a spot in the dark. Then we left a boy to keep carrion birds off until sunset; and returned home.

We were out in the morning before even the first sign of dawn. Billy rode her little mule, C. and I went afoot, Memba Sasa accompanied us because he could see whole lions where even C.'s trained eye could not make out an ear, and the syce went along to take care of the mule. The heavens were ablaze with the thronging stars of the tropics, so we found we could make out the skyline of the distant butte over the rise of the plains. The earth itself was a pool of absolute blackness. We could not see where we were placing our feet, and we were continually bringing up suddenly to walk around an unexpected aloe or thornbush. The night was quite still, but every once in a while from the blackness came rustlings, scamperings, low calls, and once or twice the startled barking of zebra very near at hand. The latter sounded as ridiculous as ever. It is one of the many incongruities of African life that Nature should have given so large and so impressive a creature the petulant yapping of an exasperated Pomeranian lap dog. At the end of three quarters of an hour of more or less stumbling progress, we made out against the sky the twisted treelet that served as our landmark. Billy dismounted, turned the mule over to the syce, and we crept slowly forward until within a guessed two or three hundred yards of our kill.

Nothing remained now but to wait for the daylight. It had already begun to show. Over behind the distant mountains some one was kindling the fires, and the stars were flickering out. The splendid ferocity of the African sunrise was at hand. Long bands of slate dark clouds lay close along the horizon, and behind them glowed a heart of fire, as on a small scale the lamplight glows through a metal-worked shade. On either side the sky was pale green-blue, translucent and pure, deep as infinity itself. The earth was still black, and the top of the rise near at hand was clear edged. On that edge, and by a strange chance accurately in the centre of illumination, stood the uncouth massive form of a shaggy wildebeeste, his head raised, staring to the east. He did not move; nothing of that fire and black world moved; only instant by instant it changed, swelling in glory toward some climax until one expected at any moment a fanfare of trumpets, the burst of triumphant culmination.

Then very far down in the distance a lion roared. The wildebeeste, without moving, bellowed back an answer or a defiance. Down in the hollow an ostrich boomed. Zebra barked, and several birds chirped strongly. The tension was breaking not in the expected fanfare and burst of triumphal music, but in a manner instantly felt to be more fitting to what was indeed a wonder, but a daily wonder for all that. At one and the same instant the rim of the sun appeared and the wildebeeste, after the sudden habit of his kind, made up his mind to go. He dropped his head and came thundering down past us at full speed. Straight to the west he headed, and so disappeared. We could hear the beat of his hoofs dying into the distance. He had gone like a Warder of the Morning whose task was finished. On the knife-edged skyline appeared the silhouette of slim-legged little Tommies, flirting their rails, sniffing at the dewy grass, dainty, slender, confiding, the open-day antithesis of the tremendous and awesome lord of the darkness that had roared its way to its lair, and to the massive shaggy herald of morning that had thundered down to the west.

## III. THE CENTRAL PLATEAU

Now is required a special quality of the imagination, not in myself, but in my readers, for it becomes necessary for them to grasp the logic of a whole country in one mental effort. The difficulties to me are very real. If I am to tell you it all in detail, your mind becomes confused to the point of mingling the ingredients of the description. The resultant mental picture is a composite; it mixes localities wide apart; it comes out, like the snake-creeper-swamp-forest thing of grammar-school South America, an unreal and deceitful impression. If, on the other hand, I try to give you a bird's-eye view-saying, here is plain, and there follows upland, and yonder succeed mountains and hills-you lose the sense of breadth and space and the toil of many days. The feeling of onward outward extending distance is gone; and that impression so indispensable to finite understanding- "here am I, and what is beyond is to be measured by the length of my legs and the toil of my days." You will not stop long enough on my plains to realize their physical extent nor their influence on the human soul. If I mention them in a sentence, you dismiss them in a thought. And that is something the plains themselves refuse to permit you to do. Yet sometimes one must become a guide-book, and bespeak his reader's imagination.

The country, then, wherein we travelled begins at the sea. Along the coast stretches a low rolling country of steaming tropics, grown with cocoanuts, bananas, mangoes, and populated by a happy, half-naked race of the Swahilis. Leaving the coast, the country rises through hills. These hills are at first fertile and green and wooded. Later they turn into an almost unbroken plateau of thorn scrub, cruel, monotonous, almost impenetrable. Fix thorn scrub in your mind, with rhino trails, and occasional openings for game, and a few rivers flowing through palms and narrow jungle strips; fix it in your mind until your mind is filled with it, until you are convinced that nothing else can exist in the world but more and more of the monotonous, terrible, dry, onstretching desert of thorn.

Then pass through this to the top of the hills inland, and journey over these hills to the highland plains.

Now sense and appreciate these wide seas of and the hills and ranges of mountains rising from them, and their infinite diversity of country-their rivers marked by ribbons of jungle, their scattered-bush and their thick-bush areas, their grass expanses, and their great distances extending far over exceedingly wide horizons. Realize how many weary hours you must travel to gain the nearest butte, what days of toil the view from its top will disclose. Savour the fact that you can spend months in its veriest corner without exhausting its possibilities. Then, and not until then, raise your eyes to the low rising transverse range that bands it to the west as the thorn desert bands it to the east.

And on these ranges are the forests, the great bewildering forests. In what looks like a grove lying athwart a little hill you can lose yourself for days. Here dwell millions of savages in an apparently untouched wilderness. Here rises a snow mountain on the equator. Here are tangles and labyrinths, great bamboo forests lost in folds of the mightiest hills. Here are the elephants. Here are the swinging vines, the jungle itself.

Yet finally it breaks. We come out on the edge of things and look down on a great gash in the earth. It is like a sunken kingdom in itself, miles wide, with its own mountain ranges, its own rivers, its own landscape features. Only on either side of it rise the escarpments which are the true level of the plateau. One can spend two months in this valley, too, and in the countries south to which it leads. And on its farther side are the high plateau plains again, or the forests, or the desert, or the great lakes that lie at the source of the Nile.

So now, perhaps, we are a little prepared to go ahead. The guide-book work is finished for good and all. There is the steaming hot low coast belt, and the hot dry thorn desert belt, and the varied immense plains, and the high mountain belt of the forests, and again the variegated wide country of the Rift Valley and the high plateau. To attempt to tell you seriatim and in detail just what they are like is the task of an encyclopaedist. Perhaps more indirectly you may be able to fill in the picture of the country, the people, and the beasts.

# IV. THE FIRST CAMP

Our very first start into the new country was made when we piled out from the little train standing patiently awaiting the good pleasure of our descent. That feature strikes me with ever new wonder-the accommodating way trains of the Uganda Railway have of waiting for you. One day, at a little wayside station, C. and I were idly exchanging remarks with the only white man in sight, killing time until the engine should whistle to a resumption of the journey. The guard lingered about just out of earshot. At the end of five minutes C. happened to catch his eye, whereupon he ventured to approach.

"When you have finished your conversation," said he politely, "we are all ready to go on."

On the morning in question there were a lot of us to disembark-one hundred and twenty-two, to be exact-of which four were white. We were not yet acquainted with our men, nor yet with our stores, nor with the methods of our travel. The train went off and left us in the middle of a high plateau, with low ridges running across it, and mountains in the distance. Men were squabbling earnestly for the most convenient loads to carry, and as fast as they had gained undisputed possession, they marked the loads with some private sign of their own. M'ganga, the headman, tall, fierce, big-framed and bony, clad in fez, a long black overcoat, blue puttees and boots, stood stiff as a ramrod, extended a rigid right arm and rattled off orders in a high dynamic voice. In his left hand he clasped a bulgy umbrella, the badge of his dignity and the symbol of his authority. The four askaris, big men too, with masterful high-cheekboned countenances, rushed here and there seeing that the orders were carried out. Expostulations, laughter, the sound of quarrelling rose and fell. Never could the combined volume of it all override the firecracker stream of M'ganga's eloquence.

We had nothing to do with it all, but stood a little dazed, staring at the novel scene. Our men were of many tribes, each with its own cast of features, its own notions of what befitted man's performance of his duties here below. They stuck together each in its clan. A fine free individualism of personal adornment characterized them. Every man dressed for his own satisfaction solely. They hung all sorts of things in the distended lobes of their ears. One had succeeded in inserting a fine big glittering tobacco tin. Others had invented elaborate topiary designs in their hair, shaving their heads so as to leave strange tufts, patches, crescents on the most unexpected places. Of the intricacy of these designs they seemed absurdly proud. Various sorts of treasure trove hung from them-a bunch of keys to which there were no locks, discarded hunting knives, tips of antelope horns, discharged brass cartridges, a hundred and one valueless trifles plucked proudly from the rubbish heap. They were all clothed. We had supplied each with a red blanket, a blue jersey, and a water bottle. The blankets they were twisting most ingeniously into turbans.

14

Beside these they sported a great variety of garments. Shooting coats that had seen better days, a dozen shabby overcoats-worn proudly through the hottest noons-raggety breeches and trousers made by some London tailor, queer baggy homemades of the same persuasion, or quite simply the square of cotton cloth arranged somewhat like a short tight skirt, or nothing at all as the man's taste ran. They were many of them amusing enough; but somehow they did not look entirely farcical and ridiculous, like our negroes putting on airs. All these things were worn with a simplicity of quiet confidence in their entire fitness. And beneath the red blanket turbans the half-wild savage faces peered out.

Now Mahomet approached. Mahomet was my personal boy. He was a Somali from the Northwest coast, dusky brown, with the regular clear-cut features of a Greek marble god. His dress was of neat khaki, and he looked down on savages; but, also, as with all the dark-skinned races, up to his white master. Mahomet was with me during all my African stay, and tested out nobly. As yet, of course, I did not know him.

"Chakula taiari," said he.

That is Swahili. It means literally "food is ready." After one has hunted in Africa for a few months, it means also "paradise is opened," "grief is at an end," "joy and thanksgiving are now in order," and similar affairs. Those two words are never forgotten, and the veriest beginner in Swahili can recognize them without the slightest effort.

We followed Mahomet. Somehow, without orders, in all this confusion, the personal staff had been quietly and efficiently busy. Drawn a little to one side stood a table with four chairs. The table was covered with a white cloth, and was set with a beautiful white enamel service. We took our places. Behind each chair straight as a ramrod stood a neat khaki-clad boy. They brought us food, and presented it properly on the left side, waiting like well-trained butlers. We might have been in a London restaurant. As three of us were Americans, we felt a trifle dazed. The porters, having finished the distribution of their loads, squatted on their heels and watched us respectfully.

And then, not two hundred yards away, four ostriches paced slowly across the track, paying not the slightest attention to us-our first real wild ostriches, scornful of oranges, careless of tourists, and rightful guardians of their own snowy plumes. The passage of these four solemn birds seemed somehow to lend this strange open-air meal an exotic flavour. We were indeed in Africa; and the ostriches helped us to realize it.

We finished breakfast and arose from our chairs. Instantly a half dozen men sprang forward. Before our amazed eyes the table service, the chairs and the table itself disappeared into neat packages. M'ganga arose to his feet.

"Bandika!" he cried.

The askaris rushed here and there actively.

"Bandika! bandika! bandika!" they cried repeatedly.

The men sprang into activity. A struggle heaved the varicoloured multitude-and, lo! each man stood upright, his load balanced on his head. At the same moment the syces led up our horses, mounted and headed across the little plain whence had come the four ostriches. Our African journey had definitely begun.

Behind us, all abreast marched the four gunbearers; then the four syces; then the safari single file, an askari at the head bearing proudly his ancient musket and our banner, other askaris flanking, M'ganga bringing up the rear with his mighty umbrella and an unsuspected rhinoceros-hide whip. The tent boys and the cook scattered along the flank anywhere, as befitted the free and independent who had nothing to do with the serious business of marching. A measured sound of drumming followed the beating of loads with a hundred sticks; a wild, weird chanting burst from the ranks and died down again as one or another individual or group felt moved to song. One lot had a formal chant and response. Their leader, in a high falsetto, said something like,

15

"Kuna koma kuno,"

and all his tribesmen would follow with a single word in a deep gruff tone,

"Za-la-nee!"

All of which undoubtedly helped immensely.

The country was a bully country, but somehow it did not look like Africa. That is to say, it looked altogether too much like any amount of country at home. There was nothing strange and exotic about it. We crossed a little plain, and up over a small hill, down into a shallow canyon that seemed to be wooded with live oaks, across a grass valley or so, and around a grass hill. Then we went into camp at the edge of another grass valley, by a stream across which rose some ordinary low cliffs.

That is the disconcerting thing about a whole lot of this country-it is so much like home. Of course, there are many wide districts exotic enough in all conscience-the jungle beds of the rivers, the bamboo forests, the great tangled forests themselves, the banana groves down the aisles of which dance savages with shields-but so very much of it is familiar. One needs only church spires and a red-roofed village or so to imagine one's self in Surrey. There is any amount of country like Arizona, and more like the uplands of Wyoming, and a lot of it resembling the smaller landscapes of New England. The prospects of the whole world are there, so that somewhere every wanderer can find the countryside of his own home repeated. And, by the same token, that is exactly what makes a good deal of it so startling. When a man sees a file of spear-armed savages, or a pair of snorty old rhinos, step out into what has seemed practically his own back yard home, he is even more startled than if he had encountered them in quite strange surroundings.

We rode into the grass meadow and picked camp site. The men trailed in and dumped down their loads in a row.

At a signal they set to work. A dozen to each tent got them up in a jiffy. A long file brought firewood from the stream bed. Others carried water, stones for the cook, a dozen other matters. The tent boys rescued our boxes; they put together the cots and made the beds, even before the tents were raised from the ground. Within an incredibly short space of time the three green tents were up and arranged, each with its bed made, its mosquito bar hung, its personal box open, its folding washstand ready with towels and soap, the table and chairs unlimbered. At a discreet distance flickered the cook campfire, and at a still discreeter distance the little tents of the men gleamed pure white against the green of the high grass.

# V. MEMBA SASA

I wish I could plunge you at once into the excitements of big game in Africa, but I cannot truthfully do so. To be sure, we went hunting that afternoon, up over the low cliffs, and we saw several of a very lively little animal known as the Chandler's reedbuck. This was not supposed to be a game country, and that was all we did see. At these we shot several times-disgracefully. In fact, for several days we could not shoot at all, at any range, nor at anything. It was very sad, and very aggravating. Afterward we found that this is an invariable experience to the newcomer. The light is new, the air is different, the

16

sizes of the game are deceiving. Nobody can at first hit anything. At the end of five days we suddenly began to shoot our normal gait. Why, I do not know.

But in this afternoon tramp around the low cliffs after the elusive reedbuck, I for the first time became acquainted with a man who developed into a real friend.

His name is Memba Sasa. Memba Sasa are two Swahili words meaning "now a crocodile." Subsequently, after I had learned to talk Swahili, I tried to find out what he was formerly, before he was a crocodile, but did not succeed.

He was of the tribe of the Monumwezi, of medium height, compactly and sturdily built, carried himself very erect, and moved with a concentrated and vigorous purposefulness. His countenance might be described as pleasing but not handsome, of a dark chocolate brown, with the broad nose of the negro, but with a firm mouth, high cheekbones, and a frowning intentness of brow that was very fine. When you talked to him he looked you straight in the eye. His own eyes were shaded by long, soft, curling lashes behind which they looked steadily and gravely-sometimes fiercely-on the world. He rarely smiled-never merely in understanding or for politeness' sake-and never laughed unless there was something really amusing. Then he chuckled from deep in his chest, the most contagious laughter you can imagine. Often we, at the other end of the camp, have laughed in sympathy, just at the sound of that deep and hearty ho! ho! ho! of Memba Sasa. Even at something genuinely amusing he never laughed much, nor without a very definite restraint. In fact, about him was no slackness, no sprawling abandon of the native in relaxation; but always a taut efficiency and a never-failing self-respect.

Naturally, behind such a fixed moral fibre must always be some moral idea. When a man lives up to a real, not a pompous, dignity some ideal must inform it. Memba Sasa's ideal was that of the Hunter.

He was a gunbearer; and he considered that a good gunbearer stood quite a few notches above any other human being, save always the white man, of course. And even among the latter Memba Sasa made great differences. These differences he kept to himself, and treated all with equal respect. Nevertheless, they existed, and Memba Sasa very well knew that fact. In the white world were two classes of masters: those who hunted well, and those who were considered by them as their friends and equals. Why they should be so considered Memba Sasa did not know, but he trusted the Hunter's judgment. These were the bwanas, or masters. All the rest were merely mazungos, or, "white men." To their faces he called them bwana, but in his heart he considered them not.

Observe, I say those who hunted well. Memba Sasa, in his profession as gunbearer, had to accompany those who hunted badly. In them he took no pride; from them he held aloof in spirit; but for them he did his conscientious best, upheld by the dignity of his profession.

For to Mamba Sasa that profession was the proudest to which a black man could aspire. He prided himself on mastering its every detail, in accomplishing its every duty minutely and exactly. The major virtues of a gunbearer are not to be despised by anybody; for they comprise great physical courage, endurance, and loyalty: the accomplishments of a gunbearer are worthy of a man's best faculties, for they include the ability to see and track game, to take and prepare properly any sort of a trophy, field taxidermy, butchering game meat, wood and plainscraft, the knowledge of how properly to care for firearms in all sorts of circumstances, and a half hundred other like minutiae. Memba Sasa knew these things, and he performed them with the artist's love for details; and his keen eyes were always spying for new ways.

At a certain time I shot an egret, and prepared to take the skin. Memba Sasa asked if he might watch me do it. Two months later, having killed a really gaudy peacocklike member of the guinea fowl tribe, I handed it over to him with instructions to take off the breast feathers before giving it to the cook. In a half hour he brought me the complete skin, I examined it carefully, and found it to be well done in every respect. Now in skinning a bird there are a number of delicate and unusual operations, such as stripping the primary quills from the bone, cutting the ear cover, and the like. I had explained none of them; and yet Memba Sasa, unassisted, had grasped their method from a single demonstration and had remembered them all two months later! C. had a trick in making the second skin incision of a trophy head that had the effect of giving a better purchase to the knife. Its exact description would be out of place here, but it actually consisted merely in inserting the point of the knife two inches away from the place it is ordinarily inserted. One day we noticed that Memba Sasa was making his incisions in that manner. I went to Africa fully determined to care for my own rifle. The modern high-velocity gun needs rather especial treatment; mere wiping out will not do. I found that Memba Sasa already knew all about boiling water, and the necessity for having it really boiling, about subsequent metal sweating, and all the rest. After watching him at work I concluded, rightly, that he would do a lot better job than I.

To the new employer Memba Sasa maintained an attitude of strict professional loyalty. His personal respect was upheld by the necessity of every man to do his job in the world. Memba Sasa did his. He cleaned the rifles; he saw that everything was in order for the day's march; he was at my elbow all ways with more cartridges and the spare rifle; he trailed and looked conscientiously. In his attitude was the stolidity of the wooden Indian. No action of mine, no joke on the part of his companions, no circumstance in the varying fortunes of the field gained from him the faintest flicker of either approval, disapproval, or interest. When we returned to camp he deposited my water bottle and camera, seized the cleaning implements, and departed to his own campfire. In the field he pointed out game that I did not see, and waited imperturbably the result of my shot.

As I before stated, the result of that shot for the first five days was very apt to be nil. This, at the time, puzzled and grieved me a lot. Occasionally I looked at Memba Sasa to catch some sign of sympathy, disgust, contempt, or-rarely-triumph at a lucky shot. Nothing. He gently but firmly took away my rifle, reloaded it, and handed it back; then waited respectfully for my next move. He knew no English, and I no Swahili.

But as time went on this attitude changed. I was armed with the new Springfield rifle, a weapon with 2,700 feet velocity, and with a marvellously flat trajectory. This commanding advantage, combined with a very long familiarity with firearms, enabled me to do some fairish shooting, after the strangeness of these new conditions had been mastered. Memba Sasa began to take a dawning interest in me as a possible source of pride. We began to develop between us a means of communication. I set myself deliberately to learn his language, and after he had cautiously determined that I really meant it, he took the greatest pains-always gravely-to teach me. A more human feeling sprang up between us.

But we had still the final test to undergo-that of danger and the tight corner.

In close quarters the gunbearer has the hardest job in the world. I have the most profound respect for his absolute courage. Even to a man armed and privileged to shoot and defend himself, a charging lion is an awesome thing, requiring a certain amount of coolness and resolution to face effectively. Think of the gunbearer at his elbow, depending not on himself but on the courage and coolness of another. He cannot do one solitary thing to defend himself. To bolt for the safety of a tree is to beg the question completely, to brand himself as a shenzi forever; to fire a gun in any circumstances is to beg the question also, for the white man must be able to depend absolutely on his second gun in an emergency. Those things are outside consideration, even, of any respectable gunbearer. In addition, he must keep cool. He must see clearly in the thickest excitement; must be ready unobtrusively to pass up the second gun in the position most convenient for immediate use, to seize the other and to perform the finicky task of reloading correctly while some rampageous beast is raising particular thunder a few yards away. All this in absolute dependence on the ability of his bwana to deal with the situation. I can confess very truly that once or twice that little unobtrusive touch of Memba Sasa crouched close to my elbow steadied me with the thought of how little right I-with a rifle in my hand-had to be scared. And the best compliment I ever received I overheard by chance. I had wounded a lion when out by myself, and had returned to camp for a heavier rifle and for Memba Sasa to do the trailing. From my tent I overheard the following conversation between Memba Sasa and the cook:

"The grass is high," said the cook. "Are you not afraid to go after a wounded lion with only one white man?"

"My one white man is enough," replied Memba Sasa.

It is a quality of courage that I must confess would be quite beyond me-to depend entirely on the other fellow, and not at all on myself. This courage is always remarkable to me, even in the case of the gunbearer who knows all about the man whose heels he follows. But consider that of the gunbearer's first experience with a stranger. The former has no idea of how the white man will act; whether he will get nervous, get actually panicky, lose his shooting ability, and generally mess things up. Nevertheless, he follows his master in, and he stands by. If the hunter fails, the gunbearer will probably die. To me it is rather fine: for he does it, not from the personal affection and loyalty which will carry men far, but from a sheer sense of duty and pride of caste. The quiet pride of the really good men, like Memba Sasa, is easy to understand.

And the records are full of stories of the white man who has not made good: of the coward who bolts, leaving his black man to take the brunt of it, or who sticks but loses his head. Each new employer must be very closely and interestedly scrutinized. In the light of subsequent experience, I can no longer wonder at Memba Sasa's first detached and impersonal attitude.

As time went on, however, and we grew to know each other better, this attitude entirely changed. At first the change consisted merely in dropping the disinterested pose as respects game. For it was a pose. Memba Sasa was most keenly interested in game whenever it was an object of pursuit. It did not matter how common the particular species might be: if we wanted it, Memba Sasa would look upon it with eager ferocity; and if we did not want it, he paid no attention to it at all. When we started in the morning, or in the relaxation of our return at night, I would mention casually a few of the things that might prove acceptable.

"To-morrow we want kongoni for boys' meat, or zebra; and some meat for masters-Tommy, impala, oribi," and Memba Sasa knew as well as I did what we needed to fill out our trophy collection. When he caught sight of one of these animals his whole countenance changed. The lines of his face set, his lips drew back from his teeth, his eyes fairly darted fire in the fixity of their gaze. He was like a fine pointer dog on birds, or like the splendid savage he was at heart.

"M'palla!" he hissed; and then after a second, in a restrained fierce voice, "Na-ona? Do you see?"

If I did not see he pointed cautiously. His own eyes never left the beast. Rarely he stayed put while I made the stalk. More often he glided like a snake at my heels. If the bullet hit, Memba Sasa always exhaled a grunt of satisfaction-"hah!"-in which triumph and satisfaction mingled with a faint derision at the unfortunate beast. In case of a trophy he squatted anxiously at the animal's head while I took my measurements, assisting very intelligently with the tape line. When I had finished, he always looked up at me with wrinkled brow.

19

"Footie n'gapi?" he inquired. This means literally, "How many feet?", footie being his euphemistic invention of a word for the tape. I would tell him how many "footie" and how many "inchie" the measurement proved to be. From the depths of his wonderful memory he would dig up the measurements of another beast of the same sort I had killed months back, but which he had remembered accurately from a single hearing.

The shooting of a beast he always detailed to his few cronies in camp: the other gunbearers, and one or two from his own tribe. He always used the first person plural, "we" did so and so; and took an inordinate pride in making out his bwana as being an altogether superior person to any of the other gunbearer's bwanas. Over a miss he always looked sad; but with a dignified sadness as though we had met with undeserved misfortune sent by malignant gods. If there were any possible alleviating explanation, Memba Sasa made the most of it, provided our fiasco was witnessed. If we were alone in our disgrace, he buried the incident fathoms deep. He took an inordinate pride in our using the minimum number of cartridges, and would explain to me in a loud tone of voice that we had cartridges enough in the belt. When we had not cartridges enough, he would sneak around after dark to get some more. At times he would even surreptitiously "lift" a few from B.'s gunbearer!

When in camp, with his "cazi" finished, Memba Sasa did fancy work! The picture of this powerful half-savage, his fierce brows bent over a tiny piece of linen, his strong fingers fussing with little stitches, will always appeal to my sense of the incongruous. Through a piece of linen he punched holes with a porcupine quill. Then he "buttonhole" stitched the holes, and embroidered patterns between them with fine white thread. The result was an openwork pattern heavily encrusted with beautiful fine embroidery. It was most astounding stuff, such as you would expect from a French convent, perhaps, but never from an African savage. He did a circular piece and a long narrow piece. They took him three months to finish, and then he sewed them together to form a skull cap. Billy, entranced with the lacelike delicacy of the work, promptly captured it; whereupon Memba Sasa philosophically started another.

By this time he had identified himself with my fortunes. We had become a firm whose business it was to carry out the affairs of a single personality-me. Memba Sasa, among other things, undertook the dignity. When I walked through a crowd, Memba Sasa zealously kicked everybody out of my royal path. When I started to issue a command, Memba Sasa finished it and amplified it and put a snapper on it. When I came into camp, Memba Sasa saw to it personally that my tent went up promptly and properly, although that was really not part of his "cazi" at all. And when somewhere beyond my ken some miserable boy had committed a crime, I never remained long in ignorance of that fact.

Perhaps I happened to be sitting in my folding chair idly smoking a pipe and reading a book. Across the open places of the camp would stride Memba Sasa, very erect, very rigid, moving in short indignant jerks, his eye flashing fire. Behind him would sneak a very hang-dog boy. Memba Sasa marched straight up to me, faced right, and drew one side, his silence sparkling with honest indignation.

"Just look at THAT!" his attitude seemed to say, "Could you believe such human depravity possible? And against OUR authority?"

He always stood, quite rigid, waiting for me to speak.

"Well, Memba Sasa?" I would inquire, after I had enjoyed the show a little.

In a few restrained words he put the case before me, always briefly, always with a scornful dignity. This shenzi has done so-and-so.

We will suppose the case fairly serious. I listened to the man's story, if necessary called a few witnesses, delivered judgment. All the while Memba Sasa stood at rigid attention, fairly bristling virtue, like the good dog standing by at the punishment of the bad dogs.

20

And in his attitude was a subtle triumph, as one would say: "You see! Fool with my bwana, will you! Just let anybody try to get funny with US!" Judgment pronounced-we have supposed the case serious, you remember-Memba Sasa himself applied the lash. I think he really enjoyed that; but it was a restrained joy. The whip descended deliberately, without excitement.

The man's devotion in unusual circumstances was beyond praise. Danger or excitement incite a sort of loyalty in any good man; but humdrum, disagreeable difficulty is a different matter.

One day we marched over a country of thorn-scrub desert. Since two days we had been cut loose from water, and had been depending on a small amount carried in zinc drums. Now our only reasons for faring were a conical hill, over the horizon, and the knowledge of a river somewhere beyond. How far beyond, or in what direction, we did not know. We had thirty men with us, a more or less ragtag lot, picked up anyhow in the bazaars. They were soft, ill-disciplined and uncertain. For five or six hours they marched well enough. Then the sun began to get very hot, and some of them began to straggle. They had, of course, no intention of deserting, for their only hope of surviving lay in staying with us; but their loads had become heavy, and they took too many rests. We put a good man behind, but without much avail. In open country a safari can be permitted to straggle over miles, for always it can keep in touch by sight; but in this thorn-scrub desert, that looks all alike, a man fifty yards out of sight is fifty yards lost. We would march fifteen or twenty minutes, then sit down to wait until the rearmost men had straggled in, perhaps a half hour later. And we did not dare move on until the tale of our thirty was complete. At this rate progress was very slow, and as the fierce equatorial sun increased in strength, became always slower still. The situation became alarming. We were quite out of water, and we had no idea where water was to be found. To complicate matters, the thornbrush thickened to a jungle.

My single companion and I consulted. It was agreed that I was to push on as rapidly as possible to locate the water, while he was to try to hold the caravan together. Accordingly, Memba Sasa and I marched ahead. We tried to leave a trail to follow; and we hoped fervently that our guess as to the stream's course would prove to be a good one. At the end of two hours and a half we found the water-a beautiful jungle-shaded stream-and filled ourselves up therewith. Our duty was accomplished, for we had left a trail to be followed. Nevertheless, I felt I should like to take back our full canteens to relieve the worst cases. Memba Sasa would not hear of it, and even while I was talking to him seized the canteens and disappeared.

At the end of two hours more camp was made, after a fashion; but still four men had failed to come in. We built a smudge in the hope of guiding them; and gave them up. If they had followed our trail, they should have been in long ago; if they had missed that trail, heaven knows where they were, or where we should go to find them. Dusk was falling, and, to tell the truth, we were both very much done up by a long day at 115 degrees in the shade under an equatorial sun. The missing men would climb trees away from the beasts, and we would organize a search next day. As we debated these things, to us came Memba Sasa.

"I want to take 'Winchi,'" said he. "Winchi" is his name for my Winchester 405.

"Why?" we asked.

"If I can take Winchi, I will find the men," said he.

This was entirely voluntary on his part. He, as well as we, had had a hard day, and he had made a double journey for part of it. We gave him Winchi and he departed. Sometime after midnight he returned with the missing men.

Perhaps a dozen times all told he volunteered for these special services; once in particular, after a fourteen-hour day, he set off at nine o'clock at night in a soaking rainstorm, wandered until two o'clock, and returned unsuccessful, to rouse me and report gravely that he could not find them. For these services he neither received nor expected special reward. And catch him doing anything outside his strict "cazi" except for US.

We were always very ceremonious and dignified in our relations on such occasions. Memba Sasa would suddenly appear, deposit the rifle in its place, and stand at attention.

"Well, Memba Sasa?" I would inquire.

"I have found the men; they are in camp."

Then I would give him his reward. It was either the word "assanti," or the two words "assanti sana," according to the difficulty and importance of the task accomplished. They mean simply "thank you" and "thank you very much."

Once or twice, after a particularly long and difficult month or so, when Memba Sasa has been almost literally my alter ego, I have called him up for special praise. "I am very pleased with you, Memba Sasa," said I. "You have done your cazi well. You are a good man."

He accepted this with dignity, without deprecation, and without the idiocy of spoken gratitude. He agreed perfectly with everything I said! "Yes" was his only comment. I liked it.

On our ultimate success in a difficult enterprise Memba Sasa set great store; and his delight in ultimate success was apparently quite apart from personal considerations. We had been hunting greater kudu for five weeks before we finally landed one. The greater kudu is, with the bongo, easily the prize beast in East Africa, and very few are shot. By a piece of bad luck, for him, I had sent Memba Sasa out in a different direction to look for signs the afternoon we finally got one. The kill was made just at dusk. C. and I, with Mavrouki, built a fire and stayed, while Kongoni went to camp after men. There he broke the news to Memba Sasa that the great prize had been captured, and he absent. Memba Sasa was hugely delighted, nor did he in any way show what must have been a great disappointment to him. After repeating the news triumphantly to every one in camp, he came out to where we were waiting, arrived quite out of breath, and grabbed me by the hand in heartiest congratulation.

Memba Sasa went in not at all for personal ornamentation, any more than he allowed his dignity to be broken by anything resembling emotionalism. No tattoo marks, no ear ornaments, no rings nor bracelets. He never even picked up an ostrich feather for his head. On the latter he sometimes wore an old felt hat; sometimes, more picturesquely, an orange-coloured fillet. Khaki shirt, khaki "shorts," blue puttees, besides his knife and my own accoutrements: that was all. In town he was all white clad, a long fine linen robe reaching to his feet; and one of the lacelike skull caps he was so very skilful at making.

That will do for a preliminary sketch. If you follow these pages, you will hear more of him; he is worth it.

# VI. THE FIRST GAME CAMP

In the review of "first" impressions with which we are concerned, we must now skip a week or ten days to stop at what is known in our diaries as the First Ford of the Guaso Nyero River.

These ten days were not uneventful. We had crossed the wide and undulating plains, had paused at some tall beautiful falls plunging several hundred feet into the mysteriousness of a dense forest on which we looked down. There we had enjoyed some duck, goose and snipe shooting; had made the acquaintance of a few of the Masai, and had looked with awe on our first hippo tracks in the mud beside a tiny ditchlike stream. Here and there were small game herds. In the light of later experience we now realize that these were nothing at all; but at the time the sight of full-grown wild animals out in plain sight was quite wonderful. At the close of the day's march we always wandered out with our rifles to see what we could find. Everything was new to us, and we had our men to feed. Our shooting gradually improved until we had overcome the difficulties peculiar to this new country and were doing as well as we could do anywhere.

Now, at the end of a hard day through scrub, over rolling bold hills, and down a scrub brush slope, we had reached the banks of the Guaso Nyero.

At this point, above the junction of its principal tributary rivers, it was a stream about sixty or seventy feet wide, flowing swift between high banks. A few trees marked its course, but nothing like a jungle. The ford was in swift water just above a deep still pool suspected of crocodiles. We found the water about waist deep, stretched a rope across, and forcibly persuaded our eager boys that one at a time was about what the situation required. On the other side we made camp on an open flat. Having marched so far continuously, we resolved to settle down for a while. The men had been without sufficient meat; and we desired very much to look over the country closely, and to collect a few heads as trophies.

Perhaps a word might not come amiss as to the killing of game. The case is here quite different from the condition of affairs at home. Here animal life is most extraordinarily abundant; it furnishes the main food supply to the traveller; and at present is probably increasing slightly, certainly holding its own. Whatever toll the sportsman or traveller take is as nothing compared to what he might take if he were an unscrupulous game hog. If his cartridges and his shoulder held out, he could easily kill a hundred animals a day instead of the few he requires. In that sense, then, no man slaughters indiscriminately. During the course of a year he probably shoots from two hundred to two hundred and fifty beasts, provided he is travelling with an ordinary sized caravan. This, the experts say, is about the annual toll of one lion. If the traveller gets his lion, he plays even with the fauna of the country; if he gets two or more lions, he has something to his credit. This probably explains why the game is still so remarkably abundant near the road and on the very outskirts of the town.

We were now much in need of a fair quantity of meat, both for immediate consumption of our safari, and to make biltong or jerky. Later, in like circumstances, we should have sallied forth in a businesslike fashion, dropped the requisite number of zebra and hartebeeste as near camp as possible, and called it a job. Now, however, being new to the game, we much desired good trophies in variety. Therefore, we scoured the country far and wide for desirable heads; and the meat waited upon the acquisition of the trophy.

This, then, might be called our first Shooting Camp. Heretofore we had travelled every day. Now the boys settled down to what the native porter considers the height of bliss: a permanent camp with plenty to eat. Each morning we were off before daylight, riding our

23

horses, and followed by the gunbearers, the syces, and fifteen or twenty porters. The country rose from the river in a long gentle slope grown with low brush and scattered candlestick euphorbias. This slope ended in a scattered range of low rocky buttes. Through any one of the various openings between them, we rode to find ourselves on the borders of an undulating grass country of low rounded hills with wide valleys winding between them. In these valleys and on these hills was the game.

Daylight of the day I would tell about found us just at the edge of the little buttes. Down one of the slopes the growing half light revealed two oryx feeding, magnificent big creatures, with straight rapier horns three feet in length. These were most exciting and desirable, so off my horse I got and began to sneak up on them through the low tufts of grass. They fed quite calmly. I congratulated myself, and slipped nearer. Without even looking in my direction, they trotted away. Somewhat chagrined, I returned to my companions, and we rode on.

Then across a mile-wide valley we saw two dark objects in the tall grass; and almost immediately identified these as rhinoceroses, the first we had seen. They stood there side by side, gazing off into space, doing nothing in a busy morning world. After staring at them through our glasses for some time, we organized a raid. At the bottom of the valley we left the horses and porters; lined up, each with his gunbearer at his elbow; and advanced on the enemy. B. was to have the shot According to all the books we should have been able, provided we were downwind and made no noise, to have approached within fifty or sixty yards undiscovered. However, at a little over a hundred yards they both turned tail and departed at a swift trot, their heads held well up and their tails sticking up straight and stiff in the most ridiculous fashion. No good shooting at them in such circumstances, so we watched them go, still keeping up their slashing trot, growing smaller and smaller in the distance until finally they disappeared over the top of a swell.

We set ourselves methodically to following them. It took us over an hour of steady plodding before we again came in sight of them. They were this time nearer the top of a hill, and we saw instantly that the curve of the slope was such that we could approach within fifty yards before coming in sight at all. Therefore, once more we dismounted, lined up in battle array, and advanced.

Sensations? Distinctly nervous, decidedly alert, and somewhat self-congratulatory that I was not more scared. No man can predicate how efficient he is going to be in the presence of really dangerous game. Only the actual trial will show. This is not a question of courage at all, but of purely involuntary reaction of the nerves. Very few men are physical cowards. They will and do face anything. But a great many men are rendered inefficient by the way their nervous systems act under stress. It is not a matter for control by will power in the slightest degree. So the big game hunter must determine by actual trial whether it so happens that the great excitement of danger renders his hand shaky or steady. The excitement in either case is the same. No man is ever "cool" in the sense that personal danger is of the same kind of indifference to him as clambering aboard a street car. He must always be lifted above himself, must enter an extra normal condition to meet extra normal circumstances. He can always control his conduct; but he can by no means always determine the way the inevitable excitement will affect his coordinations. And unfortunately, in the final result it does not matter how brave a man is, but how closely he can hold. If he finds that his nervous excitement renders him unsteady, he has no business ever to tackle dangerous game alone. If, on the other hand, he discovers that IDENTICALLY THE SAME nervous excitement happens to steady his front sight to rocklike rigidity-a rigidity he could not possibly attain in normal conditions-then he will probably keep out of trouble.

To amplify this further by a specific instance: I hunted for a short time in Africa with a man who was always eager for exciting encounters, whose pluck was admirable in every way, but whose nervous reaction so manifested itself that he was utterly unable to do even decent shooting at any range. Furthermore, his very judgment and power of observation were so obscured that he could not remember afterward with any accuracy what had happened-which way the beast was pointing, how many there were of them, in which direction they went, how many shots were fired, in short all the smaller details of the affair. He thought he remembered. After the show was over it was quite amusing to get his version of the incident. It was almost always so wide of the fact as to be little recognizable. And, mind you, he was perfectly sincere in his belief, and absolutely courageous. Only he was quite unfitted by physical make-up for a big game hunter; and I was relieved when, after a short time, his route and mine separated.

Well, we clambered up that slope with a fine compound of tension, expectation, and latent uneasiness as to just what was going to happen, anyway. Finally, we raised the backs of the beasts, stooped, sneaked a little nearer, and finally at a signal stood upright perhaps forty yards from the brutes.

For the first time I experienced a sensation I was destined many times to repeat-that of the sheer size of the animals. Menagerie rhinoceroses had been of the smaller Indian variety; and in any case most menagerie beasts are more or less stunted. These two, facing us, their little eyes blinking, looked like full-grown ironclads on dry land. The moment we stood erect B. fired at the larger of the two. Instantly they turned and were off at a tearing run. I opened fire, and B. let loose his second barrel. At about two hundred and fifty yards the big rhinoceros suddenly fell on his side, while the other continued his flight. It was all over-very exciting because we got excited, but not in the least dangerous.

The boys were delighted, for here was meat in plenty for everybody. We measured the beast, photographed him, marvelled at his immense size, and turned him over to the gunbearers for treatment. In half an hour or so a long string of porters headed across the hills in the direction of camp, many miles distant, each carrying his load either of meat, or the trophies. Rhinoceros hide, properly treated, becomes as transparent as amber, and so from it can be made many very beautiful souvenirs, such as bowls, trays, paper knives, table tops, whips, canes, and the like. And, of course, the feet of one's first rhino are always saved for cigar boxes or inkstands.

Already we had an admiring and impatient audience. From all directions came the carrion birds. They circled far up in the heavens; they shot downward like plummets from a great height with an inspiring roar of wings; they stood thick in a solemn circle all around the scene of the kill; they rose with a heavy flapping when we moved in their direction. Skulking forms flashed in the grass, and occasionally the pointed ears of a jackal would rise inquiringly.

It was by now nearly noon. The sun shone clear and hot; the heat shimmer rose in clouds from the brown surface of the hills. In all directions we could make out small gameherds resting motionless in the heat of the day, the mirage throwing them into fantastic shapes. While the final disposition was being made of the defunct rhinoceros I wandered over the edge of the hill to see what I could see, and fairly blundered on a herd of oryx at about a hundred and fifty yards range. They looked at me a startled instant, then leaped away to the left at a tremendous speed. By a lucky shot, I bowled one over. He was a beautiful beast, with his black and white face and his straight rapierlike horns nearly three feet long, and I was most pleased to get him. Memba Sasa came running at the sound of the shot. We set about preparing the head.

Then through a gap in the hills far to the left we saw a little black speck moving rapidly in our direction. At the end of a minute we could make it out as the second rhinoceros. He had run heaven knows how many miles away, and now he was returning; whether with some idea of rejoining his companion or from sheer chance, I do not know. At any rate, here he was, still ploughing along at his swinging trot. His course led him along a side hill about four hundred yards from where the oryx lay. When he was directly opposite I took the Springfield and fired, not at him, but at a spot five or six feet in front of his nose. The bullet threw up a column of dust. Rhino brought up short with astonishment, wheeled to the left, and made off at a gallop. I dropped another bullet in front of him. Again he stopped, changed direction, and made off. For the third time I hit the ground in front of him. Then he got angry, put his head down and charged the spot.

Five more shots I expended on the amusement of that rhinoceros; and at the last had run furiously charging back and forth in a twenty-yard space, very angry at the little puffing, screeching bullets, but quite unable to catch one. Then he made up his mind and departed the way he had come, finally disappearing as a little rapidly moving black speck through the gap in the hills where we had first caught sight of him.

We finished caring for the oryx, and returned to camp. To our surprise we found we were at least seven or eight miles out.

In this fashion days passed very quickly. The early dewy start in the cool of the morning, the gradual grateful warming up of sunrise, and immediately after, the rest during the midday heats under a shady tree, the long trek back to camp at sunset, the hot bath after the toilsome day-all these were very pleasant. Then the swift falling night, and the gleam of many tiny fires springing up out of the darkness; with each its sticks full of meat roasting, and its little circle of men, their skins gleaming in the light. As we sat smoking, we would become aware that M'ganga, the headman, was standing silent awaiting orders. Some one would happen to see the white of his eyes, or perhaps he might smile so that his teeth would become visible. Otherwise he might stand there an hour, and no one the wiser, for he was respectfully silent, and exactly the colour of the night.

We would indicate to him our plans for the morrow, and he would disappear. Then at a distance of twenty or thirty feet from the front of our tents a tiny tongue of flame would lick up. Dark figures could be seen manipulating wood. A blazing fire sprang up, against which we could see the motionless and picturesque figure of Saa-sita (Six o'Clock), the askari of the first night watch, leaning on his musket. He was a most picturesque figure, for his fancy ran to original headdresses, and at the moment he affected a wonderful upstanding structure made of marabout wings.

At this sign that the night had begun, we turned in. A few hyenas moaned, a few jackals barked: otherwise the first part of the night was silent, for the hunters were at their silent business, and the hunted were "layin' low and sayin' nuffin'."

Day after day we rode out, exploring the country in different directions. The great uncertainty as to what of interest we would find filled the hours with charm. Sometimes we clambered about the cliffs of the buttes trying to find klipspringers; again we ran miles pursuing the gigantic eland. I in turn got my first rhinoceros, with no more danger than had attended the killing of B.'s. On this occasion, however, I had my first experience of the lightning skill of the first-class gunbearer. Having fired both barrels, and staggered the beast, I threw open the breech and withdrew the empty cartridges, intending, of course, as my next move to fish two more out of my belt. The empty shells were hardly away from the chambers, however, when a long brown arm shot over my right shoulder and popped two fresh cartridges in the breech. So astonished was I at this unexpected apparition, that for a second or so I actually forgot to close the gun.

# VII. ON THE MARCH

After leaving the First Game Camp, we travelled many hours and miles over rolling hills piling ever higher and higher until they broke through a pass to illimitable plains. These plains were mantled with the dense scrub, looking from a distance and from above like the nap of soft green velvet. Here and there this scrub broke in round or oval patches of grass plain. Great mountain ranges peered over the edge of a horizon. Lesser mountain peaks of fantastic shapes-sheer Yosemite cliffs, single buttes, castles-had ventured singly from behind that same horizon barricade. The course of a river was marked by a meandering line of green jungle.

It took us two days to get to that river. Our intermediate camp was halfway down the pass. We ousted a hundred indignant straw-coloured monkeys and twice as many baboons from the tiny flat above the water hole. They bobbed away cursing over their shoulders at us. Next day we debouched on the plains. They were rolling, densely grown, covered with volcanic stones, swarming with game of various sorts. The men marched well. They were happy, for they had had a week of meat; and each carried a light lunch of sun-dried biltong or jerky. Some mistaken individuals had attempted to bring along some "fresh" meat. We found it advisable to pass to windward of these; but they themselves did not seem to mind.

It became very hot; for we were now descending to the lower elevations. The marching through long grass and over volcanic stones was not easy. Shortly we came out on stumbly hills, mostly rock, very dry, grown with cactus and discouraged desiccated thorn scrub. Here the sun reflected powerfully and the bearers began to flag.

Then suddenly, without warning, we pitched over a little rise to the river.

No more marvellous contrast could have been devised. From the blasted barren scrub country we plunged into the lush jungle. It was not a very wide jungle, but it was sufficient. The trees were large and variegated, reaching to a high and spacious upper story above the ground tangle. From the massive limbs hung vines, festooned and looped like great serpents. Through this upper corridor flitted birds of bright hue or striking variegation. We did not know many of them by name, nor did we desire to; but were content with the impression of vivid flashing movement and colour. Various monkeys swung, leaped and galloped slowly away before our advance; pausing to look back at us curiously, the ruffs of fur standing out all around their little black faces. The lower half of the forest jungle, however, had no spaciousness at all, but a certain breathless intimacy. Great leaved plants as tall as little trees, and trees as small as big plants, bound together by vines, made up the "deep impenetrable jungle" of our childhood imagining. Here were rustlings, sudden scurryings, half-caught glimpses, once or twice a crash as some greater animal made off. Here and there through the thicket wandered well beaten trails, wide, but low, so that to follow them one would have to bend double. These were the paths of rhinoceroses. The air smelt warm and moist and earthy, like the odour of a greenhouse.

We skirted this jungle until it gave way to let the plain down to the river. Then, in an open grove of acacias, and fairly on the river's bank, we pitched our tents.

These acacia trees were very noble big chaps, with many branches and a thick shade. In their season they are wonderfully blossomed with white, with yellow, sometimes even with vivid red flowers. Beneath them was only a small matter of ferns to clear away.

Before us the sodded bank rounded off ten feet the river itself. At this point far up in its youth it was a friendly river. Its noble width ran over shallows of yellow sand or of small pebbles. Save for unexpected deep holes one could wade across it anywhere. Yet it was very wide, with still reaches of water, with islands of gigantic papyrus, with sand bars dividing the current, and with always the vista for a greater or lesser distance down through the jungle along its banks. From our canvas chairs we could look through on one side to the arid country, and on the other to this tropical wonderland.

Yes, at this point in its youth it was indeed a friendly river in every sense of the word. There are three reasons, ordinarily, why one cannot bathe in the African rivers. In the first place, they are nearly all disagreeably muddy; in the second place, cold water in a tropical climate causes horrible congestions; in the third place they swarm with crocodiles and hippos. But this river was as yet unpolluted by the alluvial soil of the lower countries; the sun on its shallows had warmed its waters almost to blood heat; and the beasts found no congenial haunts in these clear shoals. Almost before our tents were up the men were splashing. And always my mental image of that river's beautiful expanse must include round black heads floating like gourds where the water ran smoothest.

Our tents stood all in a row facing the stream, the great trees at their backs. Down in the grove the men had pitched their little white shelters. Happily they settled down to ease. Settling down to ease, in the case of the African porter, consists in discarding as many clothes as possible. While on the march he wears everything he owns; whether from pride or a desire to simplify transportation I am unable to say. He is supplied by his employer with a blanket and jersey. As supplementals he can generally produce a half dozen white man's ill-assorted garments: an old shooting coat, a ragged pair of khaki breeches, a kitchen tablecloth for a skirt, or something of the sort. If he can raise an overcoat he is happy, especially if it happen to be a long, thick WINTER overcoat. The possessor of such a garment will wear it conscientiously throughout the longest journey and during the hottest noons. But when he relaxes in camp, he puts away all these prideful possessions and turns out in the savage simplicity of his red blanket. Draped negligently, sometimes very negligently, in what may be termed semi-toga fashion, he stalks about or squats before his little fire in all the glory of a regained savagery. The contrast of the red with his red bronze or black skin, the freedom and grace of his movements, the upright carriage of his fine figure, and the flickering savagery playing in his eyes are very effective.

Our men occupied their leisure variously and happily. A great deal of time they spent before their tiny fires roasting meat and talking. This talk was almost invariably of specific personal experiences. They bathed frequently and with pleasure. They slept. Between times they fashioned ingenious affairs of ornament or use: bows and arrows, throwing clubs, snuff-boxes of the tips of antelope horns, bound prettily with bright wire, wooden swords beautifully carved in exact imitation of the white man's service weapon, and a hundred other such affairs. At this particular time also they were much occupied in making sandals against the thorns. These were flat soles of rawhide, the edges pounded to make them curl up a trifle over the foot, fastened by thongs; very ingenious, and very useful. To their task they brought song. The labour of Africa is done to song; weird minor chanting starting high in the falsetto to trickle unevenly down to the lower registers, or where the matter is one of serious effort, an antiphony of solo and chorus. From all parts of the camp come these softly modulated chantings, low and sweet, occasionally breaking into full voice as the inner occasion swells, then almost immediately falling again to the murmuring undertone of more concentrated attention.

The red blanket was generally worn knotted from one shoulder or bound around the waist Malay fashion. When it turned into a cowl, with a miserable and humpbacked expression, it became the Official Badge of Illness. No matter what was the matter that was the proper thing to do-to throw the blanket over the head and to assume as miserable a demeanour as possible. A sore toe demanded just as much concentrated woe as a case of pneumonia. Sick call was cried after the day's work was finished. Then M'ganga or one of the askaris lifted up his voice.

"N'gonjwa! n'gonjwa!" he shouted; and at the shout the red cowls gathered in front of the tent. Three things were likely to be the matter: too much meat, fever, or pus infection from slight wounds. To these in the rainy season would be added the various sorts of colds. That meant either Epsom salts, quinine, or a little excursion with the lancet and permanganate. The African traveller gets to be heap big medicine man within these narrow limits.

All the red cowls squatted miserably, oh, very miserably, in a row. The headman stood over them rather fiercely. We surveyed the lot contemplatively, hoping to heaven that nothing complicated was going to turn up. One of the tent boys hovered in the background as dispensing chemist.

"Well," said F. at last, "what's the matter with you?"

The man indicated pointed to his head and the back of his neck and groaned. If he had a slight headache he groaned just as much as though his head were splitting. F. asked a few questions, and took his temperature. The clinical thermometer is in itself considered big medicine, and often does much good.

"Too much meat, my friend," remarked F. in English, and to his boy in Swahili, "bring the cup."

He put in this cup a triple dose of Epsom salts. The African requires three times a white man's dose. This, pathologically, was all that was required: but psychologically the job was just begun. Your African can do wonderful things with his imagination. If he thinks he is going to die, die he will, and very promptly, even though he is ailing of the most trivial complaint. If he thinks he is going to get well, he is very apt to do so in face of extraordinary odds. Therefore the white man desires not only to start his patient's internal economy with Epsom salts, but also to stir his faith. To this end F. added to that triple dose of medicine a spoonful of Chutney, one of Worcestershire sauce, a few grains of quinine, Sparklets water and a crystal or so of permanganate to turn the mixture a beautiful pink. This assortment the patient drank with gratitude-and the tears running down his cheeks.

"He will carry a load to-morrow," F. told the attentive M'ganga.

The next patient had fever. This one got twenty grains of quinine in water.

"This man carries no load to-morrow," was the direction, "but he must not drop behind."

Two or three surgical cases followed. Then a big Kavirondo rose to his feet.

"Nini?" demanded F.

"Homa-fever," whined the man.

F. clapped his hand on the back of the other's neck.

"I think," he remarked contemplatively in English, "that you're a liar, and want to get out of carrying your load."

The clinical thermometer showed no evidence of temperature.

"I'm pretty near sure you're a liar," observed F. in the pleasantest conversational tone and still in English, "but you may be merely a poor diagnostician. Perhaps your poor insides couldn't get away with that rotten meat I saw you lugging around. We'll see."

So he mixed a pint of medicine.

"There's Epsom salts for the real part of trouble," observed F., still talking to himself, "and here's a few things for the fake."

He then proceeded to concoct a mixture whose recoil was the exact measure of his imagination. The imagination was only limited by the necessity of keeping the mixture harmless. Every hot, biting, nauseous horror in camp went into that pint measure.

"There," concluded F., "if you drink that and come back again to-morrow for treatment, I'll believe you ARE sick."

Without undue pride I would like to record that I was the first to think of putting in a peculiarly nauseous gun oil, and thereby acquired a reputation of making tremendous medicine.

So implicit is this faith in white man's medicine that at one of the Government posts we were approached by one of the secondary chiefs of the district. He was a very nifty savage, dressed for calling, with his hair done in ropes like a French poodle's, his skin carefully oiled and reddened, his armlets and necklets polished, and with the ceremonial ball of black feathers on the end of his long spear. His gait was the peculiar mincing teeter of savage conventional society. According to custom, he approached unsmiling, spat carefully in his palm, and shook hands. Then he squatted and waited.

"What is it?" we asked after it became evident he really wanted something besides the pleasure of our company.

"N'dowa-medicine," said he.

"Why do you not go the Government dispensary?" we demanded.

"The doctor there is an Indian; I want REAL medicine, white man's medicine," he explained.

Immensely flattered, of course, we wanted further to know what ailed him.

"Nothing," said he blandly, "nothing at all; but it seemed an excellent chance to get good medicine."

After the clinic was all attended to, we retired to our tents and the screeching-hot bath so grateful in the tropics. When we emerged, in our mosquito boots and pajamas, the daylight was gone. Scores of little blazes licked and leaped in the velvet blackness round about, casting the undergrowth and the lower branches of the trees into flat planes like the cardboard of a stage setting. Cheerful, squatted figures sat in silhouette or in the relief of chance high light. Long switches of meat roasted before the fires. A hum of talk, bursts of laughter, the crooning of minor chants mingled with the crackling of thorns. Before our tents stood the table set for supper. Beyond it lay the pile of firewood, later to be burned on the altar of our safety against beasts. The moonlight was casting milky shadows over the river and under the trees opposite. In those shadows gleamed many fireflies. Overhead were millions of stars, and a little breeze that wandered through upper branches.

But in Equatorial Africa the simple bands of velvet black, against the spangled brightnesses that make up the visual night world, must give way in interest to the other world of sound. The air hums with an undertone of insects; the plain and hill and jungle are populous with voices furtive or bold. In daytime one sees animals enough, in all conscience, but only at night does he sense the almost oppressive feeling of the teeming life about him. The darkness is peopled. Zebra bark, bucks blow or snort or make the weird noises of their respective species; hyenas howl; out of an immense simian silence a group of monkeys suddenly break into chatterings; ostriches utter their deep hollow boom; small things scurry and squeak; a certain weird bird of the curlew or plover sort wails like a lonesome soul. Especially by the river, as here, are the boomings of the weirdest of weird bullfrogs, and the splashings and swishings of crocodile and hippopotamus. One is impressed with the busyness of the world surrounding him; every bird or beast, the hunter and the hunted, is the centre of many important affairs. The world swarms.

And then, some miles away a lion roars, the earth and air vibrating to the sheer power of the sound. The world falls to a blank dead silence. For a full minute every living creature of the jungle or of the veldt holds its breath. Their lord has spoken.

After dinner we sat in our canvas chairs, smoking. The guard fire in front of our tent had been lit. On the other side of it stood one of our askaris leaning on his musket. He and his three companions, turn about, keep the flames bright against the fiercer creatures.

After a time we grew sleepy. I called Saa-sita and entrusted to him my watch. On the crystal of this I had pasted a small piece of surgeon's plaster. When the hour hand reached the surgeon's plaster, he must wake us up. Saa-sita was a very conscientious and careful man. One day I took some time hitching my pedometer properly to his belt: I could not wear it effectively myself because I was on horseback. At the end of the ten-hour march it registered a mile and a fraction. Saa-sita explained that he wished to take especial care of it, so he had wrapped it in a cloth and carried it all day in his hand!

We turned in. As I reached over to extinguish the lantern I issued my last command for the day.

"Watcha kalele, Saa-sita," I told the askari; at once he lifted up his voice to repeat my words. "Watcha kalele!" Immediately from the Responsible all over camp the word came back-from gunbearers, from M'ganga, from tent boys-"kalele! kalele! kalele!"

Thus commanded, the boisterous fun, the croon of intimate talk, the gently rising and falling tide of melody fell to complete silence. Only remained the crackling of the fire and the innumerable voices of the tropical night.

# VIII. THE RIVER JUNGLE

We camped along this river for several weeks, poking indefinitely and happily around the country in all directions to see what we could see. Generally we went together, for neither B. nor myself had been tried out as yet on dangerous game-those easy rhinos hardly counted-and I think we both preferred to feel that we had backing until we knew what our nerves were going to do with us. Nevertheless, occasionally, I would take Memba Sasa and go out for a little purposeless stroll a few miles up or down river. Sometimes we skirted the jungle, sometimes we held as near as possible to the river's bank, sometimes we cut loose and rambled through the dry, crackling scrub over the low volcanic hills of the arid country outside.

Nothing can equal the intense interest of the most ordinary walk in Africa. It is the only country I know of where a man is thoroughly and continuously alive. Often when riding horseback with the dogs in my California home I have watched them in envy of the keen, alert interest they took in every stone, stick, and bush, in every sight, sound, and smell. With equal frequency I have expressed that envy, but as something unattainable to a human being's more phlegmatic make-up. In Africa one actually rises to continuous alertness. There are dozy moments-except you curl up in a safe place for the PURPOSE of dozing; again just like the dog! Every bush, every hollow, every high tuft of grass, every deep shadow must be scrutinized for danger. It will not do to pass carelessly any possible lurking place. At the same time the sense of hearing must be on guard; so that no break of twig or crash of bough can go unremarked. Rhinoceroses conceal themselves most cannily, and have a deceitful habit of leaping from a nap into their swiftest stride. Cobras and puff adders are scarce, to be sure, but very deadly. Lions will generally give way, if not shot at or too closely pressed; nevertheless there is always the chance of cubs or too close a surprise. Buffalo lurk daytimes in the deep thickets, but occasionally a rogue bull lives where your trail will lead. These things do not happen often, but in the long run they surely do happen, and once is quite enough provided the beast gets in.

At first this continual alertness and tension is rather exhausting; but after a very short time it becomes second nature. A sudden rustle the other side a bush no longer brings you up all standing with your heart in your throat; but you are aware of it, and you are facing the possible danger almost before your slower brain has issued any orders to that effect.

In rereading the above, I am afraid that I am conveying the idea that one here walks under the shadow of continual uneasiness. This is not in the least so. One enjoys the sun, and the birds and the little things. He cultivates the great leisure of mind that shall fill the breadth of his outlook abroad over a newly wonderful world. But underneath it all is the alertness, the responsiveness to quick reflexes of judgment and action, the intimate correlations to immediate environment which must characterize the instincts of the higher animals. And it is good to live these things.

Along the edge of that river jungle were many strange and beautiful affairs. I could slip along among the high clumps of the thicker bushes in such a manner as to be continually coming around unexpected bends. Of such maneouvres are surprises made. The graceful red impalla were here very abundant. I would come on them, their heads up, their great ears flung forward, their noses twitching in inquiry of something they suspected but could not fully sense. When slightly alarmed or suspicious the does always stood compactly in a herd, while the bucks remained discreetly in the background, their beautiful, branching, widespread horns showing over the backs of their harems. The impalla is, in my opinion, one of the most beautiful and graceful of the African bucks, a perpetual delight to watch either standing or running. These beasts are extraordinarily agile, and have a habit of breaking their ordinary fast run by unexpectedly leaping high in the air. At a distance they give somewhat the effect of dolphins at sea, only their leaps are higher and more nearly perpendicular. Once or twice I have even seen one jump over the back of another. On another occasion we saw a herd of twenty-five or thirty cross a road of which, evidently, they were a little suspicious. We could not find a single hoof mark in the dust! Generally these beasts frequent thin brush country; but I have three or four times seen them quite out in the open flat plains, feeding with the hartebeeste and zebra. They are about the size of our ordinary deer, are delicately fashioned, and can utter the most incongruously grotesque of noises by way of calls or ordinary conversation.

The lack of curiosity, or the lack of gallantry, of the impalla bucks was, in my experience, quite characteristic. They were almost always the farthest in the background and the first away when danger threatened. The ladies could look out for themselves. They had no horns to save; and what do the fool women mean by showing so little sense, anyway! They deserve what they get! It used to amuse me a lot to observe the utter abandonment of all responsibility by these handsome gentlemen. When it came time to depart, they departed. Hang the girls! They trailed along after as fast as they could.

The waterbuck-a fine large beast about the size of our caribou, a well-conditioned buck resembling in form and attitude the finest of Landseer's stags-on the other hand, had a little more sense of responsibility, when he had anything to do with the sex at all. He was hardly what you might call a strictly domestic character. I have hunted through a country for several days at a time without seeing a single mature buck of this species, although there were plenty of does, in herds of ten to fifty, with a few infants among them just sprouting horns. Then finally, in some small grassy valley, I would come on the Men's Club. There they were, ten, twenty, three dozen of them, having the finest kind of an untramelled masculine time all by themselves. Generally, however, I will say for them, they took care of their own peoples. There would quite likely be one big old fellow, his harem of varying numbers, and the younger subordinate bucks all together in a happy family. When some one of the lot announced that something was about, and they had all lined up to stare in the suspected direction, the big buck was there in the foreground of inquiry. When finally they made me out, it was generally the big buck who gave the signal. He went first, to be sure, but his going first was evidently an act of leadership, and not merely a disgraceful desire to get away before the rest did.

But the waterbuck had to yield in turn to the plains gazelles; especially to the Thompson's gazelle, familiarly-and affectionately-known as the "Tommy." He is a quaint little chap, standing only a foot and a half tall at the shoulder, fawn colour on top, white beneath, with a black, horizontal stripe on his side, like a chipmunk, most lightly and gracefully built. When he was first made, somebody told him that unless he did something characteristic, like waggling his little tail, he was likely to be mistaken by the undiscriminating for his bigger cousin, the Grant's gazelle. He has waggled his tail ever since, and so is almost never mistaken for a Grant's gazelle, even by the undiscriminating. Evidently his religion is Mohammedan, for he always has a great many wives. He takes good care of them, however. When danger appears, even when danger threatens, he is the last to leave the field. Here and there he dashes frantically, seeing that the women and children get off. And when the herd tops the hill, Tommy's little horns bring up the rear of the procession. I like Tommy. He is a cheerful, gallant, quaint little person, with the air of being quite satisfied with his own solution of this complicated world.

Among the low brush at the edge of the river jungle dwelt also the dik-dik, the tiniest miniature of a deer you could possibly imagine. His legs are lead pencil size, he stands only about nine inches tall, he weighs from five to ten pounds; and yet he is a perfect little antelope, horns and all. I used to see him singly or in pairs standing quite motionless and all but invisible in the shade of bushes; or leaping suddenly to his feet and scurrying away like mad through the dry grass. His personal opinion of me was generally expressed in a loud clear whistle. But then nobody in this strange country talks the language you would naturally expect him to talk! Zebra bark, hyenas laugh, impallas grunt, ostriches boom like drums, leopards utter a plaintive sigh, hornbills cry like a stage child, bushbucks sound like a cross between a dog and a squawky toy-and so on. There is only one safe rule of the novice in Africa: NEVER BELIEVE A WORD THE JUNGLE AND VELDT PEOPLE TELL YOU.

These two-the impalla and the waterbuck-were the principal buck we would see close to the river. Occasionally, however, we came on a few oryx, down for a drink, beautiful big antelope, with white and black faces, roached manes, and straight, nearly parallel, rapier horns upward of three feet long. A herd of these creatures, the light gleaming on their weapons, held all at the same slant, was like a regiment of bayonets in the sun. And there were also the rhinoceroses to be carefully espied and avoided. They lay obliterated beneath the shade of bushes, and arose with a mighty blow-off of steam. Whereupon we withdrew silently, for we wanted to shoot no more rhinos, unless we had to.

Beneath all these obvious and startling things, a thousand other interesting matters were afoot. In the mass and texture of the jungle grew many strange trees and shrubs. One most scrubby, fat and leafless tree, looking as though it were just about to give up a discouraged existence, surprised us by putting forth, apparently directly from its bloated wood, the most wonderful red blossoms. Another otherwise self-respecting tree hung itself all over with plump bologna sausages about two feet long and five inches thick. A curious vine hung like a rope, with Turk's-head knots about a foot apart on its whole length, like the hand-over-hand ropes of gymnasiums. Other ropes were studded all over with thick blunt bosses, resembling much the outbreak on one sort of Arts-and-Crafts door: the sort intended to repel Mail-clad Hosts.

The monkeys undoubtedly used such obvious highways through the trees. These little people were very common. As we walked along, they withdrew before us. We could make out their figures galloping hastily across the open places, mounting bushes and stubs to take a satisfying backward look, clambering to treetops, and launching themselves across the abysses between limbs. If we went slowly, they retired in silence. If we hurried at all, they protested in direct ratio to the speed of our advance. And when later the whole safari, loads on heads, marched inconsiderately through their jungle! We happened to be hunting on a parallel course a half mile away, and we could trace accurately the progress of our men by the outraged shrieks, chatterings, appeals to high heaven for at least elemental justice to the monkey people.

Often, too, we would come on concourses of the big baboons. They certainly carried on weighty affairs of their own according to a fixed polity. I never got well enough acquainted with them to master the details of their government, but it was indubitably built on patriarchal lines. When we succeeded in approaching without being discovered, we would frequently find the old men baboons squatting on their heels in a perfect circle, evidently discussing matters of weight and portent. Seen from a distance, their group so much resembled the council circles of native warriors that sometimes, in a native country, we made that mistake. Outside this solemn council, the women, young men and children went about their daily business, whatever that was. Up convenient low trees or bushes roosted sentinels.

We never remained long undiscovered. One of the sentinels barked sharply. At once the whole lot loped away, speedily but with a curious effect of deliberation. The men folks held their tails in a proud high sideways arch; the curious youngsters clambered up bushes to take a hasty look; the babies clung desperately with all four feet to the thick fur on their mothers' backs; the mothers galloped along imperturbably unheeding of infantile troubles aloft. The side hill was bewildering with the big bobbing black forms.

In this lower country the weather was hot, and the sun very strong. The heated air was full of the sounds of insects; some of them comfortable, like the buzzing of bees, some of them strange and unusual to us. One cicada had a sustained note, in quality about like that of our own August-day's friend, but in quantity and duration as the roar of a train to the gentle hum of a good motor car. Like all cicada noises it did not usurp the sound world, but constituted itself an underlying basis, so to speak. And when it stopped the silence seemed to rush in as into a vacuum!

We had likewise the aeroplane beetle. He was so big that he would have made good wing-shooting. His manner of flight was the straight-ahead, heap-of-buzz, plenty-busy, don't-stop-a-minute-or-you'll-come-down method of the aeroplane; and he made the same sort of a hum. His first-cousin, mechanically, was what we called the wind-up-the-watch insect. This specimen possessed a watch-an old-fashioned Waterbury, evidently-that he was continually winding. It must have been hard work for the poor chap, for it sounded like a very big watch.

All these things were amusing. So were the birds. The African bird is quite inclined to be didactic. He believes you need advice, and he means to give it. To this end he repeats the same thing over and over until he thinks you surely cannot misunderstand. One chap especially whom we called the lawyer bird, and who lived in the treetops, had four phrases to impart. He said them very deliberately, with due pause between each; then he repeated them rapidly; finally he said them all over again with an exasperated bearing-down emphasis. The joke of it is I cannot now remember just how they went! Another feathered pedagogue was continually warning us to go slow; very good advice near an African jungle. "Poley-poley! Poley-poley!" he warned again and again; which is good Swahili for "slowly! slowly!" We always minded him. There were many others, equally impressed with their own wisdom, but the one I remember with most amusement was a dilatory person who apparently never got around to his job until near sunset. Evidently he had contracted to deliver just so many warnings per diem; and invariably he got so busy chasing insects, enjoying the sun, gossiping with a friend and generally footling about that the late afternoon caught him unawares with never a chirp accomplished. So he sat in a bush and said his say over and over just as fast as he could without pause for breath or recreation. It was really quite a feat. Just at dusk, after two hours of gabbling, he would reach the end of his contracted number. With final relieved chirp he ended.

It has been said that African birds are "songless." This is a careless statement that can easily be read to mean that African birds are silent. The writer evidently must have had in mind as a criterion some of our own or the English great feathered soloists. Certainly the African jungle seems to produce no individual performers as sustained as our own bob-o-link, our hermit thrush, or even our common robin. But the African birds are vocal enough, for all that. Some of them have a richness and depth of timbre perhaps unequalled elsewhere. Of such is the chime-bird with his deep double note; or the bell-bird tolling like a cathedral in the blackness of the forest; or the bottle bird that apparently pours gurgling liquid gold from a silver jug. As the jungle is exceedingly populous of these feathered specialists, it follows that the early morning chorus is wonderful. Africa may not possess the soloists, but its full orchestrial effects are superb.

Naturally under the equator one expects and demands the "gorgeous tropical plumage" of the books. He is not disappointed. The sun-birds of fifty odd species, the brilliant blue starlings, the various parrots, the variegated hornbills, the widower-birds, and dozens of others whose names would mean nothing flash here and there in the shadow and in the open. With them are hundreds of quiet little bodies just as interesting to one who likes birds. From the trees and bushes hang pear-shaped nests plaited beautifully of long grasses, hard and smooth as hand-made baskets, the work of the various sorts of weaver-birds. In the tops of the trees roosted tall marabout storks like dissipated, hairless old club-men in well-groomed, correct evening dress.

And around camp gathered the swift brown kites. They were robbers and villains, but we could not hate them. All day long they sailed back and forth spying sharply. When they thought they saw their chance, they stooped with incredible swiftness to seize a piece of meat. Sometimes they would snatch their prize almost from the hands of its rightful owner, and would swoop triumphantly upward again pursued by polyglot maledictions and a throwing stick. They were very skilful on their wings. I have many times seen them, while flying, tear up and devour large chunks of meat. It seems to my inexperience as an aviator rather a nice feat to keep your balance while tearing with your beak at meat held in your talons. Regardless of other landmarks, we always knew when we were nearing camp, after one of our strolls, by the gracefully wheeling figures of our kites.

# IX. THE FIRST LION

One day we all set out to make our discoveries: F., B., and I with our gunbearers, Memba Sasa, Mavrouki, and Simba, and ten porters to bring in the trophies, which we wanted very much, and the meat, which the men wanted still more. We rode our horses, and the syces followed. This made quite a field force-nineteen men all told. Nineteen white men would be exceedingly unlikely to get within a liberal half mile of anything; but the native has sneaky ways.

At first we followed between the river and the low hills, but when the latter drew back to leave open a broad flat, we followed their line. At this point they rose to a clifflike headland a hundred and fifty feet high, flat on top. We decided to investigate that mesa, both for the possibilities of game, and for the chance of a view abroad.

The footing was exceedingly noisy and treacherous, for it was composed of flat, tinkling little stones. Dried-up, skimpy bushes just higher than our heads made a thin but regular cover. There seemed not to be a spear of anything edible, yet we caught the flash of red as a herd of impalla melted away at our rather noisy approach. Near the foot of the hill we dismounted, with orders to all the men but the gunbearers to sit down and make themselves comfortable. Should we need them we could easily either signal or send word. Then we set ourselves toilsomely to clamber up that volcanic hill.

It was not particularly easy going, especially as we were trying to walk quietly. You see, we were about to surmount a skyline. Surmounting a skyline is always most exciting anywhere, for what lies beyond is at once revealed as a whole and contains the very essence of the unknown; but most decidedly is this true in Africa. That mesa looked flat, and almost anything might be grazing or browsing there. So we proceeded gingerly, with due regard to the rolling of the loose rocks or the tinkling of the little pebbles.

But long before we had reached that alluring skyline we were halted by the gentle snapping of Mavrouki's fingers. That, strangely enough, is a sound to which wild animals seem to pay no attention, and is therefore most useful as a signal. We looked back. The three gunbearers were staring to the right of our course. About a hundred yards away, on the steep side hill, and partly concealed by the brush, stood two rhinoceroses.

They were side by side, apparently dozing. We squatted on our heels for a consultation.

The obvious thing, as the wind was from them, was to sneak quietly by, saying nuffin' to nobody. But although we wanted no more rhino, we very much wanted rhino pictures. A discussion developed no really good reason why we should not kodak these especial rhinos-except that there were two of them. So we began to worm our way quietly through the bushes in their direction.

F. and B. deployed on the flanks, their double-barrelled rifles ready for instant action. I occupied the middle with that dangerous weapon the 3A kodak. Memba Sasa followed at my elbow, holding my big gun.

Now the trouble with modern photography is that it is altogether too lavish in its depiction of distances. If you do not believe it, take a picture of a horse at as short a range as twenty-five yards. That equine will, in the development, have receded to a respectable middle distance. Therefore it had been agreed that the advance of the battle line was to cease only when those rhinoceroses loomed up reasonably large in the finder. I kept looking into the finder, you may be sure. Nearer and nearer we crept. The great beasts were evidently basking in the sun. Their little pig eyes alone gave any sign of life. Otherwise they exhibited the complete immobility of something done in granite. Probably no other beast impresses one with quite this quality. I suppose it is because even the little motions peculiar to other animals are with the rhinoceros entirely lacking. He is not in the least of a nervous disposition, so he does not stamp his feet nor change his position. It is useless for him to wag his tail; for, in the first place, the tail is absurdly inadequate; and, in the second place, flies are not among his troubles. Flies wouldn't bother you either, if you had a skin two inches thick. So there they stood, inert and solid as two huge brown rocks, save for the deep, wicked twinkle of their little eyes.

Yes, we were close enough to "see the whites of their eyes," if they had had any: and also to be within the range of their limited vision. Of course we were now stalking, and taking advantage of all the cover.

Those rhinoceroses looked to me like two Dreadnaughts. The African two-horned rhinoceros is a bigger animal anyway than our circus friend, who generally comes from India. One of these brutes I measured went five feet nine inches at the shoulder, and was

36

thirteen feet six inches from bow to stern. Compare these dimensions with your own height and with the length of your motor car. It is one thing to take on such beasts in the hurry of surprise, the excitement of a charge, or to stalk up to within a respectable range of them with a gun at ready. But this deliberate sneaking up with the hope of being able to sneak away again was a little too slow and cold-blooded. It made me nervous. I liked it, but I knew at the time I was going to like it a whole lot better when it was triumphantly over.

We were now within twenty yards (they were standing starboard side on), and I prepared to get my picture. To do so I would either have to step quietly out into sight, trusting to the shadow and the slowness of my movements to escape observation, or hold the camera above the bush, directing it by guess work. It was a little difficult to decide. I knew what I OUGHT to do—

Without the slightest premonitory warning those two brutes snorted and whirled in their tracks to stand facing in our direction. After the dead stillness they made a tremendous row, what with the jerky suddenness of their movements, their loud snorts, and the avalanche of echoing stones and boulders they started down the hill.

This was the magnificent opportunity. At this point I should boldly have stepped out from behind my bush, levelled my trusty 3A, and coolly snapped the beasts, "charging at fifteen yards." Then, if B.'s and F.'s shots went absolutely true, or if the brutes didn't happen to smash the camera as well as me, I, or my executors as the case might be, would have had a fine picture.

But I didn't. I dropped that expensive 3A Special on some hard rocks, and grabbed my rifle from Memba Sasa. If you want really to know why, go confront your motor car at fifteen or twenty paces, multiply him by two, and endow him with an eagerly malicious disposition.

They advanced several yards, halted, faced us for perhaps five or six seconds, uttered snort, whirled with the agility of polo ponies, departed at a swinging trot and with surprising agility along the steep side hill.

I recovered the camera, undamaged, and we continued our climb.

The top of the mesa was disappointing as far as game was concerned. It was covered all over with red stones, round, and as large as a man's head. Thornbushes found some sort of sustenance in the interstices.

But we had gained to a magnificent view. Below us lay the narrow flat, then the winding jungle of our river, then long rolling desert country, gray with thorn scrub, sweeping upward to the base of castellated buttes and one tremendous riven cliff mountain, dropping over the horizon to a very distant blue range. Behind us eight or ten miles away was the low ridge through which our journey had come. The mesa on which we stood broke back at right angles to admit another stream flowing into our own. Beyond this stream were rolling hills, and scrub country, the hint of blue peaks and illimitable distances falling away to the unknown Tara Desert and the sea.

There seemed to be nothing much to be gained here, so we made up our minds to cut across the mesa, and from the other edge of it to overlook the valley of the tributary river. This we would descend until we came to our horses.

Accordingly we stumbled across a mile or so of those round and rolling stones. Then we found ourselves overlooking a wide flat or pocket where the stream valley widened. It extended even as far as the upward fling of the barrier ranges. Thick scrub covered it, but erratically, so that here and there were little openings or thin places. We sat down, manned our trusty prism glasses, and gave ourselves to the pleasing occupation of looking the country over inch by inch.

This is great fun. It is a game a good deal like puzzle pictures. Re-examination generally develops new and unexpected beasts. We repeated to each other aloud the results of our scrutiny, always without removing the glasses from our eyes.

"Oryx, one," said F.; "oryx, two."

"Giraffe," reported B., "and a herd of impalla."

I saw another giraffe, and another oryx, then two rhinoceroses.

The three bearers squatted on their heels behind us, their fierce eyes staring straight ahead, seeing with the naked eye what we were finding with six-power glasses.

We turned to descend the hill. In the very centre of the deep shade of a clump of trees, I saw the gleam of a waterbuck's horns. While I was telling of this, the beast stepped from his concealment, trotted a short distance upstream and turned to climb a little ridge parallel to that by which we were descending. About halfway up he stopped, staring in our direction, his head erect, the slight ruff under his neck standing forward. He was a good four hundred yards away. B., who wanted him, decided the shot too chancy. He and F. slipped backward until they had gained the cover of the little ridge, then hastened down the bed of the ravine. Their purpose was to follow the course already taken by the waterbuck until they should have sneaked within better range. In the meantime I and the gunbearers sat down in full view of the buck. This was to keep his attention distracted.

We sat there a long time. The buck never moved but continued to stare at what evidently puzzled him. Time passes very slowly in such circumstances, and it seemed incredible that the beast should continue much longer to hold his fixed attitude. Nevertheless B. and F. were working hard. We caught glimpses of them occasionally slipping from bush to bush. Finally B. knelt and levelled his rifle. At once I turned my glasses on the buck. Before the sound of the rifle had reached me, I saw him start convulsively, then make off at the tearing run that indicates a heart hit. A moment later the crack of the rifle and the dull plunk of the hitting bullet struck my ear.

We tracked him fifty yards to where he lay dead. He was a fine trophy, and we at once set the boys to preparing it and taking the meat. In the meantime we sauntered down to look at the stream. It was a small rapid affair, but in heavy papyrus, with sparse trees, and occasional thickets, and dry hard banks. The papyrus should make a good lurking place for almost anything; but the few points of access to the water failed to show many interesting tracks. Nevertheless we decided to explore a short distance.

For an hour we walked among high thornbushes, over baking hot earth. We saw two or three dik-dik and one of the giraffes. At that time it had become very hot, and the sun was bearing down on us as with the weight of a heavy hand. The air had the scorching, blasting quality of an opened furnace door. Our mouths were getting dry and sticky in that peculiar stage of thirst on which no luke-warm canteen water in necessarily limited quantity has any effect. So we turned back, picked up the men with the waterbuck, and plodded on down the little stream, or, rather, on the red-hot dry valley bottom outside the stream's course, to where the syces were waiting with our horses. We mounted with great thankfulness. It was now eleven o'clock, and we considered our day as finished.

The best way for a distance seemed to follow the course of the tributary stream to its point of junction with our river. We rode along, rather relaxed in the suffocating heat. F. was nearest the stream. At one point it freed itself of trees and brush and ran clear, save for low papyrus, ten feet down below a steep eroded bank. F. looked over and uttered a startled exclamation. I spurred my horse forward to see.

Below us, about fifteen yards away, was the carcass of a waterbuck half hidden in the foot-high grass. A lion and two lionesses stood upon it, staring up at us with great yellow eyes. That picture is a very vivid one in my memory, for those were the first wild lions I had ever seen. My most lively impression was of their unexpected size. They seemed to bulk fully a third larger than my expectation.

The magnificent beasts stood only long enough to see clearly what had disturbed them, then turned, and in two bounds had gained the shelter of the thicket.

Now the habit in Africa is to let your gunbearers carry all your guns. You yourself stride along hand free. It is an English idea, and is pretty generally adopted out there by every one, of whatever nationality. They will explain it to you by saying that in such a climate a man should do only necessary physical work, and that a good gunbearer will get a weapon into your hand so quickly and in so convenient a position that you will lose no time. I acknowledge the gunbearers are sometimes very skilful at this, but I do deny that there is no loss of time. The instant of distracted attention while receiving a weapon, the necessity of recollecting the nervous correlations after the transfer, very often mark just the difference between a sure instinctive snapshot and a lost opportunity. It reasons that the man with the rifle in his hand reacts instinctively, in one motion, to get his weapon into play. If the gunbearer has the gun, HE must first react to pass it up, the master must receive it properly, and THEN, and not until then, may go on from where the other man began. As for physical labour in the tropics: if a grown man cannot without discomfort or evil effects carry an eight-pound rifle, he is too feeble to go out at all. In a long Western experience I have learned never to be separated from my weapon; and I believe the continuance of this habit in Africa saved me a good number of chances.

At any rate, we all flung ourselves off our horses. I, having my rifle in my hand, managed to throw a shot after the biggest lion as he vanished. It was a snap at nothing, and missed. Then in an opening on the edge a hundred yards away appeared one of the lionesses. She was trotting slowly, and on her I had time to draw a hasty aim. At the shot she bounded high in the air, fell, rolled over, and was up and into the thicket before I had much more than time to pump up another shell from the magazine. Memba Sasa in his eagerness got in the way-the first and last time he ever made a mistake in the field.

By this time the others had got hold of their weapons. We fronted the blank face of the thicket.

The wounded animal would stand a little waiting. We made a wide circle to the other side of the stream. There we quickly picked up the trail of the two uninjured beasts. They had headed directly over the hill, where we speedily lost all trace of them on the flint-like surface of the ground. We saw a big pack of baboons in the only likely direction for a lion to go. Being thus thrown back on a choice of a hundred other unlikely directions, we gave up that slim chance and returned to the thicket.

This proved to be a very dense piece of cover. Above the height of the waist the interlocking branches would absolutely prevent any progress, but by stooping low we could see dimly among the simpler main stems to a distance of perhaps fifteen or twenty feet. This combination at once afforded the wounded lioness plenty of cover in which to hide, plenty of room in which to charge home, and placed us under the disadvantage of a crouched or crawling attitude with limited vision. We talked the matter over very thoroughly. There was only one way to get that lioness out; and that was to go after her. The job of going after her needed some planning. The lion is cunning and exceeding fierce. A flank attack, once we were in the thicket, was as much to be expected as a frontal charge.

We advanced to the thicket's edge with many precautions. To our relief we found she had left us a definite trail. B. and I kneeling took up positions on either side, our rifles ready. F. and Simba crawled by inches eight or ten feet inside the thicket. Then, having executed this manoeuvre safely, B. moved up to protect our rear while I, with Memba Sasa, slid down to join F.

From this point we moved forward alternately. I would crouch, all alert, my rifle ready, while F. slipped by me and a few feet ahead. Then he get organized for battle while I passed him. Memba Sasa and Simba, game as badgers, their fine eyes gleaming with excitement, their faces shining, crept along at the rear. B. knelt outside the thicket, straining his eyes for the slightest movement either side of the line of our advance. Often these wily animals will sneak back in a half circle to attack their pursuers from behind. Two or three of the bolder porters crouched alongside B., peering eagerly. The rest had quite properly retired to the safe distance where the horses stood.

We progressed very, very slowly. Every splash of light or mottled shadow, every clump of bush stems, every fallen log had to be examined, and then examined again. And how we did strain our eyes in a vain attempt to penetrate the half lights, the duskinesses of the closed-in thicket not over fifteen feet away! And then the movement forward of two feet would bring into our field of vision an entirely new set of tiny vistas and possible lurking places.

Speaking for myself, I was keyed up to a tremendous tension. I stared until my eyes ached; every muscle and nerve was taut. Everything depended on seeing the beast promptly, and firing quickly. With the manifest advantage of being able to see us, she would spring to battle fully prepared. A yellow flash and a quick shot seemed about to size up that situation. Every few moments, I remember, I surreptitiously held out my hand to see if the constantly growing excitement and the long-continued strain had affected its steadiness.

The combination of heat and nervous strain was very exhausting. The sweat poured from me; and as F. passed me I saw the great drops standing out on his face. My tongue got dry, my breath came laboriously. Finally I began to wonder whether physically I should be able to hold out. We had been crawling, it seemed, for hours. I dared not look back, but we must have come a good quarter mile. Finally F. stopped.

"I'm all in for water," he gasped in a whisper.

Somehow that confession made me feel a lot better. I had thought that I was the only one. Cautiously we settled back on our heels. Memba Sasa and Simba wiped the sweat from their faces. It seemed that they too had found the work severe. That cheered me up still more.

Simba grinned at us, and, worming his way backward with the sinuosity of a snake, he disappeared in the direction from which we had come. F. cursed after him in a whisper both for departing and for taking the risk. But in a moment he had returned carrying two canteens of blessed water. We took a drink most gratefully.

I glanced at my watch. It was just under two hours since I had fired my shot. I looked back. My supposed quarter mile had shrunk to not over fifty feet!

After resting a few moments longer, we again took up our systematic advance. We made perhaps another fifty feet. We were ascending a very gentle slope. F. was for the moment ahead. Right before us the lion growled; a deep rumbling like the end of a great thunder roll, fathoms and fathoms deep, with the inner subterranean vibrations of a heavy train of cars passing a man inside a sealed building. At the same moment over F.'s shoulder I saw a huge yellow head rise up, the round eyes flashing anger, the small black-tipped ears laid back, the great fangs snarling. The beast was not over twelve feet distant. F. immediately fired. His shot, hitting an intervening twig, went wild. With the utmost coolness he immediately pulled the other trigger of his double barrel. The cartridge snapped.

"If you will kindly stoop down-" said I, in what I now remember to be rather an exaggeratedly polite tone. As F.'s head disappeared, I placed the little gold bead of my

405 Winchester where I thought it would do the most good, and pulled trigger. She rolled over dead.

The whole affair had begun and finished with unbelievable swiftness. From the growl to the fatal shot I don't suppose four seconds elapsed, for our various actions had followed one another with the speed of the instinctive. The lioness had growled at our approach, had raised her head to charge, and had received her deathblow before she had released her muscles in the spring. There had been no time to get frightened.

We sat back for a second. A brown hand reached over my shoulder.

"Mizouri-mizouri sana!" cried Memba Sasa joyously. I shook the hand.

"Good business!" said F. "Congratulate you on your first lion."

We then remembered B., and shouted to him that all was over. He and the other men wriggled in to where we were lying. He made this distance in about fifteen seconds. It had taken us nearly an hour.

We had the lioness dragged out into the open. She was not an especially large beast, as compared to most of the others I killed later, but at that time she looked to me about as big as they made them. As a matter of fact she was quite big enough, for she stood three feet two inches at the shoulder-measure that against the wall-and was seven feet and six inches in length. My first bullet had hit her leg, and the last had reached her heart.

Every one shook me by the hand. The gunbearers squatted about the carcass, skilfully removing the skin to an undertone of curious crooning that every few moments broke out into one or two bars of a chant. As the body was uncovered, the men crouched about to cut off little pieces of fat. These they rubbed on their foreheads and over their chests, to make them brave, they said, and cunning, like the lion.

We remounted and took up our interrupted journey to camp. It was a little after two, and the heat was at its worst. We rode rather sleepily, for the reaction from the high tension of excitement had set in. Behind us marched the three gunbearers, all abreast, very military and proud. Then came the porters in single file, the one carrying the folded lion skin leading the way; those bearing the waterbuck trophy and meat bringing up the rear. They kept up an undertone of humming in a minor key; occasionally breaking into a short musical phrase in full voice.

We rode an hour. The camp looked very cool and inviting under its wide high trees, with the river slipping by around the islands of papyrus. A number of black heads bobbed about in the shallows. The small fires sent up little wisps of smoke. Around them our boys sprawled, playing simple games, mending, talking, roasting meat. Their tiny white tents gleamed pleasantly among the cool shadows.

I had thought of riding nonchalantly up to our own tents, of dismounting with a careless word of greeting—

"Oh, yes," I would say, "we did have a good enough day. Pretty hot. Roy got a fine waterbuck. Yes, I got a lion." (Tableau on part of Billy.)

But Memba Sasa used up all the nonchalance there was. As we entered camp he remarked casually to the nearest man.

"Bwana na piga simba-the master has killed a lion."

The man leaped to his feet.

"Simba! simba! simba!" he yelled. "Na piga simba!"

Every one in camp also leaped to his feet, taking up the cry. From the water it was echoed as the bathers scrambled ashore. The camp broke into pandemonium. We were surrounded by a dense struggling mass of men. They reached up scores of black hands to grasp my own; they seized from me everything portable and bore it in triumph before me-my water bottle, my rifle, my camera, my whip, my field glasses, even my hat, everything that was detachable. Those on the outside danced and lifted up their voices in song, improvised for the most part, and in honor of the day's work. In a vast swirling, laughing, shouting, triumphant mob we swept through the camp to where Billy-by now not very much surprised-was waiting to get the official news. By the measure of this extravagant joy could we gauge what the killing of a lion means to these people who have always lived under the dread of his rule.

# X. LIONS

A very large lion I killed stood three feet and nine inches at the withers, and of course carried his head higher than that. The top of the table at which I sit is only two feet three inches from the floor. Coming through the door at my back that lion's head would stand over a foot higher than halfway up. Look at your own writing desk; your own door. Furthermore, he was nine feet and eleven inches in a straight line from nose to end of tail, or over eleven feet along the contour of the back. If he were to rise on his hind feet to strike a man down, he would stand somewhere between seven and eight feet tall, depending on how nearly he straightened up. He weighed just under six hundred pounds, or as much as four well-grown specimens of our own "mountain lion." I tell you this that you may realize, as I did not, the size to which a wild lion grows. Either menagerie specimens are stunted in growth, or their position and surroundings tend to belittle them, for certainly until a man sees old Leo in the wilderness he has not understood what a fine old chap he is.

This tremendous weight is sheer strength. A lion's carcass when the skin is removed is a really beautiful sight. The great muscles lie in ropes and bands; the forearm thicker than a man's leg, the lithe barrel banded with brawn; the flanks overlaid by the long thick muscles. And this power is instinct with the nervous force of a highly organized being. The lion is quick and intelligent and purposeful; so that he brings to his intenser activities the concentration of vivid passion, whether of anger, of hunger or of desire.

So far the opinions of varied experience will jog along together. At this point they diverge.

Just as the lion is one of the most interesting and fascinating of beasts, so concerning him one may hear the most diverse opinions. This man will tell you that any lion is always dangerous. Another will hold the king of beasts in the most utter contempt as a coward and a skulker.

In the first place, generalization about any species of animal is an exceedingly dangerous thing. I believe that, in the case of the higher animals at least, the differences in individual temperament are quite likely to be more numerous than the specific likenesses. Just as individual men are bright or dull, nervous or phlegmatic, cowardly or brave, so individual animals vary in like respect. Our own hunters will recall from their personal experiences how the big bear may have sat down and bawled harmlessly for mercy, while the little unconsidered fellow did his best until finished off: how one buck dropped instantly to a wound that another would carry five miles: how of two equally matched warriors of the herd one will give way in the fight, while still uninjured, before his perhaps badly wounded antagonist. The casual observer might-and often does-say that all bears are cowardly, all bucks are easily killed, or the reverse, according as the god of chance has treated him to one spectacle or the other. As well try to generalize on the human race-as is a certain ecclesiastical habit-that all men are vile or noble, dishonest or upright, wise or foolish.

The higher we go in the scale the truer this individualism holds. We are forced to reason not from the bulk of observations, but from their averages. If we find ten bucks who will go a mile wounded to two who succumb in their tracks from similar hurts, we are justified in saying tentatively that the species is tenacious of life. But as experience broadens we may modify that statement; for strange indeed are runs of luck.

For this reason a good deal of the wise conclusion we read in sportsmen's narratives is worth very little. Few men have experience enough with lions to rise to averages through the possibilities of luck. ESPECIALLY is this true of lions. No beast that roams seems to go more by luck than felis leo. Good hunters may search for years without seeing hide nor hair of one of the beasts. Selous, one of the greatest, went to East Africa for the express purpose of getting some of the fine beasts there, hunted six weeks and saw none. Holmes of the Escarpment has lived in the country six years, has hunted a great deal and has yet to kill his first. One of the railroad officials has for years gone up and down the Uganda Railway on his handcar, his rifle ready in hopes of the lion that never appeared; though many are there seen by those with better fortune. Bronson hunted desperately for this great prize, but failed. Rainsford shot no lions his first trip, and ran into them only three years later. Read Abel Chapman's description of his continued bad luck at even seeing the beasts. MacMillan, after five years' unbroken good fortune, has in the last two years failed to kill a lion, although he has made many trips for the purpose. F. told me he followed every rumour of a lion for two years before he got one. Again, one may hear the most marvellous of yarns the other way about-of the German who shot one from the train on the way up from Mombasa; of the young English tenderfoot who, the first day out, came on three asleep, across a river, and potted the lot; and so on. The point is, that in the case of lions the element of sheer chance seems to begin earlier and last longer than is the case with any other beast. And, you must remember, experience must thrust through the luck element to the solid ground of averages before it can have much value in the way of generalization. Before he has reached that solid ground, a man's opinions depend entirely on what kind of lions he chances to meet, in what circumstances, and on how matters happen to shape in the crowded moments.

But though lack of sufficiently extended experience has much to do with these decided differences of opinion, I believe that misapprehension has also its part. The sportsman sees lions on the plains. Likewise the lions see him, and promptly depart to thick cover or rocky butte. He comes on them in the scrub; they bound hastily out of sight. He may even meet them face to face, but instead of attacking him, they turn to right and left and make off in the long grass. When he follows them, they sneak cunningly away. If, added to this, he has the good luck to kill one or two stone dead at a single shot each, he begins to think there is not much in lion shooting after all, and goes home proclaiming the king of beasts a skulking coward.

After all, on what grounds does he base this conclusion? In what way have circumstances been a test of courage at all? The lion did not stand and fight, to be sure; but why should he? What was there in it for lions? Behind any action must a motive exist. Where is the possible motive for any lion to attack on sight? He does not-except in unusual cases-eat men; nothing has occurred to make him angry. The obvious thing is to avoid trouble, unless there is a good reason to seek it. In that one evidences the lion's good sense, but not his lack of courage. That quality has not been called upon at all.

But if the sportsman had done one of two or three things, I am quite sure he would have had a taste of our friend's mettle. If he had shot at and even grazed the beast; if he had happened upon him where an exit was not obvious; or IF HE HAD EVEN FOLLOWED THE LION UNTIL THE LATTER HAD BECOME TIRED OF THE ANNOYANCE, he would very soon have discovered that Leo is not all good nature, and that once on his courage will take him in against any odds. Furthermore, he may be astonished and dismayed to discover that of a group of several lions, two or three besides the wounded animal are quite likely to take up the quarrel and charge too. In other words, in my opinion, the lion avoids trouble when he can, not from cowardice but from essential indolence or good nature; but does not need to be cornered* to fight to the death when in his mind his dignity is sufficiently assailed.

* This is an important distinction in estimating the inherent
courage of man or beast. Even a mouse will fight when
cornered.

For of all dangerous beasts the lion, when once aroused, will alone face odds to the end. The rhinoceros, the elephant, and even the buffalo can often be turned aside by a shot. A lion almost always charges home.* Slower and slower he comes, as the bullets strike; but he comes, until at last he may be just hitching himself along, his face to the enemy, his fierce spirit undaunted. When finally he rolls over, he bites the earth in great mouthfuls; and so passes fighting to the last. The death of a lion is a fine sight.

* I seem to be generalizing here, but all these conclusions
must be understood to take into consideration the liability
of individual variation.

No, I must confess, to me the lion is an object of great respect; and so, I gather, he is to all who have had really extensive experience. Those like Leslie Tarleton, Lord Delamere, W. N. MacMillan, Baron von Bronsart, the Hills, Sir Alfred Pease, who are great lion men, all concede to the lion a courage and tenacity unequalled by any other living beast. My own experience is of course nothing as compared to that of these men. Yet I saw in my nine months afield seventy-one lions. None of these offered to attack when unwounded or not annoyed. On the other hand, only one turned tail once the battle was on, and she proved to be a three quarters grown lioness, sick and out of condition.

It is of course indubitable that where lions have been much shot they become warier in the matter of keeping out of trouble. They retire to cover earlier in the morning, and they keep more than a perfunctory outlook for the casual human being. When hunters first began to go into the Sotik the lions there would stand imperturbable, staring at the intruder with curiosity or indifference. Now they have learned that such performances are not healthy-and they have probably satisfied their curiosity. But neither in the Sotik, nor even in the plains around Nairobi itself, does the lion refuse the challenge once it has been put up to him squarely. Nor does he need to be cornered. He charges in quite blithely from the open plain, once convinced that you are really an annoyance.

As to habits! The only sure thing about a lion is his originality. He has more exceptions to his rules than the German language. Men who have been mighty lion hunters for many years, and who have brought to their hunting close observation, can only tell you what a lion MAY do in certain circumstances. Following very broad principles, they may even predict what he is APT to do, but never what he certainly WILL do. That is one thing that makes lion hunting interesting.

In general, then, the lion frequents that part of the country where feed the great game herds. From them he takes his toll by night, retiring during the day into the shallow ravines, the brush patches, or the rocky little buttes. I have, however, seen lions miles from game, slumbering peacefully atop an ant hill. Indeed, occasionally, a pack of lions likes to live high in the tall-grass ridges where every hunt will mean for them a four- or five-mile jaunt out and back again. He needs water, after feeding, and so rarely gets farther than eight or ten miles from that necessity.

He hunts at night. This is as nearly invariable a rule as can be formulated in regard to lions. Yet once, and perhaps twice, I saw lionesses stalking through tall grass as early as three o'clock in the afternoon. This eagerness may, or may not, have had to do with the possession of hungry cubs. The lion's customary harmlessness in the daytime is best evidenced, however, by the comparative indifference of the game to his presence then. From a hill we watched three of these beasts wandering leisurely across the plains below. A herd of kongonis feeding directly in their path, merely moved aside right and left, quite deliberately, to leave a passage fifty yards or so wide, but otherwise paid not the slightest attention. I have several times seen this incident, or a modification of it. And yet, conversely, on a number of occasions we have received our first intimation of the presence of lions by the wild stampeding of the game away from a certain spot.

However, the most of his hunting is done by dark. Between the hours of sundown and nine o'clock he and his comrades may be heard uttering the deep coughing grunt typical of this time of night. These curious, short, far-sounding calls may be mere evidences of intention, or they may be a sort of signal by means of which the various hunters keep in touch. After a little they cease. Then one is quite likely to hear the petulant, alarmed barking of zebra, or to feel the vibrations of many hoofs. There is a sense of hurried, flurried uneasiness abroad on the veldt.

The lion generally springs on his prey from behind or a little off the quarter. By the impetus his own weight he hurls his victim forward, doubling its head under, and very neatly breaking its neck. I have never seen this done, but the process has been well observed and attested; and certainly, of the many hundreds of lion kills I have taken the pains to inspect, the majority had had their necks broken. Sometimes, but apparently more rarely, the lion kills its prey by a bite in the back of the neck. I have seen zebra killed in this fashion, but never any of the buck. It may be possible that the lack of horns makes it more difficult to break a zebra's neck because of the corresponding lack of leverage when its head hits the ground sidewise; the instances I have noted may have been those in which the lion's spring landed too far back to throw the victim properly; or perhaps they were merely examples of the great variability in the habits of felis leo.

Once the kill is made, the lion disembowels the beast very neatly indeed, and drags the entrails a few feet out of the way. He then eats what he wants, and, curiously enough, seems often to be very fond of the skin. In fact, lacking other evidence, it is occasionally possible to identify a kill as being that of a lion by noticing whether any considerable portion of the hide has been devoured. After eating he drinks. Then he is likely to do one of two things: either he returns to cover near the carcass and lies down, or he wanders slowly and with satisfaction toward his happy home. In the latter case the hyenas, jackals, and carrion birds seize their chance. The astute hunter can often diagnose the case by the general actions and demeanour of these camp followers. A half dozen sour and disgusted looking hyenas seated on their haunches at scattered intervals, and treefuls of mournfully humpbacked vultures sunk in sadness, indicate that the lion has decided to save the rest of his zebra until to-morrow and is not far away. On the other hand, a grand flapping, snarling Kilkenny-fair of an aggregation swirling about one spot in the grass means that the principal actor has gone home.

It is ordinarily useless to expect to see the lion actually on his prey. The feeding is done before dawn, after which the lion enjoys stretching out in the open until the sun is well up, and then retiring to the nearest available cover. Still, at the risk of seeming to be perpetually qualifying, I must instance finding three lions actually on the stale carcass of a waterbuck at eleven o'clock in the morning of a piping hot day! In an undisturbed country, or one not much hunted, the early morning hours up to say nine o'clock are quite likely to show you lions sauntering leisurely across the open plains toward their lairs. They go a little, stop a little, yawn, sit down a while, and gradually work their way home. At those times you come upon them unexpectedly face to face, or, seeing them from afar, ride them down in a glorious gallop. Where the country has been much hunted, however, the lion learns to abandon his kill and seek shelter before daylight, and is almost never seen abroad. Then one must depend on happening upon him in his cover.

In the actual hunting of his game the lion is apparently very clever. He understands the value of cooperation. Two or more will manoeuvre very skilfully to give a third the chance to make an effective spring; whereupon the three will share the kill. In a rough country, or one otherwise favourable to the method, a pack of lions will often deliberately drive game into narrow ravines or cul de sacs where the killers are waiting.

At such times the man favoured by the chance of an encampment within five miles or so can hear a lion's roar.

Otherwise I doubt if he is apt often to get the full-voiced, genuine article. The peculiar questioning cough of early evening is resonant and deep in vibration, but it is a call rather than a roar. No lion is fool enough to make a noise when he is stalking. Then afterward, when full fed, individuals may open up a few times, but only a few times, in sheer satisfaction, apparently, at being well fed. The menagerie row at feeding time, formidable as it sounds within the echoing walls, is only a mild and gentle hint. But when seven or eight lions roar merely to see how much noise they can make, as when driving game, or trying to stampede your oxen on a wagon trip, the effect is something tremendous. The very substance of the ground vibrates; the air shakes. I can only compare it to the effect of a very large deep organ in a very small church. There is something genuinely awe-inspiring about it; and when the repeated volleys rumble into silence, one can imagine the veldt crouched in a rigid terror that shall endure.

# XI. LIONS AGAIN

As to the dangers of lion hunting it is also difficult to write. There is no question that a cool man, using good judgment as to just what he can or cannot do, should be able to cope with lion situations. The modern rifle is capable of stopping the beast, provided the bullet goes to the right spot. The right spot is large enough to be easy to hit, if the shooter keeps cool. Our definition of a cool man must comprise the elements of steady nerves under super-excitement, the ability to think quickly and clearly, and the mildly strategic quality of being able to make the best use of awkward circumstances. Such a man, barring sheer accidents, should be able to hunt lions with absolute certainty for just as long as he does not get careless, slipshod or over-confident. Accidents-real accidents, not merely unexpected happenings-are hardly to be counted. They can occur in your own house.

But to the man not temperamentally qualified, lion shooting is dangerous enough. The lion, when he takes the offensive, intends to get his antagonist. Having made up his mind to that, he charges home, generally at great speed. The realization that it is the man's life or the beast's is disconcerting. Also the charging lion is a spectacle much more awe-inspiring in reality than the most vivid imagination can predict. He looks very large, very determined, and has uttered certain rumbling, blood-curdling threats as to what he is going to do about it. It suddenly seems most undesirable to allow that lion to come any closer, not even an inch! A hasty, nervous shot misses—

An unwounded lion charging from a distance is said to start rather slowly, and to increase his pace only as he closes. Personally I have never been charged by an unwounded beast, but I can testify that the wounded animal comes very fast. Cuninghame puts the rate at about seven seconds to the hundred yards. Certainly I should say that a man charged from fifty yards or so would have little chance for a second shot, provided he missed the first. A hit seemed, in my experience, to the animal, by sheer force of impact, long enough to permit me to throw in another cartridge. A lioness thus took four frontal bullets starting at about sixty yards. An initial miss would probably have permitted her to close.

Here, as can be seen, is a great source of danger to a flurried or nervous beginner. He does not want that lion to get an inch nearer; he fires at too long a range, misses, and is killed or mauled before he can reload. This happened precisely so to two young friends of MacMillan. They were armed with double-rifles, let them off hastily as the beast started at them from two hundred yards, and never got another chance. If they had possessed the experience to have waited until the lion had come within fifty yards they would have had the almost certainty of four barrels at close range. Though I have seen a lion missed clean well inside those limits.

From such performances are so-called lion accidents built. During my stay in Africa I heard of six white men being killed by lions, and a number of others mauled. As far as possible I tried to determine the facts of each case. In every instance the trouble followed either foolishness or loss of nerve. I believe I should be quite safe in saying that from identically the same circumstances any of the good lion men-Tarleton, Lord Delamere, the Hills, and others-would have extricated themselves unharmed.

This does not mean that accidents may not happen. Rifles jam, but generally because of flurried manipulation! One may unexpectedly meet the lion at too close quarters; a foot may slip, or a cartridge prove defective. So may one fall downstairs or bump one's head in the dark. Sufficient forethought and alertness and readiness would go far in either case to prevent bad results.

The wounded beast, of course, offers the most interesting problem to the lion hunter. If it sees the hunter, it is likely to charge him at once. If hit while making off, however, it is more apt to take cover. Then one must summon all his good sense and nerve to get it out. No rules can be given for this; nor am I trying to write a text book for lion hunters. Any good lion hunter knows a lot more about it than I do. But always a man must keep in mind three things: that a lion can hide in cover so short that it seems to the novice as though a jack-rabbit would find scant concealment there; that he charges like lightning, and that he can spring about fifteen feet. This spring, coming unexpectedly from an unseen beast, is about impossible to avoid. Sheer luck may land a fatal shot; but even then the lion will probably do his damage before he dies. The rush from a short distance a good quick shot ought to be able to cope with.

Therefore the wise hunter assures himself of at least twenty feet-preferably more-of neutral zone all about him. No matter how long it takes, he determines absolutely that the lion is not within that distance. The rest is alertness and quickness.

As I have said, the amount of cover necessary to conceal a lion is astonishingly small. He can flatten himself out surprisingly; and his tawny colour blends so well with the brown grasses that he is practically invisible. A practised man does not, of course, look for lions at all. He is after unusual small patches, especially the black ear tips or the black of the mane. Once guessed at, it is interesting to see how quickly the hitherto unsuspected animal sketches itself out in the cover.

I should, before passing on to another aspect of the matter, mention the dangerous poisons carried by the lion's claws. Often men have died from the most trivial surface wounds. The grooves of the claws carry putrefying meat from the kills. Every sensible man in a lion country carries a small syringe, and either permanganate or carbolic. And those mild little remedies he uses full strength!

The great and overwhelming advantage is of course with the hunter. He possesses as deadly a weapon: and that weapon will kill at a distance. This is proper, I think. There are more lions than hunters; and, from our point of view, the man is more important than the beast. The game is not too hazardous. By that I mean that, barring sheer accident, a man is sure to come out all right provided he does accurately the right thing. In other words, it is a dangerous game of skill, but it does not possess the blind danger of a forest in a hurricane, say. Furthermore, it is a game that no man need play unless he wants to. In the lion country he may go about his business-daytime business-as though he were home at the farm.

Such being the case, may I be pardoned for intruding one of my own small ethical ideas at this point, with the full realization that it depends upon an entirely personal point of view. As far as my own case goes, I consider it poor sportsmanship ever to refuse a lion-chance merely because the advantages are not all in my favour. After all, lion hunting is on a different plane from ordinary shooting: it is a challenge to war, a deliberate seeking for mortal combat. Is it not just a little shameful to pot old felis leo at long range, in the open, near his kill, and wherever we have him at an advantage-nine times, and then to back out because that advantage is for once not so marked? I have so often heard the phrase, "I let him (or them) alone. It was not good enough," meaning that the game looked a little risky.

Do not misunderstand. I am not advising that you bull ahead into the long grass, or that alone you open fire on a half dozen lions in easy range. Kind providence endowed you with strategy, and certainly you should never go in where there is no show for you to use your weapon effectively. But occasionally the odds will be against you and you will be called upon to take more or less of a chance. I do not think it is quite square to quit playing merely because for once your opponent has been dealt the better cards. If here are too many of them see if you cannot manoeuvre them; if the grass is long, try every means in your power to get them out. Stay with them. If finally you fail, you will at least have the satisfaction of knowing that circumstances alone have defeated you. If you do not like that sort of a game, stay out of it entirely.

# XII. MORE LIONS

Nor do the last remarks of the preceding chapter mean that you shall not have your trophy in peace. Perhaps excitement and a slight doubt as to whether or not you are going to survive do not appeal to you; but nevertheless you would like a lion skin or so. By all means shoot one lion, or two, or three in the safest fashion you can. But after that you ought to play the game.

The surest way to get a lion is to kill a zebra, cut holes in him, fill the holes with strychnine, and come back next morning. This method is absolutely safe.

The next safest way is to follow the quarry with a pack of especially trained dogs. The lion is so busy and nervous over those dogs that you can walk up and shoot him in the ear. This method has the excitement of riding and following, the joy of a grand and noisy row, and the fun of seeing a good dog-fight. The same effect can be got chasing wart-hogs, hyenas, jackals-or jack-rabbits. The objection is that it wastes a noble beast in an inferior game. My personal opinion is that no man is justified in following with dogs any large animal that can be captured with reasonable certainty without them. The sport of coursing is another matter; but that is quite the same in essence whatever the size of the quarry. If you want to kill a lion or so quite safely, and at the same time enjoy a glorious and exciting gallop with lots of accompanying row, by all means follow the sport with hounds. But having killed one or two by that method, quit. Do not go on and clean up the country. You can do it. Poison and hounds are the SURE methods of finding any lion there may be about; and AFTER THE FIRST FEW, one is about as justifiable as the other. If you want the undoubtedly great joy of cross country pursuit, send your hounds in after less noble game.

The third safe method of killing a lion is nocturnal. You lay out a kill beneath a tree, and climb the tree. Or better, you hitch out a pig or donkey as live bait. When the lion comes to this free lunch, you try to see him; and, if you succeed in that, you try to shoot him. It is not easy to shoot at night; nor is it easy to see in the dark. Furthermore, lions only occasionally bother to come to bait. You may roost up that tree many nights before you get a chance. Once up, you have to stay up; for it is most decidedly not safe to go home after dark. The tropical night in the highlands is quite chilly. Branches seem to be quite as cramping and abrasive under the equator as in the temperate zones. Still, it is one method.

Another is to lay out a kill and visit it in the early morning. There is more to this, for you are afoot, must generally search out your beast in nearby cover, and can easily find any amount of excitement in the process.

The fourth way is to ride the lion. The hunter sees his quarry returning home across the plains, perhaps; or jumps it from some small bushy ravine. At once he spurs his horse in pursuit. The lion will run but a short distance before coming to a stop, for he is not particularly long either of wind or of patience. From this stand he almost invariably charges. The astute hunter, still mounted, turns and flees. When the lion gets tired of chasing, which he does in a very short time, the hunter faces about. At last the lion sits down in the grass, waiting for the game to develop. This is the time for the hunter to dismount and to take his shot. Quite likely he must now stand a charge afoot, and drop his beast before it gets to him.

This is real fun. It has many elements of safety, and many of danger.

To begin with, the hunter at this game generally has companions to back him: often he employs mounted Somalis to round the lion up and get it to stand. The charging lion is quite apt to make for the conspicuous mounted men-who can easily escape-ignoring the hunter afoot. As the game is largely played in the open, the movements of the beast are easily followed.

On the other hand, there is room for mistake. The hunter, for example, should never follow directly in the rear of his lion, but rather at a parallel course off the beast's flank. Then, if the lion stops suddenly, the man does not overrun before he can check his mount. He should never dismount nearer than a hundred and fifty yards from the embayed animal; and should never try to get off while the lion is moving in his direction. Then, too, a hard gallop is not conducive to the best of shooting. It is difficult to hold the front bead steady; and it is still more difficult to remember to wait, once the lion charges, until he has come near enough for a sure shot. A neglect in the inevitable excitement of the moment to remember these and a dozen other small matters may quite possibly cause trouble.

Two or three men together can make this one of the most exciting mounted games on earth; with enough of the give and take of real danger and battle to make it worth while. The hunter, however, who employs a dozen Somalis to ride the beast to a standstill, after which he goes to the front, has eliminated much of the thrill. Nor need that man's stay-at-home family feel any excessive uneasiness over Father Killing Lions in Africa.

The method that interested me more than any other is one exceedingly difficult to follow except under favourable circumstances. I refer to tracking them down afoot. This requires that your gunbearer should be an expert trailer, for, outside the fact that following a soft-padded animal over all sorts of ground is a very difficult thing to do, the hunter should be free to spy ahead. It is necessary also to possess much patience and to endure under many disappointments. But on the other hand there is in this sport a continuous keen thrill to be enjoyed in no other; and he who single handed tracks down and kills his lion thus, has well earned the title of shikari-the Hunter.

And the last method of all is to trust to the God of Chance. The secret of success is to be always ready to take instant advantage of what the moment offers.

An occasional hunting story is good in itself: and the following will also serve to illustrate what I have just been saying.

We were after that prize, the greater kudu, and in his pursuit had penetrated into some very rough country. Our hunting for the time being was over broad bench, perhaps four or five miles wide, below a range of mountains. The bench itself broke down in sheer cliffs some fifteen hundred feet, but one did not appreciate that fact unless he stood fairly on the edge of the precipice. To all intents and purposes we were on a rolling grassy plain, with low hills and cliffs, and a most beautiful little stream running down it beneath fine trees.

Up to now our hunting had gained us little beside information: that kudu had occasionally visited the region, that they had not been there for a month, and that the direction of their departure had been obscure. So we worked our way down the stream, trying out the possibilities. Of other game there seemed to be a fair supply: impalla, hartebeeste, zebra, eland, buffalo, wart-hog, sing-sing, and giraffe we had seen. I had secured a wonderful eland and a very fine impalla, and we had had a gorgeous close-quarters fight with a cheetah.* Now C. had gone out, a three weeks' journey, carrying to medical attendance a porter injured in the cheetah fracas. Billy and I were continuing the hunt alone.

* This animal quite disproved the assertion that cheetahs

never assume the aggressive. He charged repeatedly.

We had marched two hours, and were pitching camp under a single tree near the edge of the bench. After seeing everything well under way, I took the Springfield and crossed the stream, which here ran in a deep canyon. My object was to see if I could get a sing-sing that had bounded away at our approach. I did not bother to take a gunbearer, because I did not expect to be gone five minutes.

The canyon proved unexpectedly deep and rough, and the stream up to my waist. When I had gained the top, I found grass growing patchily from six inches to two feet high; and small, scrubby trees from four to ten feet tall, spaced regularly, but very scattered. These little trees hardly formed cover, but their aggregation at sufficient distance limited the view.

The sing-sing had evidently found his way over the edge of the bench. I turned to go back to camp. A duiker-a small grass antelope-broke from a little patch of the taller grass, rushed, head down headlong after their fashion, suddenly changed his mind, and dashed back again. I stepped forward to see why he had changed his mind-and ran into two lions!

They were about thirty yards away, and sat there on their haunches, side by side, staring at me with expressionless yellow eyes. I stared back. The Springfield is a good little gun, and three times before I had been forced to shoot lions with it, but my real "lion gun" with which I had done best work was the 405 Winchester. The Springfield is too light for such game. Also there were two lions, very close. Also I was quite alone.

As the game stood, it hardly looked like my move; so I held still and waited. Presently one yawned, they looked at each other, turned quite leisurely, and began to move away at a walk.

This was a different matter. If I had fired while the two were facing me, I should probably have had them both to deal with. But now that their tails were turned toward me, I should very likely have to do with only the one: at the crack of the rifle the other would run the way he was headed. So I took a careful bead at the lioness and let drive.

My aim was to cripple the pelvic bone, but, unfortunately, just as I fired, the beast wriggled lithely sidewise to pass around a tuft of grass, so that the bullet inflicted merely a slight flesh wound on the rump. She whirled like a flash, and as she raised her head high to locate me, I had time to wish that the Springfield hit a trifle harder blow. Also I had time to throw another cartridge in the barrel.

The moment she saw me she dropped her head and charged. She was thoroughly angry and came very fast. I had just enough time to steady the gold bead on her chest and to pull trigger.

At the shot, to my great relief, she turned bottom up, and I saw her tail for an instant above the grass-an almost sure indication of a bad hit. She thrashed around, and made a tremendous hullabaloo of snarls and growls. I backed out slowly, my rifle ready. It was no place for me, for the grass was over knee high.

Once at a safe distance I blazed a tree with my hunting knife and departed for camp, well pleased to be out of it. At camp I ate lunch and had a smoke; then with Memba Sasa and Mavrouki returned to the scene of trouble. I had now the 405 Winchester, a light and handy weapon delivering a tremendous blow.

We found the place readily enough. My lioness had recovered from the first shock and had gone. I was very glad I had gone first.

The trail was not very plain, but it could be followed a foot or so at a time, with many faults and casts back. I walked a yard to one side while the men followed the spoor. Owing to the abundance of cover it was very nervous work, for the beast might be almost anywhere, and would certainly charge. We tried to keep a neutral zone around ourselves by tossing stones ahead of and on both sides of our line of advance. My own position was not bad, for I had the rifle ready in my hand, but the men were in danger. Of course I was protecting them as well as I could, but there was always a chance that the lioness might spring on them in such a manner that I would be unable to use my weapon. Once I suggested that as the work was dangerous, they could quit if they wanted to.

"Hapana!" they both refused indignantly.

We had proceeded thus for half a mile when to our relief, right ahead of us, sounded the commanding, rumbling half-roar, half-growl of the lion at bay.

Instantly Memba Sasa and Mavrouki dropped back to me. We all peered ahead. One of the boys made her out first, crouched under a bush thirty-two yards away. Even as I raised the rifle she saw us and charged. I caught her in the chest before she had come ten feet. The heavy bullet stopped her dead. Then she recovered and started forward slowly, very weak, but game to the last. Another shot finished her.

51

The remarkable point of this incident was the action of the little Springfield bullet. Evidently the very high velocity of this bullet from its shock to the nervous system had delivered a paralyzing blow sufficient to knock out the lioness for the time being. Its damage to tissue, however, was slight. Inasmuch as the initial shock did not cause immediate death, the lioness recovered sufficiently to be able, two hours later, to take the offensive. This point is of the greatest interest to the student of ballistics; but it is curious to even the ordinary reader.

That is a very typical example of finding lions by sheer chance. Generally a man is out looking for the smallest kind of game when he runs up against them. Now happened to follow an equally typical example of tracking.

The next day after the killing of the lioness Memba Sasa, Kongoni and I dropped off the bench, and hunted greater kudu on a series of terraces fifteen hundred feet below. All we found were two rhino, some sing-sing, a heard of impalla, and a tremendous thirst. In the meantime, Mavrouki had, under orders, scouted the foothills of the mountain range at the back. He reported none but old tracks of kudu, but said he had seen eight lions not far from our encounter of the day before.

Therefore, as soon next morning as we could see plainly, we again crossed the canyon and the waist-deep stream. I had with me all three of the gun men, and in addition two of the most courageous porters to help with the tracking and the looking.

About eight o'clock we found the first fresh pad mark plainly outlined in an isolated piece of soft earth. Immediately we began that most fascinating of games-trailing over difficult ground. In this we could all take part, for the tracks were some hours old, and the cover scanty. Very rarely could we make out more than three successive marks. Then we had to spy carefully for the slightest indication of direction. Kongoni in especial was wonderful at this, and time and again picked up a broken grass blade or the minutest inch-fraction of disturbed earth. We moved slowly, in long hesitations and castings about, and in swift little dashes forward of a few feet; and often we went astray on false scents, only to return finally to the last certain spot. In this manner we crossed the little plain with the scattered shrub trees and arrived at the edge of the low bluff above the stream bottom.

This bottom was well wooded along the immediate bank of the stream itself, fringed with low thick brush, and in the open spaces grown to the edges with high, green, coarse grass.

As soon as we had managed to follow without fault to this grass, our difficulties of trailing were at an end. The lions' heavy bodies had made distinct paths through the tangle. These paths went forward sinuously, sometimes separating one from the other, sometimes intertwining, sometimes combining into one for a short distance. We could not determine accurately the number of beasts that had made them.

"They have gone to drink water," said Memba Sasa.

We slipped along the twisting paths, alert for indications; came to the edge of the thicket, stooped through the fringe, and descended to the stream under the tall trees. The soft earth at the water's edge was covered with tracks, thickly overlaid one over the other. The boys felt of the earth, examined, even smelled, and came to the conclusion that the beasts must have watered about five o'clock. If so, they might be ten miles away, or as many rods.

We had difficulty in determining just where the party left this place, until finally Kongoni caught sight of suspicious indications over the way. The lions had crossed the stream. We did likewise, followed the trail out of the thicket, into the grass, below the little cliffs parallel to the stream, back into the thicket, across the river once more, up the other side, in the thicket for a quarter mile, then out into the grass on that side, and so on.

They were evidently wandering, rather idly, up the general course of the stream. Certainly, unlike most cats, they did not mind getting their feet wet, for they crossed the stream four times.

At last the twining paths in the shoulder-high grass fanned out separately. We counted.

"You were right, Mavrouki," said I, "there were eight."

At the end of each path was a beaten-down little space where evidently the beasts had been lying down. With an exclamation the three gunbearers darted forward to investigate. The lairs were still warm! Their occupants had evidently made off only at our approach!

Not five minutes later we were halted by a low warning growl right ahead. We stopped. The boys squatted on their heels close to me, and we consulted in whispers.

Of course it would be sheer madness to attack eight lions in grass so high we could not see five feet in front of us. That went without saying. On the other hand, Mavrouki swore that he had yesterday seen no small cubs with the band, and our examination of the tracks made in soft earth seemed to bear him out. The chances were therefore that, unless themselves attacked or too close pressed, the lions would not attack us. By keeping just in their rear we might be able to urge them gently along until they should enter more open cover. Then we could see.

Therefore we gave the owner of that growl about five minutes to forget it, and then advanced very cautiously. We soon found where the objector had halted, and plainly read by the indications where he had stood for a moment or so, and then moved on. We slipped along after.

For five hours we hung at the heels of that band of lions, moving very slowly, perfectly willing to halt whenever they told us to, and going forward again only when we became convinced that they too had gone on. Except for the first half hour, we were never more than twenty or thirty yards from the nearest lion, and often much closer. Three or four times I saw slowly gliding yellow bodies just ahead of me, but in the circumstances it would have been sheer stark lunacy to have fired. Probably six or eight times-I did not count-we were commanded to stop, and we did stop.

It was very exciting work, but the men never faltered. Of course I went first, in case one of the beasts had the toothache or otherwise did not play up to our calculations on good nature. One or the other of the gunbearers was always just behind me. Only once was any comment made. Kongoni looked very closely into my face.

"There are very many lions," he remarked doubtfully.

"Very many lions," I agreed, as though assenting to a mere statement of fact.

Although I am convinced there was no real danger, as long as we stuck to our plan of campaign, nevertheless it was quite interesting to be for so long a period so near these great brutes. They led us for a mile or so along the course of the stream, sometimes on one side, sometimes on the other. Several times they emerged into better cover, and even into the open, but always ducked back into the thick again before we ourselves had followed their trail to the clear.

At noon we were halted by the usual growl just as we had reached the edge of the river. So we sat down on the banks and had lunch.

Finally our chance came. The trail led us, for the dozenth time, from the high grass into the thicket along the river. We ducked our heads to enter. Memba Sasa, next my shoulder, snapped his fingers violently. Following the direction of the brown arm that shot over my shoulder, I strained my eyes into the dimness of the thicket. At first I could see nothing at all, but at length a slight motion drew my eye. Then I made out the silhouette of a lion's head, facing us steadily. One of the rear guard had again turned to halt us, but this time where he and his surroundings could be seen.

Luckily I always use a Sheard gold bead sight, and even in the dimness of the tree-shaded thicket it showed up well. The beast was only forty yards away, so I fired at his head. He rolled over without a sound.

We took the usual great precautions in determining the genuineness of his demise, then carried him into the open. Strangely enough the bullet had gone so cleanly into his left eye that it had not even broken the edge of the eyelid; so that when skinned he did not show a mark. He was a very decent maned lion, three feet four inches at the shoulder, and nine feet long as he lay. We found that he had indeed been the rear guard, and that the rest, on the other side of the thicket, had made off at the shot. So in spite of the APPARENT danger of the situation, our calculations had worked out perfectly. Also we had enjoyed a half day's sport of an intensity quite impossible to be extracted from any other method of following the lion.

In trying to guess how any particular lions may act, however, you will find yourself often at fault. The lion is a very intelligent and crafty beast, and addicted to tricks. If you follow a lion to a small hill, it is well to go around that hill on the side opposite to that taken by your quarry. You are quite likely to meet him for he is clever enough thus to try to get in your rear. He will lie until you have actually passed him before breaking off. He will circle ahead, then back to confuse his trail. And when you catch sight of him in the distance, you would never suspect that he knew of your presence at all. He saunters slowly, apparently aimlessly, along pausing often, evidently too bored to take any interest in life. You wait quite breathlessly for him to pass behind cover. Then you are going to make a very rapid advance, and catch his leisurely retreat. But the moment old Leo does pass behind the cover, his appearance of idle stroller vanishes. In a dozen bounds he is gone.

That is what makes lion hunting delightful. There are some regions, very near settlements, where it is perhaps justifiable to poison these beasts. If you are a true sportsman you will confine your hound-hunting to those districts. Elsewhere, as far as playing fair with a noble beast is concerned, you may as well toss a coin to see which you shall take-your pack or a strychnine bottle.

# XIII. ON THE MANAGING OF A SAFARI

We made our way slowly down the river. As the elevation dropped, the temperature rose. It was very hot indeed during the day, and in the evening the air was tepid and caressing, and musical with the hum of insects. We sat about quite comfortably in our pajamas, and took our fifteen grains of quinine per week against the fever.

The character of the jungle along the river changed imperceptibly, the dhum palms crowding out the other trees; until, at our last camp, were nothing but palms. The wind in them sounded variously like the patter or the gathering onrush of rain. On either side the country remained unchanged, however. The volcanic hills rolled away to the distant ranges. Everywhere grew sparsely the low thornbrush, opening sometimes into clear plains, closing sometimes into dense thickets. One morning we awoke to find that many supposedly sober-minded trees had burst into blossom fairly over night. They were red, and yellow and white that before were green, a truly gorgeous sight.

Then we turned sharp to the right and began to ascend a little tributary brook coming down the wide flats from a cleft in the hills. This was prettily named the Isiola, and, after the first mile or so, was not big enough to afford the luxury of a jungle of its own. Its banks were generally grassy and steep, its thickets few, and its little trees isolated in parklike spaces. To either side of it, and almost at its level, stretched plains, but plains grown with scattered brush and shrubs so that at a mile or two one's vista was closed. But for all its scant ten feet of width the Isiola stood upon its dignity as a stream. We discovered that when we tried to cross. The men floundered waist-deep on uncertain bottom; the syces received much unsympathetic comment for their handling of the animals, and we had to get Billy over by a melodramatic "bridge of life" with B., F., myself, and Memba Sasa in the title roles.

Then we pitched camp in the open on the other side, sent the horses back from the stream until after dark, in fear of the deadly tsetse fly, and prepared to enjoy a good exploration of the neighbourhood. Whereupon M'ganga rose up to his gaunt and terrific height of authority, stretched forth his bony arm at right angles, and uttered between eight and nine thousand commands in a high dynamic monotone without a single pause for breath. These, supplemented by about as many more, resulted in (a) a bridge across the stream, and (b) a banda.

A banda is a delightful African institution. It springs from nothing in about two hours, but it takes twenty boys with a vitriolic M'ganga back of them to bring it about. Some of them carry huge backloads of grass, or papyrus, or cat-tail rushes, as the case may be; others lug in poles of various lengths from where their comrades are cutting them by means of their panga. A panga, parenthetically, is the safari man's substitute for axe, shovel, pick, knife, sickle, lawn-mower, hammer, gatling gun, world's library of classics, higher mathematics, grand opera, and toothpicks. It looks rather like a machete with a very broad end and a slight curved back. A good man can do extraordinary things with it. Indeed, at this moment, two boys are with this apparently clumsy implement delicately peeling some of the small thorn trees, from the bared trunks of which they are stripping long bands of tough inner bark.

With these three raw materials-poles, withes, and grass-M'ganga and his men set to work. They planted their corner and end poles, they laid their rafters, they completed their framework, binding all with the tough withes; then deftly they thatched it with the grass. Almost before we had settled our own affairs, M'ganga was standing before us smiling. Gone now was his mien of high indignation and swirling energy.

"Banda naquisha," he informed us.

And we moved in our table and our canvas chairs; hung up our water bottles; Billy got out her fancy work. Nothing could be pleasanter nor more appropriate to the climate than this wide low arbour, open at either end to the breezes, thatched so thickly that the fierce sun could nowhere strike through.

The men had now settled down to a knowledge of what we were like; and things were going smoothly. At first the African porter will try it on to see just how easy you are likely to prove. If he makes up his mind that you really are easy, then you are in for infinite petty annoyance, and possibly open mutiny. Therefore, for a little while, it is necessary to be extremely vigilant, to insist on minute performance in all circumstances where later you might condone an omission. For the same reason punishment must be more frequent and more severe at the outset. It is all a matter of watching the temper of the men. If they are cheerful and willing, you are not nearly as particular as you would be were their spirit becoming sullen. Then the infraction is not so important in itself as an excuse for the punishment. For when your men get sulky, you watch vigilantly for the first and faintest EXCUSE to inflict punishment.

55

This game always seemed to me very fascinating, when played right. It is often played wrong. People do not look far enough. Because they see that punishment has a most salutary effect on morale, and is sometimes efficacious in getting things done that otherwise would lag, they jump to the conclusion that the only effective way to handle a safari is by penalties. By this I do not at all mean that they act savagely, or punish to brutal excess. Merely they hold rigidly to the letter of the work and the day's discipline. Because it is sometimes necessary to punish severely slight infractions when the men's tempers need sweetening, they ALWAYS punish slight infractions severely.

And in ordinary circumstances this method undoubtedly results in a very efficient safari. Things are done smartly, on time, with a snap. The day's march begins without delay; there is a minimum of straggling; on arrival the tents are immediately got up and the wood and water fetched. But in a tight place, men so handled by invariable rule are very apt to sit down apathetically, and put the whole thing up to the white man. When it comes time to help out they are not there. The contrast with a well-disposed safari cannot be appreciated by one who has not seen both.

The safari-man loves a master. He does not for a moment understand any well-meant but misplaced efforts on your part to lighten his work below the requirements of custom. Always he will beg you to ease up on him, to accord him favour; and always he will despise you if you yield. The relations of man to man, of man to work, are all long since established by immemorial distauri-custom-and it is not for you or him to change them lightly. If you know what he should or can do, and hold him rigidly to it, he will respect and follow you.

But in order to keep him up to the mark, it is not always advisable to light into him with a whip, necessary as the whip often is. If he is sullen, or inclined to make mischief, then that is the crying requirement. But if he is merely careless, or a little slow, or tired, you can handle him in other ways. Ridicule before his comrades is very effective: a sort of good-natured guying, I mean. "Ah! very tired!" uttered in the right tone of voice has brought many a loiterer to his feet as effectively as the kick some men feel must always be bestowed, and quite without anger, mind you! For days at a time we have kept our men travelling at good speed by commenting, as though by the way, after we had arrived in camp, on which tribe happened to come in at the head.

"Ah! Kavirondos came in first to-night," we would remark. "Last night the Monumwezis were ahead."

And once, actually, by this method we succeeded in working up such a feeling of rivalry that the Kikuyus, the unambitious, weak and despised Kikuyus, led the van!

But the first hint of insubordination, of intended insolence, of willful shirking must be met by instant authority. Occasionally, when the situation is of the quick and sharp variety, the white man may have to mix in the row himself. He must never hesitate an instant; for the only reason he alone can control so many is that he has always controlled them. F. had a very effective blow, or shove, which I found well worth adopting. It is delivered with the heel of the palm to the man's chin, and is more of a lifting, heaving shove than an actual blow. Its effect is immediately upsetting. Impertinence is best dealt with in this manner on the spot. Evidently intended slowness in coming when called is also best treated by a flick of the whip-and forgetfulness. And so with a half dozen others. But any more serious matter should be decided from the throne of the canvas chair, witness should be heard, judgment formally pronounced, and execution intrusted to the askaris or gunbearers.

It is, as I have said, a most interesting game. It demands three sorts of knowledge: first what a safari man is capable of doing; second, what he customarily should or should not do; third, an ability to read the actual intention or motive back of his actions. When you are able to punish or hold your hand on these principles, and not merely because things have or have not gone smoothly or right, then you are a good safari manager. There are mighty few of them.

As for punishment, that is quite simply the whip. The average writer on the country speaks of this with hushed voice and averted face as a necessity but as something to be deprecated and passed over as quickly as possible. He does this because he thinks he ought to. As a matter of fact, such an attitude is all poppycock. In the flogging of a white man, or a black who suffers from such a punishment in his soul as well as his body, this is all very well. But the safari man expects it, it doesn't hurt his feelings in the least, it is ancient custom. As well sentimentalize over necessary schoolboy punishment, or over father paddy-whacking little Willie when little Willie has been a bad boy. The chances are your porter will leap to his feet, crack his heels together and depart with a whoop of joy, grinning from ear to ear. Or he may draw himself up and salute you, military fashion, again with a grin. In any case his "soul" is not "scared" a little bit, and there is no sense in yourself feeling about it as though it were.

At another slant the justice you will dispense to your men differs from our own. Again this is because of the teaching long tradition has made part of their mental make-up. Our own belief is that it is better to let two guilty men go than to punish one innocent. With natives it is the other way about. If a crime is committed the guilty MUST be punished. Preferably he alone is to be dealt with; but in case it is impossible to identify him, then all the members of the first inclusive unit must be brought to account. This is the native way of doing things; is the only way the native understands; and is the only way that in his mind true justice is answered. Thus if a sheep is stolen, the thief must be caught and punished. Suppose, however it is known to what family the thief belongs, but the family refuses to disclose which of its members committed the theft: then each member must be punished for sheep stealing; or, if not the family, then the tribe must make restitution. But punishment MUST be inflicted.

There is an essential justice to recommend this, outside the fact that it has with the native all the solidity of accepted ethics, and it certainly helps to run the real criminal to earth. The innocent sometimes suffers innocently, but not very often; and our own records show that in that respect with us it is the same. This is not the place to argue the right or wrong of the matter from our own standpoint but to recognize the fact that it is right from theirs, and to act accordingly. Thus in cast of theft of meat, or something that cannot be traced, it is well to call up the witnesses, to prove the alibis, and then to place the issue squarely up to those that remain. There may be but two, or there may be a dozen.

"I know you did not all steal the meat," you must say, "but I know that one of you did. Unless I know which one that is by to-morrow morning, I will kiboko all of you. Bass!"

Perhaps occasionally you may have to kiboko the lot, in the full knowledge that most are innocent. That seems hard; and your heart will misgive you. Harden it. The "innocent" probably know perfectly well who the guilty man is. And the incident builds for the future.

I had intended nowhere to comment on the politics or policies of the country. Nothing is more silly than the casual visitor's snap judgments on how a country is run. Nevertheless, I may perhaps be pardoned for suggesting that the Government would strengthen its hand, and aid its few straggling settlers by adopting this native view of retributions. For instance, at present it is absolutely impossible to identify individual sheep and cattle stealers. They operate stealthily and at night. If the Government cannot identify the actual thief, it gives the matter up. As a consequence a great hardship is inflicted on the settler and an evil increases. If, however, the Government would hold the village, the district, or the tribe responsible, and exact just compensation from such units in every case, the evil would very suddenly come to an end. And the native's respect for the white man would climb in the scale.

Once the safari man gets confidence in his master, that confidence is complete. The white man's duties are in his mind clearly defined. His job is to see that the black man is fed, is watered, is taken care of in every way. The ordinary porter considers himself quite devoid of responsibility. He is also an improvident creature, for he drinks all his water when he gets thirsty, no matter how long and hot the journey before him; he eats his rations all up when he happens to get hungry, two days before next distribution time; he straggles outrageously at times and has to be rounded up; he works three months and, on a whim, deserts two days before the end of his journey, thus forfeiting all his wages. Once two porters came to us for money.

"What for?" asked C.

"To buy a sheep," said they.

For two months we had been shooting them all the game meat they could eat, but on this occasion two days had intervened since the last kill. If they had been on trading safari they would have had no meat at all. A sheep cost six rupees in that country, and they were getting but ten rupees a month as wages. In view of the circumstances, and for their own good, we refused. Another man once insisted on purchasing a cake of violet-scented soap for a rupee. Their chief idea of a wild time in Nairobi, after return from a long safari, is to SIT IN A CHAIR and drink tea. For this they pay exorbitantly at the Somali so-called "hotels." It is a strange sight. But then, I have seen cowboys off the range or lumberjacks from the river do equally extravagant and foolish things.

On the other hand they carry their loads well, they march tremendously, they know their camp duties and they do them. Under adverse circumstances they are good-natured. I remember C. and I, being belated and lost in a driving rain. We wandered until nearly midnight. The four or five men with us were loaded heavily with the meat and trophy of a roan. Certainly they must have been very tired; for only occasionally could we permit them to lay down their loads. Most of the time we were actually groping, over boulders, volcanic rocks, fallen trees and all sorts of tribulation. The men took it as a huge joke, and at every pause laughed consumedly.

In making up a safari one tries to mix in four or five tribes. This prevents concerted action in case of trouble, for no one tribe will help another. They vary both in tribal and individual characteristics, of course. For example, the Kikuyus are docile but mediocre porters; the Kavirondos strong carriers but turbulent and difficult to handle. You are very lucky if you happen on a camp jester, one of the sort that sings, shouts, or jokes while on the march. He is probably not much as a porter, but he is worth his wages nevertheless. He may or may not aspire to his giddy eminence. We had one droll-faced little Kavirondo whose very expression made one laugh, and whose rueful remarks on the harshness of his lot finally ended by being funny. His name got to be a catchword in camp.

"Mualo! Mualo!" the men would cry, as they heaved their burdens to their heads; and all day long their war cry would ring out, "Mualo!" followed by shrieks of laughter.

Of the other type was Sulimani, a big, one-eyed Monumwezi, who had a really keen wit coupled with an earnest, solemn manner. This man was no buffoon, however; and he was a good porter, always at or near the head of the procession. In the great jungle south of Kenia we came upon Cuninghame. When the head of our safari reached the spot Sulimani left the ranks and, his load still aloft danced solemnly in front of Cuninghame, chanting something in a loud tone of voice. Then with a final deep "Jambo!" to his old master he rejoined the safari. When the day had stretched to weariness and the men had fallen to a sullen plodding, Sulimani's vigorous song could always set the safari sticks tapping the sides of the chop boxes.

He carried part of the tent, and the next best men were entrusted with the cook outfit and our personal effects. It was a point of honour with these men to be the first in camp. The rear, the very extreme and straggling rear, was brought up by worthless porters with loads of cornmeal-and the weary askaris whose duty it was to keep astern and herd the lot in.

# XIV. A DAY ON THE ISIOLA

Early one morning-we were still on the Isiola-we set forth on our horses to ride across the rolling, brush-grown plain. Our intention was to proceed at right angles to our own little stream until we had reached the forest growth of another, which we could dimly make out eight or ten miles distant. Billy went with us, so there were four a-horseback. Behind us trudged the gunbearers, and the syces, and after them straggled a dozen or fifteen porters.

The sun was just up, and the air was only tepid as yet. From patches of high grass whirred and rocketed grouse of two sorts. They were so much like our own ruffed grouse and prairie chicken that I could with no effort imagine myself once more a boy in the coverts of the Middle West. Only before us we could see the stripes of trotting zebra disappearing; and catch the glint of light on the bayonets of the oryx. Two giraffes galumphed away to the right. Little grass antelope darted from clump to clump of grass. Once we saw gerenuk-oh, far away in an impossible distance. Of course we tried to stalk them; and as usual we failed. The gerenuk we had come to look upon as our Lesser Hoodoo.

The beast is a gazelle about as big as a black-tailed deer. His peculiarity is his excessively long neck, a good deal on the giraffe order. With it he crops browse above high tide mark of other animals, especially when as often happens he balances cleverly on his hind legs. By means of it also he can, with his body completely concealed, look over the top of ordinary cover and see you long before you have made out his inconspicuous little head. Then he departs. He seems to have a lamentable lack of healthy curiosity about you. In that respect he should take lessons from the kongoni. After that you can follow him as far as you please; you will get only glimpses at three or four hundred yards.

We remounted sadly and rode on. The surface of the ground was rather soft, scattered with round rocks the size of a man's head, and full of pig holes.

"Cheerful country to ride over at speed," remarked Billy. Later in the day we had occasion to remember that statement.

The plains led us ever on. First would be a band of scattered brush growing singly and in small clumps: then a little open prairie; then a narrow, long grass swale; then perhaps a low, long hill with small single trees and rough, volcanic footing. Ten thousand things kept us interested. Game was everywhere, feeding singly, in groups, in herds, game of all sizes and descriptions. The rounded ears of jackals pointed at us from the grass. Hundreds of birds balanced or fluttered about us, birds of all sizes from the big ground hornbill to the littlest hummers and sun birds. Overhead, across the wonderful variegated sky of Africa the broad-winged carrion hunters and birds of prey wheeled. In all our stay on the Isiola we had not seen a single rhino track, so we rode quite care free and happy.

Finally, across a glade, not over a hundred and fifty yards away, we saw a solitary bull oryx standing under a bush. B. wanted an oryx. We discussed this one idly. He looked to be a decent oryx, but nothing especial. However, he offered a very good shot; so B., after some hesitation, decided to take it. It proved to be by far the best specimen we shot, the horns measuring thirty-six and three fourths inches! Almost immediately after, two of the rather rare striped hyenas leaped from the grass and departed rapidly over the top of a hill. We opened fire, and F. dropped one of them. By the time these trophies were prepared, the sun had mounted high in the heavens, and it was getting hot.

Accordingly we abandoned that still distant river and swung away in a wide circle to return to camp.

Several minor adventures brought us to high noon and the heat of the day. B. had succeeded in drawing a prize, one of the Grevy's or mountain zebra. He and the gunbearers engaged themselves with that, while we sat under the rather scanty shade of a small thorn tree and had lunch. Here we had a favourable chance to observe that very common, but always wonderful phenomenon, the gathering of the carrion birds. Within five minutes after the stoop of the first vulture above the carcass, the sky immediately over that one spot was fairly darkened with them. They were as thick as midges-or as ducks used to be in California. All sizes were there from the little carrion crows to the great dignified vultures and marabouts and eagles. The small fry flopped and scolded, and rose and fell in a dense mass; the marabouts walked with dignified pace to and fro through the grass all about. As far as the eye could penetrate the blue, it could make out more and yet more of the great soarers stooping with half bent wings. Below we could see uncertainly through the shimmer of the mirage the bent forms of the men.

We ate and waited; and after a little we dozed. I was awakened suddenly by a tremendous rushing roar, like the sound of a not too distant waterfall. The group of men were plodding toward us carrying burdens. And like plummets the birds were dropping straight down from the heavens, spreading wide their wings at the last moment to check their speed. This made the roaring sound that had awakened me.

A wide spot in the shimmer showed black and struggling against the ground. I arose and walked over, meeting halfway B. and the men carrying the meat. It took me probably about two minutes to reach the place where the zebra had been killed. Hundreds, perhaps thousands, of the great birds were standing idly about; a dozen or so were flapping and scrambling in the centre. I stepped into view. With a mighty commotion they all took wing clumsily, awkwardly, reluctantly. A trampled, bloody space and the larger bones, picked absolutely clean, was all that remained! In less than two minutes the job had been done!

"You're certainly good workmen!" I exclaimed, "but I wonder how you all make a living!"

We started the men on to camp with the meat, and ourselves rested under the shade. The day had been a full and interesting one; but we considered it as finished. Remained only the hot journey back to camp.

After a half hour we mounted again and rode on slowly. The sun was very strong and a heavy shimmer clothed the plain. Through this shimmer we caught sight of something large and black and flapping. It looked like a crow-or, better, a scare-crow-crippled, half flying, half running, with waving wings or arms, now dwindling, now gigantic as the mirage caught it up or let it drop. As we watched, it developed, and we made it out to be a porter, clad in a long, ragged black overcoat, running zigzag through the bushes in our direction.

The moment we identified it we spurred our horses forward. As my horse leaped, Memba Sasa snatched the Springfield from my left hand and forced the 405 Winchester upon me. Clever Memba Sasa! He no more than we knew what was up, but shrewdly concluded that whatever it was it needed a heavy gun.

As we galloped to meet him, the porter stopped. We saw him to be a very long-legged, raggedy youth whom we had nicknamed the Marabout because of his exceedingly long, lean legs, the fact that his breeches were white, short and baggy, and because he kept his entire head shaved close. He called himself Fundi, which means The Expert, a sufficient indication of his confidence in himself.

He awaited us leaning on his safari stick, panting heavily, the sweat running off his face in splashes. "Simba!"* said he, and immediately set off on a long, easy lope ahead of us. We pulled down to a trot and followed him.

&ast; Lion

At the end of a half mile we made out a man up a tree. Fundi, out of breath, stopped short and pointed to this man. The latter, as soon as he had seen us, commenced to scramble down. We spurred forward to find out where the lions had been last seen.

Then Billy covered herself with glory by seeing them first. She apprised us of that fact with some excitement. We saw the long, yellow bodies of two of them disappearing in the edge of the brush about three hundred yards away. With a wild whoop we tore after them at a dead run.

Then began a wild ride. Do you remember Billy's remark about the nature of the footing? Before long we closed in near enough to catch occasional glimpses of the beasts, bounding easily along. At that moment B.'s horse went down in a heap. None of us thought for a moment of pulling up. I looked back to see B. getting up again, and thought I caught fragments of encouraging-sounding language. Then my horse went down. I managed to hold my rifle clear, and to cling to the reins. Did you ever try to get on a somewhat demoralized horse in a frantic hurry, when all your friends were getting farther away every minute, and so lessening your chances of being in the fun? I began to understand perfectly B.'s remarks of a moment before. However, on I scrambled, and soon overtook the hunt.

We dodged in and out of bushes, and around and over holes. Every few moments we would catch a glimpse of one of those silently bounding lions, and then we would let out a yell. Also every few moments one or the other of us would go down in a heap, and would scramble up and curse, and remount hastily. Billy had better luck. She had no gun, and belonged a little in the rear anyway, but was coming along game as a badger for all that.

My own horse had the legs of the others quite easily, and for that reason I was ahead far enough to see the magnificent sight of five lions sideways on, all in a row, standing in the grass gazing at me with a sort of calm and impersonal dignity. I wheeled my horse immediately so as to be ready in case of a charge, and yelled to the others to hurry up. While I sat there, they moved slowly off one after the other, so that by the time the men had come, the lions had gone. We now had no difficulty in running into them again. Once more my better animal brought me to the lead, so that for the second time I drew up facing the lions, and at about one hundred yards range. One by one they began to leave as before, very leisurely and haughtily, until a single old maned fellow remained. He, however, sat there, his great round head peering over the top of the grass.

"Well," he seemed to say, "here I am, what do you intend to do about it?"

The others arrived, and we all dismounted. B. had not yet killed his lion, so the shot was his. Billy very coolly came up behind and held his horse. I should like here to remark that Billy is very terrified of spiders. F. and I stood at the ready, and B. sat down.

Riding fast an exciting mile or so, getting chucked on your head two or three times, and facing your first lion are none of them conducive to steady shooting. The first shot therefore went high, but the second hit the lion square in the chest, and he rolled over dead.

We all danced a little war dance, and congratulated B. and turned to get the meaning of a queer little gurgling gasp behind us. There was Fundi! That long-legged scarecrow, not content with running to get us and then back again, had trailed us the whole distance of our mad chase over broken ground at terrific speed in order to be in at the death. And he was just about all in at the death. He could barely gasp his breath, his eyes stuck out; he looked close to apoplexy.

"Bwana! bwana!" was all he could say. "Master! master!"

We shook hands with Fundi.

"My son," said I, "you're a true sport, and you'll surely get yours later."

He did not understand me, but he grinned. The gunbearers began to drift in, also completely pumped. They set up a feeble shout when they saw the dead lion. It was a good maned beast, three feet six inches at the shoulder, and nine feet long.

We left Fundi with the lion, instructing him to stay there until some of the other men came up. We remounted and pushed on slowly in hopes of coming on one of the others.

Here and there we rode, our courses interweaving, looking eagerly. And lo! through a tiny opening in the brush we espied one of those elusive gerenuk standing not over one hundred yards away. Whereupon I dismounted and did some of the worst shooting I perpetrated in Africa, for I let loose three times at him before I landed. But land I did, and there was one Lesser Hoodoo broken. Truly this was our day.

We measured him and started to prepare the trophy, when to us came Mavrouki and a porter, quite out of breath, but able to tell us that they had been scouting around and had seen two of the lions. Then, instead of leaving one up a tree to watch, both had come pell-mell to tell us all about it. We pointed this out to them, and called their attention to the fact that the brush was wide, that lions are not stationary objects, and that, unlike the leopard, they can change their spots quite readily. However, we remounted and went to take a look.

Of course there was nothing. So we rode on, rather aimlessly, weaving in and out of the bushes and open spaces. I think we were all a little tired from the long day and the excitement, and hence a bit listless. Suddenly we were fairly shaken out of our saddles by an angry roar just ahead. Usually a lion growls, low and thunderous, when he wants, to warn you that you have gone about far enough; but this one was angry all through at being followed about so much, and he just plain yelled at us.

He crouched near a bush forty yards away, and was switching his tail. I had heard that this was a sure premonition of an instant charge, but I had not before realized exactly what "switching the tail" meant. I had thought of it as a slow sweeping from side to side, after the manner of the domestic cat. This lion's tail was whirling perpendicularly from right to left, and from left to right with the speed and energy of a flail actuated by a particularly instantaneous kind of machinery. I could see only the outline of the head and this vigorous tail; but I took instant aim and let drive. The whole affair sank out of sight.

We made a detour around the dead lion without stopping to examine him, shouting to one of the men to stay and watch the carcass. Billy alone seemed uninfected with the now prevalent idea that we were likely to find lions almost anywhere. Her skepticism was justified. We found no more lions; but another miracle took place for all that. We ran across the second imbecile gerenuk, and B. collected it! These two were the only ones we ever got within decent shot of, and they sandwiched themselves neatly with lions. Truly, it WAS our day.

After a time we gave it up, and went back to measure and photograph our latest prize. It proved to be a male, maneless, two inches shorter than that killed by B., and three feet five and one half inches tall at the shoulder. My bullet had reached the brain just over the left eye.

Now, toward sunset, we headed definitely toward camp. The long shadows and beautiful lights of evening were falling across the hills far the other side the Isiola. A little breeze with a touch of coolness breathed down from distant unseen Kenia. We plodded on through the grass quite happily, noting the different animals coming out to the cool of the evening. The line of brush that marked the course of the Isiola came imperceptibly nearer until we could make out the white gleam of the porters' tents and wisps of smoke curling upward.

Then a small black mass disengaged itself from the camp and came slowly across the prairie in our direction. As it approached we made it out to be our Monumwezis, twenty strong. The news of the lions had reached them, and they were coming to meet us. They were huddled in a close knot, their heads inclined toward the centre. Each man carried upright a peeled white wand. They moved in absolute unison and rhythm, on a slanting zigzag in our direction: first three steps to the right, then three to the left, with a strong stamp of the foot between. Their bodies swayed together. Sulimani led them, dancing backward, his wand upheld.

"Sheeka!" he enunciated in a piercing half whistle.

And the swaying men responded in chorus, half hushed, rumbling, with strong aspiration.

"Goom zoop! goom zoop!"

When fifty yards from us, however, the formation broke and they rushed us with a yell. Our horses plunged in astonishment, and we had hard work to prevent their bolting, small blame to 'em! The men surrounded us, shaking our hands frantically. At once they appropriated everything we or our gunbearers carried. One who got left otherwise insisted on having Billy's parasol. Then we all broke for camp at full speed, yelling like fiends, firing our revolvers in the air. It was a grand entry, and a grand reception. The rest of the camp poured out with wild shouts. The dark forms thronged about us, teeth flashing, arms waving. And in the background, under the shadows of the trees were the Monumwezis, their formation regained, close gathered, heads bent, two steps swaying to the right-stamp! two steps swaying to the left-stamp!-the white wands gleaming, and the rumble of their lion song rolling in an undertone:

"Goom zoop! goom zoop!"

# XV. THE LION DANCE

We took our hot baths and sat down to supper most gratefully, for we were tired. The long string of men, bearing each a log of wood, filed in from the darkness to add to our pile of fuel. Saa-sita and Shamba knelt and built the night fire. In a moment the little flame licked up through the carefully arranged structure. We finished the meal, and the boys whisked away the table.

Then out in the blackness beyond our little globe of light we became aware of a dull confusion, a rustling to and fro. Through the shadows the eye could guess at movement.

The confusion steadied to a kind of rhythm, and into the circle of the fire came the group of Monumwezis. Again they were gathered together in a compact little mass; but now they were bent nearly double, and were stripped to the red blankets about their waists. Before them writhed Sulimani, close to earth, darting irregularly now to right, now to left, wriggling, spreading his arms abroad. He was repeating over and over two phrases; or rather the same phrase in two such different intonations that they seemed to convey quite separate meanings.

"Ka soompeele?" he cried with a strongly appealing interrogation.

"Ka soompeele!" he repeated with the downward inflection of decided affirmation.

And the bent men, their dark bodies gleaming in the firelight, stamping in rhythm every third step, chorused in a deep rumbling bass:

"Goom zoop! goom zoop!"

Thus they advanced; circled between us and the fire, and withdrew to the half darkness, where tirelessly they continued the same reiterations.

Hardly had they withdrawn when another group danced forward in their places. These were the Kikuyus. They had discarded completely their safari clothes, and now came forth dressed out in skins, in strips of white cloth, with feathers, shells and various ornaments. They carried white wands to represent spears, and they sang their tribal lion song. A soloist delivered the main argument in a high wavering minor and was followed by a deep rumbling emphatic chorus of repetition, strongly accented so that the sheer rhythm of it was most pronounced:

"An-gee a Ka ga An-gee a Ka ga An-gee a Ka ga Ki ya Ka ga Ka ga an gee ya!"

Solemnly and loftily, their eyes fixed straight before them they made the circle of the fire, passed before our chairs, and withdrew to the half light. There, a few paces from the stamping, crouching Monumwezis, they continued their performance.

The next to appear were the Wakambas. These were more histrionic. They too were unrecognizable as our porters, for they too had for the lion discarded their work-a-day garments in favour of savage. They produced a pantomime of the day's doings, very realistic indeed, ending with a half dozen of dark swaying bodies swinging and shuddering in the long grass as lions, while the "horses" wove in and out among the crouching forms, all done to the beat of rhythm. Past us swept the hunt, and in its turn melted into the half light.

The Kavirondos next appeared, the most fantastically caparisoned of the lot, fine big black men, their eyes rolling with excitement. They had captured our flag from its place before the big tent, and were rallied close about this, dancing fantastically. Before us they leaped and stamped and shook their spears and shouted out their full-voiced song, while the other three tribes danced each its specialty dimly in the background.

The dance thus begun lasted for fully two hours. Each tribe took a turn before us, only to give way to the next. We had leisure to notice minutiae, such as the ingenious tail one of the "lions" had constructed from a sweater. As time went on, the men worked themselves to a frenzy. From the serried ranks every once in a while one would break forth with a shriek to rush headlong into the fire, to beat the earth about him with his club, to rush over to shake one of us violently by the hand, or even to seize one of our feet between his two palms. Then with equal abruptness back he darted to regain his place among the dancers. Wilder and wilder became the movements, higher rose the voices. The mock lion hunt grew more realistic, and the slaughter on both sides something tremendous. Lower and lower crouched the Monumwezi, drawing apart with their deep "goom"; drawing suddenly to a common centre with the sharp "zoop!" Only the Kikuyus held their lofty bearing as they rolled forth their chant, but the mounting excitement showed in their tense muscles and the rolling of their eyes. The sweat

64

glistened on naked black and bronze bodies. Among the Monumwezi to my astonishment I saw Memba Sasa, stripped like the rest, and dancing with all abandon. The firelight leaped high among the logs that eager hands cast on it; and the shadows it threw from the swirling, leaping figures wavered out into a great, calm darkness.

The night guard understood a little of the native languages, so he stood behind our chairs and told us in Swahili the meaning of some of the repeated phrases.

"This has been a glorious day; few safaris have had so glorious a day."

"The masters looked upon the fierce lions and did not run away."

"Brave men without other weapons will nevertheless kill with a knife."

"The masters' mothers must be brave women, the masters are so brave."

"The white woman went hunting, and so were many lions killed."

The last one pleased Billy. She felt that at last she was appreciated.

We sat there spellbound by the weird savagery of the spectacle-the great licking fire, the dancing, barbaric figures, the rise and fall of the rhythm, the dust and shuffle, the ebb and flow of the dance, the dim, half-guessed groups swaying in the darkness-and overhead the calm tropic night.

At last, fairly exhausted, they stopped. Some one gave a signal. The men all gathered in one group, uttered a final yell, very like a cheer, and dispersed.

We called up the heroes of the day-Fundi and his companion-and made a little speech, and bestowed appropriate reward. Then we turned in.

# XVI. FUNDI

Fundi, as I have suggested, was built very much on the lines of the marabout stork. He was about twenty years old, carried himself very erect, and looked one straight in the eye. His total assets when he came to us were a pair of raggedy white breeches, very baggy, and an old mesh undershirt, ditto ditto. To this we added a jersey, a red blanket, and a water bottle. At the first opportunity he constructed himself a pair of rawhide sandals.

Throughout the first part of the trip he had applied himself to business and carried his load. He never made trouble. Then he and his companion saw five lions; and the chance Fundi had evidently long been awaiting came to his hand. He ran himself almost into coma, exhibited himself game, and so fell under our especial and distinguished notice. After participating whole-heartedly in the lion dance he and his companion were singled out for Our Distinguished Favour, to the extent of five rupees per. Thus far Fundi's history reads just like the history of any ordinary Captain of Industry.

Next morning, after the interesting ceremony of rewarding the worthy, we moved on to a new camp. When the line-up was called for, lo! there stood Fundi, without a load, but holding firmly my double-barrelled rifle. Evidently he had seized the chance of favour-and the rifle-and intended to be no longer a porter but a second gunbearer.

This looked interesting, so we said nothing. Fundi marched the day through very proudly. At evening he deposited the rifle in the proper place, and set to work with a will at raising the big tent.

The day following he tried it again. It worked. The third day he marched deliberately up past the syce to take his place near me. And the fourth day, as we were going hunting,

Fundi calmly fell in with the rest. Nothing had been said, but Fundi had definitely grasped his chance to rise from the ranks. In this he differed from his companion in glory. That worthy citizen pocketed his five rupees and was never heard from again; I do not even remember his name nor how he looked.

I killed a buck of some sort, and Memba Sasa, as usual, stepped forward to attend to the trophy. But I stopped him.

"Fundi," said I, "if you are a gunbearer, prepare this beast."

He stepped up confidently and set to work. I watched him closely. He did it very well, without awkwardness, though he made one or two minor mistakes in method.

"Have you done this before?" I inquired.

"No, bwana."

"How did you learn to do it?"

"I have watched the gunbearers when I was a porter bringing in meat."*

> * Except in the greatest emergencies a gunbearer would never
>
> think of carrying any sort of a burden.

This was pleasing, but it would never do, at this stage of the game, to let him think so, neither on his own account nor that of the real gunbearers.

"You will bring in meat today also," said I, for I was indeed a little shorthanded, "and you will learn how to make the top incision straighter."

When we had reached camp I handed him the Springfield.

"Clean this," I told him.

He departed with it, returning it after a time for my inspection. It looked all right. I catechized him on the method he had employed-for high velocities require very especial treatment-and found him letter perfect.

"You learned this also by watching?"

"Yes, bwana, I watched the gunbearers by the fire, evenings."

Evidently Fundi had been preparing for his chance.

Next day, as he walked alongside, I noticed that he had not removed the leather cap, or sight protector, that covers the end of the rifle and is fastened on by a leather thong. Immediately I called a halt.

"Fundi," said I, "do you know that the cover should be in your pocket? Suppose a rhinoceros jumps up very near at hand: how can you get time to unlace the thong and hand me the rifle?"

He thrust the rifle at me suddenly. In some magical fashion the sight cover had disappeared!

"I have thought of this," said he, "and I have tied the thong, so, in order that it come away with one pull; and I snatch it off, so, with my left hand while I am giving you the gun with my right hand. It seemed good to keep the cover on, for there are many branches, and the sight is very easy to injure."

Of course this was good sense, and most ingenious; Fundi bade fair to be quite a boy, but the native African is very easily spoiled. Therefore, although my inclination was strongly to praise him, I did nothing of the sort.

"A gunbearer carries the gun away from the branches," was my only comment.

Shortly after occurred an incident by way of deeper test. We were all riding rather idly along the easy slope below the foothills. The grass was short, so we thought we could see easily everything there was to be seen; but, as we passed some thirty yards from a small tree, an unexpected and unnecessary rhinoceros rose from an equally unexpected and unnecessary green hollow beneath the tree, and charged us. He made straight for Billy. Her mule, panic-stricken, froze with terror in spite of Billy's attack with a parasol. I spurred my own animal between her and the charging brute, with some vague idea of slipping off the other side as the rhino struck. F. and B. leaped from their own animals, and F., with a little.28 calibre rifle, took a hasty shot at the big brute. Now, of course a.28 calibre rifle would hardly injure a rhino, but the bullet happened to catch his right shoulder just as he was about to come down on his right foot. The shock tripped him up as neatly as though he had been upset by a rope. At the same instant Billy's mule came to its senses and bolted, whereupon I too jumped off. The whole thing took about two finger snaps of time. At the instant I hit the ground, Fundi passed the double rifle across the horse's back to me.

Note two things to the credit of Fundi: in the first place, he had not bolted; in the second place, instead of running up to the left side of my mount and perhaps colliding with and certainly confusing me, he had come up on the right side and passed the rifle to me ACROSS the horse. I do not know whether or not he had figured this out beforehand, but it was cleverly done.

The rhinoceros rolled over and over, like a shot rabbit, kicked for a moment, and came to his feet. We were now all ready for him, in battle array, but he had evidently had enough. He turned at right angles and trotted off, apparently-and probably-none the worse for the little bullet in his shoulder.

Fundi now began acquiring things that he supposed befitting to his dignity. The first of these matters was a faded fez, in which he stuck a long feather. From that he progressed in worldly wealth. How he got it all, on what credit, or with what hypnotic power, I do not know. Probably he hypothecated his wages, certainly he had his five rupees.

At any rate he started out with a ragged undershirt and a pair of white, baggy breeches. He entered Nairobi at the end of the trip with a cap, a neat khaki shirt, two water bottles, a cartridge belt, a sash with a tassel, a pair of spiral puttees, an old pair of shoes, and a personal private small boy, picked up en route from some of the savage tribes, to carry his cooking pot, make his fires, draw his water, and generally perform his lordly behests. This was indeed "more-than-oriental-splendour!"

From now on Fundi considered himself my second gunbearer. I had no use for him, but Fundi's development interested me, and I wanted to give him a chance. His main fault at first was eagerness. He had to be rapped pretty sharply and a good number of times before he discovered that he really must walk in the rear. His habit of calling my attention to perfectly obvious things I cured by liberal sarcasm. His intense desire to take his own line as perhaps opposed to mine when we were casting about on trail, I abated kindly but firmly with the toe of my boot. His evident but mistaken tendency to consider himself on an equality with Memba Sasa we both squelched by giving him the hard and dirty work to do. But his faults were never those of voluntary omission, and he came on surprisingly; in fact so surprisingly that he began to get quite cocky over it. Not that he was ever in the least aggressive or disrespectful or neglectful-it would have been easy to deal with that sort of thing-but he carried his head pretty high, and evidently began to have mental reservations. Fundi needed a little wholesome discipline. He was forgetting his porter days, and was rapidly coming to consider himself a full-fledged gunbearer.

The occasion soon arose. We were returning from a buffalo hunt and ran across two rhinoceroses, one of which carried a splendid horn. B. wanted a well developed specimen very much, so we took this chance. The approach was easy enough, and at seventy yards or so B. knocked her flat with a bullet from his.465 Holland. The beast was immediately afoot, but was as promptly smothered by shots from us all. So far the affair was very simple, but now came complication. The second rhinoceros refused to leave. We did not want to kill it, so we spent a lot of time and pains shooing it away. We showered rocks and clods of earth in his direction; we yelled sharply and whistled shrilly. The brute faced here and there, his pig eyes blinking, his snout upraised, trying to locate us, and declining to budge. At length he gave us up as hopeless, and trotted away slowly. We let him go, and when we thought he had quite departed, we approached to examine B.'s trophy.

Whereupon the other craftily returned; and charged us, snorting like an engine blowing off steam. This was a genuine premeditated charge, as opposed to a blind rush, and it is offered as a good example of the sort.

The rhinoceros had come fairly close before we got into action. He headed straight for F. and myself, with B. a little to one side. Things happened very quickly. F. and I each planted a heavy bullet in his head; while B. sent a lighter Winchester bullet into the ribs. The rhino went down in a heap eleven yards away, and one of us promptly shot him in the spine to finish him.

Personally I was entirely concentrated in the matter at hand-as is always the way in crises requiring action-and got very few impressions from anything outside. Nevertheless I imagined, subconsciously that I had heard four shots. F. and B. disclaimed more than one apiece, so I concluded myself mistaken, exchanged my heavy rifle with Fundi for the lighter Winchester, and we started for camp, leaving all the boys to attend to the dead rhinos. At camp I threw down the lever of my Winchester-and drew out an exploded shell!

Here was a double crime on Fundi's part. In the first place, he had fired the gun, a thing no bearer is supposed ever to do in any circumstances short of the disarmament and actual mauling of his master. Naturally this is so, for the white man must be able in an emergency to depend ABSOLUTELY on his second gun being loaded and ready for his need. In the second place, Fundi had given me an empty rifle to carry home. Such a weapon is worse than none in case of trouble; at least I could have gone up a tree in the latter case. I would have looked sweet snapping that old cartridge at anything dangerous!

Therefore after supper we stationed ourselves in a row before the fire, seated in our canvas chairs, and with due formality sent word that we wanted all the gunbearers. They came and stood before us. Memba Sasa erect, military, compact, looking us straight in the eye; Mavrouki slightly bent forward, his face alive with the little crafty, calculating smile peculiar to him; Simba, tall and suave, standing with much social ease; and Fundi, a trifle frightened, but uncertain as to whether or not he had been found out.

We stated the matter in a few words.

"Gunbearers, this man Fundi, when the rhinoceros charged, fired Winchi. Was this the work of a gunbearer?"

The three seasoned men looked at each other with shocked astonishment that such depravity could exist.

"And being frightened, he gave back Winchi with the exploded cartridge in her. Was that the work of a gunbearer?"

"No, bwana," said Fundi humbly.

"You, the gunbearers, have been called because we wish to know what should be done with this man Fundi."

It should be here explained that it is not customary to kiboko, or flog, men of the gunbearer class. They respect themselves and their calling, and would never stand that sort of punishment. When one blunders, a sarcastic scolding is generally sufficient; a more serious fault may be punished on the spot by the white man's fist; or a really bad dereliction may cause the man's instant degradation from the post. With this in mind we had called the council of gunbearers. Memba Sasa spoke.

"Bwana," said he, "this man is not a true gunbearer. He is no longer a true porter. He carries a gun in the field, like a gunbearer; and he knows much of the duty of gunbearer. Also he does not run away nor climb trees. But he carries in the meat; and he is not a real gunbearer. He is half porter and half gunbearer."

"What punishment shall he have?"

"Kiboko," said they.

"Thank you. Bass!"

They went, leaving Fundi. We surveyed him, quietly.

"You a gunbearer!" said we at last. "Memba Sasa says you are half gunbearer. He was wrong. You are all porter; and you know no more than they do. It is in our mind to put you back to carrying a load. If you do not wish to taste the kiboko, you can take a load to-morrow."

"The kiboko, bwana," pleaded Fundi, very abashed and humble.

"Furthermore," we added crushingly, "you did not even hit the rhinoceros!"

So with all ceremony he got the kiboko. The incident did him a lot of good, and toned down his exuberance somewhat. Nevertheless he still required a good deal of training, just as does a promising bird dog in its first season. Generally his faults were of over-eagerness. Indeed, once he got me thoroughly angry in face of another rhinoceros by dancing just out of reach with the heavy rifle, instead of sticking close to me where I could get at him. I temporarily forgot the rhino, and advanced on Fundi with the full intention of knocking his fool head off. Whereupon this six feet something of most superb and insolent pride wilted down to a small boy with his elbow before his face.

"Don't hit, bwana! Don't hit!" he begged.

The whole thing was so comical, especially with Memba Sasa standing by virtuous and scornful, that I had hard work to keep from laughing. Fortunately the rhinoceros behaved himself.

The proud moment of Fundi's life was when safari entered Nairobi at the end of the first expedition. He had gone forth with a load on his head, rags on his back, and his only glory was the self-assumed one of the name he had taken-Fundi, the Expert. He returned carrying a rifle, rigged from top to toe in new garments and fancy accoutrements, followed by a toro, or small boy, he had bought from some of the savage tribes to carry his blanket and cooking pot for him. To the friends who darted out to the line of march, he was gracious, but he held his head high, and had no time for mere persiflage.

I did not take Fundi on my second expedition, for I had no real use for a second gunbearer. Several times subsequently I saw him on the streets of Nairobi. Always he came up to greet me, and ask solicitously if I would not give him a job. This I was unable to do. When we paid off, I had made an addition to his porter's wages, and had written him a chit. This said that the boy had the makings of a gunbearer with further training. It would have been unfair to possible white employers to have said more. Fundi was, when I left the country, precisely in the position of any young man who tries to rise in the world. He would not again take a load as porter, and he was not yet skilled enough or known enough to pick up more than stray jobs as gunbearer. Before him was struggle and hard times, with a certainty of a highly considered profession if he won through. Behind him was steady work without outlets for ambition. It was distinctly up to him to prove whether he had done well to reach for ambition, or whether he would have done better in contentment with his old lot. And that is in essence a good deal like our own world isn't it?

# XVII. NATIVES

Up to this time, save for a few Masai at the very beginning of our trip, we had seen no natives at all. Only lately, the night of the lion dance, one of the Wanderobo-the forest hunters-had drifted in to tell us of buffalo and to get some meat. He was a simple soul, small and capable, of a beautiful red-brown, with his hair done up in a tight, short queue. He wore three skewers about six inches long thrust through each of his ears, three strings of blue beads on his neck, a bracelet tight around his upper arm, a bangle around his ankle, a pair of rawhide sandals, and about a half yard of cotton cloth which he hung from one shoulder. As weapons he carried a round-headed, heavy club, or runga, and a long-bladed spear. He led us to buffalo, accepted a thirty-three cent blanket, and made fire with two sticks in about thirty seconds. The only other evidences of human life we had come across were a few beehives suspended in the trees. These were logs, bored hollow and stopped at either end. Some of them were very quaintly carved. They hung in the trees like strange fruits.

Now, however, after leaving the Isiola, we were to quit the game country and for days travel among the swarming millions of the jungle.

A few preliminary and entirely random observations may be permitted me by way of clearing the ground for a conception of these people. These observations do not pretend to be ethnological, nor even common logical.

The first thing for an American to realize is that our own negro population came mainly from the West Coast, and differed utterly from these peoples of the highlands in the East. Therefore one must first of all get rid of the mental image of our own negro "dressed up" in savage garb. Many of these tribes are not negro at all-the Somalis, the Nandi, and the Masai, for example-while others belong to the negroid and Nilotic races. Their colour is general cast more on the red-bronze than the black, though the Kavirondos and some others are black enough. The texture of their skin is very satiny and wonderful. This perfection is probably due to the constant anointing of the body with oils of various sorts. As a usual thing they are a fine lot physically. The southern Masai will average between six and seven feet in height, and are almost invariably well built. Of most tribes the physical development is remarkably strong and graceful; and a great many of the women will display a rounded, firm, high-breasted physique in marked contrast to the blacks of the lowlands. Of the different tribes possibly the Kikuyus are apt to count the most weakly and spindly examples: though some of these people, perhaps a majority, are well made.

Furthermore, the native differentiates himself still further in impression from our negro in his carriage and the mental attitude that lies behind it. Our people are trying to pattern themselves on white men, and succeed in giving a more or less shambling imitation thereof. The native has standards, ideas, and ideals that perfectly satisfy him, and that antedated the white man's coming by thousands of years. The consciousness of this reflects itself in his outward bearing. He does not shuffle; he is not either obsequious or impudent. Even when he acknowledges the white man's divinity and pays it appropriate respect, he does not lose the poise of his own well-worked-out attitude toward life and toward himself.

We are fond of calling these people primitive. In the world's standard of measurement they are primitive, very primitive indeed. But ordinarily by that term, we mean also undeveloped, embryonic. In that sense we are wrong. Instead of being at the very dawn of human development, these people are at the end-as far as they themselves are concerned. The original racial impulse that started them down the years toward development has fulfilled its duty and spent its force. They have worked out all their problems, established all their customs, arranged the world and its phenomena in a philosophy to their complete satisfaction. They have lived, ethnologists tell us, for thousands, perhaps hundreds of thousands of years, just as we find them to-day. From our standpoint that is in a hopeless intellectual darkness, for they know absolutely nothing of the most elementary subjects of knowledge. From their standpoint, however, they have reached the highest DESIRABLE pinnacle of human development. Nothing remains to be changed. Their customs, religions, and duties have been worked out and immutably established long ago; and nobody dreams of questioning either their wisdom or their imperative necessity. They are the conservatives of the world.

Nor must we conclude-looking at them with the eyes of our own civilization-that the savage is, from his standpoint, lazy and idle. His life is laid out more rigidly than ours will be for a great many thousands of years. From childhood to old age he performs his every act in accord with prohibitions and requirements. He must remember them all; for ignorance does not divert consequences. He must observe them all; in pain of terrible punishments. For example, never may he cultivate on the site of a grave; and the plants that spring up from it must never be cut.* He must make certain complicated offerings before venturing to harvest a crop. On crossing the first stream of a journey he must touch his lips with the end of his wetted bow, wade across, drop a stone on the far side, and then drink. If he cuts his nails, he must throw the parings into a thicket. If he drink from a stream, and also cross it, he must eject a mouthful of water back into the stream. He must be particularly careful not to look his mother-in-law in the face. Hundreds of omens by the manner of their happening may modify actions, as, on what side of the road a woodpecker calls, or in which direction a hyena or jackal crosses the path, how the ground hornbill flies or alights, and the like. He must notice these things, and change his plans according to their occurrence. If he does not notice them, they exercise their influence just the same. This does not encourage a distrait mental attitude. Also it goes far to explain otherwise unexplainable visitations. Truly, as Hobley says in his unexcelled work on the A-Kamba, "the life of a savage native is a complex matter, and he is hedged round by all sorts of rules and prohibitions, the infringement of which will probably cause his death, if only by the intense belief he has in the rules which guide his life."

> \* Customs are not universal among the different tribes. I am
> merely illustrating.

For these rules and customs he never attempts to give a reason. They are; and that is all there is to it. A mere statement: "This is the custom" settles the matter finally. There is no necessity, nor passing thought even, of finding any logical cause. The matter was worked out in the mental evolution of remote ancestors. At that time, perhaps, insurgent and Standpatter, Conservative and Radical fought out the questions of the day, and the Muckrakers swung by their tails and chattered about it. Those days are all long since over. The questions of the world are settled forever. The people have passed through the struggles of their formative period to the ultimate highest perfection of adjustment to material and spiritual environment of which they were capable under the influence of their original racial force.

Parenthetically, it is now a question whether or not an added impulse can be communicated from without. Such an impulse must (a) unsettle all the old beliefs, (b)

71

inspire an era of skepticism, (c) reintroduce the old struggle of ideas between the Insurgent and the Standpatter, and Radical and the Conservative, (d) in the meantime furnish, from the older civilization, materials, both in the thought-world and in the object-world, for building slowly a new set of customs more closely approximating those we are building for ourselves. This is a longer and slower and more complicated affair than teaching the native to wear clothes and sing hymns; or to build houses and drink gin; but it is what must be accomplished step by step before the African peoples are really civilized. I, personally, do not think it can be done.

Now having, a hundred thousand years or so ago, worked out the highest good of the human race, according to them, what must they say to themselves and what must their attitude be when the white man has come and has unrolled his carpet of wonderful tricks? The dilemma is evident. Either we, as black men, must admit that our hundred-thousand-year-old ideas as to what constitutes the highest type of human relation to environment is all wrong, or else we must evolve a new attitude toward this new phenomena. It is human nature to do the latter. Therefore the native has not abandoned his old gods; nor has he adopted a new. He still believes firmly that his way is the best way of doing things, but he acknowledges the Superman.

To the Superman, with all races, anything is possible. Only our Superman is an idea, and ideal. The native has his Superman before him in the actual flesh.

We will suppose that our own Superman has appeared among us, accomplishing things that apparently contravene all our established tenets of skill, of intellect, of possibility. It will be readily acknowledged that such an individual would at first create some astonishment. He wanders into a crowded hotel lobby, let us say, evidently with the desire of going to the bar. Instead of pushing laboriously through the crowd, he floats just above their heads, gets his drink, and floats out again! That is levitation, and is probably just as simple to him as striking a match is to you and me. After we get thoroughly accustomed to him and his life, we are no longer vastly astonished, though always interested, at the various manifestations of his extraordinary powers. We go right along using the marvellous wireless, aeroplanes, motor cars, constructive machinery, and the like that make us confident-justly, of course-in that we are about the smartest lot of people on earth. And if we see red, white, and blue streamers of light crossing the zenith at noon, we do not manifest any very profound amazement. "There's that confounded Superman again," we mutter, if we happen to be busy. "I wonder what stunt he's going to do now!"

A consideration of the above beautiful fable may go a little way toward explaining the supposed native stolidity in the face of the white man's wonders. A few years ago some misguided person brought a balloon to Nairobi. The balloon interested the white people a lot, but everybody was chiefly occupied wondering what the natives would do when they saw THAT! The natives did not do anything. They gathered in large numbers, and most interestedly watched it go up, and then went home again. But they were not stricken with wonder to any great extent. So also with locomotives, motor cars, telephones, phonographs-any of our modern ingenuities. The native is pleased and entertained, but not astonished. "Stupid creature, no imagination," say we, because our pride in showing off is a wee bit hurt.

Why should he be astonished? His mental revolution took place when he saw the first match struck. It is manifestly impossible for any one to make fire instantaneously by rubbing one small stick. When for the first time he saw it done, he was indeed vastly astounded. The immutable had been changed. The law had been transcended. The impossible had been accomplished. And then, as logical sequence, his mind completed the syllogism. If the white man can do this impossibility, why not all the rest? To defy the laws of nature by flying in the air or forcing great masses of iron to transport one, is no more wonderful than to defy them by striking a light. Since the white man can provedly do one, what earthly reason exists why he should not do anything else that hits his fancy? There is nothing to get astonished at.

This does not necessarily mean that the native looks on the white man as a god. On the contrary, your African is very shrewd in the reading of character. But indubitably white men possess great magic, uncertain in its extent.

That is as far as I should care to go, without much deeper acquaintance, into the attitude of the native mind toward the whites. A superficial study of it, beyond the general principals I have enunciated, discloses many strange contradictions. The native respects the white man's warlike skill, he respects his physical prowess, he certainly acknowledges tacitly his moral superiority in the right to command. In case of dispute he likes the white man's adjudication; in case of illness the man's medicine; in case of trouble the white man's sustaining hand. Yet he almost never attempts to copy the white man's appearance or ways of doing things. His own savage customs and habits he fulfils with as much pride as ever in their eternal fitness. Once I was badgering Memba Sasa, asking him whether he thought the white skin or the black skin the more ornamental. "You are not white," he retorted at last. "That," pointing to a leaf of my notebook, "is white. You are red. I do not like the looks of red people."

They call our speech the "snake language," because of its hissing sound. Once this is brought to your attention, indeed, you cannot help noticing the superabundance of the sibilants.

A queer melange the pigeonholes of an African's brain must contain-fear and respect, strongly mingled with clear estimate of intrinsic character of individuals and a satisfaction with his own standards.

Nor, I think, do we realize sufficiently the actual fundamental differences between the African and our peoples. Physically they must be in many ways as different from our selves as though they actually belonged to a different species. The Masai are a fine big race, enduring, well developed and efficient. They live exclusively on cow's milk mixed with blood; no meat, no fruit, no vegetables, no grain; just that and nothing more. Obviously they must differ from us most radically, or else all our dietetic theories are wrong. It is a well-known fact that any native requires a triple dose of white man's medicine. Furthermore a native's sensitiveness to pain is very much less than the white man's. This is indubitable. For example, the Wakamba file-or, rather, chip, by means of a small chisel-all their front teeth down to needle points, When these happen to fall out, the warrior substitutes an artificial tooth which he drives down into the socket. If the savage got the same effects from such a performance that a white man's dental system would arouse, even "savage stoicism" would hardly do him much good. There is nothing to be gained by multiplying examples. Every African traveller can recall a thousand.

Incidentally, and by the way, I want to add to the milk-and-blood joke on dietetics another on the physical culturists. We are all familiar with the wails over the loss of our toe nails. You know what I mean; they run somewhat like this: shoes are the curse of civilization; if we wear them much longer we shall not only lose the intended use of our feet, but we shall lose our toe nails as well; the savage man, etc., etc., etc. Now I saw a great many of said savage men in Africa, and I got much interested in their toe nails, because I soon found that our own civilized "imprisoned" toe nails were very much better developed. In fact, a large number of the free and untramelled savages have hardly any toe nails at all! Whether this upsets a theory, nullifies a sentimental protest, or merely stands as an exception, I should not dare guess. But the fact is indubitable.

# XVIII. IN THE JUNGLE

(a) THE MARCH TO MERU

Now, one day we left the Isiola River and cut across on a long upward slant to the left. In a very short time we had left the plains, and were adrift in an ocean of brown grass that concealed all but the bobbing loads atop the safari, and over which we could only see when mounted. It was glorious feed, apparently, but it contained very few animals for all that. An animal could without doubt wax fat and sleek therein: but only to furnish light and salutary meals to beasts of prey. Long grass makes easy stalking. We saw a few ostriches, some giraffe, and three or four singly adventurous oryx. The ripening grasses were softer than a rippling field grain; and even more beautiful in their umber and browns. Although apparently we travelled a level, nevertheless in the extreme distance the plains of our hunting were dropping below, and the far off mountains were slowly rising above the horizon. On the other side were two very green hills, looking nearly straight up and down, and through a cleft the splintered snow-clad summit of Mt. Kenia.

At length this gentle foothill slope broke over into rougher country. Then, in the pass, we came upon many parallel beaten paths, wider and straighter than the game trails-native tracks. That night we camped in a small, round valley under some glorious trees, with green grass around us; a refreshing contrast after the desert brown. In the distance ahead stood a big hill, and at its base we could make out amid the tree-green, the straight slim smoke of many fires and the threads of many roads.

We began our next morning's march early, and we dropped over the hill into a wide, cultivated valley. Fields of grain, mostly rape, were planted irregularly among big scattered trees. The morning air, warming under the sun, was as yet still, and carried sound well. The cooing, chattering and calling of thousands of birds mingled with shouts and the clapping together of pieces of wood. As we came closer we saw that every so often scaffolds had been erected overlooking the grain, and on these scaffolds naked boys danced and yelled and worked clappers to scare the birds from the crops. They seemed to put a great deal of rigour into the job; whether from natural enthusiasm or efficient direful supervision I could not say. Certainly they must have worked in watches, however; no human being could keep up that row continuously for a single day, let alone the whole season of ripening grain. As we passed they fell silent and stared their fill.

On the banks of a boggy little stream that we had to flounder across we came on a gentleman and lady travelling. They were a tall, well formed pair, mahogany in colour, with the open, pleasant expression of most of these jungle peoples. The man wore a string around his waist into which was thrust a small leafy branch; the woman had on a beautiful skirt made by halving a banana leaf, using the stem as belt, and letting the leaf part hang down as a skirt. Shortly after meeting these people we turned sharp to the right on a well beaten road.

For nearly two weeks we were to follow this road, so it may be as well to get an idea of it. Its course was a segment of about a sixth of the circle of Kenia's foothills. With Kenia itself as a centre, this road swung among the lower elevations about the base of that great mountain. Its course was mainly down and up hundreds of the canyons radiating from the main peak, and over the ridges between them. No sooner were we down, than we had to climb up; and no sooner were we up, than once more down we had to plunge. At times, however, we crossed considerable plateaus. Most of this country was dense jungle, so dense that we could not see on either side more than fifteen or twenty feet. Occasionally, atop the ridges, however, we would come upon small open parks. In these jungles live millions of human beings.

At once, as soon as we had turned into the main road, we began to meet people. In the grain fields of the valley we saw only the elevated boys, and a few men engaged in weaving a little house perched on stilts. We came across some of these little houses all completed, with conical roofs. They were evidently used for granaries. As we mounted the slope on the other side, however, the trees closed in, and we found ourselves marching down the narrow aisle of the jungle itself.

It was a dense and beautiful jungle, with very tall trees and the deepest shade; and the impenetrable tangle to the edge of the track. Among the trees were the broad leaves of bananas and palms, the fling of leafy vines. Over the track these leaned, so that we rode through splashing and mottling shade. Nothing could have seemed wilder than this apparently impenetrable and yet we had ridden but a short distance before we realized that we were in fact passing through cultivated land. It was, again, only a difference in terms. Native cultivation in this district rarely consists of clearing land and planting crops in due order, but in leaving the forest proper as it is, and in planting foodstuffs haphazard wherever a tiny space can be made for even three hills of corn or a single banana. Thus they add to rather than subtract from the typical density of the jungle. At first, we found, it took some practice to tell a farm when we saw it.

From the track narrow little paths wound immediately out of sight. Sometimes we saw a wisp of smoke rising above the undergrowth and eddying in the tops of the trees. Long vine ropes swung from point to point, hung at intervals with such matters as feathers, bones, miniature shields, carved sticks, shells and clappers: either as magic or to keep off the birds. From either side the track we were conscious always of bright black eyes watching us. Sometimes we caught a glimpse of their owners crouched in the bush, concealed behind banana leaves, motionless and straight against a tree trunk. When they saw themselves observed they vanished without a sound.

The upper air was musical with birds, and bright with the flutter of their wings. Rarely did we see them long enough to catch a fair idea of their size and shape. They flashed from shade to shade, leaving only an impression of brilliant colour. There were some exceptions: as the widower-bird, dressed all in black, with long trailing wing-plumes of which he seemed very proud; and the various sorts of green pigeons and parrots. There were many flowering shrubs and trees, and the air was laden with perfume. Strange, too, it seemed to see tall trees with leaves three or four feet long and half as many wide.

We were riding a mile or so ahead of the safari. At first we were accompanied only by our gunbearers and syces. Before long, however, we began to accumulate a following.

This consisted at first of a very wonderful young man, probably a chief's son. He carried a long bright spear, wore a short sword thrust through a girdle, had his hair done in three wrapped queues, one over each temple and one behind, and was generally brought to a high state of polish by means of red earth and oil. About his knee he wore a little bell that jingled pleasingly at every step. From one shoulder hung a goat-skin cloak embroidered with steel beads. A small package neatly done up in leaves probably contained his lunch. He teetered along with a mincing up and down step, every movement, and the expression of his face displaying a fatuous self-satisfaction. When we looked back again this youth had magically become two. Then appeared two women and a white goat. All except the goat were dressed for visiting, with long chains of beads, bracelets and anklets, and heavy ornaments in the distended ear lobes. The manner people sprang apparently out of the ground was very disconcerting. It was a good deal like those fairy-story moving pictures where a wave of the wand produces beautiful ladies. By half an hour we had acquired a long retinue-young warriors, old men, women and innumerable children. After we had passed, the new recruits stepped quietly from the shadow of the jungle and fell in. Every one with nothing much to do evidently made up his mind he might as well go to Meru now as any other time.

Also we met a great number of people going in the other direction. Women were bearing loads of yams. Chiefs' sons minced along, their spears poised in their left hands at just the proper angle, their bangles jingling, their right hands carried raised in a most affected manner. Their social ease was remarkable, especially in contrast with the awkwardness of the lower poverty-stricken or menial castes. The latter drew one side to let us pass, and stared. Our chiefs' sons, on the other hand, stepped springingly and beamingly forward; spat carefully in their hands (we did the same); shook hands all down the line: exchanged a long-drawn "moo-o-ga!" with each of us; and departed at the same springing rapid gait. The ordinary warriors greeted us, but did not offer to shake hands, thank goodness! There were a great many of them. Across the valleys and through the open spaces the sun, as it struck down the trail, was always flashing back from distant spears. Twice we met flocks of sheep being moved from one point to another. Three or four herdsmen and innumerable small boys seemed to be in charge. Occasionally we met a real chief or headman of a village, distinguished by the fact that he or a servant carried a small wooden stool. With these dignitaries we always stopped to exchange friendly words.

These comprised the travelling public. The resident public also showed itself quite in evidence. Once our retainers had become sufficiently numerous to inspire confidence, the jungle people no longer hid. On the contrary, they came out to the very edge of the track to exchange greetings. They were very good-natured, exceedingly well-formed, and quite jocular with our boys. Especially did our suave and elegant Simba sparkle. This resident public, called from its daily labours and duties, did not always show as gaudy a make-up as did the dressed-up travelling public. Banana leaves were popular wear, and seemed to us at once pretty and fresh. To be sure some had rather withered away; but even wool will shrink. We saw some grass skirts, like the Sunday-school pictures.

At noon we stopped under a tree by a little stream for lunch. Before long a dozen women were lined up in front of us staring at Billy with all their might. She nodded and smiled at them. Thereupon they sent one of their number away. The messenger returned after a few moments carrying a bunch of the small eating bananas which she laid at our feet. Billy fished some beads out of her saddle bags, and presented them. Friendly relations having been thus fully established, two or three of the women scurried hastily away, to return a few moments later each with her small child. To these infants they carefully and earnestly pointed out Billy and her wonders, talking in a tongue unknown to us. The admonition undoubtedly ran something like this:

"Now, my child, look well at this: for when you get to be a very old person you will be able to look back at the day when with your own eyes you beheld a white woman. See all the strange things she wears-and HASN'T she a funny face?"

We offered these bung-eyed and totally naked youngsters various bribes in the way of beads, the tinfoil from chocolate, and even a small piece of the chocolate itself. Most of them howled and hid their faces against their mothers. The mothers looked scandalized, and hypocritically astounded, and mortified.

They made remarks, still in an unknown language, but which much past experience enabled me to translate very readily:

"I don't know what has got into little Willie," was the drift of it. "I have never known him to act this way before. Why, only yesterday I was saying to his father that it really seemed as though that child NEVER cried-"

It made me feel quite friendly and at home.

Now at last came two marvellous and magnificent personages before whom the women and children drew back to a respectful distance. These potentates squatted down and smiled at us engagingly. Evidently this was a really important couple, so we called up Simba, who knew the language, and had a talk.

They were old men, straight, and very tall, with the hawk-faced, high-headed dignity of the true aristocrat. Their robes were voluminous, of some short-haired skins, beautifully embroidered. Around their arms were armlets of polished buffalo horn. They wore most elaborate ear ornaments, and long cased marquise rings extending well beyond the first joints of the fingers. Very fine old gentlemen. They were quite unarmed.

After appropriate greetings, we learned that these were the chief and his prime minister of a nearby village hidden in the jungle. We exchanged polite phrases; then offered tobacco. This was accepted. From the jungle came a youth carrying more bananas. We indicated our pleasure. The old men arose with great dignity and departed, sweeping the women and children before them.

We rode on. Our acquired retinue, which had waited at a respectful distance, went on too. I suppose they must have desired the prestige of being attached to Our Persons. In the depths of the forest Billy succumbed to the temptation to bargain, and made her first trade. Her prize was a long water gourd strapped with leather and decorated with cowry shells. Our boys were completely scandalized at the price she paid for it, so I fear the wily savage got ahead of her.

About the middle of the afternoon we sat down to wait for the safari to catch up. It would never do to cheat our boys out of their anticipated grand entrance to the Government post at Meru. We finally debouched from the forest to the great clearing at the head of a most impressive procession, flags flying, oryx horns blowing, boys chanting and beating the sides of their loads with the safari sticks. As there happened to be gathered, at this time, several thousand of warriors for the purpose of a council, or shauri, with the District Commissioner we had just the audience to delight our barbaric hearts.

(b) MERU

The Government post at Meru is situated in a clearing won from the forest on the first gentle slopes of Kenia's ranges. The clearing is a very large one, and on it the grass grows green and short, like a lawn. It resembles, as much as anything else, the rolling, beautiful downs of a first-class country club, and the illusion is enhanced by the Commissioner's house among some trees atop a hill. Well-kept roadways railed with rustic fences lead from the house to the native quarters lying in the hollow and to the Government offices atop another hill. Then also there are the quarters of the Nubian troops; round low houses with conical grass roofs.

These, and the presence everywhere of savages, rather take away from the first country-club effect. A corral seemed full of a seething mob of natives; we found later that this was the market, a place of exchange. Groups wandered idly here and there across the greensward; and other groups sat in circles under the shade of trees, each man's spear stuck in the ground behind him. At stated points were the Nubians, fine, tall, black, soldierly men, with red fez, khaki shirt, and short breeches, bare knees and feet, spiral puttees, and a broad red sash of webbing. One of these soldiers assigned us a place to camp. We directed our safari there, and then immediately rode over to pay our respects to the Commissioner.

The latter, Horne by name, greeted us with the utmost cordiality, and offered us cool drinks. Then we accompanied him to a grand shauri or council of chiefs.

Horne was a little chap, dressed in flannels and a big slouch hat, carrying only a light rawhide whip, with very little of the dignity and "side" usually considered necessary in dealing with wild natives. The post at Meru had been established only two years, among a people that had always been very difficult, and had only recently ceased open hostilities. Nevertheless in that length of time Horne's personal influence had won them over to positive friendliness. He had, moreover, done the entire construction work of the post itself; and this we now saw to be even more elaborate than we had at first realized. Irrigating ditches ran in all directions brimming with clear mountain water; the roads and paths were rounded, graded and gravelled; the houses were substantial, well built and well kept; fences, except of course the rustic, were whitewashed; the native quarters and "barracks" were well ranged and in perfect order. The place looked ten years old instead of only two.

We followed Horne to an enclosure, outside the gate of which were stacked a great number of spears. Inside we found the owners of those spears squatted before the open side of a small, three-walled building containing a table and a chair. Horne placed himself in the chair, lounged back, and hit the table smartly with his rawhide whip. From the centre of the throng an old man got up and made quite a long speech. When he had finished another did likewise. All was carried out with the greatest decorum. After four or five had thus spoken, Horne, without altering his lounging attitude, spoke twenty or thirty words, rapped again on the table with his rawhide whip, and immediately came over to us.

"Now," said he cheerfully, "we'll have a game of golf."

That was amusing, but not astonishing. Most of us have at one time or another laid out a scratch hole or so somewhere in the vacant lot. We returned to the house, Horne produced a sufficiency of clubs, and we sallied forth. Then came the surprise of our life! We played eighteen holes-eighteen, mind you-over an excellently laid-out and kept-up course! The fair greens were cropped short and smooth by a well-managed small herd of sheep; the putting greens were rolled, and in perfect order; bunkers had been located at the correct distances; there were water hazards in the proper spots. In short, it was a genuine, scientific, well-kept golf course. Over it played Horne, solitary except on the rare occasions when he and his assistant happened to be at the post at the same time. The nearest white man was six days' journey; the nearest small civilization 196 miles.* The whole affair was most astounding.

    * Which was, in turn, over three hundred miles from the

        next.

Our caddies were grinning youngsters a good deal like the Gold Dust Twins. They wore nothing but our golf bags. Afield were other supernumerary caddies: one in case we sliced, one in case we pulled, and one in case we drove straight ahead. Horne explained that unlimited caddies were easier to get than unlimited golf balls. I can well believe it.

F. joined forces with Horne against B. and me for a grand international match. I regret to state that America was defeated by two holes.

We returned to find our camp crowded with savages. In a short time we had established trade relations and were doing a brisk business. Two years before we should have had to barter exclusively; but now, thanks to Horne's attempt to collect an annual hut tax, money was some good. We had, however, very good luck with bright blankets and cotton cloth. Our beads did not happen here to be in fashion. Probably three months earlier or later we might have done better with them. The feminine mind here differs in no basic essential from that of civilization. Fashions change as rapidly, as often and as completely in the jungle as in Paris. The trader who brings blue beads when blue beads have "gone out" might just as well have stayed at home. We bought a number of the pretty "marquise" rings for four cents apiece (our money), some war clubs or rungas for the same, several spears, armlets, stools and the like. Billy thought one of the short, soft skin cloaks embroidered with steel beads might be nice to hang on the wall. We offered a youth two rupees for one. This must have been a high price, for every man in hearing of the words snatched off his cloak and rushed forward holding it out. As that reduced his costume to a few knick-knacks, Billy retired from the busy mart until we could arrange matters.

We dined with Horne. His official residence was most interesting. The main room was very high to beams and a grass-thatched roof, with a well-brushed earth floor covered with mats. It contained comfortable furniture, a small library, a good phonograph, tables, lamps and the like. When the mountain chill descended, Horne lit a fire in a coal-oil can with a perforated bottom. What little smoke was produced by the clean burning wood lost itself far aloft. Leopard skins and other trophies hung on the wall. We dined in another room at a well-appointed table. After dinner we sat up until the unheard of hour of ten o'clock discussing at length many matters that interested us. Horne told us of his personal bodyguard consisting of one son from each chief of his wide district. These youths were encouraged to make as good an appearance as possible, and as a consequence turned out in the extreme of savage gorgeousness. Horne spoke of them carelessly as a "matter of policy in keeping the different tribes well disposed," but I thought he was at heart a little proud of them. Certainly, later and from other sources, we heard great tales of their endurance, devotion and efficiency. Also we heard that Horne had cut in half his six months' leave (earned by three years' continuous service in the jungle) to hurry back from England because he could not bear the thought of being absent from the first collection of the hut tax! He is a good man.

We said good-night to him and stepped from the lighted house into the vast tropical night. The little rays of our lantern showed us the inequalities of the ground, and where to step across the bubbling, little irrigation streams. But thousands of stars insisted on a simplification. The broad, rolling meadows of the clearing lay half guessed in the dim light; and about its edge was the velvet band of the forest, dark and mysterious, stretching away for leagues into the jungle. From it near at hand, far away, came the rhythmic beating of solemn great drums, and the rising and falling chants of the savage peoples.

(C) THE CHIEFS

We left Meru well observed by a very large audience, much to the delight of our safari boys, who love to show off. We had acquired fourteen more small boys, or totos, ranging in age from eight to twelve years. These had been fitted out by their masters to alleviate their original shenzi appearance of savagery. Some had ragged blankets, which they had already learned to twist turban wise around their heads; others had ragged old jerseys reaching to their knees, or the wrecks of full-grown undershirts; one or two even sported baggy breeches a dozen sizes too large. Each carried his little load, proudly, atop his head like a real porter, sufurias or cooking pots, the small bags of potio, and the like. Inside a mile they had gravitated together and with the small boy's relish for imitation and for playing a game, had completed a miniature safari organization of their own. Thenceforth they marched in a compact little company, under orders of their "headman." They marched very well, too, straight and proud and tireless. Of course we inspected their loads to see that they were not required to carry too much for their strength; but, I am bound to say, we never discovered an attempt at overloading. In fact, the toto brigade was treated very well indeed. M'ganga especially took great interest in their education and welfare. One of my most vivid camp recollections is that of M'ganga, very benign and didactic, seated on a chop box and holding forth to a semicircle of totos squatted on the ground before him. On reaching camp totos had several clearly defined duties: they must pick out good places for their masters' individual camps, they must procure cooking stones, they must collect kindling wood and start fires, they must fill the sufurias with water and set them over to boil. In the meantime, their masters were attending to the pitching of the bwana's camp. The rest of the time the toto played about quite happily, and did light odd jobs, or watched most attentively while his master showed him small details of a safari-boy's duty, or taught him simple handicraft. Our boys seemed to take great pains with their totos and to try hard to teach them.

Also at Meru we had acquired two cocks and four hens of the ridiculously small native breed. These rode atop the loads: their feet were tied to the cords and there they swayed and teetered and balanced all day long, apparently quite happy and interested. At each new camp site they were released and went scratching and clucking around among the tents. They lent our temporary quarters quite a settled air of domesticity. We named the cocks Gaston and Alphonse and somehow it was rather fine, in the blackness before dawn, to hear these little birds crowing stout-heartedly against the great African wilderness. Neither Gaston, Alphonse nor any of their harem were killed and eaten by their owners; but seemed rather to fulfil the function of household pets.

Along the jungle track we met swarms of people coming in to the post. One large native safari composed exclusively of women were transporting loads of trade goods for the Indian trader. They carried their burdens on their backs by means of a strap passing over the top of the head; our own "tump line" method. The labour seemed in no way to have dashed their spirits, for they grinned at us, and joked merrily with our boys. Along the way, every once in a while, we came upon people squatted down behind small stocks of sugarcane, yams, bananas, and the like. With these our boys did a brisk trade. Little paths led mysteriously into the jungle. Down them came more savages to greet us. Everybody was most friendly and cheerful, thanks to Horne's personal influence. Two years before this same lot had been hostile. From every hidden village came the headmen or chiefs. They all wanted to shake hands-the ordinary citizen never dreamed of aspiring to that honour-and they all spat carefully into their palms before they did so. This all had to be done in passing; for ordinary village headmen it was beneath Our Dignity to draw rein. Once only we broke over this rule. That was in the case of an old fellow with white hair who managed to get so tangled up in the shrubbery that he could not get to us. He was so frantic with disappointment that we made an exception and waited.

About three miles out, we lost one of our newly acquired totos. Reason: an exasperated parent who had followed from Meru for the purpose of reclaiming his runaway offspring. The latter was dragged off howling. Evidently he, like some of his civilized cousins, had "run away to join the circus." As nearly as we could get at it, the rest of the totos, as well as the nine additional we picked up before we quitted the jungle, had all come with their parents' consent. In fact, we soon discovered that we could buy any amount of good sound totos, not house broke however, for an average of half a rupee (16-1/2 cents) apiece.

The road was very much up and down hill over the numerous ridges that star-fish out from Mt. Kenia. We would climb down steep trails from 200 to 800 feet (measured by aneroid), cross an excellent mountain stream of crystalline dashing water, and climb out again. The trails of course had no notion of easy grades. It was very hard work, especially for men with loads; and it would have been impossible on account of the heat were it not for the numerous streams. On the slopes and in the bottoms were patches of magnificent forest; on the crests was the jungle, and occasionally an outlook over extended views. The birds and the strange tropical big-leaved trees were a constant delight-exotic and strange. Billy was in a heaven of joy, for her specialty in Africa was plants, seeds and bulbs, for her California garden. She had syces, gunbearers and tent boys all climbing, shaking branches, and generally pawing about.

This idiosyncracy of Billy's puzzled our boys hugely. At first they tried telling her that everything was poisonous; but when that did not work, they resigned themselves to their fate. In fact, some of the most enterprising like Memba Sasa, Kitaru, and, later, Kongoni used of their own accord to hunt up and bring in seeds and blossoms. They did not in the least understand what it was for; and it used to puzzle them hugely until out of sheer pity for their uneasiness, I implied that the Memsahib collected "medicine." That was rational, so the wrinkled brow of care was smoothed. From this botanical trait, Billy got her native name of "Beebee Kooletta"-"The Lady Who Says: Go Get That." For in Africa every white man has a name by which he is known among the native people. If you would get news of your friends, you must know their local cognomens-their own white man names will not do at all. For example, I was called either Bwana Machumwani or Bwana N'goma. The former means merely Master Four-eyes, referring to my glasses. The precise meaning of the latter is a matter much disputed between myself and Billy. An N'goma is a native dance, consisting of drum poundings, chantings, and hoppings around. Therefore I translate myself (most appropriately) as the Master who Makes Merry. On the other hand, Billy, with true feminine indirectness, insists that it means "The Master who Shouts and Howls." I leave it to any fairminded reader.

About the middle of the morning we met a Government runner, a proud youth, young, lithe, with many ornaments and bangles; his red skin glistening; the long blade of his spear, bound around with a red strip to signify his office, slanting across his shoulder; his buffalo hide shield slung from it over his back; the letter he was bearing stuck in a cleft stick and carried proudly before him as a priest carries a cross to the heathen-in the pictures. He was swinging along at a brisk pace, but on seeing us drew up and gave us a smart military salute.

At one point where the path went level and straight for some distance, we were riding in an absolute solitude. Suddenly from the jungle on either side and about fifty yards ahead of us leaped a dozen women. They were dressed in grass skirts, and carried long narrow wooden shields painted white and brown. These they clashed together, shrieked shrilly, and charged down on us at full speed. When within a few yards of our horses noses they came to a sudden halt, once more clashed their shields, shrieked, turned and scuttled away as fast as their legs could carry them. At a hundred yards they repeated the performance; and charged back at us again. Thus advancing and retreating, shrieking high, hitting the wooden shields with resounding crash, they preceded our slow advance for a half mile or so. Then at some signal unperceived by us they vanished abruptly into the jungle. Once more we rode forward in silence and in solitude. Why they did it I could not say.

Of this tissue were our days made. At noon our boys plucked us each two or three banana leaves which they spread down for us to lie on. Then we dozed through the hot hours in great comfort, occasionally waking to blue sky through green trees, or to peer idly into the tangled jungle. At two o'clock or a little later we would arouse ourselves reluctantly and move on. The safari we had dimly heard passing us an hour before. In this country of the direct track we did not attempt to accompany our men.

The end of the day's march found us in a little clearing where we could pitch camp. Generally this was atop a ridge, so that the boys had some distance to carry water; but that disadvantage was outweighed by the cleared space. Sometimes we found ourselves hemmed in by a wall of jungle. Again we enjoyed a broad outlook. One such in especial took in the magnificent, splintered, snow-capped peak of Kenia on the right, a tremendous gorge and rolling forested mountains straight ahead, and a great drop to a plain with other and distant mountains to the left. It was as fine a panoramic view as one could imagine.

Our tents pitched, and ourselves washed and refreshed, we gave audience to the resident chief, who had probably been waiting. With this potentate we conversed affably, after the usual expectoratorial ceremonies. Billy, being a mere woman, did not always come in for this; but nevertheless she maintained what she called her "quarantine gloves,"

81

and kept them very handy. We had standing orders with our boys for basins of hot water to be waiting always behind our tents. After the usual polite exchanges we informed the chief of our needs-firewood, perhaps, milk, a sheep or the like. These he furnished. When we left we made him a present of a few beads, a knife, a blanket or such according to the value of his contribution.

To me these encounters were some of the most interesting of our many experiences, for each man differed radically from every other in his conceptions of ceremony, in his ideas, and in his methods. Our coming was a good deal of an event, always, and each chief, according to his temperament and training, tried to do things up properly. And in that attempt certain basic traits of human nature showed in the very strongest relief. Thus there are three points of view to take in running any spectacle: that of the star performer, the stage manager, or the truly artistic. We encountered well-marked specimens of each. I will tell you about them.

The star performer knew his stagecraft thoroughly; and in the exposition of his knowledge he showed incidentally how truly basic are the principles of stagecraft anywhere.

We were seated under a tree near the banks of a stream eating our lunch. Before us appeared two tall and slender youths, wreathed in smiles, engaging, and most attentive to the small niceties of courtesy. We returned their greeting from our recumbent positions, whereupon they made preparation to squat down beside us.

"Are you sultans?" we demanded sternly, "that you attempt to sit in Our Presence," and we lazily kicked the nearest.

Not at all abashed, but favourably impressed with our transcendent importance-as we intended-they leaned gracefully on their spears and entered into conversation. After a few trifles of airy persiflage they got down to business.

"This," said they, indicating the tiny flat, "is the most beautiful place to camp in all the mountains."

We doubted it.

"Here is excellent water."

We agreed to that.

"And there is no more water for a journey."

"You are liars," we observed politely.

"And near is the village of our chief, who is a great warrior, and will bring you many presents; the greatest man in these parts."

"Now you're getting to it," we observed in English; "you want trade." Then in Swahili, "We shall march two hours longer."

After a few polite phrases they went away. We finished lunch, remounted, and rode up the trail. At the edge of the canyon we came to a wide clearing, at the farther side of which was evidently the village in question. But the merry villagers, down to the last toro, were drawn up at the edge of the track in a double line through which we rode. They were very wealthy savages, and wore it all. Bright neck, arm, and leg ornaments, yards and yards of cowry shells in strings, blue beads of all sizes (blue beads were evidently "in"), odd scraps and shapes of embroidered skins, clean shaves and a beautiful polish characterized this holiday gathering. We made our royal progress between the serried ranks. About eight or ten seconds after we had passed the last villager-just the proper dramatic pause, you observe-the bushes parted and a splendid, straight, springy young man came into view and stepped smilingly across the space that separated us. And about eight or ten seconds after his emergence-again just the right dramatic pause-the bushes parted again to give entrance to four of the quaintest little dolls of wives. These advanced all abreast, parted, and took up positions two either side the smiling chief. This youth was evidently in the height of fashion, his hair braided in a tight queue bound with skin, his ears dangling with ornaments, heavy necklaces around his neck, and armlets etc., ad lib. His robe was of fine monkey skin embroidered with rosettes of beads, and his spear was very long, bright and keen. He was tall and finely built carried himself with a free, lithe swing. As the quintette came to halt, the villagers fell silent and our shauri began.

We drew up and dismounted. We all expectorated as gentlemen.

"These," said he proudly, "are my beebees."

We replied that they seemed like excellent beebees and politely inquired the price of wives thereabout, and also the market for totos. He gave us to understand that such superior wives as these brought three cows and twenty sheep apiece, but that you could get a pretty good toto for half a rupee.

"When we look upon our women," he concluded grandly, "we find them good; but when we look upon the white women they are as nothing!" He completely obliterated the poor little beebees with a magnificent gesture. They looked very humble and abashed. I was, however, a bit uncertain as to whether this was intended as a genuine tribute to Billy, or was meant to console us for having only one to his four.

Now observe the stagecraft of all this: entrance of diplomats, preliminary conversation introducing the idea of the greatness of N'Zahgi (for that was his name), chorus of villagers, and, as climax, dramatic entrance of the hero and heroines. It was pretty well done.

Again we stopped about the middle of the afternoon in an opening on the rounded top of a hill. While waiting for the safari to come up, Billy wandered away fifty or sixty yards to sit under a big tree. She did not stay long. Immediately she was settled, a dozen women and young girls surrounded her. They were almost uproariously good-natured, but Billy was probably the first white woman they had ever seen, and they intended to make the most of her. Every item of her clothes and equipment they examined minutely, handled and discussed. When she told them with great dignity to go away, they laughed consumedly, fairly tumbling into each other's arms with excess of joy. Billy tried to gather her effects for a masterly retreat, but found the press of numbers too great. At last she had to signal for help. One of us wandered over with a kiboko with which lightly he flicked the legs of such damsels as he could reach. They scattered like quail, laughing hilariously. Billy was escorted back to safety.

Shortly after the Chief and his Prime Minister came in. He was a little old gray-haired gentleman, as spry as a cricket, quite nervous, and very chatty. We indicated our wants to him, and he retired after enunciating many words. The safari came in, made camp. We had tea and a bath. The darkness fell; and still no Chief, no milk, no firewood, no promises fulfilled. There were plenty of natives around camp, but when we suggested that they get out and rustle on our behalf, they merely laughed good-naturedly. We seriously contemplated turning the whole lot out of camp.

Finally we gave it up, and sat down to our dinner. It was now quite dark. The askaris had built a little campfire out in front.

Then, far in the distance of the jungle's depths, we heard a faint measured chanting as of many people coming nearer. From another direction this was repeated. The two processions approached each other; their paths converged; the double chanting became a chorus that grew moment by moment. We heard beneath the wild weird minors the rhythmic stamping of feet, and the tapping of sticks. The procession debouched from the jungle's edge into the circle of the firelight. Our old chief led, accompanied by a bodyguard in all the panoply of war: ostrich feather circlets enclosing the head and face, shields of bright heraldry, long glittering spears. These were followed by a dozen of the quaintest solemn dolls of beebees dressed in all the white cowry shells, beads and brass the royal treasury afforded, very earnest, very much on inspection, every little head uplifted, singing away just as hard as ever they could. Each carried a gourd of milk, a bunch of bananas, some sugarcane, yams or the like. Straight to the fire marched the pageant. Then the warriors dividing right and left, drew up facing each other in two lines, struck their spears upright in the ground, and stood at attention. The quaint brown little women lined up to close the end of this hollow square, of which our group was, roughly speaking, the fourth side. Then all came to attention. The song now rose to a wild and ecstatic minor chanting. The beebees, still singing, one by one cast their burdens between the files and at our feet in the middle of the hollow square. Then they continued their chant, singing away at the tops of their little lungs, their eyes and teeth showing, their pretty bodies held rigidly upright. The warriors, very erect and military, stared straight ahead.

And the chief? Was he the centre of the show, the important leading man, to the contemplation of whom all these glories led? Not at all! This particular chief did not have the soul of a leading man, but rather the soul of a stage manager. Quite forgetful of himself and his part in the spectacle, his brow furrowed with anxiety, he was flittering from one to another of the performers. He listened carefully to each singer in turn, holding his hand behind his ear to catch the individual note, striking one on the shoulder in admonition, nodding approval at another. He darted unexpectedly across to scrutinize a warrior, in the chance of catching a flicker of the eyelid even. Nary a flicker! They did their stage manager credit, and stood like magnificent bronzes. He even ran across to peer into our own faces to see how we liked it.

With a sudden crescendo the music stopped. Involuntarily we broke into handclapping. The old boy looked a bit startled at this, but we explained to him, and he seemed very pleased. We then accepted formally the heap of presents, by touching them-and in turn passed over a blanket, a box of matches, and two needles, together with beads for the beebees. Then F., on an inspiration, produced his flashlight. This made a tremendous sensation. The women tittered and giggled and blinked as its beams were thrown directly into their eyes; the chief's sons grinned and guffawed; the chief himself laughed like a pleased schoolboy, and seemed never to weary of the sudden shutting on and off of the switch. But the trusty Spartan warriors, standing still in their formation behind their planted spears, were not to be shaken. They glared straight in front of them, even when we held the light within a few inches of their eyes, and not a muscle quivered!

"It is wonderful! wonderful!" the old man repeated. "Many Government men have come here, but none have had anything like that! The bwanas must be very great sultans!"

After the departure of our friends, we went rather grandly to bed. We always did after any one had called us sultans.

But our prize chief was an individual named M'booley.* Our camp here also was on a fine cleared hilltop between two streams. After we had traded for a while with very friendly and prosperous people M'booley came in. He was young, tall, straight, with a beautiful smooth lithe form, and his face was hawklike and cleverly intelligent. He carried himself with the greatest dignity and simplicity, meeting us on an easy plane of familiarity. I do not know how I can better describe his manner toward us than to compare it to the manner the member of an exclusive golf club would use to one who is a stranger, but evidently a guest. He took our quality for granted; and supposed we must do the same by him, neither acting as though he considered us "great white men," nor yet standing aloof and too respectful. And as the distinguishing feature of all, he was absolutely without personal ornament.

    \* Pronounce each o separately.

Pause for a moment to consider what a real advance in esthetic taste that one little fact stands for. All M'booley's attendants were the giddiest and gaudiest savages we had yet seen, with more colobus fur, sleighbells, polished metal, ostrich plumes, and red paint than would have fitted out any two other royal courts of the jungle. The women too were wealthy and opulent without limit. It takes considerable perception among our civilized people to realize that severe simplicity amid ultra magnificence makes the most effective distinguishing of an individual. If you do not believe it, drop in at the next ball to which you are invited. M'booley had fathomed this, and what was more he had the strength of mind to act on it. Any savage loves finery for its own sake. His hair was cut short, and shaved away at the edges to leave what looked like an ordinary close-fitting skull cap. He wore one pair of plain armlets on his left upper arm and small simple ear-rings. His robe was black. He had no trace of either oil or paint, nor did he even carry a spear.

He greeted us with good-humoured ease, and inquired conversationally if we wanted anything. We suggested wood and milk, whereupon still smiling, he uttered a few casual words in his own language to no one in particular. There was no earthly doubt that he was chief. Three of the most gorgeous and haughty warriors ran out of camp. Shortly long files of women came in bringing loads of firewood; and others carrying bananas, yams, sugarcane and a sheep. Truly M'booley did things on a princely scale. We thanked him. He accepted the thanks with a casual smile, waved his hand and went on to talk of something else. In due order our M'ganga brought up one of our best trade blankets, to which we added a half dozen boxes of matches and a razor.

Now into camp filed a small procession: four women, four children, and two young men. These advanced to where M'booley was standing smoking with great satisfaction one of B's tailor-made cigarettes. M'booley advanced ten feet to meet them, and brought them up to introduce them one by one in the most formal fashion. These were of course his family, and we had to confess that they "saw" N'Zahgi's outfit of ornaments and "raised" him beyond the ceiling. We gave them each in turn the handshake of ceremony, first with the palms as we do it, and then each grasping the other's upright thumb. The "little chiefs" were proud, aristocratic little fellows, holding themselves very straight and solemn. I think one would have known them for royalty anywhere.

It was quite a social occasion. None of our guests was in the least ill at ease; in fact, the young ladies were quite coy and flirtatious. We had a great many jokes. Each of the little ladies received a handful of prevailing beads. M'booley smiled benignly at these delightful femininities. After a time he led us to the edge of the hill and showed us his houses across the cation, perched on a flat about halfway up the wall. They were of the usual grass-thatched construction, but rather larger and neater than most. Examining them through the glasses we saw that a little stream had been diverted to flow through the front yard. M'booley waved his hand abroad and gave us to understand that he considered the outlook worth looking at. It was; but an appreciation of that fact is foreign to the average native. Next morning, when we rode by very early, we found the little flat most attractively cleared and arranged. M'booley was out to shake us by the hand in farewell, shivering in the cold of dawn. The flirtatious and spoiled little beauties were not in evidence.

One day after two very deep canyons we emerged from the forest jungle into an up and down country of high jungle bush-brush. From the top of a ridge it looked a good deal like a northern cut-over pine country grown up very heavily to blackberry vines; although, of course, when we came nearer, the "blackberry vines" proved to be ten or twenty feet high. This was a district of which Horne had warned us. The natives herein were reported restless and semi-hostile; and in fact had never been friendly. They probably needed the demonstration most native tribes seem to require before they are content to settle down and be happy. At any rate safaris were not permitted in their district; and we ourselves were allowed to go through merely because we were a large party, did not intend to linger, and had a good reputation with natives.

It is very curious how abruptly, in Central Africa, one passes from one condition to another, from one tribe or race to the next. Sometimes, as in the present case, it is the traversing of a deep cañon; at others the simple crossing of a tiny brook is enough. Moreover the line of demarcation is clearly defined, as boundaries elsewhere are never defined save in wartime.

Thus we smiled our good-bye to a friendly numerous people, descended a hill, and ascended another into a deserted track. After a half mile we came unexpectedly on to two men carrying each a load of reeds. These they abandoned and fled up the hillside through the jungle, in spite of our shouted assurances. A moment later they reappeared at some distance above us, each with a spear he had snatched from somewhere; they were unarmed when we first caught sight of them. Examined through the glasses they proved to be sullen looking men, copper coloured, but broad across the cheekbones, broad in the forehead, more decidedly of the negro type than our late hosts.

Aside from these two men we travelled through an apparently deserted jungle. I suspect, however, that we were probably well watched; for when we stopped for noon we heard the gunbearers beyond the screen of leaves talking to some one. On learning from our boys that these were some of the shenzis, we told them to bring the savages in for a shauri; but in this our men failed, nor could they themselves get nearer than fifty yards or so to the wild people. So until evening our impression remained that of two distant men, and the indistinct sound of voices behind a leafy screen.

We made camp comparatively early in a wide open space surrounded by low forest. Almost immediately then the savages commenced to drift in, very haughty and arrogant. They were fully armed. Besides the spear and decorated shield, some of them carried the curious small grass spears. These are used to stab upward from below, the wielder lying flat in the grass. Some of these men were fantastically painted with a groundwork ochre, on which had been drawn intricate wavy designs on the legs, like stockings, and varied stripes across the face. One particularly ingenious individual, stark naked, had outlined a roughly entire skeleton! He was a gruesome object! They stalked here and there through the camp, looking at our men and their activities with a lofty and silent contempt.

You may be sure we had our arrangements, though they did not appear on the surface. The askaris, or native soldiers, were posted here and there with their muskets; the gunbearers also kept our spare weapons by them. The askaris could not hit a barn, but they could make a noise. The gunbearers were fair shots.

Of course the chief and his prime minister came in. They were evil-looking savages. To them we paid not the slightest attention, but went about our usual business as though they did not exist. At the end of an hour they of their own initiative greeted us. We did not hear them. Half an hour later they disappeared, to return after an interval, followed by a string of young men bearing firewood. Evidently our bearing had impressed them, as we had intended. We then unbent far enough to recognize them, carried on a formal conversation for a few moments, gave them adequate presents and dismissed them. Then we ordered the askaris to clear camp and to keep it clear. No women had appeared. Even the gifts of firewood had been carried by men, a most unusual proceeding.

As soon as dark fell the drums began roaring in the forest all about our clearing, and the chanting to rise. We instructed our men to shoot first and inquire afterward, if a shenzi so much as showed himself in the clearing. This was not as bad as it sounded; the shenzi stood in no immediate danger. Then we turned in to a sleep rather light and broken by uncertainty. I do not think we were in any immediate danger of a considered attack, for these people were not openly hostile; but there was always a chance that the savages might by their drum pounding and dancing work themselves into a frenzy. Then we might have to do a little rapid shooting. Not for one instant the whole night long did those misguided savages cease their howling and dancing. At any rate we cost them a night's sleep.

Next morning we took up our march through the deserted tracks once more. Not a sign of human life did we encounter. About ten o'clock we climbed down a tremendous gash of a box canyon with precipitous cliffs. From below we looked back to see, perched high against the skyline, the motionless figures of many savages watching us from the crags. So we had had company after all, and we had not known it. This canyon proved to be the boundary line. With the same abruptness we passed again into friendly country.

(d) OUT THE OTHER SIDE

We left the jungle finally when we turned on a long angle away from Kenia. At first the open country of the foothills was closely cultivated with fields of rape and maize. We saw some of the people breaking new soil by means of long pointed sticks. The plowmen quite simply inserted the pointed end in the ground and pried. It was very slow hard work. In other fields the grain stood high and good. From among the stalks, as from a miniature jungle, the little naked totos stared out, and the good-natured women smiled at us. The magnificent peak of Kenia had now shaken itself free of the forests. On its snow the sunrises and sunsets kindled their fires. The flames of grass fires, too, could plainly be made out, incredible distances away, and at daytime, through the reek, were fascinating suggestions of distant rivers, plains, jungles, and hills. You see, we were still practically on the wide slope of Kenia's base, though the peak was many days away, and so could look out over wide country.

The last half day of this we wandered literally in a rape field. The stalks were quite above our heads, and we could see but a few yards in any direction. In addition the track had become a footpath not over two feet wide. We could occasionally look back to catch glimpses of a pack or so bobbing along on a porter's head. From our own path hundreds of other paths branched; we were continually taking the wrong fork and moving back to set the safari right before it could do likewise. This we did by drawing a deep double line in the earth across the wrong trail. Then we hustled on ahead to pioneer the way a little farther; our difficulties were further complicated by the fact that we had sent our horses back to Nairobi for fear of the tsetse fly, so we could not see out above the corn. All we knew was that we ought to go down hill.

At the ends of some of our false trails we came upon fascinating little settlements: groups of houses inside brush enclosures, with low wooden gateways beneath which we had to stoop to enter. Within were groups of beehive houses with small naked children and perhaps an old woman or old man seated cross-legged under a sort of veranda. From them we obtained new-and confusing-directions.

After three o'clock we came finally out on the edge of a cliff fifty or sixty feet high, below which lay uncultivated bottom lands like a great meadow and a little meandering stream. We descended the cliff, and camped by the meandering stream.

By this time we were fairly tired from long walking in the heat, and so were content to sit down under our tent-fly before our little table, and let Mahomet bring us sparklets and lime juice. Before us was the flat of a meadow below the cliffs and the cliffs themselves. Just below the rise lay a single patch of standing rape not over two acres in extent, the only sign of human life. It was as though this little bit had overflowed from the countless millions on the plateau above. Beyond it arose a thin signal of smoke.

We sipped our lime juice and rested. Soon our attention was attracted by the peculiar actions of a big flock of very white birds. They rose suddenly from one side of the tiny rape field, wheeled and swirled like leaves in the wind, and dropped down suddenly on the other side the patch. After a few moments they repeated the performance. The sun caught the dazzling white of their plumage. At first we speculated on what they might be, then on what they were doing, to behave in so peculiar a manner. The lime juice and the armchair began to get in their recuperative work. Somehow the distance across that flat did not seem quite as tremendous as at first. Finally I picked up the shotgun and sauntered across to investigate. The cause of action I soon determined. The owner of that rape field turned out to be an emaciated, gray-haired but spry old savage. He was armed with a spear; and at the moment his chief business in life seemed to be chasing a large flock of white birds off his grain. Since he had no assistance, and since the birds held his spear in justifiable contempt as a fowling piece, he was getting much exercise and few results. The birds gave way before his direct charge, flopped over to the other side, and continued their meal. They had already occasioned considerable damage; the rape heads were bent and destroyed for a space of perhaps ten feet from the outer edge of the field. As this grain probably constituted the old man's food supply for a season, I did not wonder at the vehemence with which he shook his spear at his enemies, nor the apparent flavour of his language, though I did marvel at his physical endurance. As for the birds, they had become cynical and impudent; they barely fluttered out of the way.

I halted the old gentleman and hastened to explain that I was neither a pirate, a robber, nor an oppressor of the poor. This as counter-check to his tendency to flee, leaving me in sole charge. He understood a little Swahili, and talked a few words of something he intended for that language. By means of our mutual accomplishment in that tongue, and through a more efficient sign language, I got him to understand the plan of campaign. It was very simple. I squatted down inside the rape, while he went around the other side to scare them up.

The white birds uttered their peculiarly derisive cackle at the old man and flapped over to my side. Then they were certainly an astonished lot of birds. I gave them both barrels and dropped a pair; got two more shots as they swung over me and dropped another pair, and brought down a straggling single as a grand finale. The flock, with shrill, derogatory remarks, flew in an airline straight away. They never deviated, as far as I could follow them with the eye. Even after they had apparently disappeared, I could catch an occasional flash of white in the sun.

Now the old gentleman came whooping around with long, undignified bounds to fall on his face and seize my foot in an excess of gratitude. He rose and capered about, he rushed out and gathered in the slain one by one and laid them in a pile at my feet. Then he danced a jig-step around them and reviled them, and fell on his face once more, repeating the word "Bwana! bwana! bwana!" over and over-"Master! master! master!" We returned to camp together, the old gentleman carrying the birds, and capering about like a small boy, pouring forth a flood of his sort of Swahili, of which I could understand only a word here and there. Memba Sasa, very dignified and scornful of such performances, met us halfway and took my gun. He seemed to be able to understand the old fellow's brand of Swahili, and said it over again in a brand I could understand. From it I gathered that I was called a marvellously great sultan, a protector of the poor, and other Arabian Nights titles.

The birds proved to be white egrets. Now at home I am strongly against the killing of these creatures, and have so expressed myself on many occasions. But, looking from the beautiful white plumage of these villainous marauders, to the wrinkled countenance of the grateful weary old savage, I could not fan a spark of regret. And from the straight line of their retreating flight I like to think that the rest of the flock never came back, but took their toll from the wider fields of the plateau above.

Next day we reentered the game-haunted wilderness, nor did we see any more native villages until many weeks later we came into the country of the Wakamba.

# XIX. THE TANA RIVER

Our first sight of the Tana River was from the top of a bluff. It flowed below us a hundred feet, bending at a sharp elbow against the cliff on which we stood. Out of the jungle it crept sluggishly and into the jungle it crept again, brown, slow, viscid, suggestive of the fevers and the lurking beasts by which, indeed, it was haunted. From our elevation we could follow its course by the jungle that grew along its banks. At first this was intermittent, leaving thin or even open spaces at intervals, but lower down it extended away unbroken and very tall. The trees were many of them beginning to come into flower.

Either side of the jungle were rolling hills. Those to the left made up to the tremendous slopes of Kenia. Those to the right ended finally in a low broken range many miles away called the Ithanga Hills. The country gave one the impression of being clothed with small trees; although here and there this growth gave space to wide grassy plains. Later we discovered that the forest was more apparent than real. The small trees, even where continuous, were sparse enough to permit free walking in all directions, and open enough to allow clear sight for a hundred yards or so. Furthermore, the shallow wide valleys between the hills were almost invariably treeless and grown to very high thick grass.

Thus the course of the Tana possessed advantages to such as we. By following in general the course of the stream we were always certain of wood and water. The river itself was full of fish-not to speak of hundreds of crocodiles and hippopotamuses. The thick river jungle gave cover to such animals as the bushbuck, leopard, the beautiful colobus, some of the tiny antelope, waterbuck, buffalo and rhinoceros. Among the thorn and acacia trees of the hillsides one was certain of impalla, eland, diks-diks, and giraffes. In the grass bottoms were lions, rhinoceroses, a half dozen varieties of buck, and thousands and thousands of game birds such as guinea fowl and grouse. On the plains fed zebra, hartebeeste, wart-hog, ostriches, and several species of the smaller antelope. As a sportsman's paradise this region would be hard to beat.

We were now afoot. The dreaded tsetse fly abounded here, and we had sent our horses in via Fort Hall. F. had accompanied them, and hoped to rejoin us in a few days or weeks with tougher and less valuable mules. Pending his return we moved on leisurely, camping long at one spot, marching short days, searching the country far and near for the special trophies of which we stood in need.

It was great fun. Generally we hunted each in his own direction and according to his own ideas. The jungle along the river, while not the most prolific in trophies, was by all odds the most interesting. It was very dense, very hot, and very shady. Often a thorn thicket would fling itself from the hills right across to the water's edge, absolutely and hopelessly impenetrable save by way of the rhinoceros tracks. Along these then we would slip, bent double, very quietly and gingerly, keeping a sharp lookout for the rightful owners of the trail. Again we would wander among lofty trees through the tops of which the sun flickered on festooned serpent-like vines. Every once in a while we managed a glimpse of the sullen oily river through the dense leaf screen on its banks. The water looked thick as syrup, of a deadly menacing green. Sometimes we saw a loathsome crocodile lying with his nose just out of water, or heard the snorting blow of a hippopotamus coming up for air. Then the thicket forced us inland again. We stepped

89

very slowly, very alertly, our ears cocked for the faintest sound, our eyes roving. Generally, of course, the creatures of the jungle saw us first. We became aware of them by a crash or a rustling or a scamper. Then we stood stock listening with all our ears for some sound distinguishing to the species. Thus I came to recognize the queer barking note of the bushbuck, for example, and to realize how profane and vulgar that and the beautiful creature, the impala, can be when he forgets himself. As for the rhinoceros, he does not care how much noise he makes, nor how badly he scares you.

Personally, I liked very well to circle out in the more open country until about three o'clock, then to enter the river jungle and work my way slowly back toward camp. At that time of day the shadows were lengthening, the birds and animals were beginning to stir about. In the cooling nether world of shadow we slipped silently from thicket to thicket, from tree to tree; and the jungle people fled from us, or withdrew, or gazed curiously, or cursed us as their dispositions varied.

While thus returning one evening I saw my first colobus. He was swinging rapidly from one tree to another, his long black and white fur shining against the sun. I wanted him very much, and promptly let drive at him with the 405 Winchester. I always carried this heavier weapon in the dense jungle. Of course I missed him, but the roar of the shot so surprised him that he came to a stand. Memba Sasa passed me the Springfield, and I managed to get him in the head. At the shot another flashed into view, high up in the top of a tree. Again I aimed and fired. The beast let go and fell like a plummet. "Good shot," said I to myself. Fifty feet down the colobus seized a limb and went skipping away through the branches as lively as ever. In a moment he stopped to look back, and by good luck I landed him through the body. When we retrieved him we found that the first shot had not hit him at all!

At the time I thought he must have been frightened into falling; but many subsequent experiences showed me that this sheer let-go-all-holds drop is characteristic of the colobus and his mode of progression. He rarely, as far as my observation goes, leaps out and across as do the ordinary monkeys, but prefers to progress by a series of slanting ascents followed by breath-taking straight drops to lower levels. When closely pressed from beneath, he will go as high as he can, and will then conceal himself in the thick leaves.

B. and I procured our desired number of colobus by taking advantage of this habit-as soon as we had learned it. Shooting the beasts with our rifles we soon found to be not only very difficult, but also destructive of the skins. On the other hand, a man could not, save by sheer good fortune, rely on stalking near enough to use a shotgun. Therefore we evolved a method productive of the maximum noise, row, barked shins, thorn wounds, tumbles, bruises-and colobus! It was very simple. We took about twenty boys into the jungle with us, and as soon as we caught sight of a colobus we chased him madly. That was all there was to it.

And yet this method, simple apparently to the point of imbecility, had considerable logic back of it after all; for after a time somebody managed to get underneath that colobus when he was at the top of a tree. Then the beast would hide.

Consider then a tumbling riotous mob careering through the jungle as fast as the jungle would let it, slipping, stumbling, falling flat, getting tangled hopelessly, disentangling with profane remarks, falling behind and catching up again, everybody yelling and shrieking. Ahead of us we caught glimpses of the sleek bounding black and white creature, running up the long slanting limbs, and dropping like a plummet into the lower branches of the next tree. We white men never could keep up with the best of our men at this sort of work, although in the open country I could hold them well enough. We could see them dashing through the thick cover at a great rate of speed far ahead of us. After an interval came a great shout in chorus. By this we knew that the quarry had been definitely brought to a stand. Arriving at the spot we craned our heads backward, and proceeded to get a crick in the neck trying to make out invisible colobus in the very tops of the trees above us. For gaudily marked beasts the colobus were extraordinarily difficult to see. This was in no sense owing to any far-fetched application of protective colouration; but to the remarkable skill the animals possessed in concealing themselves behind apparently the scantiest and most inadequate cover. Fortunately for us our boys' ability to see them was equally remarkable. Indeed, the most difficult part of their task was to point the game out to us. We squinted, and changed position, and tried hard to follow directions eagerly proffered by a dozen of the men. Finally one of us would, by the aid of six power-glasses, make out, or guess at a small tuft of white or black hair showing beyond the concealment of a bunch of leaves. We would unlimber the shotgun and send a charge of BB into that bunch. Then down would plump the game, to the huge and vociferous delight of all the boys. Or, as occasionally happened, the shot was followed merely by a shower of leaves and a chorus of expostulations indicating that we had mistaken the place, and had fired into empty air.

In this manner we gathered the twelve we required between us. At noon we sat under the bank, with the tangled roots of trees above us, and the smooth oily river slipping by. You may be sure we always selected a spot protected by very shoal water, for the crocodiles were numerous. I always shot these loathsome creatures whenever I got a chance, whenever the sound of a shot would not alarm more valuable game. Generally they were to be seen in midstream, just the tip of their snouts above water, and extraordinarily like anything but crocodiles. Often it took several close scrutinies through the glass to determine the brutes. This required rather nice shooting. More rarely we managed to see them on the banks, or only half submerged. In this position, too, they were all but undistinguishable as living creatures. I think this is perhaps because of their complete immobility. The creatures of the woods, standing quite still, are difficult enough to see; but I have a notion that the eye, unknown to itself, catches the sum total of little flexings of the muscles, movements of the skin, winkings, even the play of wind and light in the hair of the coat, all of which, while impossible of analysis, together relieve the appearance of dead inertia. The vitality of a creature like the crocodile, however, seems to have withdrawn into the inner recesses of its being. It lies like a log of wood, and for a log of wood it is mistaken.

Nevertheless the crocodile has stored in it somewhere a fearful vitality. The swiftness of its movements when seizing prey is most astonishing; a swirl of water, the sweep of a powerful tail, and the unfortunate victim has disappeared. For this reason it is especially dangerous to approach the actual edge of any of the great rivers, unless the water is so shallow that the crocodile could not possibly approach under cover, as is its cheerful habit. We had considerable difficulty in impressing this elementary truth on our hill-bred totos until one day, hearing wild shrieks from the direction of the river, I rushed down to find the lot huddled together in the very middle of a sand spit that reached well out into the stream. Inquiry developed that while paddling in the shallows they had been surprised by the sudden appearance of an ugly snout and well drenched by the sweep of an eager tail. The stroke fortunately missed. We stilled the tumult, sat down quietly to wait, and at the end of ten minutes had the satisfaction of abating that croc.

Generally we killed the brutes where we found them and allowed them to drift away with the current. Occasionally however we wanted a piece of hide, and then tried to retrieve them. One such occasion showed very vividly the tenacity of life and the primitive nervous systems of these great saurians.

I discovered the beast, head out of water, in a reasonable sized pool below which were shallow rapids. My Springfield bullet hit him fair, whereupon he stood square on his head and waved his tail in the air, rolled over three or four times, thrashed the water, and disappeared. After waiting a while we moved on downstream. Returning four hours later I sneaked up quietly. There the crocodile lay sunning himself on the sand bank. I supposed he must be dead; but when I accidentally broke a twig, he immediately commenced to slide off into the water. Thereupon I stopped him with a bullet in the spine. The first shot had smashed a hole in his head, just behind the eye, about the size of an ordinary coffee cup. In spite of this wound, which would have been instantly fatal to any warm-blooded animal, the creature was so little affected that it actually reacted to a slight noise made at some distance from where it lay. Of course the wound would probably have been fatal in the long run.

The best spot to shoot at, indeed, is not the head but the spine immediately back of the head.

These brutes are exceedingly powerful. They are capable of taking down horses and cattle, with no particular effort. This I know from my own observation. Mr. Fleischman, however, was privileged to see the wonderful sight of the capture and destruction of a full-grown rhinoceros by a crocodile. The photographs he took of this most extraordinary affair leave no room for doubt. Crossing a stream was always a matter of concern to us. The boys beat the surface of the water vigorously with their safari sticks. On occasion we have even let loose a few heavy bullets to stir up the pool before venturing in.

A steep climb through thorn and brush would always extricate us from the river jungle when we became tired of it. Then we found ourselves in a continuous but scattered growth of small trees. Between the trunks of these we could see for a hundred yards or so before their numbers closed in the view. Here was the favourite haunt of numerous beautiful impalla. We caught glimpses of them, flashing through the trees; or occasionally standing, gazing in our direction, their slender necks stretched high, their ears pointed for us. These curious ones were generally the does. The bucks were either more cautious or less inquisitive. A herd or so of eland also liked this covered country; and there were always a few waterbuck and rhinoceroses about. Often too we here encountered stragglers from the open plains-zebra or hartebeeste, very alert and suspicious in unaccustomed surroundings.

A great deal of the plains country had been burned over; and a considerable area was still afire. The low bright flames licked their way slowly through the grass in a narrow irregular band extending sometimes for miles. Behind it was blackened soil, and above it rolled dense clouds of smoke. Always accompanied it thousands of birds wheeling and dashing frantically in and out of the murk, often fairly at the flames themselves. The published writings of a certain worthy and sentimental person waste much sympathy over these poor birds dashing frenziedly about above their destroyed nests. As a matter of fact they are taking greedy advantage of a most excellent opportunity to get insects cheap. Thousands of the common red-billed European storks patrolled the grass just in front of the advancing flames, or wheeled barely above the fire. Grasshoppers were their main object, although apparently they never objected to any small mammals or reptiles that came their way. Far overhead wheeled a few thousand more assorted soarers who either had no appetite or had satisfied it.

The utter indifference of the animals to the advance of a big conflagration always impressed me. One naturally pictures the beasts as fleeing wildly, nostrils distended, before the devouring element. On the contrary I have seen kongoni grazing quite peacefully with flames on three sides of them. The fire seems to travel rather slowly in the tough grass; although at times and for a short distance it will leap to a wild and roaring life. Beasts will then lope rapidly away to right or left, but without excitement.

On these open plains we were more or less pestered with ticks of various sizes. These clung to the grass blades; but with no invincible preference for that habitat; trousers did them just as well. Then they ascended looking for openings. They ranged in size from little red ones as small as the period of a printed page to big patterned fellows the size of a pea. The little ones were much the most abundant. At times I have had the front of my breeches so covered with them that their numbers actually imparted a reddish tinge to the surface of the cloth. This sounds like exaggeration, but it is a measured statement. The process of de-ticking (new and valuable word) can then be done only by scraping with the back of a hunting knife.

Some people, of tender skin, are driven nearly frantic by these pests. Others, of whom I am thankful to say I am one, get off comparatively easy. In a particularly bad tick country, one generally appoints one of the youngsters as "tick toto." It is then his job in life to de-tick any person or domestic animal requiring his services. His is a busy existence. But though at first the nuisance is excessive, one becomes accustomed to it in a remarkably short space of time. The adaptability of the human being is nowhere better exemplified. After a time one gets so that at night he can remove a marauding tick and cast it forth into the darkness without even waking up. Fortunately ticks are local in distribution. Often one may travel weeks or months without this infliction.

I was always interested and impressed to observe how indifferent the wild animals seem to be to these insects. Zebra, rhinoceros and giraffe seem to be especially good hosts. The loathsome creatures fasten themselves in clusters wherever they can grip their fangs. Thus in a tick country a zebra's ears, the lids and corners of his eyes, his nostrils and lips, the soft skin between his legs and body, and between his hind legs, and under his tail are always crusted with ticks as thick as they can cling. One would think the drain on vitality would be enormous, but the animals are always plump and in condition. The same state of affairs obtains with the other two beasts named. The hartebeeste also carries ticks but not nearly in the same abundance; while such creatures as the waterbuck, impalla, gazelles and the smaller bucks seem either to be absolutely free from the pests, or to have a very few. Whether this is because such animals take the trouble to rid themselves, or because they are more immune from attack it would be difficult to say. I have found ticks clinging to the hair of lions, but never fastened to the flesh. It is probable that they had been brushed off from the grass in passing. Perhaps ticks do not like lions, waterbuck, Tommies, et al., or perhaps only big coarse-grained common brutes like zebra and rhinos will stand them at all.

# XX. DIVERS ADVENTURES ALONG THE TANA

Late one afternoon I shot a wart-hog in the tall grass. The beast was an unusually fine specimen, so I instructed Fundi and the porters to take the head, and myself started for camp with Memba Sasa. I had gone not over a hundred yards when I was recalled by wild and agonized appeals of "Bwana! bwana!" The long-legged Fundi was repeatedly leaping straight up in the air to an astonishing height above the long grass, curling his legs up under him at each jump, and yelling like a steam-engine. Returning promptly, I found that the wart-hog had come to life at the first prick of the knife. He was engaged in charging back and forth in an earnest effort to tusk Fundi, and the latter was jumping high in an equally earnest effort to keep out of the way. Fortunately he proved agile enough to do so until I planted another bullet in the aggressor.

These wart-hogs are most comical brutes from whatever angle one views them. They have a patriarchal, self-satisfied, suburban manner of complete importance. The old gentleman bosses his harem outrageously, and each and every member of the tribe walks about with short steps and a stuffy parvenu small-town self-sufficiency. One is quite certain that it is only by accident that they have long tusks and live in Africa, instead of rubber-plants and self-made business and a pug-dog within commuters' distance of New York. But at the slightest alarm this swollen and puffy importance breaks down completely. Away they scurry, their tails held stiffly and straightly perpendicular, their short legs scrabbling the small stones in a frantic effort to go faster than nature had intended them to go. Nor do they cease their flight at a reasonable distance, but keep on going over hill and dale, until they fairly vanish in the blue. I used to like starting them off this way, just for the sake of contrast, and also for the sake of the delicious but impossible vision of seeing their human prototypes do likewise.

When a wart-hog is at home, he lives down a hole. Of course it has to be a particularly large hole. He around and backs down it. No more peculiar sight can be imagined than the sardonically toothsome countenance of a wart-hog fading slowly in the dimness of a deep burrow, a good deal like Alice's Cheshire Cat. Firing a revolver, preferably with smoky black powder, just in front of the hole annoys the wart-hog exceedingly. Out he comes full tilt, bent on damaging some one, and it takes quick shooting to prevent his doing so.

Once, many hundreds of miles south of the Tana, and many months later, we were riding quite peaceably through the country, when we were startled by the sound of a deep and continuous roaring in a small brush patch to our left. We advanced cautiously to a prospective lion, only to discover that the roaring proceeded from the depths of a wart-hog burrow. The reverberation of our footsteps on the hollow ground had alarmed him. He was a very nervous wart-hog.

On another occasion, when returning to camp from a solitary walk, I saw two wart-hogs before they saw me. I made no attempt to conceal myself, but stood absolutely motionless. They fed slowly nearer and nearer until at last they were not over twenty yards away. When finally they made me out, their indignation and amazement and utter incredulity were very funny. In fact, they did not believe in me at all for some few snorty moments. Finally they departed, their absurd tails stiff upright.

One afternoon F. and I, hunting along one of the wide grass bottom lands, caught sight of a herd of an especially fine impalla. The animals were feeding about fifty yards the other side of a small solitary bush, and the bush grew on the sloping bank of the slight depression that represented the dry stream bottom. We could duck down into the depression, sneak along it, come up back of the little bush, and shoot from very close range. Leaving the gunbearers, we proceeded to do this.

So quietly did we move that when we rose up back of the little bush a lioness lying under it with her cub was as surprised as we were!

Indeed, I do not think she knew what we were, for instead of attacking, she leaped out the other side the bush, uttering a startled snarl. At once she whirled to come at us, but the brief respite had allowed us to recover our own scattered wits. As she turned I caught her broadside through the heart. Although this shot knocked her down, F. immediately followed it with another for safety's sake. We found that actually we had just missed stepping on her tail!

The cub we caught a glimpse of. He was about the size of a setter dog. We tried hard to find him, but failed. The lioness was an unusually large one, probably about as big as the female ever grows, measuring nine feet six inches in length, and three feet eight inches tall at the shoulder.

Billy had her funny times housekeeping. The kitchen department never quite ceased marvelling at her. Whenever she went to the cook-camp to deliver her orders she was surrounded by an attentive and respectful audience. One day, after holding forth for some time in Swahili, she found that she had been standing hobnailed on one of the boy's feet.

"Why, Mahomet!" she cried. "That must hurt you! Why didn't you tell me?"

"Memsahib," he smiled politely, "I think perhaps you move some time!"

On another occasion she was trying to tell the cook, through Mahomet as interpreter, that she wanted a tough old buffalo steak pounded, boarding-house style. This evidently puzzled all hands. They turned to in an earnest discussion of what it was all about, anyway. Billy understood Swahili well enough at that time to gather that they could not understand the Memsahib's wanting the meat "kibokoed"-FLOGGED. Was it a religious rite, or a piece of revenge? They gave it up.

"All right," said Mahomet patiently at last. "He say he do it. WHICH ONE IS IT?"

Part of our supplies comprised tins of dehydrated fruit. One evening Billy decided to have a grand celebration, so she passed out a tin marked "rhubarb" and some cornstarch, together with suitable instructions for a fruit pudding. In a little while the cook returned.

"Nataka m'tund-I want fruit," said he.

Billy pointed out, severely, that he already had fruit. He went away shaking his head. Evening and the pudding came. It looked good, and we congratulated Billy on her culinary enterprise. Being hungry, we took big mouthfuls. There followed splutterings and investigations. The rhubarb can proved to be an old one containing heavy gun grease!

When finally we parted with our faithful cook we bought him a really wonderful many bladed knife as a present. On seeing it he slumped to the ground-six feet of lofty dignity-and began to weep violently, rocking back and forth in an excess of grief.

"Why, what is it?" we inquired, alarmed.

"Oh, Memsahib!" he wailed, the tears coursing down his cheeks, "I wanted a watch!"

One morning about nine o'clock we were riding along at the edge of a grass-grown savannah, with a low hill to our right and another about four hundred yards ahead. Suddenly two rhinoceroses came to their feet some fifty yards to our left out in the high grass, and stood looking uncertainly in our direction.

"Look out! Rhinos!" I warned instantly.

"Why-why!" gasped Billy in an astonished tone of voice, "they have manes!"

In some concern for her sanity I glanced in her direction. She was staring, not to her left, but straight ahead. I followed the direction of her gaze, to see three lions moving across the face of the hill.

Instantly we dropped off our horses. We wanted a shot at those lions very much indeed, but were hampered in our efforts by the two rhinoceroses, now stamping, snorting, and moving slowly in our direction. The language we muttered was racy, but we dropped to a kneeling position and opened fire on the disappearing lions. It was most distinctly a case of divided attention, one eye on those menacing rhinos, and one trying to attend to the always delicate operation of aligning sights and signalling from a rather distracted brain just when to pull the trigger. Our faithful gunbearers crouched by us, the heavy guns ready.

One rhino seemed either peaceable or stupid. He showed no inclination either to attack or to depart, but was willing to back whatever play his friend might decide on. The friend charged toward us until we began to think he meant battle, stopped, thought a moment, and then, followed by his companion, trotted slowly across our bows about eighty yards away, while we continued our long range practice at the lions over their backs.

In this we were not winning many cigars. F. had a 280-calibre rifle shooting the Ross cartridge through the much advertised grooveless oval bore. It was little accurate beyond a hundred yards. Memba Sasa had thrust the 405 into my hand, knowing it for the "lion gun," and kept just out of reach with the long-range Springfield. I had no time to argue the matter with him. The 405 has a trajectory like a rainbow at that distance, and I was guessing at it, and not making very good guesses either. B. had his Springfield and made closer practice, finally hitting a leg of one of the beasts. We saw him lift his paw and shake it, but he did not move lamely afterward, so the damage was probably confined to a simple scrape. It was a good shot anyway. Then they disappeared over the top of the hill.

We walked forward, regretting rhinos. Thirty yards ahead of me came a thunderous and roaring growl, and a magnificent old lion reared his head from a low bush. He evidently intended mischief, for I could see his tail switching. However, B. had killed only one lion and I wanted very much to give him the shot. Therefore, I held the front sight on the middle of his chest, and uttered a fervent wish to myself that B. would hurry up. In about ten seconds the muzzle of his rifle poked over my shoulder, so I resigned the job.

At B.'s shot the lion fell over, but was immediately up and trying to get at us. Then we saw that his hind quarters were paralyzed. He was a most magnificent sight as he reared his fine old head, roaring at us full mouthed so that the very air trembled. Billy had a good look at a lion in action. B. took up a commanding position on an ant hill to one side with his rifle levelled. F. and I advanced slowly side by side. At twelve feet from the wounded beast stopped, F. unlimbered the kodak, while I held the bead of the 405 between the lion's eyes, ready to press trigger at the first forward movement, however slight. Thus we took several exposures in the two cameras. Unfortunately one of the cameras fell in the river the next day. The other contained but one exposure. While not so spectacular as some of those spoiled, it shows very well the erect mane, the wicked narrowing of the eyes, the flattening of the ears of an angry lion. You must imagine, furthermore, the deep rumbling diapason of his growling.

We backed away, and B. put in the finishing shot. The first bullet, we then found, had penetrated the kidneys, thus inflicting a temporary paralysis.

When we came to skin him we found an old-fashioned lead bullet between the bones of his right forepaw. The entrance wound had so entirely healed over that hardly the trace of a scar remained. From what I know of the character of these beasts, I have no doubt that this ancient injury furnished the reason for his staying to attack us instead of departing with the other three lions over the hill.

Following the course of the river, we one afternoon came around a bend on a huge herd of mixed game that had been down to water. The river, a quite impassable barrier lay to our right, and an equally impassable precipitous ravine barred their flight ahead. They were forced to cross our front, quite close, within the hundred yards. We stopped to watch them go, a seemingly endless file of them, some very much frightened, bounding spasmodically as though stung; others more philosophical, loping easily and unconcernedly; still others to a few-even stopping for a moment to get a good view of us. The very young creatures, as always, bounced along absolutely stiff-legged, exactly like wooden animals suspended by an elastic, touching the ground and rebounding high, without a bend of the knee nor an apparent effort of the muscles. Young animals seem to have to learn how to bend their legs for the most efficient travel. The same is true of human babies as well. In this herd were, we estimated, some four or five hundred beasts.

While hunting near the foothills I came across the body of a large eagle suspended by one leg from the crotch of a limb. The bird's talon had missed its grip, probably on alighting, the tarsus had slipped through the crotch beyond the joint, the eagle had fallen forward, and had never been able to flop itself back to an upright position!

# XXI. THE RHINOCEROS

The rhinoceros is, with the giraffe, the hippopotamus, the gerenuk, and the camel, one of Africa's unbelievable animals. Nobody has bettered Kipling's description of him in the Just-so Stories: "A horn on his nose, piggy eyes, and few manners." He lives a self-centred life, wrapped up in the porcine contentment that broods within nor looks abroad over the land. When anything external to himself and his food and drink penetrates to his intelligence he makes a flurried fool of himself, rushing madly and frantically here and there in a hysterical effort either to destroy or get away from the cause of disturbance. He is the incarnation of a living and perpetual Grouch.

Generally he lives by himself, sometimes with his spouse, more rarely still with a third that is probably a grown-up son or daughter. I personally have never seen more than three in company. Some observers have reported larger bands, or rather collections, but, lacking other evidence, I should be inclined to suspect that some circumstances of food or water rather than a sense of gregariousness had attracted a number of individuals to one locality.

The rhinoceros has three objects in life: to fill his stomach with food and water, to stand absolutely motionless under a bush, and to imitate ant hills when he lies down in the tall grass. When disturbed at any of these occupations he snorts. The snort sounds exactly as though the safety valve of a locomotive had suddenly opened and as suddenly shut again after two seconds of escaping steam. Then he puts his head down and rushes madly in some direction, generally upwind. As he weighs about two tons, and can, in spite of his appearance, get over the ground nearly as fast as an ordinary horse, he is a truly imposing sight, especially since the innocent bystander generally happens to be upwind, and hence in the general path of progress. This is because the rhino's scent is his keenest sense, and through it he becomes aware, in the majority of times, of man's presence. His sight is very poor indeed; he cannot see clearly even a moving object much beyond fifty yards. He can, however, hear pretty well.

The novice, then, is subjected to what he calls a "vicious charge" on the part of the rhinoceros, merely because his scent was borne to the beast from upwind, and the rhino naturally runs away upwind. He opens fire, and has another thrilling adventure to relate. As a matter of fact, if he had approached from the other side, and then aroused the animal with a clod of earth, the beast would probably have "charged" away in identically the same direction. I am convinced from a fairly varied experience that this is the basis for most of the thrilling experiences with rhinoceroses.

But whatever the beast's first mental attitude, the danger is quite real. In the beginning he rushes, upwind in instinctive reaction against the strange scent. If he catches sight of the man at all, it must be after he has approached to pretty close range, for only at close range are the rhino's eyes effective. Then he is quite likely to finish what was at first a blind dash by a genuine charge. Whether this is from malice or from the panicky feeling that he is now too close to attempt to get away, I never was able determine. It is probably in the majority of cases the latter. This seems indicated by the fact that the rhino, if avoided in his first rush, will generally charge right through and keep on going. Occasionally, however, he will whirl and come back to the attack. There can then be no doubt that he actually intends mischief.

Nor must it be forgotten that with these animals, AS WITH ALL OTHERS, not enough account is taken of individual variation. They, as well as man, and as well as other animals, have their cowards, their fighters, their slothful and their enterprising. And, too, there seem to be truculent and peaceful districts. North of Mt. Kenia, between that peak and the Northern Guaso Nyero River, we saw many rhinos, none of which showed the slightest disposition to turn ugly. In fact, they were so peaceful that they scrabbled off as fast as they could go every time they either scented, heard, or SAW us; and in their flight they held their noses up, not down. In the wide angle between the Tana and Thika rivers, and comprising the Yatta Plains, and in the thickets of the Tsavo, the rhinoceroses generally ran nose down in a position of attack and were much inclined to let their angry passions master them at the sight of man. Thus we never had our safari scattered by rhinoceroses in the former district, while in the latter the boys were up trees six times in the course of one morning! Carl Akeley, with a moving picture machine, could not tease a charge out of a rhino in a dozen tries, while Dugmore, in a different part of the country, was so chivied about that he finally left the district to avoid killing any more of the brutes in self-defence!

The fact of the matter is that the rhinoceros is neither animated by the implacable man-destroying passion ascribed to him by the amateur hunter, nor is he so purposeless and haphazard in his rushes as some would have us believe. On being disturbed his instinct is to get away. He generally tries to get away in the direction of the disturbance, or upwind, as the case may be. If he catches sight of the cause of disturbance he is apt to try to trample and gore it, whatever it is. As his sight is short, he will sometimes so inflict punishment on unoffending bushes. In doing this he is probably not animated by a consuming destructive blind rage, but by a naturally pugnacious desire to eliminate sources of annoyance. Missing a definite object, he thunders right through and disappears without trying again to discover what has aroused him.

This first rush is not a charge in the sense that it is an attack on a definite object. It may not, and probably will not, amount to a charge at all, for the beast will blunder through without ever defining more clearly the object of his blind dash. That dash is likely, however, at any moment, to turn into a definite charge should the rhinoceros happen to catch sight of his disturber. Whether the impelling motive would then be a mistaken notion that on the part of the beast he was so close he had to fight, or just plain malice, would not matter. At such times the intended victim is not interested in the rhino's mental processes.

Owing to his size, his powerful armament, and his incredible quickness the rhinoceros is a dangerous animal at all times, to be treated with respect and due caution. This is proved by the number of white men, out of a sparse population, that are annually tossed and killed by the brutes, and by the promptness with which the natives take to trees-thorn trees at that!-when the cry of faru! is raised. As he comes rushing in your direction, head down and long weapon pointed, tail rigidly erect, ears up, the earth trembling with his tread and the air with his snorts, you suddenly feel very small and ineffective.

If you keep cool, however, it is probable that the encounter will result only in a lot of mental perturbation for the rhino and a bit of excitement for yourself. If there is any cover you should duck down behind it and move rapidly but quietly to one side or another of the line of advance. If there is no cover, you should crouch low and hold still. The chances are he will pass to one side or the other of you, and go snorting away into the distance. Keep your eye on him very closely. If he swerves definitely in your direction, AND DROPS HIS HEAD A LITTLE LOWER, it would be just as well to open fire. Provided the beast was still far enough away to give me "sea-room," I used to put a small bullet in the flesh of the outer part of the shoulder. The wound thus inflicted was not at all serious, but the shock of the bullet usually turned the beast. This was generally in the direction of the wounded shoulder, which would indicate that the brute turned toward the apparent source of the attack, probably for the purpose of getting even. At any rate, the shot turned the rush to one side, and the rhinoceros, as usual, went right on through. If, however, he seemed to mean business, or was too close for comfort, the point to aim for was the neck just above the lowered horn.

In my own experience I came to establish a "dead line" about twenty yards from myself. That seemed to be as near as I cared to let the brutes come. Up to that point I let them alone on the chance that they might swerve or change their minds, as they often did. But inside of twenty yards, whether the rhinoceros meant to charge me, or was merely running blindly by, did not particularly matter. Even in the latter case he might happen to catch sight of me and change his mind. Thus, looking over my notebook records, I find that I was "charged" forty odd times-that is to say, the rhinoceros rushed in my general direction. Of this lot I can be sure of but three, and possibly four, that certainly meant mischief. Six more came so directly at us, and continued so to come, that in spite of ourselves we were compelled to kill them. The rest were successfully dodged.

As I have heard old hunters of many times my experience, affirm that only in a few instances have they themselves been charged indubitably and with malice aforethought, it might be well to detail my reasons for believing myself definitely and not blindly attacked.

The first instance was that when B. killed his second trophy rhinoceros. The beast's companion refused to leave the dead body for a long time, but finally withdrew. On our approaching, however, and after we had been some moments occupied with the trophy, it returned and charged viciously. It was finally killed at fifteen yards.

The second instance was of a rhinoceros that got up from the grass sixty yards away, and came headlong in my direction. At the moment I was standing on the edge of a narrow eroded ravine, ten feet deep, with perpendicular sides. The rhinoceros came on bravely to the edge of this ravine-and stopped. Then he gave an exhibition of unmitigated bad temper most amusing to contemplate-from my safe position. He snorted, and stamped, and pawed the earth, and tramped up and down at a great rate. I sat on the opposite bank and laughed at him. This did not please him a bit, but after many short rushes to the edge of the ravine, he gave it up and departed slowly, his tail very erect and rigid. From the persistency with which he tried to get at me, I cannot but think he intended something of the sort from the first.

The third instance was much more aggravating. In company with Memba Sasa and Fundi I left camp early one morning to get a waterbuck. Four or five hundred yards out, however, we came on fresh buffalo signs, not an hour old. To one who knew anything of buffaloes' habits this seemed like an excellent chance, for at this time of the morning they should be feeding not far away preparatory to seeking cover for the day. Therefore we immediately took up the trail.

It led us over hills, through valleys, high grass, burned country, brush, thin scrub, and small woodland alternately. Unfortunately we had happened on these buffalo just as they were about changing district, and they were therefore travelling steadily. At times the trail was easy to follow and at other times we had to cast about very diligently to find traces of the direction even such huge animals had taken. It was interesting work, however, and we drew on steadily, keeping a sharp lookout ahead in case the buffalo had come to a halt in some shady thicket out of the sun. As the latter ascended the heavens and the scorching heat increased, our confidence in nearing our quarry ascended likewise, for we knew that buffaloes do not like great heat. Nevertheless this band continued straight on its way. I think now they must have got scent of our camp, and had therefore decided to move to one of the alternate and widely separated feeding grounds every herd keeps in its habitat. Only at noon, and after six hours of steady trailing, covering perhaps a dozen miles, did we catch them up.

From the start we had been bothered with rhinoceroses. Five times did we encounter them, standing almost squarely on the line of the spoor we were following. Then we had to make a wide quiet circle to leeward in order to avoid disturbing them, and were forced to a very minute search in order to pick up the buffalo tracks again on the other side. This was at once an anxiety and a delay, and we did not love those rhino.

Finally, at the very edge of the Yatta Plains we overtook the herd, resting for noon in a scattered thicket. Leaving Fundi, I, with Memba Sasa, stalked down to them. We crawled and crept by inches flat to the ground, which was so hot that it fairly burned the hand. The sun beat down on us fiercely, and the air was close and heavy even among the scanty grass tufts in which we were trying to get cover. It was very hard work indeed, but after a half hour of it we gained a thin bush not over thirty yards from a half dozen dark and indeterminate bodies dozing in the very centre of a brush patch. Cautiously I wiped the sweat from my eyes and raised my glasses. It was slow work and patient work, picking out and examining each individual beast from the mass. Finally the job was done. I let fall my glasses.

"Monumookee y'otey-all cows," I whispered to Memba Sasa.

We backed out of there inch by inch, with intention of circling a short distance to the leeward, and then trying the herd again lower down. But some awkward slight movement, probably on my part, caught the eye of one of those blessed cows. She threw up her head; instantly the whole thicket seemed alive with beasts. We could hear them crashing and stamping, breaking the brush, rushing headlong and stopping again; we could even catch momentary glimpses of dark bodies. After a few minutes we saw the mass of the herd emerge from the thicket five hundred yards away and flow up over the hill. There were probably a hundred and fifty of them, and, looking through my glasses, I saw among them two fine old bulls. They were of course not much alarmed, as only the one cow knew what it was all about anyway, and I suspected they would stop at the next thicket.

We had only one small canteen of water with us, but we divided that. It probably did us good, but the quantity was not sufficient to touch our thirst. For the remainder of the day we suffered rather severely, as the sun was fierce.

After a short interval we followed on after the buffaloes. Within a half mile beyond the crest of the hill over which they had disappeared was another thicket. At the very edge of the thicket, asleep under an outlying bush, stood one of the big bulls!

Luck seemed with us at last. The wind was right, and between us and the bull lay only four hundred yards of knee-high grass. All we had to do was to get down on our hands and knees, and, without further precautions, crawl up within range and pot him. That meant only a bit of hard, hot work.

When we were about halfway a rhinoceros suddenly arose from the grass between us and the buffalo, and about one hundred yards away.

What had aroused him, at that distance and upwind, I do not know. It hardly seemed possible that he could have heard us, for we were moving very quietly, and, as I say, we were downwind. However, there he was on his feet, sniffing now this way, now that, in search for what had alarmed him. We sank out of sight and lay low, fully expecting that the brute would make off.

For just twenty-five minutes by the watch that rhinoceros looked and looked deliberately in all directions while we lay hidden waiting for him to get over it. Sometimes he would start off quite confidently for fifty or sixty yards, so that we thought at last we were rid of him, but always he returned to the exact spot where we had first seen him, there to stamp, and blow. The buffalo paid no attention to these manifestations. I suppose everybody in jungleland is accustomed to rhinoceros bad temper over nothing. Twice he came in our direction, but both times gave it up after advancing twenty-five yards or so. We lay flat on our faces, the vertical sun slowly roasting us, and cursed that rhino.

Now the significance of this incident is twofold: first, the fact that, instead of rushing off at the first intimation of our presence, as would the average rhino, he went methodically to work to find us; second, that he displayed such remarkable perseverance as to keep at it nearly a half hour. This was a spirit quite at variance with that finding its expression in the blind rush or in the sudden passionate attack. From that point of view it seems to me that the interest and significance of the incident can hardly be overstated.

Four or five times we thought ourselves freed of the nuisance, but always, just as we were about to move on, back he came, as eager as ever to nose us out. Finally he gave it up, and, at a slow trot, started to go away from there. And out of the three hundred and sixty degrees of the circle where he might have gone he selected just our direction. Note that this was downwind for him, and that rhinoceroses usually escape upwind.

We laid very low, hoping that, as before, he would change his mind as to direction. But now he was no longer looking, but travelling. Nearer and nearer he came. We could see plainly his little eyes, and hear the regular swish, swish, swish of his thick legs brushing through the grass. The regularity of his trot never varied, but to me lying there directly in his path, he seemed to be coming on altogether too fast for comfort. From our low level he looked as big as a barn. Memba Sasa touched me lightly on the leg. I hated to shoot, but finally when he loomed fairly over us I saw it must be now or never. If I allowed him to come closer, he must indubitably catch the first movement of my gun and so charge right on us before I would have time to deliver even an ineffective shot. Therefore, most reluctantly, I placed the ivory bead of the great Holland gun just to the point of his shoulder and pulled the trigger. So close was he that as he toppled forward I instinctively, though unnecessarily of course, shrank back as though he might fall on me. Fortunately I had picked my spot properly, and no second shot was necessary. He fell just twenty-seven feet-nine yards—from where we lay!

The buffalo vanished into the blue. We were left with a dead rhino, which we did not want, twelve miles from camp, and no water. It was a hard hike back, but we made it finally, though nearly perished from thirst.

This beast, be it noted, did not charge us at all, but I consider him as one of the three undoubtedly animated by hostile intentions. Of the others I can, at this moment, remember five that might or might not have been actually and maliciously charging when they were killed or dodged. I am no mind reader for rhinoceros. Also I am willing to believe in their entirely altruistic intentions. Only, if they want to get the practical results of their said altruistic intentions they must really refrain from coming straight at me nearer than twenty yards. It has been stated that if one stands perfectly still until the rhinoceros is just six feet away, and then jumps sideways, the beast will pass him. I never happened to meet anybody who had acted on this theory. I suppose that such exist: though I doubt if any persistent exponent of the art is likely to exist long. Personally I like my own method, and stoutly maintain that within twenty yards it is up to the rhinoceros to begin to do the dodging.

# XXII. THE RHINOCEROS-(continued)

At first the traveller is pleased and curious over rhinoceros. After he has seen and encountered eight or ten, he begins to look upon them as an unmitigated nuisance. By the time he has done a week in thick rhino-infested scrub he gets fairly to hating them.

They are bad enough in the open plains, where they can be seen and avoided, but in the tall grass or the scrub they are a continuous anxiety. No cover seems small enough to reveal them. Often they will stand or lie absolutely immobile until you are within a very short distance, and then will outrageously break out. They are, in spite of their clumsy build, as quick and active as polo ponies, and are the only beasts I know of capable of leaping into full speed ahead from a recumbent position. In thorn scrub they are the worst, for there, no matter how alert the traveller may hold himself, he is likely to come around a bush smack on one. And a dozen times a day the throat-stopping, abrupt crash and smash to right or left brings him up all standing, his heart racing, the blood pounding through his veins. It is jumpy work, and is very hard on the temper. In the natural reaction from being startled into fits one snaps back to profanity. The cumulative effects of the epithets hurled after a departing and inconsiderately hasty rhinoceros may have done something toward ruining the temper of the species. It does not matter whether or not the individual beast proves dangerous; he is inevitably most startling. I have come in at night with my eyes fairly aching from spying for rhinos during a day's journey through high grass.

And, as a friend remarked, rhinos are such a mussy death. One poor chap, killed while we were away on our first trip, could not be moved from the spot where he had been trampled. A few shovelfuls of earth over the remains was all the rhinoceros had left possible.

Fortunately, in the thick stuff especially, it is often possible to avoid the chance rhinoceros through the warning given by the rhinoceros birds. These are birds about the size of a robin that accompany the beast everywhere. They sit in a row along his back occupying themselves with ticks and a good place to roost. Always they are peaceful and quiet until a human being approaches. Then they flutter a few feet into the air uttering a peculiar rapid chattering. Writers with more sentiment than sense of proportion assure us that this warns the rhinoceros of approaching danger! On the contrary, I always looked at it the other way. The rhinoceros birds thereby warned ME of danger, and I was duly thankful.

The safari boys stand quite justly in a holy awe of the rhino. The safari is strung out over a mile or two of country, as a usual thing, and a downwind rhino is sure to pierce some part of the line in his rush. Then down go the loads with a smash, and up the nearest trees swarm the boys. Usually their refuges are thorn trees, armed, even on the main trunk, with long sharp spikes. There is no difficulty in going up, but the gingerly coming down, after all the excitement has died, is a matter of deliberation and of voices uplifted in woe. Cuninghame tells of an inadequate slender and springy, but solitary, sapling into which swarmed half his safari on the advent of a rambunctious rhino. The tree swayed and bent and cracked alarmingly, threatening to dump the whole lot on the ground. At each crack the boys yelled. This attracted the rhinoceros, which immediately charged the tree full tilt. He hit square, the tree shivered and creaked, the boys wound their arms and legs around the slender support and howled frantically. Again and again rhinoceros drew back to repeat his butting of that tree. By the time Cuninghame reached the spot, the tree, with its despairing burden of black birds, was clinging to the soil by its last remaining roots.

In the Nairobi Club I met a gentleman with one arm gone at the shoulder. He told his story in a slightly bored and drawling voice, picking his words very carefully, and evidently most occupied with neither understating nor overstating the case. It seems he had been out, and had killed some sort of a buck. While his men were occupied with this, he strolled on alone to see what he could find. He found a rhinoceros, that charged viciously, and into which he emptied his gun.

"When I came to," he said, "it was just coming on dusk, and the lions were beginning to grunt. My arm was completely crushed, and I was badly bruised and knocked about. As near as I could remember I was fully ten miles from camp. A circle of carrion birds stood all about me not more than ten feet away, and a great many others were flapping over me and fighting in the air. These last were so close that I could feel the wind from their wings. It was rawther gruesome." He paused and thought a a moment, as though weighing his words. "In fact," he added with an air of final conviction, "it was QUITE gruesome!"

The most calm and imperturbable rhinoceros I ever saw was one that made us a call on the Thika River. It was just noon, and our boys were making camp after a morning's march. The usual racket was on, and the usual varied movement of rather confused industry. Suddenly silence fell. We came out of the tent to see the safari gazing spellbound in one direction. There was a rhinoceros wandering peaceably over the little knoll back of camp, and headed exactly in our direction. While we watched, he strolled through the edge of camp, descended the steep bank to the river's edge, drank, climbed the bank, strolled through camp again and departed over the hill. To us he paid not the slightest attention. It seems impossible to believe that he neither scented nor saw any evidences of human life in all that populated flat, especially when one considers how often these beasts will SEEM to become aware of man's presence by telepathy.* Perhaps he was the one exception to the whole race, and was a good-natured rhino.

    * Opposing theories are those of "instinct," and of slight
    causes, such a grasshoppers leaping before the hunter's
    feet, not noticed by the man approaching.

The babies are astonishing and amusing creatures, with blunt noses on which the horns are just beginning to form, and with even fewer manners than their parents. The mere fact of an 800-pound baby does not cease to be curious. They are truculent little creatures, and sometimes rather hard to avoid when they get on the warpath. Generally, as far as my observation goes, the mother gives birth to but one at a time. There may be occasional twin births, but I happen never to have met so interesting a family.

Rhinoceroses are still very numerous-too numerous. I have seen as many as fourteen in two hours, and probably could have found as many more if I had been searching for them. There is no doubt, however, that this species must be the first to disappear of the larger African animals. His great size combined with his 'orrid 'abits mark him for early destruction. No such dangerous lunatic can be allowed at large in a settled country, nor in a country where men are travelling constantly. The species will probably be preserved in appropriate restricted areas. It would be a great pity to have so perfect an example of the Prehistoric Pinhead wiped out completely. Elsewhere he will diminish, and finally disappear.

For one thing, and for one thing only, is the traveller indebted to the rhinoceros. The beast is lazy, large, and has an excellent eye for easy ways through. For this reason, as regards the question of good roads, he combines the excellent qualities of Public Sentiment, the Steam Roller, and the Expert Engineer. Through thorn thickets impenetrable to anything less armoured than a Dreadnaught like himself he clears excellent paths. Down and out of eroded ravines with perpendicular sides he makes excellent wide trails, tramped hard, on easy grades, often with zigzags to ease the slant. In some of the high country where the torrential rains wash hundreds of such gullies across the line of march it is hardly an exaggeration to say that travel would be practically impossible without the rhino trails wherewith to cross. Sometimes the perpendicular banks will extend for miles without offering any natural break down to the stream-bed. Since this is so I respectfully submit to Government the following proposal:

(a) That a limited number of these beasts shall be licensed as Trail Rhinos; and that all the rest shall be killed from the settled and regularly travelled districts.

(b) That these Trail Rhinos shall be suitably hobbled by short steel chains.

(c) That each Trail Rhino shall carry painted conspicuously on his side his serial number.

(d) That as a further precaution for public safety each Trail Rhino shall carry firmly attached to his tail a suitable red warning flag. Thus the well-known habit of the rhinoceros of elevating his tail rigidly when about to charge, or when in the act of charging, will fly the flag as a warning to travellers.

(e) That an official shall be appointed to be known as the Inspector of Rhinos whose duty it shall be to examine the hobbles, numbers and flags of all Trail Rhinos, and to keep the same in due working order and repair.

And I do submit to all and sundry that the above resolutions have as much sense to them as have most of the petitions submitted to Government by settlers in a new country.

# XXIII. THE HIPPO POOL

For a number of days we camped in a grove just above a dense jungle and not fifty paces from the bank of a deep and wide river. We could at various points push through light low undergrowth, or stoop beneath clear limbs, or emerge on tiny open banks and promontories to look out over the width of the stream. The river here was some three or four hundred feet wide. It cascaded down through various large boulders and sluiceways to fall bubbling and boiling into deep water; it then flowed still and sluggish for nearly a half mile and finally divided into channels around a number of wooded islands of different sizes. In the long still stretch dwelt about sixty hippopotamuses of all sizes.

During our stay these hippos led a life of alarmed and angry care. When we first arrived they were distributed picturesquely on banks or sandbars, or were lying in midstream. At once they disappeared under water. By the end of four or five minutes they began to come to the surface. Each beast took one disgusted look, snorted, and sank again. So hasty was his action that he did not even take time to get a full breath; consequently up he had to come in not more than two minutes, this time. The third submersion lasted less than a minute; and at the end of half hour of yelling we had the hippos alternating between the bottom of the river and the surface of the water about as fast as they could make a round trip, blowing like porpoises. It was a comical sight. And as some of the boys were always out watching the show, those hippos had no respite during the daylight hours. From a short distance inland the explosive blowing as they came to the surface sounded like the irregular exhaust of a steam-engine.

We camped at this spot four days; and never, in that length of time, during the daytime, did those hippopotamuses take any recreation and rest. To be sure after a little they calmed down sufficiently to remain on the surface for a half minute or so, instead of gasping a mouthful of air and plunging below at once; but below was where they considered they belonged most of the time. We got to recognize certain individuals. They would stare at us fixedly for a while; and then would glump down out of sight like submarines.

When I saw them thus floating with only the very top of the head and snout out of water, I for the first time appreciated why the Greeks had named them hippopotamuses-the river horses. With the heavy jowl hidden; and the prominent nostrils, the long reverse-curved nose, the wide eyes, and the little pointed ears alone visible, they resembled more than a little that sort of conventionalized and noble charger seen on the frieze of the Parthenon, or in the prancy paintings of the Renaissance.

There were hippopotamuses of all sizes and of all colours. The little ones, not bigger than a grand piano, were of flesh pink. Those half-grown were mottled with pink and black in blotches. The adults were almost invariably all dark, though a few of them retained still a small pink spot or so-a sort of persistence in mature years of the eternal boy-, I suppose. All were very sleek and shiny with the wet; and they had a fashion of suddenly and violently wiggling one or the other or both of their little ears in ridiculous contrast to the fixed stare of their bung eyes. Generally they had nothing to say as to the situation, though occasionally some exasperated old codger would utter a grumbling bellow.

The ground vegetation for a good quarter mile from the river bank was entirely destroyed, and the earth beaten and packed hard by these animals. Landing trails had been made leading out from the water by easy and regular grades. These trails were about two feet wide and worn a foot or so deep. They differed from the rhino trails, from which they could be easily distinguished, in that they showed distinctly two parallel tracks separated from each other by a slight ridge. In other words, the hippo waddles. These trails we found as far as four and five miles inland. They were used, of course, only at night; and led invariably to lush and heavy feed. While we were encamped there, the country on our side the river was not used by our particular herd of hippos. One night, however, we were awakened by a tremendous rending crash of breaking bushes, followed by an instant's silence and then the outbreak of a babel of voices. Then we heard a prolonged sw-i-sh-sh-sh, exactly like the launching of a big boat. A hippo had blundered out the wrong side the river, and fairly into our camp.

In rivers such as the Tana these great beasts are most extraordinarily abundant. Directly in front of our camp, for example, were three separate herds which contained respectively about sixty, forty, and twenty-five head. Within two miles below camp were three other big pools each with its population; while a walk of a mile above showed about as many more. This sort of thing obtained for practically the whole length of the river-hundreds of miles. Furthermore, every little tributary stream, no matter how small, provided it can muster a pool or so deep enough to submerge so large an animal, has its faithful band. I have known of a hippo quite happily occupying a ditch pool ten feet wide and fifteen feet long. There was literally not room enough for the beast to turn around; he had to go in at one end and out at the other! Each lake, too, is alive with them; and both lakes and rivers are many.

Nobody disturbs hippos, save for trophies and an occasional supply of meat for the men or of cooking fat for the kitchen. Therefore they wax fat and sassy, and will long continue to flourish in the land.

It takes time to kill a hippo, provided one is wanted. The mark is small, and generally it is impossible to tell whether or not the bullet has reached the brain. Harmed or whole the beast sinks anyway. Some hours later the distention of the stomach will float the body. Therefore the only decent way to do is to take the shot, and then wait a half day to see whether or not you have missed. There are always plenty of volunteers in camp to watch the pool, for the boys are extravagantly fond of hippo meat. Then it is necessary to manoeuvre a rope on the carcass, often a matter of great difficulty, for the other hippos bellow and snort and try to live up to the circus posters of the Blood-sweating Behemoth of Holy Writ, and the crocodiles like dark meat very much. Usually one offers especial reward to volunteers, and shoots into the water to frighten the beasts. The volunteer dashes rapidly across the shallows, makes a swift plunge, and clambers out on the floating body as onto a raft.

Then he makes fast the rope, and everybody tails on and tows the whole outfit ashore. On one occasion the volunteer produced a fish line and actually caught a small fish from the floating carcass! This sounds like a good one; but I saw it with my own two eyes.

It was at the hippo pool camp that we first became acquainted with Funny Face.

Funny Face was the smallest, furriest little monkey you ever saw. I never cared for monkeys before; but this one was altogether engaging. He had thick soft fur almost like that on a Persian cat, and a tiny human black face, and hands that emerged from a ruff; and he was about as big as old-fashioned dolls used to be before they began to try to imitate real babies with them. That is to say, he was that big when we said farewell to him. When we first knew him, had he stood in a half pint measure he could just have seen over the rim. We caught him in a little thorn ravine all by himself, a fact that perhaps indicates that his mother had been killed, or perhaps that he, like a good little Funny Face, was merely staying where he was told while she was away. At any rate he fought savagely, according to his small powers. We took him ignominiously by the scruff of the neck, haled him to camp, and dumped him down on Billy. Billy constructed him a beautiful belt by sacrificing part of a kodak strap (mine), and tied him to a chop box filled with dry grass. Thenceforth this became Funny Face's castle, at home and on the march.

Within a few hours his confidence in life was restored. He accepted small articles of food from our hands, eyeing us intently, retired and examined them. As they all proved desirable, he rapidly came to the conclusion that these new large strange monkeys, while not so beautiful and agile as his own people, were nevertheless a good sort after all. Therefore he took us into his confidence. By next day he was quite tame, would submit to being picked up without struggling, and had ceased trying to take an end off our various fingers. In fact when the finger was presented, he would seize it in both small black hands; convey it to his mouth; give it several mild and gentle love-chews; and then, clasping it with all four hands, would draw himself up like a little athlete and seat himself upright on the outspread palm. Thence he would survey the world, wrinkling up his tiny brow.

This chastened and scholarly attitude of mind lasted for four or five days. Then Funny Face concluded that he understood all about it, had settled satisfactorily to himself all the problems of the world and his relations to it, and had arrived at a good working basis for life. Therefore these questions ceased to occupy him. He dismissed them from his mind completely, and gave himself over to light-hearted frivolity.

His disposition was flighty but full of elusive charm. You deprecated his lack of serious purpose in life, disapproved heartily of his irresponsibility, but you fell to his engaging qualities. He was a typical example of the lovable good-for-naught. Nothing retained his attention for two consecutive minutes. If he seized a nut and started for his chop box with it, the chances were he would drop it and forget all about it in the interest excited by a crawling ant or the colour of a flower. His elfish face was always alight with the play of emotions and of flashing changing interests. He was greatly given to starting off on very important errands, which he forgot before he arrived.

In this he contrasted strangely with his friend Darwin. Darwin was another monkey of the same species, caught about a week later. Darwin's face was sober and pondering, and his methods direct and effective. No side excursions into the brilliant though evanescent fields of fancy diverted him from his ends. These were, generally, to get the most and best food and the warmest corner for sleep. When he had acquired a nut, a kernel of corn, or a piece of fruit, he sat him down and examined it thoroughly and conscientiously and then, conscientiously and thoroughly, he devoured it. No extraneous interest could distract his attention; not for a moment. That he had sounded the seriousness of life is proved by the fact that he had observed and understood the flighty character of Funny Face. When Funny Face acquired a titbit, Darwin took up a hump-backed position near at hand, his bright little eyes fixed on his friend's activities. Funny Face would nibble relishingly at his prune for a moment or so; then an altogether astonishing butterfly would flitter by just overhead. Funny Face, lost in ecstasy would gaze skyward after the departing marvel. This was Darwin's opportunity. In two hops he was at Funny Face's side. With great deliberation, but most businesslike directness, Darwin disengaged Funny Face's unresisting fingers from the prune, seized it, and retired. Funny Face never knew it; his soul was far away after the blazoned wonder, and when it returned, it was not to prunes at all. They were forgotten, and his wandering eye focussed back to a bright button in the grass. Thus by strict attention to business did Darwin prosper.

Darwin's attitude was always serious, and his expression grave. When he condescended to romp with Funny Face one could see that it was not for the mere joy of sport, but for the purposes of relaxation. If offered a gift he always examined it seriously before finally accepting it, turning it over and over in his hands, and considering it with wrinkled brow. If you offered anything to Funny Face, no matter what, he dashed up, seized it on the fly, departed at speed uttering grateful low chatterings; probably dropped and forgot it in the excitement of something new before he had even looked to see what it was.

"These people," said Darwin to himself, "on the whole, and as an average, seem to give me appropriate and pleasing gifts. To be sure, it is always well to see that they don't try to bunco me with olive stones or such worthless trash, but still I believe they are worth cultivating and standing in with."

"It strikes me," observed Funny Face to himself, "that my adorable Memsahib and my beloved bwana have been very kind to me to-day, though I don't remember precisely how. But I certainly do love them!"

We cut good sized holes on each of the four sides of their chop box to afford them ventilation on the march. The box was always carried on one of the safari boy's heads: and Funny Face and Darwin gazed forth with great interest. It was very amusing to see the big negro striding jauntily along under his light burden; the large brown winking eyes glued to two of the apertures. When we arrived in camp and threw the box cover open, they hopped forth, shook themselves, examined their immediate surroundings and proceeded to take a little exercise. When anything alarmed them, such as the shadow of a passing hawk, they skittered madly up the nearest thing in sight-tent pole, tree, or human form— and scolded indignantly or chittered in a low tone according to the degree of their terror. When Funny Face was very young, indeed, the grass near camp caught fire. After the excitement was over we found him completely buried in the straw of his box, crouched, and whimpering like a child. As he could hardly, at his tender age, have had any previous experience with fire, this instinctive fear was to me very interesting.

The monkeys had only one genuine enemy. That was an innocent plush lion named Little Simba. It had been given us in joke before we left California, we had tucked it into an odd corner of our trunk, had discovered it there, carried it on safari out of sheer idleness, and lo! it had become an important member of the expedition. Every morning Mahomet or Yusuf packed it-or rather him-carefully away in the tin box. Promptly at the end of the day's march Little Simba was haled forth and set in a place of honour in the centre of the table, and reigned there-or sometimes in a little grass jungle constructed by his faithful servitors-until the march was again resumed. His job in life was to look after our hunting luck. When he failed to get us what we wanted, he was punished; when he procured us what we desired he was rewarded by having his tail sewed on afresh, or by being presented with new black thread whiskers, or even a tiny blanket of Mericani against the cold. This last was an especial favour for finally getting us the greater kudu. Naturally as we did all this in the spirit of an idle joke our rewards and punishments were rather desultory. To our surprise, however, we soon found that our boys took Little Simba quite seriously. He was a fetish, a little god, a power of good or bad luck. We did not appreciate this point until one evening, after a rather disappointing day, Mahomet came to us bearing Little Simba in his hand.

"Bwana," said he respectfully, "is it enough that I shut Simba in the tin box, or do you wish to flog him?"

On one very disgraceful occasion, when everything went wrong, we plucked Little Simba from his high throne and with him made a beautiful drop-kick out into the tall grass. There, in a loud tone of voice, we sternly bade him lie until the morrow. The camp was bung-eyed. It is not given to every people to treat its gods in such fashion: indeed, in very deed, great is the white man! To be fair, having published Little Simba's disgrace, we should publish also Little Simba's triumph: to tell how, at the end of a certain very lucky three months' safari he was perched atop a pole and carried into town triumphantly at the head of a howling, singing procession of a hundred men. He returned to America, and now, having retired from active professional life, is leading an honoured old age among the trophies he helped to procure.

Funny Face first met Little Simba when on an early investigating tour. With considerable difficulty he had shinnied up the table leg, and had hoisted himself over the awkwardly projecting table edge. When almost within reach of the fascinating affairs displayed atop, he looked straight up into the face of Little Simba! Funny Face shrieked aloud, let go all holds and fell off flat on his back. Recovering immediately, he climbed just as high as he could, and proceeded, during the next hour, to relieve his feelings by the most insulting chatterings and grimaces. He never recovered from this initial experience. All that was necessary to evoke all sorts of monkey talk was to produce Little Simba. Against his benign plush front then broke a storm of remonstrance. He became the object of slow advances and sudden scurrying, shrieking retreats, that lasted just as long as he stayed there, and never got any farther than a certain quite conservative point. Little Simba did not mind. He was too busy being a god.

# XXIV. BUFFALO

The Cape Buffalo is one of the four dangerous kinds of African big game; of which the other three are the lion, the rhinoceros, and the elephant. These latter are familiar to us in zoological gardens, although the African and larger form of the rhinoceros and elephant are seldom or never seen in captivity. But buffaloes are as yet unrepresented in our living collections. They are huge beasts, tremendous from any point of view, whether considered in height, in mass, or in power. At the shoulder they stand from just under five feet to just under six feet in height; they are short legged, heavy bodied bull necked, thick in every dimension. In colour they are black as to hair, and slate gray as to skin; so that the individual impression depends on the thickness of the coat. They wear their horns parted in the middle, sweeping smoothly away in the curves of two great bosses either side the head. A good trophy will measure in spread from forty inches to four feet. Four men will be required to carry in the head alone. As buffaloes when disturbed or suspicious have a habit of thrusting their noses up and forward, that position will cling to one's memory as the most typical of the species.

A great many hunters rank the buffalo first among the dangerous beasts. This is not my own opinion, but he is certainly dangerous enough. He possesses the size, power, and truculence of the rhinoceros, together with all that animal's keenness of scent and hearing but with a sharpness of vision the rhinoceros has not. While not as clever as either the lion or the elephant, he is tricky enough when angered to circle back for the purpose of attacking his pursuers in the rear or flank, and to arrange rather ingenious ambushes for the same purpose. He is rather more tenacious of life than the rhinoceros, and will carry away an extraordinary quantity of big bullets. Add to these considerations the facts that buffaloes go in herds; and that, barring luck, chances are about even they will have to be followed into the thickest cover, it can readily be seen that their pursuit is exciting.

The problem would be simplified were one able or willing to slip into the thicket or up to the grazing herd and kill the nearest beast that offers. As a matter of fact an ordinary herd will contain only two or three bulls worth shooting; and it is the hunter's delicate task to glide and crawl here and there, with due regard for sight, scent and sound, until he has picked one of these from the scores of undesirables. Many times will he worm his way by inches toward the great black bodies half defined in the screen of thick undergrowth only to find that he has stalked cows or small bulls. Then inch by inch he must back out again, unable to see twenty yards to either side, guiding himself by the probabilities of the faint chance breezes in the thicket. To right and left he hears the quiet continued crop, crop, crop, sound of animals grazing. The sweat runs down his face in streams, and blinds his eyes, but only occasionally and with the utmost caution can he raise his hand-or, better, lower his head-to clear his vision. When at last he has withdrawn from the danger zone, he wipes his face, takes a drink from the canteen, and tries again. Sooner or later his presence comes to the notice of some old cow. Behind the leafy screen where unsuspected she has been standing comes the most unexpected and heart-jumping crash! Instantly the jungle all about roars into life. The great bodies of the alarmed beasts hurl themselves through the thicket, smash! bang! crash! smash! as though a tornado were uprooting the forest. Then abruptly a complete silence! This lasts but ten seconds or so; then off rushes the wild stampede in another direction; only again to come to a listening halt of breathless stillness. So the hunter, unable to see anything, and feeling very small, huddles with his gunbearers in a compact group, listening to the wild surging short rushes, now this way, now that, hoping that the stampede may not run over him. If by chance it does, he has his two shots and the possibility of hugging a tree while the rush divides around him. The latter is the most likely; a single buffalo is hard enough to stop with two shots, let alone a herd. And yet, sometimes, the mere flash and noise will suffice to turn them, provided they are not actually trying to attack, but only rushing indefinitely about. Probably a man can experience few more thrilling moments than he will enjoy standing in one of the small leafy rooms of an African jungle while several hundred tons of buffalo crash back and forth all around him.

In the best of circumstances it is only rarely that having identified his big bull, the hunter can deliver a knockdown blow. The beast is extraordinarily vital, and in addition it is exceedingly difficult to get a fair, open shot. Then from the danger of being trampled down by the blind and senseless stampede of the herd he passes to the more defined peril from an angered and cunning single animal. The majority of fatalities in hunting buffaloes happen while following wounded beasts. A flank charge at close range may catch the most experienced man; and even when clearly seen, it is difficult to stop. The buffalo's wide bosses are a helmet to his brain, and the body shot is always chancy. The beast tosses his victim, or tramples him, or pushes him against a tree to crush him like a fly.

He who would get his trophy, however, is not always-perhaps is not generally-forced into the thicket to get it. When not much disturbed, buffaloes are in the habit of grazing out into the open just before dark; and of returning to their thicket cover only well after sunrise. If the hunter can arrange to meet his herd at such a time, he stands a very good chance of getting a clear shot. The job then requires merely ordinary caution and manoeuvring; and the only danger, outside the ever-present one from the wounded beast, is that the herd may charge over him deliberately. Therefore it is well to keep out of sight.

The difficulty generally is to locate your beasts. They wander all night, and must be blundered upon in the early morning before they have drifted back into the thickets. Sometimes, by sending skilled trackers in several directions, they can be traced to where they have entered cover. A messenger then brings the white man to the place, and every one tries to guess at what spot the buffaloes are likely to emerge for their evening stroll. It is remarkably easy to make a wrong guess, and the remaining daylight is rarely sufficient to repair a mistake. And also, in the case of a herd ranging a wide country with much tall grass and several drinking holes, it is rather difficult, without very good luck, to locate them on any given night or morning. A few herds, a very few, may have fixed habits, and so prove easy hunting.

These difficulties, while in no way formidable, are real enough in their small way; but they are immensely increased when the herds have been often disturbed. Disturbance need not necessarily mean shooting. In countries unvisited by white men often the pastoral natives will so annoy the buffalo by shoutings and other means, whenever they appear near the tame cattle, that the huge beasts will come practically nocturnal. In that case only the rankest luck will avail to get a man a chance in the open. The herds cling to cover until after sundown and just at dusk; and they return again very soon after the first streaks of dawn. If the hunter just happens to be at the exact spot, he may get a twilight shot when the glimmering ivory of his front sight is barely visible. Otherwise he must go into the thicket.

As an illustration of the first condition might be instanced an afternoon on the Tana. The weather was very hot. We had sent three lots of men out in different directions, each under the leadership of one of the gunbearers, to scout, while we took it easy in the shade of our banda, or grass shelter, on the bank of the river. About one o'clock a messenger came into camp reporting that the men under Mavrouki had traced a herd to its lying-down place. We took our heavy guns and started.

The way led through thin scrub up the long slope of a hill that broke on the other side into undulating grass ridges that ended in a range of hills. These were about four or five miles distant, and thinly wooded on sides and lower slopes with what resembled a small live-oak growth. Among these trees, our guide told us, the buffalo had first been sighted.

The sun was very hot, and all the animals were still. We saw impalla in the scrub, and many giraffes and bucks on the plains. After an hour and a half's walk we entered the parklike groves at the foot of the hills, and our guide began to proceed more cautiously. He moved forward a few feet, peered about, retraced his steps. Suddenly his face broke into a broad grin. Following his indication we looked up, and there in a tree almost above us roosted one of our boys sound asleep! We whistled at him. Thereupon he awoke, tried to look very alert, and pointed in the direction we should go. After an interval we picked up another sentinel, and another, and another until, passed on thus from one to the next, we traced the movements of the herd. Finally we came upon Mavrouki and Simba under a bush. From them, in whispers, we learned that the buffalo were karibu sana-very near; that they had fed this far, and were now lying in the long grass just ahead. Leaving the men, we now continued our forward movement on hands and knees, in single file. It was very hot work, for the sun beat square down on us, and the tall grass kept off every breath of air. Every few moments we rested, lying on our faces. Occasionally, when the grass shortened, or the slant of ground tended to expose us, we lay quite flat and hitched forward an inch at a time by the strength of our toes. This was very severe work indeed, and we were drenched in perspiration. In fact, as I had been feeling quite ill all day, it became rather doubtful whether I could stand the pace.

However after a while we managed to drop down into an eroded deep little ravine. Here the air was like that of a furnace, but at least we could walk upright for a few rods. This we did, with the most extraordinary precautions against even the breaking of a twig or the rolling of a pebble. Then we clambered to the top of the bank, wormed our way forward another fifty feet to the shelter of a tiny bush, and stretched out to recuperate. We lay there some time, sheltered from the sun. Then ahead of us suddenly rumbled a deep bellow. We were fairly upon the herd!

Cautiously F., who was nearest the centre of the bush, raised himself alongside the stem to look. He could see where the beasts were lying, not fifty yards away, but he could make out nothing but the fact of great black bodies taking their ease in the grass under the shade of trees. So much he reported to us; then rose again to keep watch.

Thus we waited the rest of the afternoon. The sun dipped at last toward the west, a faint irregular breeze wandered down from the hills, certain birds awoke and uttered their clear calls, an unsuspected kongoni stepped from the shade of a tree over the way and began to crop the grass, the shadows were lengthening through the trees. Then ahead of us an uneasiness ran through the herd. We in the grass could hear the mutterings and grumblings of many great animals. Suddenly F. snapped his fingers, stooped low and darted forward. We scrambled to our feet and followed.

Across a short open space we ran, bent double to the shelter of a big ant hill. Peering over the top of this we found ourselves within sixty yards of a long compact column of the great black beasts, moving forward orderly to the left, the points of the cow's horns, curved up and in, tossing slowly as the animals walked. On the flank of the herd was a big gray bull.

It had been agreed that B. was to have the shot. Therefore he opened fire with his 405 Winchester, a weapon altogether too light for this sort of work. At the shot the herd dashed forward to an open grass meadow a few rods away, wheeled and faced back in a compact mass, their noses thrust up and out in their typical fashion, trying with all their senses to locate the cause of the disturbance.

Taking advantage both of the scattered cover, and the half light of the shadows we slipped forward as rapidly and as unobtrusively as we could to the edge of the grass meadow. Here we came to a stand eighty yards from the buffaloes. They stood compactly like a herd of cattle, staring, tossing their heads, moving slightly, their wild eyes searching for us. I saw several good bulls, but always they moved where it was impossible to shoot without danger of getting the wrong beast. Finally my chance came; I planted a pair of Holland bullets in the shoulder of one of them.

The herd broke away to the right, sweeping past us at close range. My bull ran thirty yards with them, then went down stone dead. When we examined him we found the hole made by B.'s Winchester bullet; so that quite unintentionally and by accident I had fired at the same beast. This was lucky. The trophy, by hunter's law, of course, belonged to B.

Therefore F. and I alone followed on after the herd. It was now coming on dusk. Within a hundred yards we began to see scattered beasts. The formation of the herd had broken.

Some had gone on in flight, while others in small scattered groups would stop to stare back, and would then move slowly on for a few paces before stopping again. Among these I made out a bull facing us about a hundred and twenty-five yards away, and managed to stagger him, but could not bring him down.

Now occurred an incident which I should hesitate to relate were it not that both F. and myself saw it. We have since talked it over, compared our recollections, and found them to coincide in every particular.

As we moved cautiously in pursuit of the slowly retreating herd three cows broke back and came running down past us. We ducked aside and hid, of course, but noticed that of the three two were very young, while one was so old that she had become fairly emaciated, a very unusual thing with buffaloes. We then followed the herd for twenty minutes, or until twilight, when we turned back. About halfway down the slope we again met the three cows, returning. They passed us within twenty yards, but paid us no attention whatever. The old cow was coming along very reluctantly, hanging back at every step, and every once in a while swinging her head viciously at one or the other of her two companions. These escorted her on either side, and a little to the rear. They were plainly urging her forward, and did not hesitate to dig her in the ribs with their horns whenever she turned especially obstinate. In fact they acted exactly like a pair of cowboys HERDING a recalcitrant animal back to its band and I have no doubt at all that when they first by us the old lady was making a break for liberty in the wrong direction, AND THAT THE TWO YOUNGER COWS WERE TRYING TO ROUND HER BACK! Whether they were her daughters or not is problematical; but it certainly seemed that they were taking care of her and trying to prevent her running back where it was dangerous to go. I never heard of a similar case, though Herbert Ward* mentions, without particulars that elephants AND BUFFALOES will assist each other WHEN WOUNDED.

   * A Voice from the Congo.

After passing these we returned to where B. and the men, who had now come up, had prepared the dead bull for transportation. We started at once, travelling by the stars, shouting and singing to discourage the lions, but did not reach camp until well into the night.


## XXV. THE BUFFALO-continued


Some months later, and many hundreds of miles farther south, Billy and I found ourselves alone with twenty men, and two weeks to pass until C.-our companion at the time-should return from a long journey out with a wounded man. By slow stages, and relaying back and forth, we landed in a valley so beautiful in every way that we resolved to stay as long as possible. This could be but five days at most. At the end of that time we must start for our prearranged rendezvous with C.

The valley was in the shape of an ellipse, the sides of which were formed by great clifflike mountains, and the other two by hills lower, but still of considerable boldness and size. The longest radius was perhaps six or eight miles, and the shortest three or four. At one end a canyon dropped away to a lower level, and at the other a pass in the hills gave over to the country of the Narassara River. The name of the valley was Lengeetoto.

From the great mountains flowed many brooks of clear sparkling water, that ran beneath the most beautiful of open jungles, to unite finally in one main stream that disappeared down the canyon. Between these brooks were low broad rolling hills, sometimes grass covered, sometimes grown thinly with bushes. Where they headed in the mountains, long stringers of forest trees ran up to blocklike groves, apparently pasted like wafers against the base of the cliffs, but in reality occupying spacious slopes below them.

We decided to camp at the foot of a long grass slant within a hundred yards of the trees along one of the small streams. Before us we had the sweep of brown grass rising to a clear cut skyline; and all about us the distant great hills behind which the day dawned and fell. One afternoon a herd of giraffes stood silhouetted on this skyline quite a half hour gazing curiously down on our camp. Hartebeeste and zebra swarmed in the grassy openings; and impalla in the brush. We saw sing-sing and steinbuck, and other animals, and heard lions nearly every night. But principally we elected to stay because a herd of buffaloes ranged the foothills and dwelt in the groves of forest trees under the cliffs. We wanted a buffalo; and as Lengeetoto is practically unknown to white men, we thought this a good chance to get one. In that I reckoned without the fact that at certain seasons the Masai bring their cattle in, and at such times annoy the buffalo all they can.

We started out well enough. I sent Memba Sasa with two men to locate the herd. About three o'clock a messenger came to camp after me. We plunged through our own jungle, crossed a low swell, traversed another jungle, and got in touch with the other two men. They reported the buffalo had entered the thicket a few hundred yards below us. Cautiously reconnoitering the ground it soon became evident that we would be forced more definitely to locate the herd. To be sure, they had entered the stream jungle at a known point, but there could be no telling how far they might continue in the thicket, nor on what side of it they would emerge at sundown. Therefore we commenced cautiously and slowly follow the trail.

The going was very thick, naturally, and we could not see very far ahead. Our object was not now to try for a bull, but merely to find where the herd was feeding, in order that we might wait for it to come out. However, we were brought to a stand, in the middle of a jungle of green leaves, by the cropping sound of a beast grazing just the other side of a bush. We could not see it, and we stood stock still in the hope of escaping discovery ourselves. But an instant later a sudden crash of wood told us we had been seen. It was near work. The gunbearers crouched close to me. I held the heavy double gun ready. If the beast had elected to charge I would have had less than ten yards within which to stop it. Fortunately it did not do so. But instantly the herd was afoot and off at full speed. A locomotive amuck in a kindling pile could have made no more appalling a succession of rending crashes than did those heavy animals rushing here and there through the thick woody growth. We could see nothing. Twice the rush started in our direction, but stopped as suddenly as it had begun, to be succeeded by absolute stillness when everything, ourselves included, held its breath to listen. Finally, the first panic over, the herd started definitely away downstream. We ran as fast as we could out of the jungle to a commanding position on the hill. Thence we could determine the course of the herd. It continued on downstream as far as we could follow the sounds in the convolutions of the hills. Realizing that it would improbably recover enough from its alarmed condition to resume its regular habits that day, we returned to camp.

Next morning Memba Sasa and I were afield before daylight. We took no other men. In hunting I am a strong disbeliever in the common habit of trailing along a small army. It is simple enough, in case the kill is made, to send back for help. No matter how skilful your men are at stalking, the chances of alarming the game are greatly increased by numbers; while the possibilities of misunderstanding the plan of campaign, and so getting into the wrong place at the wrong time, are infinite. Alone, or with one gunbearer, a man can slip in and out a herd of formidable animals with the least chances of danger. Merely going out after camp meat is of course a different matter.

We did not follow in the direction taken by the herd the night before, but struck off toward the opposite side of the valley. For two hours we searched the wooded country at the base of the cliff mountains, working slowly around the circle, examining every inlet, ravine and gully. Plenty of other sorts of game we saw, including elephant tracks not a half hour old; but no buffalo. About eight o'clock, however, while looking through my glasses, I caught sight of some tiny chunky black dots crawling along below the mountains diagonally across the valley, and somewhat over three miles away. We started in that direction as fast as we could walk. At the end of an hour we surmounted the last swell, and stood at the edge of a steep drop. Immediately below us flowed a good-sized stream through a high jungle over the tops of which we looked to a triangular gentle slope overgrown with scattered bushes and high grass. Beyond this again ran another jungle, angling up hill from the first, to end in a forest of trees about thirty or forty acres in extent. This jungle and these trees were backed up against the slope of the mountain. The buffaloes we had first seen above the grove: they must now have sought cover among either the trees or the lower jungle, and it seemed reasonable that the beasts would emerge on the grass and bush area late in the afternoon. Therefore Memba Sasa and I selected good comfortable sheltered spots, leaned our backs against rocks, and resigned ourselves to long patience. It was now about nine o'clock in the morning, and we could not expect our game to come out before half past three at earliest. We could not, however, go away to come back later because of the chance that the buffaloes might take it into their heads to go travelling. I had been fooled that way before. For this reason, also, it was necessary, every five minutes or so, to examine carefully all our boundaries; lest the beasts might be slipping away through the cover.

The hours passed very slowly. We made lunch last as long as possible. I had in my pocket a small edition of Hawthorne's "The House of the Seven Gables," which I read, pausing every few minutes to raise my glasses for the periodical examination of the country. The mental focussing back from the pale gray half light of Hawthorne's New England to the actuality of wild Africa was a most extraordinary experience.

Through the heat of the day the world lay absolutely silent. At about half-past three, however, we heard rumblings and low bellows from the trees a half mile away. I repocketed Hawthorne, and aroused myself to continuous alertness.

The ensuing two hours passed more slowly than all the rest of the day, for we were constantly on the lookout. The buffaloes delayed most singularly, seemingly reluctant to leave their deep cover. The sun dropped behind the mountains, and their shadow commenced to climb the opposite range. I glanced at my watch. We had not more than a half hour of daylight left.

Fifteen minutes of this passed. It began to look as though our long and monotonous wait had been quite in vain; when, right below us, and perhaps five hundred yards away, four great black bodies fed leisurely from the bushes. Three of them we could see plainly. Two were bulls of fair size. The fourth, half concealed in the brush, was by far the biggest of the lot.

In order to reach them we would have to slip down the face of the hill on which we sat, cross the stream jungle at the bottom, climb out the other side, and make our stalk to within range. With a half hour more of daylight this would have been comparatively easy, but in such circumstances it is difficult to move at the same time rapidly and unseen. However, we decided to make the attempt. To that end we disencumbered ourselves of all our extras-lunch box, book, kodak, glasses, etc.-and wormed our way as rapidly as possible toward the bottom of the hill. We utilized the cover as much as we were able, but nevertheless breathed a sigh of relief when we had dropped below the line of the jungle. We wasted very little time crossing the latter, save for precautions against noise. Even in my haste, however, I had opportunity to notice its high and austere character, with the arching overhead vines, and the clear freedom from undergrowth in its heart. Across this cleared space we ran at full speed, crouching below the grasp of the vines, splashed across the brook and dashed up the other bank. Only a faint glimmer of light lingered in the jungle. At the upper edge we paused, collected ourselves, and pushed cautiously through the thick border-screen of bush.

The twilight was just fading into dusk. Of course we had taken our bearings from the other hill; so now, after reassuring ourselves of them, we began to wriggle our way at a great pace through the high grass. Our calculations were quite accurate. We stalked successfully, and at last, drenched in sweat, found ourselves lying flat within ten yards of a small bush behind which we could make out dimly the black mass of the largest beast we had seen from across the way.

Although it was now practically dark, we had the game in our own hands. From our low position the animal, once it fed forward from behind the single small bush, would be plainly outlined against the sky, and at ten yards I should be able to place my heavy bullets properly, even in the dark. Therefore, quite easy in our minds, we lay flat and rested. At the end of twenty seconds the animal began to step forward. I levelled my double gun, ready to press trigger the moment the shoulder appeared in the clear. Then against the saffron sky emerged the ugly outline and two upstanding horns of a rhinoceros!

"Faru!" I whispered disgustedly to Memba Sasa. With infinite pains we backed out, then retreated to a safe distance. It was of course now too late to hunt up the three genuine buffaloes of this ill-assorted group.

In fact our main necessity was to get through the river jungle before the afterglow had faded from the sky, leaving us in pitch darkness. I sent Memba Sasa across to pick up the effects we had left on the opposite ridge, while I myself struck directly across the flat toward camp.

I had plunged ahead thus, for two or three hundred yards, when I was brought up short by the violent snort of a rhinoceros just off the starboard bow. He was very close, but I was unable to locate him in the dusk. A cautious retreat and change of course cleared me from him, and I was about to start on again full speed when once more I was halted by another rhinoceros, this time dead ahead. Attempting to back away from him, I aroused another in my rear; and as though this were not enough a fourth opened up to the left.

It was absolutely impossible to see anything ten yards away unless it happened to be silhouetted against the sky. I backed cautiously toward a little bush, with a vague idea of having something to dodge around. As the old hunter said when, unarmed, he met the bear, "Anything, even a newspaper, would have come handy." To my great joy I backed against a conical ant hill four or five feet high. This I ascended and began anti-rhino demonstrations. I had no time to fool with rhinos, anyway. I wanted to get through that jungle before the leopards left their family circles. I hurled clods of earth and opprobrious shouts and epithets in the four directions of my four obstreperous friends, and I thought I counted four reluctant departures. Then, with considerable doubt, I descended from my ant hill and hurried down the slope, stumbling over grass hummocks, colliding with bushes, tangling with vines, but progressing in a gratifyingly rhinoless condition. Five minutes cautious but rapid feeling my way brought me through the jungle. Shortly after I raised the campfires; and so got home.

The next two days were repetitions, with slight variation, of this experience, minus the rhinos! Starting from camp before daylight we were only in time to see the herd-always aggravatingly on the other side of the cover, no matter which side we selected for our approach, slowly grazing into the dense jungle. And always they emerged so late and so far away that our very best efforts failed to get us near them before dark. The margin always so narrow, however, that our hopes were alive.

On the fourth day, which must be our last in Longeetoto, we found that the herd had shifted to fresh cover three miles along the base of the mountains. We had no faith in those buffaloes, but about half-past three we sallied forth dutifully and took position on a hill overlooking the new hiding place. This consisted of a wide grove of forest trees varied by occasional open glades and many dense thickets. So eager were we to win what had by now developed into a contest that I refused to shoot a lioness with a three-quarters-grown cub that appeared within easy shot from some reeds below us.

Time passed as usual until nearly sunset. Then through an opening into one of the small glades we caught sight of the herd travelling slowly but steadily from right to left. The glimpse was only momentary, but it was sufficient to indicate the direction from which we might expect them to emerge. Therefore we ran at top speed down from our own hill, tore through the jungle at its foot, and hastily, but with more caution, mounted the opposite slope through the scattered groves and high grass. We could hear occasionally indications of the buffaloes' slow advance, and we wanted to gain a good ambuscade above them before they emerged. We found it in the shape of a small conical hillock perched on the side hill itself, and covered with long grass. It commanded open vistas through the scattered trees in all directions. And the thicket itself ended not fifty yards away. No buffalo could possibly come out without our seeing him; and we had a good half hour of clear daylight before us. It really seemed that luck had changed at last.

We settled ourselves, unlimbered for action, and got our breath. The buffaloes came nearer and nearer. At length, through a tiny opening a hundred yards away, we could catch momentary glimpses of their great black bodies. I thrust forward the safety catch and waited. Finally a half dozen of the huge beasts were feeding not six feet inside the circle of brush, and only thirty-odd yards from where we lay.

And they came no farther! I never passed a more heart-breaking half hour of suspense than that in which little by little the daylight and our hopes faded, while those confounded buffaloes moved slowly out to the very edge of the thicket, turned, and moved as slowly back again. At times they came actually into view. We could see their sleek black bodies rolling lazily into sight and back again, like seals on the surface of water, but never could we make out more than that. I could have had a dozen good shots, but I could not even guess what I would be shooting at. And the daylight drained away and the minutes ticked by!

Finally, as I could see no end to this performance save that to which we had been so sickeningly accustomed in the last four days, I motioned to Memba Sasa, and together we glided like shadows into the thicket.

There it was already dusk. We sneaked breathlessly through the small openings, desperately in a hurry, almost painfully on the alert. In the dark shadow sixty yards ahead stood a half dozen monstrous bodies all facing our way. They suspected the presence of something unusual, but in the darkness and the stillness they could neither identify it nor locate it exactly. I dropped on one knee and snatched my prism glasses to my eyes. The magnification enabled me to see partially into the shadows. Every one of the group carried the sharply inturned points to the horns: they were all cows!

An instant after I had made out this fact, they stampeded across our face. The whole band thundered and crashed away.

Desperately we sprang after them, our guns atrail, our bodies stooped low to keep down in the shadow of the earth. And suddenly, without the slightest warning we plumped around a bush square on top of the entire herd. It had stopped and was staring back in our direction. I could see nothing but the wild toss of a hundred pair of horns silhouetted against such of the irregular saffron afterglow as had not been blocked off by the twigs and branches of the thicket. All below was indistinguishable blackness.

They stood in a long compact semicircular line thirty yards away, quite still, evidently staring intently into the dusk to find out what had alarmed them. At any moment they were likely to make another rush; and if they did so in the direction they were facing, they would most certainly run over us and trample us down.

Remembering the dusk I thought it likely that the unexpected vivid flash of the gun might turn them off before they got started. Therefore I raised the big double Holland, aimed below the line of heads, and was just about to pull trigger when my eye caught the silhouette of a pair of horns whose tips spread out instead of turning in. This was a bull, and I immediately shifted the gun in his direction. At the heavy double report, the herd broke wildly to right and left and thundered away. I confess I was quite relieved.

A low moaning bellow told us that our bull was down. The last few days' experience at being out late had taught us wisdom so Memba Sasa had brought a lantern. By the light of this, we discovered our bull down, and all but dead. To make sure, I put a Winchester bullet into his backbone.

We felt ourselves legitimately open to congratulations, for we had killed this bull from a practically nocturnal herd, in the face of considerable danger and more than considerable difficulty. Therefore we shook hands and made appropriate remarks to each other, lacking anybody to make them for us.

By now it was pitch dark in the thicket, and just about so outside. We had to do a little planning. I took the Holland gun, gave Memba Sasa the Winchester, and started him for camp after help. As he carried off the lantern, it was now up to me to make a fire and to make it quickly.

For the past hour a fine drizzle had been falling; and the whole country was wet from previous rains. I hastily dragged in all the dead wood I could find near, collected what ought to be good kindling, and started in to light a fire. Now, although I am no Boy Scout, I have lit several fires in my time. But never when I was at the same time in such a desperate need and hurry; and in possession of such poor materials. The harder I worked, the worse things sputtered and smouldered. Probably the relief from the long tension of the buffalo hunt had something to do with my general piffling inefficiency. If I had taken time to do a proper job once instead of a halfway job a dozen times, as I should have done and usually would have done, I would have had a fire in no time. I imagine I was somewhat scared. The lioness and her hulking cub had smelled the buffalo and were prowling around. I could hear them purring and uttering their hollow grunts. However, at last the flame held. I fed it sparingly, lit a pipe, placed the Holland gun next my hand, and resigned myself to waiting. For two hours this was not so bad. I smoked, and rested up, and dried out before my little fire. Then my fuel began to run low. I arose and tore down all the remaining dead limbs within the circle of my firelight. These were not many, so I stepped out into the darkness for more. Immediately I was warned back by a deep growl!

The next hour was not one of such solid comfort. I began to get parsimonious about my supply of firewood, trying to use it in such a manner as to keep up an adequate blaze, and at the same time to make it last until Memba Sasa should return with the men. I did it, though I got down to charred ends before I was through. The old lioness hung around within a hundred yards or so below, and the buffalo herd, returning, filed by above, pausing to stamp and snort at the fire. Finally, about nine o'clock, I made out two lanterns bobbing up to me through the trees.

The last incident to be selected from many experiences with buffaloes took place in quite an unvisited district over the mountains from the Loieta Plains. For nearly two months we had ranged far in this lovely upland country of groves and valleys and wide grass bottoms between hills, hunting for greater kudu. One day we all set out from camp to sweep the base of a range of low mountains in search of a good specimen of Newman's hartebeeste, or anything else especially desirable that might happen along. The gentle slope from the mountains was of grass cut by numerous small ravines grown with low brush. This brush was so scanty as to afford but indifferent cover for anything larger than one of the small grass antelopes. All the ravines led down a mile or so to a deeper main watercourse paralleling the mountains. Some water stood in the pools here; and the cover was a little more dense, but consisted at best of but a "stringer" no wider than a city street. Flanking the stringer were scattered high bushes for a few yards; and then the open country. Altogether as unlikely a place for the shade-loving buffalo as could be imagined.

We collected our Newmanii after rather a long hunt; and just at noon, when the heat of the day began to come on, we wandered down to the water for lunch. Here we found a good clear pool and drank. The boys began to make themselves comfortable by the water's edge; C. went to superintend the disposal of Billy's mule. Billy had sat down beneath the shade of the most hospitable of the bushes a hundred feet or so away, and was taking off her veil and gloves. I was carrying to her the lunch box. When I was about halfway from where the boys were drinking at the stream's edge to where she sat, a buffalo bull thrust his head from the bushes just the other side of her. His head was thrust up and forward, as he reached after some of the higher tender leaves on the bushes. So close was he that I could see plainly the drops glistening on his moist black nose. As for Billy, peacefully unwinding her long veil, she seemed fairly under the beast.

I had no weapon, and any moment might bring some word or some noise that would catch the animal's attention. Fortunately, for the moment, every one, relaxed in the first reaction after the long morning, was keeping silence. If the buffalo should look down, he could not fail to see Billy; and if he saw her, he would indubitably kill her.

As has been explained, snapping the fingers does not seem to reach the attention of wild animals. Therefore I snapped mine as vigorously as I knew how. Billy heard, looked toward me, turned in the direction of my gaze, and slowly sank prone against the ground. Some of the boys heard me also, and I could see the heads of all of them popping up in interest from the banks of the stream. My cautious but very frantic signals to lie low were understood: the heads dropped back. Mavrouki, a rifle in each hand, came worming his way toward me through the grass with incredible quickness and agility. A moment later he thrust the 405 Winchester into my hand.

This weapon, powerful and accurate as it is, the best of the lot for lions, was altogether too small for the tremendous brute before me. However, the Holland was in camp; and I was very glad in the circumstances to get this. The buffalo had browsed slowly forward into the clear, and was now taking the top off a small bush, and facing half away from us. It seemed to me quite the largest buffalo I had ever seen, though I should have been willing to have acknowledged at that moment that the circumstances had something to do with the estimate. However, later we found that the impression was correct. He was verily a giant of his kind. His height at the shoulder was five feet ten inches; and his build was even chunkier than the usual solid robust pattern of buffaloes. For example, his neck, just back of the horns, was two feet eight inches thick! He weighed not far from three thousand pounds.

Once the rifle was in my hands I lost the feeling of utter helplessness, and began to plan the best way out of the situation. As yet the beast was totally unconscious of our presence; but that could not continue long. There were too many men about. A chance current of air from any one of a half dozen directions could not fail to give him the scent. Then there would be lively doings. It was exceedingly desirable to deliver the first careful blow of the engagement while he was unaware. On the other hand, his present attitude-half away from me-was not favourable; nor, in my exposed position dared I move to a better place. There seemed nothing better than to wait; so wait we did. Mavrouki crouched close at my elbow, showing not the faintest indication of a desire to be anywhere but there.

The buffalo browsed for a minute or so; then swung slowly broadside on. So massive and low were the bosses of his horns that the brain shot was impossible. Therefore I aimed low in the shoulder. The shock of the bullet actually knocked that great beast off his feet! My respect for the hitting power of the 405 went up several notches. The only trouble was that he rebounded like a rubber ball. Without an instant's hesitation I gave him another in the same place. This brought him to his knees for an instant; but he was immediately afoot again. Billy had, with great good sense and courage, continued to lie absolutely flat within a few yards of the beast, Mavrouki and I had kept low, and C. and the men were out of sight. The buffalo therefore had seen none of his antagonists. He charged at a guess, and guessed wrong. As he went by I fired at his head, and, as we found out afterward, broke his jaw. A moment later C.'s great elephant gun roared from somewhere behind me as he fired by a glimpse through the brush at the charging animal. It was an excellent snapshot, and landed back of the ribs.

When the buffalo broke through the screen of brush I dashed after him, for I thought our only chance of avoiding danger lay in keeping close track of where that buffalo went. On the other side the bushes I found a little grassy opening, and then a small but dense thicket into which the animal had plunged. To my left, C. was running up, followed closely by Billy, who, with her usual good sense, had figured out the safest place to be immediately back of the guns. We came together at the thicket's edge.

The animal's movements could be plainly followed by the sound of his crashing. We heard him dash away some distance, pause, circle a bit to the right, and then come rushing back in our direction. Stooping low we peered into the darkness of the thicket. Suddenly we saw him, not a dozen yards away. He was still afoot, but very slow. I dropped the magazine of five shots into him as fast as I could work the lever. We later found all the bullet-holes in a spot as big as the palm of your hand. These successive heavy blows delivered all in the same place were too much for even his tremendous vitality; and slowly he sank on his side.

# XXVI. JUJA

Most people have heard of Juja, the modern dwelling in the heart of an African wilderness, belonging to our own countryman, Mr. W. N. McMillan. If most people are as I was before I saw the place, they have considerable curiosity and no knowledge of what it is and how it looks.

We came to Juja at the end of a wide circle that had lasted three months, and was now bringing us back again toward our starting point. For five days we had been camped on top a high bluff at the junction of two rivers. When we moved we dropped down the bluff, crossed one river, and, after some searching, found our way up the other bluff. There we were on a vast plain bounded by mountains thirty miles away. A large white and unexpected sign told us we were on Juja Farm, and warned us that we should be careful of our fires in the long grass.

For an hour we plodded slowly along. Herds of zebra and hartebeeste drew aside before us, dark heavy wildebeeste-the gnu-stood in groups at a safe distance their heads low, looking exactly like our vanished bison; ghostlike bands of Thompson's gazelles glided away with their smooth regular motion. On the vast and treeless plains single small objects standing above the general uniformity took an exaggerated value; so that, before it emerged from the swirling heat mirage, a solitary tree might easily be mistaken for a group of buildings or a grove. Finally, however, we raised above the horizon a dark straight clump of trees. It danced in the mirage, and blurred and changed form, but it persisted. A strange patch of white kept appearing and disappearing again. This resolved itself into the side of a building. A spider-legged water tower appeared above the trees.

Gradually we drew up on these. A bit later we swung to the right around a close wire fence ten feet high, passed through a gate, and rode down a long slanting avenue of young trees. Between the trees were century plants and flowers, and a clipped border ran before them. The avenue ended before a low white bungalow, with shady verandas all about it, and vines. A formal flower garden lay immediately about it, and a very tall flag pole had been planted in front. A hundred feet away the garden dropped off steep to one of the deep river canyons.

Two white-robed Somalis appeared on the veranda to inform us that McMillan was off on safari. Our own boys approaching at this moment, we thereupon led them past the house, down another long avenue of trees and flowers, out into an open space with many buildings at its edges, past extensive stables, and through another gate to the open plains once more. Here we made camp. After lunch we went back to explore.

Juja is situated on the top of a high bluff overlooking a river. In all directions are tremendous grass plains. Donya Sabuk-the Mountain of Buffaloes-is the only landmark nearer than the dim mountains beyond the edge of the world, and that is a day's journey away. A rectangle of possibly forty acres has been enclosed on three sides by animal-proof wire fence. The fourth side is the edge of the bluff. Within this enclosure have been planted many trees, now of good size; a pretty garden with abundance of flowers, ornamental shrubs, a sundial, and lawns. In the river bottom land below the bluff is a very extensive vegetable and fruit garden, with cornfields, and experimental plantings of rubber, and the like. For the use of the people of Juja here are raised a great variety and abundance of vegetables, fruits, and grains.

Juja House, as has been said, stands back a hundred feet from a bend in the bluffs that permits a view straight up the river valley. It is surrounded by gardens and trees, and occupies all one end of the enclosed rectangle. Farther down and perched on the edge of a bluff, are several pretty little bungalows for the accommodation of the superintendent and his family, for the bachelors' mess, for the farm offices and dispensary, and for the dairy room, the ice-plant and the post-office and telegraph station. Back of and inland from this row on the edge of the cliff, and scattered widely in open space, are a large store stocked with everything on earth, the Somali quarters of low whitewashed buildings, the cattle corrals, the stables, wild animal cages, granaries, blacksmith and carpenter shops, wagon sheds and the like. Outside the enclosure, and a half mile away, are the conical grass huts that make up the native village. Below the cliff is a concrete dam, an electric light plant, a pumping plant and a few details of the sort.

Such is a relief map of Juja proper. Four miles away, and on another river, is Long Juja, a strictly utilitarian affair where grow ostriches, cattle, sheep, and various irrigated things in the bottom land. All the rest of the farm, or estate, or whatever one would call it, is open plain, with here and there a river bottom, or a trifle of brush cover. But never enough to constitute more than an isolated and lonesome patch.

Before leaving London we had received from McMillan earnest assurances that he kept open house, and that we must take advantage of his hospitality should we happen his way. Therefore when one of his white-robed Somalis approached us to inquire respectfully as to what we wanted for dinner, we yielded weakly to the temptation and told him. Then we marched us boldly to the house and took possession.

All around the house ran a veranda, shaded bamboo curtains and vines, furnished with the luxurious teakwood chairs of the tropics of which you can so extend the arms as to form two comfortable and elevated rests for your feet. Horns of various animals ornamented the walls. A megaphone and a huge terrestrial telescope on a tripod stood in one corner. Through the latter one could examine at favourable times the herds of game on the plains.

And inside-mind you, we were fresh from three months in the wilderness-we found rugs, pictures, wall paper, a pianola, many books, baths, beautiful white bedrooms with snowy mosquito curtains, electric lights, running water, and above all an atmosphere of homelike comfort. We fell into easy chairs, and seized books and magazines. The Somalis brought us trays with iced and fizzy drinks in thin glasses. When the time came we crossed the veranda in the rear to enter a spacious separate dining-room. The table was white with napery, glittering with silver and glass, bright with flowers. We ate leisurely of a well-served course dinner, ending with black coffee, shelled nuts, and candied fruit. Replete and satisfied we strolled back across the veranda to the main house. F. raised his hand.

"Hark!" he admonished us.

We held still. From the velvet darkness came the hurried petulant barking of zebra; three hyenas howled.

# XXVII. A VISIT AT JUJA

Next day we left all this; and continued our march. About a month later, however, we encountered McMillan himself in Nairobi. I was just out from a very hard trip to the coast-Billy not with me-and wanted nothing so much as a few days' rest. McMillan's cordiality was not to be denied, however, so the very next day found us tucking ourselves into a buckboard behind four white Abyssinian mules. McMillan, some Somalis and Captain Duirs came along in another similar rig. Our driver was a Hottentot half-caste from South Africa. He had a flat face, a yellow skin, a quiet manner, and a competent hand. His name was Michael. At his feet crouched a small Kikuyu savage, in blanket ear ornaments and all the fixings, armed with a long lashed whip and raucous voice. At any given moment he was likely to hop out over the moving wheel, run forward, bat the off leading mule, and hop back again, all with the most extraordinary agility. He likewise hurled what sounded like very opprobrious epithets at such natives as did not get out the way quickly enough to suit him. The expression of his face, which was that of a person steeped in woe, never changed.

We rattled out of Nairobi at a great pace, and swung into the Fort Hall Road. This famous thoroughfare, one of the three or four made roads in all East Africa, is about sixty miles long. It is a strategic necessity but is used by thousands of natives on their way to see the sights of the great metropolis. As during the season there is no water for much of the distance, a great many pay for their curiosity with their lives. The road skirts the base of the hills, winding in and out of shallow canyons and about the edges of rounded hills. To the right one can see far out across the Athi Plains.

We met an almost unbroken succession of people. There were long pack trains of women, quite cheerful, bent over under the weight of firewood or vegetables, many with babies tucked away in the folds of their garments; mincing dandified warriors with poodle-dog hair, skewers in their ears, their jewelery brought to a high polish a fatuous expression of self-satisfaction on their faces, carrying each a section of sugarcane which they now used as a staff but would later devour for lunch; bearers, under convoy of straight soldierly red-sashed Sudanese, transporting Government goods; wild-eyed staring shenzis from the forest, with matted hair and goatskin garments, looking ready to bolt aside at the slightest alarm; coveys of marvellous and giggling damsels, their fine-grained skin anointed and shining with red oil, strung with beads and shells, very coquettish and sure of their feminine charm; naked small boys marching solemnly like their elders; camel trains from far-off Abyssinia or Somaliland under convoy of white-clad turbaned grave men of beautiful features; donkey safaris in charge of dirty degenerate looking East Indians carrying trade goods to some distant post-all these and many more, going one way or the other, drew one side, at the sight of our white faces, to let us pass.

About two o'clock we suddenly turned off from the road, apparently quite at random, down the long grassy interminable incline that dipped slowly down and slowly up again over great distance to form the Athi Plains. Along the road, with its endless swarm of humanity, we had seen no game, but after a half mile it began to appear. We encountered herds of zebra, kongoni, wildebeeste, and "Tommies" standing about or grazing, sometimes almost within range from the moving buckboard. After a time we made out the trees and water tower of Juja ahead; and by four o'clock had turned into the avenue of trees. Our approach had been seen. Tea was ready, and a great and hospitable table of bottles, ice, and siphons.

The next morning we inspected the stables, built of stone in a hollow square, like a fort, with box stalls opening directly into the courtyard and screened carefully against the deadly flies. The horses, beautiful creatures, were led forth each by his proud and anxious syce. We tried them all, and selected our mounts for the time of our stay. The syces were small black men, lean and well formed, accustomed to running afoot wherever their charges went, at walk, lope or gallop. Thus in a day they covered incredible distances over all sorts of country; but were always at hand to seize the bridle reins when the master wished to dismount. Like the rickshaw runners in Nairobi, they wore their hair clipped close around their bullet heads and seemed to have developed into a small compact hard type of their own. They ate and slept with their horses.

Just outside the courtyard of the stables a little barred window had been cut through. Near this were congregated a number of Kikuyu savages wrapped in their blankets, receiving each in turn a portion of cracked corn from a dusty white man behind the bars. They were a solemn, unsmiling, strange type of savage, and they performed all the manual work within the enclosure, squatting on their heels and pulling methodically but slowly at the weeds, digging with their pangas, carrying loads: to and fro, or solemnly pushing a lawn mower, blankets wrapped shamelessly about their necks. They were harried about by a red-faced beefy English gardener with a marvellous vocabulary of several native languages and a short hippo-hide whip. He talked himself absolutely purple in the face without, as far as my observation went, penetrating an inch below the surface. The Kikuyus went right on doing what they were already doing in exactly the same manner. Probably the purple Englishman was satisfied with that, but I am sure apoplexy of either the heat or thundering variety has him by now.

Before the store building squatted another group of savages. Perhaps in time one of the lot expected to buy something; or possibly they just sat. Nobody but a storekeeper would ever have time to find out. Such is the native way. The storekeeper in this case was named John. Besides being storekeeper, he had charge of the issuing of all the house supplies, and those for the white men's mess; he must do all the worrying about the upper class natives; he must occasionally kill a buck for the meat supply; and he must be prepared to take out any stray tenderfeet that happen along during McMillan's absence, and persuade them that they are mighty hunters. His domain was a fascinating place, for it contained everything from pianola parts to patent washstands. The next best equipped place of the kind I know of is the property room of a moving picture company.

We went to mail a letter, and found the postmaster to be a gentle-voiced, polite little Hindu, who greeted us smilingly, and attempted to conceal a work of art. We insisted; whereupon he deprecatingly drew forth a copy of a newspaper cartoon having to do with Colonel Roosevelt's visit. It was copied with mathematical exactness, and highly coloured in a manner to throw into profound melancholy the chauffeur of a coloured supplement press. We admired and praised; whereupon, still shyly, he produced more, and yet again more copies of the same cartoon. When we left, he was reseating himself to the painstaking valueless labour with which he filled his days. Three times a week such mail as Juja gets comes in via native runner. We saw the latter, a splendid figure, almost naked, loping easily, his little bundle held before him.

Down past the office and dispensary we strolled, by the comfortable, airy, white man's clubhouse. The headman of the native population passed us with a dignified salute; a fine upstanding deep-chested man, with a lofty air of fierce pride. He and his handful of soldiers alone of the natives, except the Somalis and syces, dwelt within the compound in a group of huts near the gate. There when off duty they might be seen polishing their arms, or chatting with their women. The latter were ladies of leisure, with wonderful chignons, much jewelery, and patterned Mericani wrapped gracefully about their pretty figures.

By the time we had seen all these things it was noon. We ate lunch. The various members of the party decided to do various things. I elected to go out with McMillan while he killed a wildebeeste, and I am very glad I did. It was a most astonishing performance.

You must imagine us driving out the gate in a buckboard behind four small but lively white Abyssinian mules. In the front seat were Michael, the Hottentot driver, and McMillan's Somali gunbearer. In the rear seat were McMillan and myself, while a small black syce perched precariously behind. Our rifles rested in a sling before us. So we jogged out on the road to Long Juju, examining with a critical eye the herds of game to right and left of us. The latter examined us, apparently, with an eye as critical. Finally, in a herd of zebra, we espied a lone wildebeeste.

The wildebeeste is the Jekyll and Hyde of the animal kingdom. His usual and familiar habit is that of a heavy, sluggish animal, like our vanished bison. He stands solid and inert, his head down; he plods slowly forward in single file, his horns swinging, each foot planted deliberately. In short, he is the personification of dignity, solid respectability, gravity of demeanour. But then all of a sudden, at any small interruption, he becomes the giddiest of created beings. Up goes his head and tail, he buck jumps, cavorts, gambols, kicks up his heels, bounds stiff-legged, and generally performs like an irresponsible infant. To see a whole herd at once of these grave and reverend seigneurs suddenly blow up into such light-headed capers goes far to destroy one's faith in the stability of institutions.

Also the wildebeeste is not misnamed. He is a conservative, and he sees no particular reason for allowing his curiosity to interfere with his preconceived beliefs. The latter are distrustful. Therefore he and his females and his young-I should say small-depart when one is yet far away. I say small, because I do not believe that any wildebeeste is ever young. They do not resemble calves, but are exact replicas of the big ones, just as Niobe's daughters are in nothing childlike, but merely smaller women.

When we caught sight of this lone wildebeeste among the zebra, I naturally expected that we would pull up the buckboard, descend, and approach to within some sort of long range. Then we would open fire. Barring luck, the wildebeeste would thereupon depart "wilder and beestier than ever," as John McCutcheon has it. Not at all! Michael, the Hottentot, turned the buckboard off the road, headed toward the distant quarry, and charged at full speed! Over stones we went that sent us feet into the air, down and out of shallow gullies that seemed as though they would jerk the pole from the vehicle with a grand rattlety-bang, every one hanging on for his life. I was entirely occupied with the state of my spinal column and the retention of my teeth, but McMillan must have been keeping his eye on the game. One peculiarity of the wildebeeste is that he cannot see behind him, and another is that he is curious. It would not require a very large bump of curiosity, however, to cause any animal to wonder what all the row was about. There could be no doubt that this animal would sooner or later stop for an instant to look for the purpose of seeing what was up in jungleland; and just before doing so he would, for a few steps, slow down from a gallop to a trot. McMillan was watching for this symptom.

"Now!" he yelled, when he saw it.

Instantly Michael threw his weight into the right rein and against the brake. We swerved so violently to the right and stopped so suddenly that I nearly landed on the broad prairies. The manoeuvre fetched us up broadside. The small black syce-and heaven knows how HE had managed to hang on-darted to the heads of the leading mules. At the same moment the wildebeeste turned, and stopped; but even before he had swung his head, McMillan had fired. It was extraordinarily good, quick work, the way he picked up the long range from the spurts of dust where the bullets hit. At the third or fourth shots he landed one. Immediately the beast was off again at a tearing run pursued by a rapid fusillade from the remaining shots. Then with a violent jerk and a wild yell we were off again.

This time, since the animal was wounded, he made for rougher country. And everywhere that wildebeeste went we too were sure to go. We hit or shaved boulders that ought to have smashed a wheel, we tore through thick brush regardless. Twice we charged unhesitatingly over apparent precipices. I do not know the name of the manufacturer of the buckboard. If I did, I should certainly recommend it here. Twice more we swerved to our broadside and cut loose the port batteries. Once more McMillan hit. Then, on the fourth "run," we gained perceptibly. The beast was weakening. When he came to a stumbling halt we were not over a hundred yards from him, and McMillan easily brought him down. We had chased him four or five miles, and McMillan had fired nineteen shots, of which two had hit. The rifle practice throughout had been remarkably good, and a treat to watch. Personally, besides the fun of attending the show, I got a mighty good afternoon's exercise.

We loaded the game aboard and jogged slowly back to the house, for the mules were pretty tired. We found a neighbour, Mr. Heatley of Kamiti Ranch who had "dropped down" twelve miles to see us. On account of a theft McMillan now had all the Somalis assembled for interrogation on the side verandas. The interrogation did not amount to much, but while it was going on the Sudanese headman and his askaris were quietly searching the boys' quarters. After a time they appeared. The suspected men had concealed nothing, but the searchers brought with them three of McMillan's shirts which they had found among the effects of another, and entirely unsuspected, boy named Abadie.

124

"How is this, Abadie?" demanded McMillan sternly.

Abadie hesitated. Then he evidently reflected that there is slight use in having a deity unless one makes use of him.

"Bwana," said he with an engaging air of belief and candour, "God must have put them there!"

That evening we planned a "general day" for the morrow. We took boys and buckboards and saddle-horses, beaters, shotguns, rifles, and revolvers, and we sallied forth for a grand and joyous time. The day from a sporting standpoint was entirely successful, the bag consisting of two waterbuck, a zebra, a big wart-hog, six hares, and six grouse. Personally I was a little hazy and uncertain. By evening the fever had me, and though I stayed at Juja for six days longer, it was as a patient to McMillan's unfailing kindness rather than as a participant in the life of the farm.

# XXVIII. A RESIDENCE AT JUJA

A short time later, at about middle of the rainy season, McMillan left for a little fishing off Catalina Island. The latter is some fourteen thousand miles of travel from Juja. Before leaving on this flying trip, McMillan made us a gorgeous offer.

"If," said he, "you want to go it alone, you can go out and use Juja as long as you please."

This offer, or, rather, a portion of it, you may be sure, we accepted promptly. McMillan wanted in addition to leave us his servants; but to this we would not agree. Memba Sasa and Mahomet were, of course, members of our permanent staff. In addition to them we picked up another house boy, named Leyeye. He was a Masai. These proud and aristocratic savages rarely condescend to take service of any sort except as herders; but when they do they prove to be unusually efficient and intelligent. We had also a Somali cook, and six ordinary bearers to do general labour. This small safari we started off afoot for Juja. The whole lot cost us about what we would pay one Chinaman on the Pacific Coast.

Next day we ourselves drove out in the mule buckboard. The rains were on, and the road was very muddy. After the vital tropical fashion the grass was springing tall in the natural meadows and on the plains and the brief-lived white lilies and an abundance of ground flowers washed the slopes with colour. Beneath the grass covering, the entire surface of the ground was an inch or so deep in water. This was always most surprising, for, apparently, the whole country should have been high and dry. Certainly its level was that of a plateau rather than a bottom land; so that one seemed always to be travelling at an elevation. Nevertheless walking or riding we were continually splashing, and the only dry going outside the occasional rare "islands" of the slight undulations we found near the very edge of the bluffs above the rivers. There the drainage seemed sufficient to carry off the excess. Elsewhere the hardpan or bedrock must have been exceptionally level and near the top of the ground.

Nothing nor nobody seemed to mind this much. The game splashed around merrily, cropping at the tall grass; the natives slopped indifferently, and we ourselves soon became so accustomed to two or three inches of water and wet feet that after the first two days we never gave those phenomena a thought.

The world above at this season of the year was magnificent. The African heavens are always widely spacious, but now they seemed to have blown even vaster than usual. In the sweep of the vision four or five heavy black rainstorms would be trailing their skirts across an infinitely remote prospect; between them white piled scud clouds and cumuli sailed like ships; and from them reflected so brilliant a sunlight and behind all showed so dazzling a blue sky that the general impression was of a fine day. The rainstorms' gray veils slanted; tremendous patches of shadow lay becalmed on the plains; bright sunshine poured abundantly its warmth and yellow light.

So brilliant with both direct and reflected light and the values of contrast were the heavens, that when one happened to stand within one of the great shadows it became extraordinarily difficult to make out game on the plains. The pupils contracted to the brilliancy overhead. Often too, near sunset, the atmosphere would become suffused with a lurid saffron light that made everything unreal and ghastly. At such times the game seemed puzzled by the unusual aspect of things. The zebra especially would bark and stamp and stand their ground, and even come nearer out of sheer curiosity. I have thus been within fifty yards of them, right out in the open. At such times it was as though the sky, instead of rounding over in the usual shape, had been thrust up at the western horizon to the same incredible height as the zenith. In the space thus created were piled great clouds through which slanted broad bands of yellow light on a diminished world.

It rained with great suddenness on our devoted heads, and with a curious effect of metamorphoslng the entire universe. One moment all was clear and smiling, with the trifling exception of distant rain squalls that amounted to nothing in the general scheme. Then the horizon turned black, and with incredible swiftness the dark clouds materialized out of nothing, rolled high to the zenith like a wave, blotted out every last vestige of brightness. A heavy oppressive still darkness breathed over the earth. Then through the silence came a faraway soft drumming sound, barely to be heard. As we bent our ears to catch this it grew louder and louder, approaching at breakneck speed like a troop of horses. It became a roar fairly terrifying in its mercilessly continued crescendo. At last the deluge of rain burst actually as a relief.

And what a deluge! Facing it we found difficulty in breathing. In six seconds every stitch we wore was soaked through, and only the notebook, tobacco, and matches bestowed craftily in the crown of the cork helmet escaped. The visible world was dark and contracted. It seemed that nothing but rain could anywhere exist; as though this storm must fill all space to the horizon and beyond. Then it swept on and we found ourselves steaming in bright sunlight. The dry flat prairie (if this was the first shower for some time) had suddenly become a lake from the surface of which projected bushes and clumps of grass. Every game trail had become the water course of a swiftly running brook.

But most pleasant were the evenings at Juja, when, safe indoors, we sat and listened to the charge of the storm's wild horsemen, and the thunder of its drumming on the tin roof. The onslaughts were as fierce and abrupt as those of Cossacks, and swept by as suddenly. The roar died away in the distance, and we could then hear the steady musical dripping of waters.

Pleasant it was also to walk out from Juja in almost any direction. The compound, and the buildings and trees within it, soon dwindled in the distances of the great flat plain. Herds of game were always in sight, grazing, lying down, staring in our direction. The animals were incredibly numerous. Some days they were fairly tame, and others exceedingly wild, without any rhyme or reason. This shyness or the reverse seemed not to be individual to one herd; but to be practically universal. On a "wild day" everything was wild from the Lone Tree to Long Juju. It would be manifestly absurd to guess at the reason. Possibly the cause might be atmospheric or electrical; possibly days of nervousness might follow nights of unusual activity by the lions; one could invent a dozen possibilities. Perhaps the kongonis decided it.

At Juja we got to know the kongonis even better than we had before. They are comical, quizzical beasts, with long-nosed humorous faces, a singularly awkward construction, a shambling gait; but with altruistic dispositions and an ability to get over the ground at an extraordinary speed. Every move is a joke; their expression is always one of grieved but humorous astonishment. They quirk their heads sidewise or down and stare at an intruder with the most comical air of skeptical wonder. "Well, look who's here!" says the expression.

"Pooh!" says the kongoni himself, after a good look, "pooh! pooh!" with the most insulting inflection.

He is very numerous and very alert. One or more of a grazing herd are always perched as sentinels atop ant hills or similar small elevations. On the slightest intimation of danger they give the alarm, whereupon the herd makes off at once, gathering in all other miscellaneous game that may be in the vicinity. They will go out of their way to do this, as every African hunter knows. It immensely complicates matters; for the sportsman must not only stalk his quarry, but he must stalk each and every kongoni as well. Once, in another part of the country, C. and I saw a kongoni leave a band of its own species far down to our right, gallop toward us and across our front, pick up a herd of zebra we were trying to approach and make off with them to safety. We cursed that kongoni, but we admired him, for he deliberately ran out of safety into danger for the purpose of warning those zebra. So seriously do they take their job as policemen of the plains that it is very common for a lazy single animal of another species to graze in a herd of kongonis simply for the sake of protection. Wildebeeste are much given to this.

The kongoni progresses by a series of long high bounds. While in midair he half tucks up his feet, which gives him the appearance of an automatic toy. This gait looks deliberate, but is really quite fast, as the mounted sportsman discovers when he enters upon a vain pursuit. If the horse is an especially good one, so that the kongoni feels himself a trifle closely pressed, the latter stops bouncing and runs. Then he simply fades away into the distance.

These beasts are also given to chasing each other all over the landscape. When a gentleman kongoni conceives a dislike for another gentleman kongoni, he makes no concealment of his emotions, but marches up and prods him in the ribs. The ensuing battle is usually fought out very stubbornly with much feinting, parrying, clashing of the lyre-shaped horns; and a good deal of crafty circling for a favourable opening. As far as I was ever able to see not much real damage is inflicted; though I could well imagine that only skilful fence prevented unpleasant punctures in soft spots. After a time one or the other feels himself weakening. He dashes strongly in, wheels while his antagonist is braced, and makes off. The enemy pursues. Then, apparently, the chase is on for the rest of the day. The victor is not content merely to drive his rival out of the country; he wants to catch him. On that object he is very intent; about as intent as the other fellow is of getting away. I have seen two such beasts almost run over a dozen men who were making no effort to keep out of sight. Long after honour is satisfied, indeed, as it seems to me, long after the dictates of common decency would call a halt that persistent and single-minded pursuer bounds solemnly and conscientiously along in the wake of his disgusted rival.

These and the zebra and wildebeeste were at Juja the most conspicuous game animals. If they could not for the moment be seen from the veranda of the house itself, a short walk to the gate was sufficient to reveal many hundreds. Among them fed herds of the smaller Thompson's gazelle, or "Tommies." So small were they that only their heads could be seen above the tall grass as they ran.

To me there was never-ending fascination in walking out over those sloppy plains in search of adventure, and in the pleasure of watching the beasts. Scarcely less fascination haunted a stroll down the river canyons or along the tops of the bluffs above them. Here the country was broken into rocky escarpments in which were caves; was clothed with low and scattered brush; or was wooded in the bottom lands. Naturally an entirely different set of animals dwelt here; and in addition one was often treated to the romance of surprise. Herds of impalla haunted these edges; graceful creatures, trim and pretty with wide horns and beautiful glowing red coats. Sometimes they would venture out on the open plains, in a very compact band, ready to break back for cover at the slightest alarm; but generally fed inside the fringe of bushes. Once from the bluff above I saw a beautiful herd of over a hundred pacing decorously along the river bottom below me, single file, the oldest buck at the head, and the miscellaneous small buck bringing up the rear after the does. I shouted at them. Immediately the solemn procession broke. They began to leap, springing straight up into the air as though from a released spring, or diving forward and upward in long graceful bounds like dolphins at sea. These leaps were incredible. Several even jumped quite over the backs of others; and all without a semblance of effort.

Along the fringe of the river, too, dwelt the lordly waterbuck, magnificent and proud as the stags of Landseer; and the tiny steinbuck and duiker, no bigger than jack-rabbits, but perfect little deer for all that. The incredibly plebeian wart-hog rooted about; and down in the bottom lands were leopards. I knocked one off a rock one day. In the river itself dwelt hippopotamuses and crocodiles. One of the latter dragged under a yearling calf just below the house itself, and while we were there. Besides these were of course such affairs as hyenas and jackals, and great numbers of small game: hares, ducks, three kinds of grouse, guinea fowl, pigeons, quail, and jack snipe, not to speak of a variety of plover.

In the drier extents of dry grass atop the bluffs the dance birds were especially numerous; each with his dance ring nicely trodden out, each leaping and falling rhythmically for hours at a time. Toward sunset great flights of sand grouse swarmed across the yellowing sky from some distant feeding ground.

Near Juja I had one of the three experiences that especially impressed on my mind the abundance of African big game. I had stalked and wounded a wildebeeste across the N'derogo River, and had followed him a mile or so afoot, hoping to be able to put in a finishing shot. As sometimes happens the animal rather gained strength as time went on; so I signalled for my horse, mounted, and started out to run him down. After a quarter mile we began to pick up the game herds. Those directly in our course ran straight away; other herds on either side, seeing them running, came across in a slant to join them. Inside of a half mile I was driving before me literally thousands of head of game of several varieties. The dust rose in a choking cloud that fairly obscured the landscape, and the drumming of the hooves was like the stampeding of cattle. It was a wonderful sight.

On the plains of Juja, also, I had my one real African Adventure, when, as in the Sunday Supplements, I Stared Death in the Face-also everlasting disgrace and much derision. We were just returning to the farm after an afternoon's walk, and as we approached I began to look around for much needed meat. A herd of zebra stood in sight; so leaving Memba Sasa I began to stalk them. My usual weapon for this sort of thing was the Springfield, for which I carried extra cartridges in my belt. On this occasion, however, I traded with Memba Sasa for the 405, simply for the purpose of trying it out. At a few paces over three hundred yards I landed on the zebra, but did not knock him down. Then I set out to follow. It was a long job and took me far, for again and again he joined other zebra, when, of course, I could not tell one from t'other. My only expedient was to frighten the lot. There upon the uninjured ones would distance the one that was hurt. The latter kept his eye on me. Whenever I managed to get within reasonable distance, I put up the rear sight of the 405, and let drive. I heard every shot hit, and after

128

each hit was more than a little astonished to see the zebra still on his feet, and still able to wobble on.* The fifth shot emptied the rifle. As I had no more cartridges for this arm, I approached to within sixty yards, and stopped to wait either for him to fall, or for a very distant Memba Sasa to come up with more cartridges. Then the zebra waked up. He put his ears back and came straight in my direction. This rush I took for a blind death flurry, and so dodged off to one side, thinking that he would of course go by me. Not at all! He swung around on the circle too, and made after me. I could see that his ears were back, eyes blazing, and his teeth snapping with rage. It was a malicious charge, and, as such, with due deliberation, I offer it to sportsman's annals. As I had no more cartridges I ran away as fast as I could go. Although I made rather better time than ever I had attained to before, it was evident that the zebra would catch me; and as the brute could paw, bite, and kick, I did not much care for the situation. Just as he had nearly reached me, and as I was trying to figure on what kind of a fight I could put up with a clubbed rifle barrel, he fell dead. To be killed by a lion is at least a dignified death; but to be mauled by a zebra!

I am sorry I did not try out this heavy-calibred rifle oftener at long range. It was a marvellously effective weapon at close quarters; but I have an idea-but only a tentative idea-that above three hundred yards its velocity is so reduced by air resistance against the big blunt bullet as greatly to impair its hitting powers.

We generally got back from our walks or rides just before dark to find the house gleaming with lights, a hot bath ready, and a tray of good wet drinks next the easy chairs. There, after changing our clothes, we sipped and read the papers-two months off the press, but fresh arrived for all that-until a white-robed, dignified figure appeared in the doorway to inform us that dinner was ready. Our ways were civilized and soft, then, until the morrow when once again, perhaps, we went forth into the African wilderness.

Juja is a place of startling contrasts-of naked savages clipping formal hedges, of windows opening from a perfectly appointed brilliantly lighted dining-room to a night whence float the lost wails of hyenas or the deep grumbling of lions, of cushioned luxurious chairs in reach of many books, but looking out on hills where the game herds feed, of comfortable beds with fine linen and soft blankets where one lies listening to the voices of an African night, or the weirder minor house noises whose origin and nature no man could guess, of tennis courts and summer houses, of lawns and hammocks, of sundials and clipped hedges separated only by a few strands of woven wire from fields identical with those in which roamed the cave men of the Pleistocene. But to Billy was reserved the most ridiculous contrast of all. Her bedroom opened to a veranda a few feet above a formal garden. This was a very formal garden, with a sundial, gravelled walks, bordered flower beds, and clipped border hedges. One night she heard a noise outside. Slipping on a warm wrap and seizing her trusty revolver she stole out on the veranda to investigate. She looked over the veranda rail. There just below her, trampling the flower beds, tracking the gravel walks, endangering the sundial, stood a hippopotamus!

We had neighbours six or seven miles away. At times they came down to spend the night and luxuriate in the comforts of civilization. They were a Lady A., and her nephew, and a young Scotch acquaintance the nephew had taken into partnership. They had built themselves circular houses of papyrus reeds with conical thatched roofs and earth floors, had purchased ox teams and gathered a dozen or so Kikuyus, and were engaged in breaking a farm in the wilderness. The life was rough and hard, and Lady A. and her nephew gently bred, but they seemed to be having quite cheerfully the time of their lives. The game furnished them meat, as it did all of us, and they hoped in time that their labours would make the land valuable and productive. Fascinating as was the life, it was also one of many deprivations. At Juja were a number of old copies of Life, the pretty girls in which so fascinated the young men that we broke the laws of propriety by presenting them, though they did not belong to us. C., the nephew, was of the finest type of young Englishman, clean cut, enthusiastic, good looking, with an air of engaging vitality and optimism. His partner, of his own age, was an insufferable youth. Brought up in some small Scottish valley, his outlook had never widened. Because he wanted to buy four oxen at a cheaper price, he tried desperately to abrogate quarantine regulations. If he had succeeded, he would have made a few rupees, but would have introduced disease in his neighbours' herds. This consideration did not affect him. He was much given to sneering at what he could not understand; and therefore, a great deal met with his disapproval. His reading had evidently brought him down only to about the middle sixties; and affairs at that date were to him still burning questions. Thus he would declaim vehemently over the Alabama claims.

"I blush with shame," he would cry, "when I think of England's attitude in that matter."

We pointed out that the dispute had been amicably settled by the best minds of the time, had passed between the covers of history, and had given way in immediate importance to several later topics.

"This vacillating policy," he swept on, "annoys me. For my part, I should like to see so firm a stand taken on all questions that in any part of the world, whenever a man, and wherever a man, said 'I am an Englishman? everybody else would draw back!'"

He was an incredible person. However, I was glad to see him; he and a few others of his kind have consoled me for a number of Americans I have met abroad. Lady A., with the tolerant philosophy of her class, seemed merely amused. I have often since wondered how this ill-assorted partnership turned out.

Two other neighbours of ours dropped in once or twice-twenty-six miles on bicycles, on which they could ride only a portion of the distance. They had some sort of a ranch up in the Ithanga Hills; and were two of the nicest fellows one would want to meet, brimful of energy, game for anything, and had so good a time always that the grumpiest fever could not prevent every one else having a good time too. Once they rode on their bicycles forty miles to Nairobi, danced half the night at a Government House ball, rode back in the early morning, and did an afternoon's plowing! They explained this feat by pointing out most convincingly that the ground was just right for plowing, but they did not want to miss the ball!

Occasionally a trim and dapper police official would drift in on horseback looking for native criminals; and once a safari came by. Twelve miles away was the famous Kamiti Farm of Heatly, where Roosevelt killed his buffalo; and once or twice Heatly himself, a fine chap, came to see us. Also just before I left with Duirs for a lion hunt on Kapiti, Lady Girouard, wife of the Governor, and her nephew and niece rode out for a hunt. In the African fashion, all these people brought their own personal servants. It makes entertaining easy. Nobody knows where all these boys sleep; but they manage to tuck away somewhere, and always show up after a mysterious system of their own whenever there is anything to be done.

We stayed at Juja a little over three weeks. Then most reluctantly said farewell and returned to Nairobi in preparation for a long trip to the south.

# XXIX. CHAPTER THE LAST

With our return from Juja to Nairobi for a breathing space, this volume comes to a logical conclusion. In it I have tried to give a fairly comprehensive impression-it could hardly be a picture of so large a subject-of a portion of East Equatorial Africa, its animals, and its people. Those who are sufficiently interested will have an opportunity in a succeeding volume of wandering with us even farther afield. The low jungly coast region; the fierce desert of the Serengetti; the swift sullen rhinoceros-haunted stretches of the Tsavo; Nairobi, the strangest mixture of the twentieth centuries A.D. and B.C.; Mombasa with its wild, barbaric passionate ebb and flow of life, of colour, of throbbing sound, the great lions of the Kapiti Plains, the Thirst of the Loieta, the Masai spearmen, the long chase for the greater kudu; the wonderful, high unknown country beyond the Narossara and other affairs will there be detailed. If the reader of this volume happens to want more, there he will find it.

# APPENDIX I

Most people are very much interested in how hot it gets in such tropics as we traversed. Unfortunately it is very difficult to tell them. Temperature tables have very little to do with the matter, for humidity varies greatly. On the Serengetti at lower reaches of the Guaso Nyero I have seen it above 110 degrees. It was hot, to be sure, but not exhaustingly so. On the other hand, at 90 or 95 degrees the low coast belt I have had the sweat run from me literally in streams; so that a muddy spot formed wherever I stood still. In the highlands, moreover, the nights were often extremely cold. I have recorded night temperatures as low as 40 at 7000 feet of elevation; and noon temperatures as low 65.

Of more importance than the actual or sensible temperature of the air is the power of the sun's rays. At all times of year this is practically constant; for the orb merely swings a few degrees north and south of the equator, and the extreme difference in time between its risings or settings is not more than twenty minutes. This power is also practically constant whatever the temperature of the air and is dangerous even on a cloudy day, when the heat waves are effectually screened off, but when the actinic rays are as active as ever. For this reason the protection of helmet and spine pad should never be omitted, no matter what the condition of the weather, between nine o'clock and four. A very brief exposure is likely to prove fatal. It should be added that some people stand these actinic rays better than others.

Such being the case, mere temperature tables could have little interest to the general reader. I append a few statistics, selected from many, and illustrative of the different conditions.

| Locality. | Elevation | 6am | noon | 8pm | Apparent conditions |
|---|---|---|---|---|---|
| Coast | — | 80 | 90 | 76 | Very hot and sticky |

| | | | | | |
|---|---|---|---|---|---|
| Isiola River | 2900 | 65 | 94 | 84 | Hot but not exhausting |
| Tans River | 3350 | 68 | 98 | 79 | Hot but not exhausting |
| Near Meru | 5450 | 62 | 80 | 70 | Very pleasant |
| Serengetti Plains | 2200 | 78 | 106 | 86 | Hot and humid |
| Narossara River | 5450 | 54 | 89 | 69 | Very pleasant |
| Narossara Mts. | 7400 | 42 | 80 | 50 | Chilly |
| Narossara Mts. | 6450 | 40 | 62 | 52 | Cold |

# APPENDIX II

## GAME ANIMALS COLLECTED

| | | |
|---|---|---|
| Lion | Bush pig | Grant's gazelle |
| Serval cat | Baboon | Thompson's gazelle |
| Cheetah | Colobus | Gerenuk gazelle |
| Black-backed jackal | Hippopotamus | Coke's hartebeests |
| Silver jackal | Rhinoceros | Jackson's hartebeests |
| Striped hyena | Crocodile | Neuman's hartebeests |
| Spotted hyena | Python | Chandler's reedbuck |
| Fennec fox | Ward's zebra | Bohur reedbuck |
| Honey badger | Grevy's zebra | Beisa ox |
| Aardewolf | Notata gazelle | Fringe-eared oryx |
| Wart-hog | Roberts' gazelle | Duiker |
| Waterbuck | Klipspringer | Harvey's duiker |
| Sing-sing | Dik-dik | Greater kudu |
| Oribi (3 varieties) | Wildebeeste | Lesser kudu |
| Eland | Roosevelt's wildebeests | Sable antelope |
| Roan antelope | Buffalo | |
| Bushbuck | Topi | |

Total, fifty-four kinds

## GAME BIRDS COLLECTED

| Marabout | Gadwall | Lesser bustard |
|---|---|---|
| Egret | European stork | Guinea fowl |
| Glossy ibis | Quail | Giant guinea fowl |
| Egyptian goose | Sand grouse | Green pigeon |
| White goose | Francolin | Blue pigeon |
| English snipe | Spur fowl | Dove (2 species) |
| Mallard duck | Greater bustard | |

Total, twenty-two kinds

# APPENDIX III

For the benefit of the sportsman and gun crank who want plain facts and no flapdoodle, the following statistics are offered. To the lay reader this inclusion will be incomprehensible; but I know my gun crank as I am one myself!

Army Springfield, model 1903 to take the 1906 cartridge, shooting the Spitzer sharp point bullet. Stocked to suit me by Ludwig Wundhammer, and fitted with Sheard gold bead front sight and Lyman aperture receiver sight. With this I did most my shooting, as the trajectory was remarkably good, and the killing power remarkable. Tried out both the old-fashioned soft point bullets and the sharp Spitzer bullets, but find the latter far the more effective. In fact the paralyzing shock given by the Spitzer is almost beyond belief. African animals are notably tenacious of life; but the Springfield dropped nearly half the animals dead with one shot; a most unusual record, as every sportsman will recognize. The bullets seemed on impact always to flatten slightly at the base, the point remaining intact-to spin widely on the axis, and to plunge off at an angle. This action of course depended on the high velocity. The requisite velocity, however seemed to keep up within all shooting ranges. A kongoni I killed at 638 paces (measured), and another at 566 paces both exhibited this action of the bullet. I mention these ranges because I have seen the statement in print that the remaining velocity beyond 350 yards would not be sufficient in this arm to prevent the bullet passing through cleanly. I should also hasten to add that I do not habitually shoot at game at the above ranges; but did so in these two instances for the precise purpose of testing the arm. Metal fouling did not bother me at all, though I had been led to expect trouble from it. The weapon was always cleaned with water so boiling hot that the heat of the barrel dried it. When occasionally flakes of metal fouling became visible a Marble brush always sufficed to remove enough of it. It was my habit to smear the bullets with mobilubricant before placing them in the magazine. This was not as much of a nuisance as it sounds. A small tin box about the size of a pill box lasted me the whole trip; and only once did I completely empty the magazine at one time. On my return I tested the rifle very thoroughly for accuracy. In spite of careful cleaning the barrel was in several places slightly corroded. For this the climate was responsible. The few small pittings, however, did not seem in any way to have affected the accuracy, as the rifle shot the following groups: 3-1/2 inches at 200 yards; 7-1/4 inches at 300 yards; and 11-1/2 inches at 500 yards.*

* It shot one five-shot 1-2/3 inch group at 200 yds., and

133

several others at all distances less than the figures given,

but I am convinced these must have been largely accidental.

These groups were not made from a machine rest, however; as none was available. The complete record with this arm for my whole stay in Africa was 307 hits out of 395 cartridges fired, representing 185 head of game killed. Most of this shooting was for meat and represented also all sorts of "varmints" as well.

The 405 Winchester. This weapon was sighted like the Springfield, and was constantly in the field as my second gun. For lions it could not be beaten; as it was very accurate, delivered a hard blow, and held five cartridges. Beyond 125 to 150 yards one had to begin to guess at distance, so for ordinary shooting I preferred the Springfield. In thick brush country, however, where one was likely to come suddenly on rhinoceroes, but where one wanted to be ready always for desirable smaller game, the Winchester was just the thing. It was short, handy, and reliable. One experience with a zebra 300-350 yards has made me question whether at long (hunting) ranges the remaining velocity of the big blunt nosed bullet is not seriously reduced; but as to that I have not enough data for a final conclusion. I have no doubt, however, that at such ranges, and beyond, the little Springfield has more shocking power. Of course at closer ranges the Winchester is by far the more powerful. I killed one rhinoceros with the 405, one buffalo and one hippo; but should consider it too light for an emergency gun against the larger dangerous animals, such as buffalo and rhinoceros. If one has time for extreme accuracy, and can pick the shot, it is plenty big; but I refer now to close quarters in a hurry. I had no trouble whatever with the mechanism of this arm; nor have I ever had trouble with any of the lever actions, although I have used them for many years. As regards speed of fire the controversy between the lever and bolt action advocates seems to me foolish in the extreme. Either action can be fired faster than it should be fired in the presence of game. It is my belief that any man, no matter how practised or how cool, can stampede himself beyond his best accuracy by pumping out his shots too rapidly. This is especially true in the face of charging dangerous game. So firmly do I believe this that I generally take the rifle from my shoulder between each shot. Even aimed rapid fire is of no great value as compared with better aimed slower fire. The first bullet delivers to an animal's nervous system about all the shock it can absorb. If the beast is not thereby knocked down and held down, subsequent shots can accomplish that desirable result only by reaching a vital spot or by tearing tissue. As an example of this I might instance a waterbuck into which I saw my companion empty five heavy 465 and double 500 bullets from cordite rifles before it fell! Thus if the game gets to its feet after the first shock, it is true that the hunter will often empty into it six or seven more bullets without apparent result, unless he aims carefully for a centrally vital point. It follows that therefore a second shot aimed with enough care to land it in that point is worth a lot more than a half dozen delivered in three or four seconds with only the accuracy necessary to group decently at very short range, even if all of them hit the beast. I am perfectly aware that this view will probably be disputed; but it is the result of considerable experience, close observation and real interest in the game. The whole record of the Winchester was 56 hits out of 70 cartridges fired; representing 27 head of game.

The 465 Holland & Holland double cordite rifle. This beautiful weapon, built and balanced like a fine hammerless shotgun, was fitted with open sights. It was of course essentially a close range emergency gun, but was capable of accurate work at a distance. I killed one buffalo dead with it, across a wide canyon, with the 300-yard leaf up on the back sight. Its game list however was limited to rhinoceroses, hippopotamuses, buffaloes and crocodiles. The recoil in spite of its weight of twelve and one half pounds, was tremendous; but unnoticeable when I was shooting at any of these brutes. Its total record was 31 cartridges fired with 29 hits representing 13 head of game.

The conditions militating against marksmanship are often severe. Hard work in the tropics is not the most steadying regime in the world, and outside a man's nerves, he is often bothered by queer lights, and the effects of the mirage that swirls from the sun-heated plain. The ranges, too, are rather long. I took the trouble to pace out about every kill, and find that antelope in the plains averaged 245 yards; with a maximum of 638 yards, while antelope in covered country averaged 148 yards, with a maximum of 311.

# APPENDIX IV. THE AMERICAN IN AFRICA

### IN WHICH HE APPEARS AS DIFFERENT FROM THE ENGLISHMAN

It is always interesting to play the other fellow's game his way, and then, in light of experience, to see wherein our way and his way modify each other.

The above proposition here refers to camping. We do considerable of it in our country, especially in our North and West. After we have been at it for some time, we evolve a method of our own. The basis of that method is to do without; to GO LIGHT. At first even the best of us will carry too much plunder, but ten years of philosophy and rainstorms, trails and trials, will bring us to an irreducible minimum. A party of three will get along with two pack horses, say; or, on a harder trip, each will carry the necessities on his own back. To take just as little as is consistent with comfort is to play the game skilfully. Any article must pay in use for its transportation.

With this ideal deeply ingrained by the test of experience, the American camper is appalled by the caravan his British cousins consider necessary for a trip into the African back country. His said cousin has, perhaps, very kindly offered to have his outfit ready for him when he arrives. He does arrive to find from one hundred to one hundred and fifty men gathered as his personal attendants.

"Great Scot!" he cries, "I want to go camping; I don't want to invade anybody's territory. Why the army?"

He discovers that these are porters, to carry his effects.

"What effects?" he demands, bewildered. As far as he knows, he has two guns, some ammunition, and a black tin box, bought in London, and half-filled with extra clothes, a few medicines, a thermometer, and some little personal knick-knacks. He has been wondering what else he is going to put in to keep things from rattling about. Of course he expected besides these to take along a little plain grub, and some blankets, and a frying pan and kettle or so.

The English friend has known several Americans, so he explains patiently.

"I know this seems foolish to you," he says, "but you must remember you are under the equator and you must do things differently here. As long as you keep fit you are safe; but if you get run down a bit you'll go. You've got to do yourself well, down here, rather better than you have to in any other climate. You need all the comfort you can get; and you want to save yourself all you can."

This has a reasonable sound and the American does not yet know the game. Recovering from his first shock, he begins to look things over. There is a double tent, folding camp chair, folding easy chair, folding table, wash basin, bath tub, cot, mosquito curtains, clothes hangers; there are oil lanterns, oil carriers, two loads of mysterious cooking utensils and cook camp stuff; there is an open fly, which his friend explains is his dining tent; and there are from a dozen to twenty boxes standing in a row, each with its padlock. "I didn't go in for luxury," apologizes the English friend. "Of course we can easily add anything you want but I remember you wrote me that you wanted to travel light."

"What are those?" our American inquires, pointing to the locked boxes.

He learns that they are chop boxes, containing food and supplies. At this he rises on his hind legs and paws the air.

"Food!" he shrieks. "Why, man alive, I'm alone, and I am only going to be out three months! I can carry all I'll ever eat in three months in one of those boxes."

But the Englishman patiently explains. You cannot live on "bacon and beans" in this country, so to speak. You must do yourself rather well, you know, to keep in condition. And you cannot pack food in bags, it must be tinned. And then, of course, such things as your sparklet siphons and lime juice require careful packing-and your champagne.

"Champagne," breathes the American in awestricken tones.

"Exactly, dear boy, an absolute necessity. After a touch of sun there's nothing picks you up better than a mouthful of fizz. It's used as a medicine, not a drink, you understand."

The American reflects again that this is the other fellow's game, and that the other fellow has been playing it for some time, and that he ought to know. But he cannot yet see why the one hundred and fifty men. Again the Englishman explains. There is the Headman to run the show. Correct: we need him. Then there are four askaris. What are they? Native soldiers. No, you won't be fighting anything; but they keep the men going, and act as sort of sub-foremen in bossing the complicated work. Next is your cook, and your own valet and that of your horse. Also your two gunbearers.

"Hold on!" cries our friend. "I have only two guns, and I'm going to carry one myself." 

But this, he learns, is quite impossible. It is never done. It is absolutely necessary, in this climate, to avoid all work.

That makes how many? Ten already, and there seem to be three tent loads, one bed load, one chair and table load, one lantern load, two miscellaneous loads, two cook loads, one personal box, and fifteen chop boxes-total twenty-six, plus the staff, as above, thirty-six. Why all the rest of the army?

Very simple: these thirty-six men have, according to regulation, seven tents, and certain personal effects, and they must have "potio" or a ration of one and a half pounds per diem. These things must be carried by more men.

"I see," murmurs the American, crushed, "and these more men have more tents and more potio, which must also be carried. It's like the House that Jack Built."

So our American concludes still once again that the other fellow knows his own game, and starts out. He learns he has what is called a "modest safari"; and spares a fleeting wonder as to what a really elaborate safari must be. The procession takes the field. He soon sees the value of the four askaris-the necessity of whom he has secretly doubted. Without their vigorous seconding the headman would have a hard time indeed. Also, when he observes the labour of tent-making, packing, washing, and general service performed by his tent boy, he abandons the notion that that individual could just as well take care of the horse as well, especially as the horse has to have all his grass cut and brought to him. At evening our friend has a hot bath, a long cool fizzly drink of lime juice and soda; he puts on the clean clothes laid out for him, assumes soft mosquito boots, and sits down to dinner. This is served to him in courses, and on enamel ware. Each course has its proper-sized plate and cutlery. He starts with soup, goes down through tinned whitebait or other fish, an entree, a roast, perhaps a curry, a sweet, and small coffee. He is certainly being "done well," and he enjoys the comfort of it.

There comes a time when he begins to wonder a little. It is all very pleasant, of course, and perhaps very necessary; they all tell him it is. But, after all, it is a little galling to the average man to think that of him. Your Englishman doesn't mind that; he enjoys being taken care of: but the sportsman of American training likes to stand on his own feet as far as he is able and conditions permit. Besides, it is expensive. Besides that, it is a confounded nuisance, especially when potio gives out and more must be sought, near or far. Then, if he is wise, he begins to do a little figuring on his own account.

My experience was very much as above. Three of us went out for eleven weeks with what was considered a very "modest" safari indeed. It comprised one hundred and eighteen men. My fifth and last trip, also with two companions, was for three months. Our personnel consisted, all told, forty men.

In essentials the Englishman is absolutely right. One cannot camp in Africa as one would at home. The experimenter would be dead in a month. In his application of that principle, however, he seems to the American point of view to overshoot. Let us examine his proposition in terms of the essentials-food, clothing, shelter. There is no doubt but that a man must keep in top condition as far as possible; and that, to do so, he must have plenty of good food. He can never do as we do on very hard trips at home: take a little tea, sugar, coffee, flour, salt, oatmeal. But on the other hand, he certainly does not need a five-course dinner every night, nor a complete battery of cutlery, napery and table ware to eat it from. Flour, sugar, oatmeal, tea and coffee, rice, beans, onions, curry, dried fruits, a little bacon, and some dehydrated vegetables will do him very well indeed-with what he can shoot. These will pack in waterproof bags very comfortably. In addition to feeding himself well, he finds he must not sleep next to the ground, he must have a hot bath every day, but never a cold one, and he must shelter himself with a double tent against the sun.

Those are the absolute necessities of the climate. In other words, if he carries a double tent, a cot, a folding bath; and gives a little attention to a properly balanced food supply, he has met the situation.

If, in addition, he takes canned goods, soda siphons, lime juice, easy chairs and all the rest of the paraphernalia, he is merely using a basic principle as an excuse to include sheer luxuries. In further extenuation of this he is apt to argue that porters are cheap, and that it costs but little more to carry these extra comforts. Against this argument, of course, I have nothing to say. It is the inalienable right of every man to carry all the luxuries he wants. My point is that the average American sportsman does not want them, and only takes them because he is overpersuaded that these things are not luxuries, but necessities. For, mark you, he could take the same things into the Sierras or the North-by paying; but he doesn't.

I repeat, it is the inalienable right of any man to travel as luxuriously as he pleases. But by the same token it is not his right to pretend that luxuries are necessities. That is to put himself into the same category with the man who always finds some other excuse for taking a drink than the simple one that he wants it.

The Englishman's point of view is that he objects to "pigging it," as he says. "Pigging it" means changing your home habits in any way. If you have been accustomed to eating your sardines after a meal, and somebody offers them to you first, that is "pigging it." In other words, as nearly as I can make out, "pigging it" does not so much mean doing things in an inadequate fashion as DOING THEM DIFFERENTLY. Therefore, the Englishman in the field likes to approximate as closely as may be his life in town, even if it takes one hundred and fifty men to do it. Which reduces the "pigging it" argument to an attempt at condemnation by calling names.

The American temperament, on the contrary, being more experimental and independent, prefers to build anew upon its essentials. Where the Englishman covers the situation blanket-wise with his old institutions, the American prefers to construct new institutions on the necessities of the case. He objects strongly to being taken care of too completely. He objects strongly to losing the keen enjoyment of overcoming difficulties and enduring hardships. The Englishman by habit and training has no such objections. He likes to be taken care of, financially, personally, and everlastingly. That is his ideal of life. If he can be taken care of better by employing three hundred porters and packing eight tin trunks of personal effects-as I have seen it done-he will so employ and take. That is all right: he likes it.

But the American does not like it. A good deal of the fun for him is in going light, in matching himself against his environment. It is no fun to him to carry his complete little civilization along with him, laboriously. If he must have cotton wool, let it be as little cotton wool as possible. He likes to be comfortable; but he likes to be comfortable with the minimum of means. Striking just the proper balance somehow adds to his interest in the game. And how he DOES object to that ever-recurring thought-that he is such a helpless mollusc that it requires a small regiment to get him safely around the country!

Both means are perfectly legitimate, of course; and neither view is open to criticism. All either man is justified in saying is that he, personally, wouldn't get much fun out of doing it the other way. As a matter of fact, human nature generally goes beyond its justifications and is prone to criticise. The Englishman waxes a trifle caustic on the subject of "pigging it"; and the American indulges in more than a bit of sarcasm on the subject of "being led about Africa like a dog on a string."

By some such roundabout mental process as the above the American comes to the conclusion that he need not necessarily adopt the other fellow's method of playing this game. His own method needs modification, but it will do. He ventures to leave out the tables and easy chair, takes a camp stool and eats off a chop box. To the best of his belief his health does not suffer from this. He gets on with a camper's allowance of plate, cup and cutlery, and so cuts out a load and a half of assorted kitchen utensils and table ware. He even does without a tablecloth and napkins! He discards the lime juice and siphons, and purchases a canvas evaporation bag to cool the water. He fires one gunbearer, and undertakes the formidable physical feat of carrying one of his rifles himself. And, above all, he modifies that grub list. The purchase of waterproof bags gets rid of a lot of tin: the staple groceries do quite as well as London fancy stuff. Golden syrup takes the place of all the miscellaneous jams, marmalades and other sweets. The canned goods go by the board. He lays in a stock of dried fruit. At the end, he is possessed of a grub list but little different from that of his Rocky Mountain trips. Some few items he has cut down; and some he has substituted; but bulk and weight are the same. For his three months' trip he has four or five chop boxes all told.

And then suddenly he finds that thus he has made a reduction all along the line. Tent load, two men; grub and kitchen, five men; personal, one man; bed, one man; miscellaneous, one or two. There is now no need for headmen and askaris to handle this little lot. Twenty more to carry food for the men-he is off with a quarter of the number of his first "modest safari."

You who are sportsmen and are not going to Africa, as is the case with most, will perhaps read this, because we are always interested in how the other fellow does it. To the few who are intending an exploration of the dark continent this concentration of a year's experience may be valuable. Remember to sleep off the ground, not to starve yourself, to protect yourself from the sun, to let negroes do all hard work but marching and hunting. Do these things your own way, using your common-sense on how to get at it. You'll be all right.

That, I conceive, covers the case. The remainder of your equipment has to do with camp affairs, and merely needs listing. The question here is not of the sort to get, but of what to take. The tents, cooking affairs, etc., are well adapted to the country. In selecting your tent, however, you will do very well to pick out one whose veranda fly reaches fairly to the ground, instead of stopping halfway.

```
1 tent and ground sheet
1 folding cot and cork mattress,
1 pillow, 3 single blankets
1 combined folding bath and ashstand ("X" brand)
1 camp stool
3 folding candle lanterns
1 gallon turpentine
3 lbs. alum
1 river rope
Sail needles and twine
3 pangas (native tools for chopping and digging)
Cook outfit (select these yourself, and cut out the
extras)
2 axes (small)
Plenty laundry soap
Evaporation bag
2 pails
10 yards cotton cloth ("Mericani")
```

These things, your food, your porters' outfits and what trade goods you may need are quite sufficient. You will have all you want, and not too much. If you take care of yourself, you ought to keep in good health. Your small outfit permits greater mobility than does that of the English cousin, infinitely less nuisance and expense. Furthermore, you feel that once more you are "next to things," instead of "being led about Africa like a dog on a string."

# APPENDIX V. THE AMERICAN IN AFRICA

## WHAT HE SHOULD TAKE

Before going to Africa I read as many books as I could get hold of on the subject, some of them by Americans. In every case the authors have given a chapter detailing the necessary outfit. Invariably they have followed the Englishman's ideas almost absolutely. Nobody has ventured to modify those ideas in any essential manner. Some have deprecatingly ventured to remark that it is as well to leave out the tinned carfare-if you do not like carfare; but that is as far as they care to go. The lists are those of the firms who make a business of equipping caravans. The heads of such firms are generally old African travellers. They furnish the equipment their customers demand; and as English sportsmen generally all demand the same thing, the firms end by issuing a printed list of essentials for shooting parties in Africa, including carfare. Travellers follow the lists blindly, and later copy them verbatim into their books. Not one has thought to empty out the whole bag of tricks, to examine them in the light of reason, and to pick out what a man of American habits, as contrasted to one of English habits, would like to have. This cannot be done a priori; it requires the test of experience to determine how to meet, in our own way, the unusual demands of climate and conditions.

And please note, when the heads of these equipment firms, these old African travellers, take the field for themselves, they pay no attention whatever to their own printed lists of "essentials."

Now, premising that the English sportsman has, by many years' experience, worked out just what he likes to take into the field; and assuring you solemnly that his ideas are not in the least the ideas of American sportsman, let us see if we cannot do something for ourselves.

At present the American has either to take over in toto the English idea, which is not adapted to him, and is-TO HIM-a nuisance, or to go it blind, without experience except that acquired in a temperate climate, which is dangerous. I am not going to copy out the English list again, even for comparison. I have not the space; and if curious enough, you can find it in any book on modern African travel. Of course I realize well that few Americans go to Africa; but I also realize well that the sportsman is a crank, a wild and eager enthusiast over items of equipment anywhere. He-and I am thinking emphatically of him-would avidly devour the details of the proper outfit for the gentle art of hunting the totally extinct whiffenpoof.

Let us begin, first of all, with:

Personal Equipment Clothes. On the top of your head you must have a sun helmet. Get it of cork, not of pith. The latter has a habit of melting unobtrusively about your ears when it rains. A helmet in brush is the next noisiest thing to a circus band, so it is always well to have, also, a double terai. This is not something to eat. It is a wide felt hat, and then another wide felt hat on top of that. The vertical-rays-of-the-tropical-sun (pronounced as one word to save time after you have heard and said it a thousand times) are supposed to get tangled and lost somewhere between the two hats. It is not, however, a good contraption to go in all day when the sun is strong.

As underwear you want the lightest Jaeger wool. Doesn't sound well for tropics, but it is an essential. You will sweat enough anyway, even if you get down to a brass wire costume like the natives. It is when you stop in the shade, or the breeze, or the dusk of evening, that the trouble comes. A chill means trouble, SURE. Two extra suits are all you want. There is no earthly sense in bringing more. Your tent boy washes them out whenever he can lay hands on them-it is one of his harmless manias.

Your shirt should be of the thinnest brown flannel. Leather the shoulders, and part way down the upper arm, with chamois. This is to protect your precious garment against the thorns when you dive through them. On the back you have buttons sewed wherewith to attach a spine pad. Before I went to Africa I searched eagerly for information or illustration of a spine pad. I guessed what it must be for, and to an extent what it must be like, but all writers maintained a conservative reticence as to the thing itself. Here is the first authorized description. A spine pad is a quilted affair in consistency like the things you are supposed to lift hot flat-irons with. On the outside it is brown flannel, like the shirt; on the inside it is a gaudy orange colour. The latter is not for aesthetic effect, but to intercept actinic rays. It is eight or ten inches wide, is shaped to button close up under your collar, and extends halfway down your back. In addition it is well to wear a silk handkerchief around the neck; as the spine and back of the head seem to be the most vulnerable to the sun.

140

For breeches, suit yourself as to material. It will have to be very tough, and of fast colour. The best cut is the "semi-riding," loose at the knees, which should be well faced with soft leather, both for crawling, and to save the cloth in grass and low brush. One pair ought to last four months, roughly speaking. You will find a thin pair of ordinary khaki trousers very comfortable as a change for wear about camp. In passing I would call your attention to "shorts." Shorts are loose, bobbed off khaki breeches, like knee drawers. With them are worn puttees or leather leggings, and low boots. The knees are bare. They are much affected by young Englishmen. I observed them carefully at every opportunity, and my private opinion is that man has rarely managed to invent as idiotically unfitted a contraption for the purpose in hand. In a country teeming with poisonous insects, ticks, fever-bearing mosquitoes; in a country where vegetation is unusually well armed with thorns, spines and hooks, mostly poisonous; in a country where, oftener than in any other a man is called upon to get down on his hands and knees and crawl a few assorted abrading miles, it would seem an obvious necessity to protect one's bare skin as much as possible. The only reason given for these astonishing garments is that they are cooler and freer to walk in. That I can believe. But they allow ticks and other insects to crawl up, mosquitoes to bite, thorns to tear, and assorted troubles to enter. And I can vouch by experience that ordinary breeches are not uncomfortably hot or tight. Indeed, one does not get especially hot in the legs anyway. I noticed that none of the old-time hunters like Cuninghame or Judd wore shorts. The real reason is not that they are cool, but that they are picturesque. Common belief to the contrary, your average practical, matter-of-fact Englishman loves to dress up. I knew one engaged in farming-picturesque farming-in our own West, who used to appear at afternoon tea in a clean suit of blue overalls! It is a harmless amusement. Our own youths do it, also, substituting chaps for shorts, perhaps. I am not criticising the spirit in them; but merely trying to keep mistaken shorts off you.

For leg gear I found that nothing could beat our American combination of high-laced boots and heavy knit socks. Leather leggings are noisy, and the rolled puttees hot and binding. Have your boots ten or twelve inches high, with a flap to buckle over the tie of the laces, with soles of the mercury-impregnated leather called "elk hide," and with small Hungarian hobs. Your tent boy will grease these every day with "dubbin," of which you want a good supply. It is not my intention to offer free advertisements generally, but I wore one pair of boots all the time I was in Africa, through wet, heat, and long, long walking. They were in good condition when I gave them away finally, and had not started a stitch. They were made by that excellent craftsman, A. A. Cutter, of Eau Claire, Wis., and he deserves and is entirely welcome to this puff. Needless to remark, I have received no especial favours from Mr. Cutter.

Six pairs of woollen socks, knit by hand, if possible-will be enough. For evening, when you come in, I know nothing better than a pair of very high moosehide moccasins. They should, however, be provided with thin soles against the stray thorn, and should reach well above the ankle by way of defence against the fever mosquito. That festive insect carries on a surreptitious guerrilla warfare low down. The English "mosquito boot" is simply an affair like a riding boot, made of suede leather, with thin soles. It is most comfortable. My objection is that it is unsubstantial and goes to pieces in a very brief time even under ordinary evening wear about camp.

You will also want a coat. In American camping I have always maintained the coat is a useless garment. There one does his own work to a large extent. When at work or travel the coat is in the way. When in camp the sweater or buckskin shirt is handier, and more easily carried. In Africa, however, where the other fellow does most of the work, a coat is often very handy. Do not make the mistake of getting an unlined light-weight garment. When you want it at all, you want it warm and substantial. Stick on all the pockets possible, and have them button securely.

For wet weather there is nothing to equal a long and voluminous cape. Straps crossing the chest and around the waist permit one to throw it off the shoulders to shoot. It covers the hands, the rifle-most of the little horses or mules one gets out there. One can sleep in or on it, and it is a most effective garment against heavy winds. One suit of pajamas is enough, considering your tent boy's commendable mania for laundry work. Add handkerchiefs and you are fixed.

You will wear most of the above, and put what remains in your "officer's box." This is a thin steel, air-tight affair with a wooden bottom, and is the ticket for African work.

Sporting. Pick out your guns to suit yourself. You want a light one and a heavy one.

When I came to send out my ammunition, I was forced again to take the other fellow's experience. I was told by everybody that I should bring plenty, that it was better to have too much than too little, etc. I rather thought so myself, and accordingly shipped a trifle over 1,500 rounds of small bore cartridges. Unfortunately, I never got into the field with any of my numerous advisers on this point, so cannot state their methods from first-hand information. Inductive reasoning leads me to believe that they consider it unsportsmanlike to shoot at a standing animal at all, or at one running nearer than 250 yards. Furthermore, it is etiquette to continue firing until the last cloud of dust has died down on the distant horizon. Only thus can I conceive of getting rid of that amount of ammunition. In eight months of steady shooting, for example-shooting for trophies, as well as to feed a safari of fluctuating numbers, counting jackals, marabout and such small trash-I got away with 395 rounds of small bore ammunition and about 100 of large. This accounted for 225 kills. That should give one an idea. Figure out how many animals you are likely to want for ANY purpose, multiply by three, and bring that many cartridges.

To carry these cartridges I should adopt the English system of a stout leather belt on which you slip various sized pockets and loops to suit the occasion. Each unit has loops for ten cartridges. You rarely want more than that; and if you do, your gunbearer is supplied. In addition to the loops, you have leather pockets to carry your watch; your money, your matches and tobacco, your compass-anything you please. They are handy and safe. The tropical climate is too "sticky" to get much comfort, or anything else, out of ordinary pockets.

In addition, you supply your gunbearer with a cartridge belt, a leather or canvas carrying bag, water bottle for him and for yourself, a sheath knife and a whetstone. In the bag are your camera, tape line, the whetstone, field cleaners and lunch. You personally carry your field glasses, sun glasses, a knife, compass, matches, police whistle and notebook. The field glasses should not be more than six power; and if possible you should get the sort with detachable prisms. The prisms are apt to cloud in a tropical climate, and the non-detachable sort are almost impossible for a layman to clean. Hang these glasses around your neck by a strap only just long enough to permit you to raise them to your eyes. The best notebook is the "loose-leaf" sort. By means of this you can keep always a fresh leaf on top; and at night can transfer your day's notes to safe keeping in your tin box. The sun glasses should not be smoked or dark-you can do nothing with them-but of the new amberol, the sort that excludes the ultra-violet rays, but otherwise makes the world brighter and gayer. Spectacle frames of non-corrosive white metal, not steel, are the proper sort.

To clean your guns you must supply plenty of oil, and then some more. The East African gunbearer has a quite proper and gratifying, but most astonishing horror for a suspicion of rust; and to use oil any faster he would have to drink it.

Other Equipment. All this has taken much time to tell about, it has not done much toward filling up that tin box. Dump in your toilet effects and a bath towel, two or three scalpels for taxidermy, a ball of string, some safety-pins, a small tool kit, sewing materials, a flask of brandy, kodak films packed in tin, a boxed thermometer, an aneroid (if you are curious as to elevations), journal, tags for labelling trophies, a few yards of gun cloth, and the medicine kit.

The latter divides into two classes: for your men and for yourself. The men will suffer from certain well defined troubles: "tumbo," or overeating; diarrhaea, bronchial colds, fever and various small injuries. For "tumbo" you want a liberal supply of Epsom's salts; for diarrhaea you need chlorodyne; any good expectorant for the colds; quinine for the fever; permanganate and plenty of bandages for the injuries. With this lot you can do wonders. For yourself you need, or may need, in addition, a more elaborate lot: Laxative, quinine, phenacetin, bismuth and soda, bromide of ammonium, morphia, camphor-ice, and aspirin. A clinical thermometer for whites and one for blacks should be included. A tin of malted milk is not a bad thing to take as an emergency ration after fever.

By this time your tin box is fairly well provided. You may turn to general supplies.

143

CPSIA information can be obtained
at www.ICGtesting.com
Printed in the USA
LVOW01s1750291015

460303LV00024B/662/P